I0699640

F. FOX NORTH

The Chaos Agents

A Novel

Fretboard Press

For Molly, my favorite song.

Fear no more the heat o' the sun,
Nor the furious winter's rages;
Thou thy worldly task hast done,
Home art gone, and ta'en thy wages:
Golden lads and girls all must,
As chimney-sweepers, come to dust.

WILLIAM SHAKESPEARE, CYMBELINE, ACT IV,
SCENE 2

Preface

How do you know when you've made something remarkable?

Is it because you've been paid for it? Is it because someone tells you it's good? Is it because of the way your audience shifts, sitting forward in their seats, their pupils flooding their eyes with black?

Is it because you find yourself revisiting it yourself over and over again? Held captive by the story as if it didn't come from you, as if you were *channeling*, as if you were merely a conduit for these people and their stories? Is it because, when you read it again - willingly - for the fifth or fifteenth or fiftieth time, you hear yourself say, *Oh, yes, this was the book I've always needed?*

I first became enamored with British mid-twentieth century music when I was eleven years old. I wasn't then capable of writing a story like this. The notion to finally write a fab book first occurred to me in 2014, between my first two published novels, but it was so far afield from my genre - young adult science fiction - and popular tastes that I could not even begin to contemplate writing it. I set the idea aside for several other books, some which meant something to me, some which didn't. I grew. I changed. And I began to realize that the story was much bigger than a fictionalization of two real boys navigating grief and identity in 1958. Baron and Eddie began to come to me through the ether, and with them, their children, their ghosts, their problems, their cats.

At last, in 2017, I set the first chapter to paper. I shared it with a friend. "Wow," she said, "You must write amazing erotica. The sexual tension!" That chapter is shared here almost unchanged, save for my realization that Baron - of course! - is a diminutive guy, a pocket human.

(And I must say, writing these books has always been like that; I don't make *choices*. I have *realizations*. The universe is already set out in perfect detail, and woe to the author who tries to change it. There is a guitar that is missing in this book by 2017. I tried to write it in. It was wrong, all wrong. I had to write an entire sequel for the characters to finally consent to sharing with me where it went.)

In 2017 I was under a deadline. I wrote here and there between other things. And, well, I didn't know what to *do* with this book. It wasn't for teenagers. It wasn't like any other book I'd read. I got halfway through, and wrote several other books in the meantime. Sensible books. Potentially lucrative books.

But every winter something would happen to me. As the weather cooled, I'd don '70s concert tees and start playing The Hollies for my family. I'd play my guitar incessantly. "The winter of Baron Templeton," my spouse would say, as the season inevitably turned to spring and I'd babbling about the private sex lives of long-dead rock stars at dinner. In 2020, I realized I was not, for the first time, contractually bound by anything else. And I let my passions carry me. That winter, writing as though possessed, until I was pulling nine, ten hour days at the keyboard, until I gave myself a sciatica flare-up. I stayed up all night. I finished Baron's story, and Naomi's story, and Ed's story, and Richard Charles' story and Sid's story, and poor, dear Cymbeline's, but I still didn't feel done. I learned to solder pick-ups and build guitars just so I could stay in the world a little longer. I mean, I *built myself* Baron's Rickenbacker Combo 800, a guitar which does not exist. I thought that might satisfy. I sent the manuscript to my agent, and told myself it was over.

My agent loved it. She read it in one sitting, crying in a coffee shop, and when she was asked by a neighboring table what she was reading, she didn't know what to say. She put it on submission and based on early interest - film and book - we felt optimistic. We waited for an offer. I told myself I had done my work, for now.

And then the next winter, the same old mood returned. Baron, I was missing Baron. In between more sensible projects, I let myself write a short story about Baron. It became two short stories. It became a novella. It became a sequel, I reluctantly admitted to myself.

And meanwhile, the offer never came from trade publishing. My agent fielded phone calls, editors saying the book was "transcendent," and "definitely had voice." But they also didn't know what to *do* with it. "Band books don't sell," "too raunchy," "not a good fit for our list," "I'm just not sure how to break it out."

I've done this dance before with other books. I told myself I could pack them away, write something else, better targeted to *the market*. For whatever reason, I can't with this book.

No, that's not true. I know the reason. The reason is Baron Templeton, borrowing my skin, my fingers, my time. Inhabiting me. Being bossy, a brat. But *right*.

You're not going to put us down, now. You think I'm going to let you do all that?

No, no, Baron. Of course not.

Good.

The truth is, I can't wait for you to read *The Chaos Agents*. I know it's remarkable. I know it will change you. I had no choice but to share it with you - Baron, *fucking* Baron, would have it no other way.

Yours as the weather starts to cool and every winter thereafter,

Fox

Acknowledgement

Thankful to the early supporters: JE, MN, VM, KA, JD, MG, AW, AG, VW, SW, KL, ST, LR, AB, JC.

And to JPM, who told me, when I was 11, to "be sure to eat your vegetables."

1 - 1957

Standing in the basement of St. Michael's & All Angels Church, the sounds of the other boys' trainers bouncing off the rafters, Baron Templeton fell in love with Edmund Hammond III.

It wasn't a pansyish sort of love. He didn't want to press his lips to Eddie's lips like he did to Sue Grasso down the street and just about every girl he saw in the movies. It wasn't a fucking love or a wanking-each-other kind of love. Baron had felt those loves before, with other boys, with a girl or two. This was not that.

But as he watched Eddie bend his body over the too-big guitar, the boy's fingers moving too-fast over the neck, as he watched Eddie's cheeks blossom like a pair of poppies against a field of white snow and heard the soft, uncertain, but pitch-perfect notes fall from his lips, he realized that he wanted to *be* Edmund Hammond III. With his skinny trousers and blue pressed shirt, one button open at the neck. With his blond and angelic curls and even more cherubic voice. *Gloria in excelsis Deo* and all of that.

Baron had borrowed his coloring from his swarthy sailor father; black hair, black eyes, and in these summer months his arms brown like wet sand. He only knew how to play the bottom four strings on the guitar he kept slung over one shoulder. His mother had taught him that, from banjo chords. And while his band mates, the Bartlebys, they called themselves, all fell in line because he knew chords at all, Baron could see that this bloke would not be so easy. Edmund Hammond III was better at it than Baron Templeton was. Better at singing, even if he sang too soft. Better at bending those strings, all six of them too. Baron sucked at his fag, shedding ash on the dusty floor of the church basement. He wanted to murder Eddie and walk around in his skin. That's what he decided, right then and there.

The boy's chords faded. For a minute, he looked around, squirrely-faced and nervous.

"Ye like it, Bongo?" Ed asked Teddy Turner, the friend who had brought him here. But before Teddy could answer, Baron let his cigarette dangle between his lips and clapped his hands together. Too hard. Too loud. Eddie jumped, just like he was supposed to.

"Good show," Baron said, still clapping. Eddie's brow went crinkly.

"Are you having a go at me?" he asked. Baron wouldn't deign to answer that. He swaggered over, fag still dangling, shedding ash and smoke all over. Then he grabbed one of the folding metal chairs for himself and plopped right down on it.

"You'll need to lose the curls," Baron said. He reached over and batted one of those angel's curlicues out of Eddie's eyes. Eddie swiped his hand away.

"I didn't ask you," he said. His cheeks were still graced by red blossoms. Baron found himself wondering if this was what the kid looked like when he cummed, all angry and breathless and uncertain. It amused him, thinking of that. He grabbed his cigarette and stubbed it out on his shoe, smirking all the while.

"Well if you want to be in me band," he began, "You can't go around looking like a lady."

Eddie's expression was still outwardly all hard and blushing. But something behind his eyes melted a little, a sad bit of desperation. This one had a tragic backstory, Baron was sure of it. A haunted look, to get the girls excited.

"Who said I wanted to be in your band?" Eddie asked. Behind them, Bongo laughed.

"Are you serious, Eddie?" he asked. "You saw them out there. They were fantastic. The girls—"

He didn't need to say the rest. The girls, in their blouses and skirts and tight tall socks had all been creaming themselves. That wasn't why Baron did it of course—the band, music, any of that. But it was an undeniable benefit.

"Listen to Bongo," Baron said, letting his lips pop over the words. Theodore Teddy-Bongo Turner wasn't his favorite individual, but he certainly had his uses.

"Five seems too many for a skiffle band," Eddie said. He looked down at his guitar, letting his fingers tickle the strings. It was an acoustic, a dreaded nought, thick-bodied, ancient. Playing coy, then. Baron grinned.

"We'll kick someone out."

"The washboard player." Eddie's eyes shot up when he said it, burning right into Baron's black soul. If he thought that Baron had a conscience, then he thought wrong.

"Dickie Ashby," Baron paused, licked his lips, nodded. "Yeh. We're a rock band, anyway. Not a skiffle band. At least, we will be. Been meaning to give him the boot."

"Have you, then?" Eddie asked. Baron shrugged. He suddenly wished he hadn't put out his cigarette. He needed to do something with his hands. So he swung his guitar around and set it on his knee. Let his fingers touch and untouch the strings. Delicate. Same way he worked at lifting up Sue Grasso's skirt.

"You tell Dickie," Eddie said, "And I'm in. I won't be your mistress."

Behind them, Bongo let out a whoop.

"I knew you blokes would be a pair," Bongo said. Over the strings, Eddie glanced up at Baron. His eyebrow cocked. Ed's blue eyes, a pair of beautiful stinking pieces of sea glass, nearly rolled. It was Baron's turn to blush. Allies. They were allies then. Against Bongo. Against the world. Forever more.

"Feck off," Baron shouted back over his shoulder. Bongo let out a wounded noise, which was good. Wounding him had been Baron's intent. Now Baron watched as a smile curled Eddie's angel-mouth, as Eddie bent over his guitar again.

"If we're going to be in a band together," Eddie said. "We should teach you some proper chords. All six strings."

Under normal circumstances, Baron would have punched Eddie in the jaw at that. The nerve, acting like he could teach Baron something, when Baron was more than a year older, when it was Baron's band, besides. But they were blokes now. Comrades. Yes. Baron licked his lips, edging forward in his seat.

"Show me," he said. Eddie edged forward too. Ed's hands cradled that guitar neck like the throat of a fallen swan, full of gentle lovingkindness. Their knees knocked. Neither one seemed to mind.

And that was the beginning of it all.

2 - 1977

Timothy was the oldest, so when they moved out of the big house he got a room all to himself. Marigold was little—she could still sleep tucked in next to Mom, her bottle leaking sour milk onto the sheets. That left Zach and Richard Charles squeezed in one tiny room together, and worse, sharing the same double bed.

Zachy knew not to say anything when he saw the stained mattress that had been wedged into the space. Mom did her best for them, working nights waiting tables after she got done stocking shelves at the pharmacy, and her best hadn't gotten any better since Dad had stopped paying child support. Zachy was thirteen and change, in middle school, but largely prepubescent. His world was still orderly. What's more, he had always understood the rules of things: sports and the order of operations and all the names for all the WWII planes in the books in the library. He knew that Mom was trying, that even taking this stinking old mattress from the church charity ladies had been a hardship for her. Zach didn't want to make her feel any worse than she already did. So he set his suitcase on top of the bed and gave her a smile.

"I like the window," he said. "The trees outside."

Mom forced a smile back. Maybe once, before Marigold, she would have ruffled his hair and said something like *that's my boy*, but something had shifted since the baby had been born and his voice had changed. Anyway, they both had Richard Charles to think about. Richie, only he wouldn't let anyone call him that anymore, fourteen, with his armpit stink and his gross hairs on the soap in the morning, Richie, who was the exact same height as his littlest brother but who seemed to always take up the whole room, Richie—rather, Richard Charles—who might have understood the rules, but didn't care about them, anyway.

"One bed? We're not a bunch of faggots, mom!" he bellowed, because he was always bellowing lately. And then, before Mom could even tell him to watch his words, he shoved Zachy's suitcase onto the floor and flopped down on the mattress, smashing his zitty face into the fabric and rubbing his dirty Jack Purcells all over.

"I've always wanted a full bed, though," he added, and grinned so wide that the hooks on the ends of his braces showed. Beside him, Zachy could feel Mom melt a little. She gave Richard Charles a gentle slap on the rear.

"No shoes," she said. Zach bent over and started picking up his clothes. He didn't want them to see how his face was burning, how his jaw had gone tight with anger. It didn't do any good to let Richard Charles know that you were mad, or jealous. It only made it all worse. And when Zach stood up, Richie had untied his laces and was handing his shoes to Mom like she was some kind of foot servant. Maybe she was. She took them, with one eyebrow arched and the other all crinkling.

"This is only temporary," she said. "You know this is only temporary."

Even though she was smiling, cradling Richie's sneakers to her chest like they were precious, there was a desperate kind of note in her voice, a sad one.

"I know, Mom," Zachy said. "We'll be fine, okay?"

"You'll be fine," Richard Charles said, "Sleeping on the sofa."

"Mom!"

A sigh. But it was hollow. The kind of sigh that makes things worse. "Richard Charles, I expect the two of you to get along. Don't make me call your father." That made Richie sit up straighter in the bed. He curled his top lip, showing puffy gums, showing wires.

"I was only fucking around."

"I know you are, sweetie," she said, and then she kissed his forehead. "I hate that I've done this to you. To all of you."

"We do, too," Richie said, at the same time Zachy told her, "It's fine, Mom."

Their eyes locked on each other, sending an armory of bullets across that gross old mattress.

"I can't believe you—" Zachy said. Richard Charles stretched his arms behind his head, laying back down. He didn't deign to answer, only echoed Zach's words back at him in a girlish whine.

"I can't believe you!"

"Boys—"

That's when the baby started crying. Mom sighed again, with urgency, this time. She left Richard Charles' shoes sitting at the end of the mattress.

"We'll talk about this later," she said, though it wasn't clear to Zachy what "this" was. Other than the fact that his brother was an asshole. Zach put his tongue between his molars, sucking in his lips as his mother left her middle children behind. He lifted up his bag and put it on the mattress again, but Richard Charles gave him a heavy-lidded look.

"What are you doing?"

"Unpacking . . ." Zachy said softly, not even wanting to get into it with his brother. Richie's overgrown eyebrows went low.

"I told you, you can sleep on the couch."

Zach didn't answer. He set his jaw for a minute, his breath coming slow through flared nostrils. He wasn't going to fight—he knew what came of fighting with Richie. He wasn't even going to sigh. He lifted up his suitcase and lugged it into the tiny living room, flinching when the bedroom door slammed hard behind him.

Marigold's wails were still echoing behind Mom's door. Timothy's was shut, too. He was probably jacking off. Zach was alone again. Always alone. He put his bag on the crusty shag carpet and pulled out his pajamas. The blankets were all packed up still. He wadded one of the throw pillows beneath his head and laid down. He heard more crying. Muffled voices from above and below. The new neighbors. He got up again and went back to his suitcase and found his little handheld radio. The only good thing that had ever come from Dad. He got back on the sofa, curling his body around the crackling sound. Fiddled with the dial, not even caring where it landed.

He closed his eyes. The music was old and familiar, but somehow he felt like it was the first time he'd ever heard this song. Marigold's cries were fading. Maybe the neighbors had finally gone to bed. Or maybe he was just getting swept up in something new, or something ancient, or something that was both things, all at once. The ragged guitar. A man's voice, hoarse from cigarettes. The bass thump, and the drums behind it. The double dutch rhythm of the lyrics, skipping over themselves. *I know that when I see you again, I'm gonna make sure that it won't be the end.* Zach sat up now in the dark living room, where boxes towered against the walls like so much ancient stone. The chorus was wailing. A second man's voice joined the first, high and reedy. But their sound together was like a pulse, streaming through Zachy's veins. *Or else I'm dead or else I'm dead or else I'm dead.*

Zach held the radio in his fist. For a moment, he was very still. Until he wasn't. He'd heard this song enough—on Dad's sacred records, on the radio in the car—that he knew it would be over soon. And then the magic would fade away. He needed to share it with someone. He needed someone else to hear.

It was as though he were transported to the door of his new bedroom by magic. He definitely didn't feel his feet make contact with the ground. Clutching the radio in one hand, he stood before the door and started pounding with the other hand. In time with the music at first, but then harder and more wildly. After what felt like a lifetime—a whole verse of alchemy over and gone forever—Richie cracked open the door.

"What the hell do you want?" his big brother demanded. Zachy held out the radio. From behind the door, Richard Charles took in his little brother's face, white as powder in the inky black.

"You need to hear this," Zachy said.

Richard Charles stood there, listening. And then he opened up the door.

3 - 1957

The Hammond abode looked unbelievably ordinary, a sturdy row home whose bricks hadn't even trembled from Hitler's bombs. The front path was lined with red and yellow tulips, garishly bright, and when Baron saw the little balding man crouched down in the dirt among them, he wondered if he might have had the wrong house. Surely, this man was too old to be any relative of Eddie's, except perhaps a grandfather, and this house seemed altogether too uncomplicated. Quaint, even. But then the old man saw Baron and stood, squinting into the sunlight for a moment. He offered one hand to Baron over the wrought iron fencing.

"You must be looking for my Edmund," he said. Baron, trying not to let his lip curl, took the man's hand and shook. Yes, that was Eddie's face all right, gone all fleshy and age-spotted. He wondered if he was seeing the other boy's future here, and it wasn't a pretty one. The old man's bones jutted, just a little too thin, past the end of his pushed-up sleeves. Like someone wasn't after him to eat enough.

"Baron," Baron said. And then added, "Templeton."

"A baron then?" said the old man. "Should I curtsy?"

You should go fuck yourself, is what Baron wanted to say—what he would have normally said. But this old ballsack was someone to Eddie, so Baron only twisted his lips.

"No, but you can kiss my ring if you'd like."

"Kiss your arse is more like it," the old fuckface said, laughing too loudly, and thumping Baron on the shoulder. Baron didn't smile, and he didn't laugh. He didn't like to be touched by strangers unless they were pretty girls or decent-enough looking boys. But if his discomfort showed, the old fuckwad didn't care.

"Now you're probably wonderin'," the old fuckmanc said, "How Eddie got such a young and handsome brother. I'm really his father, of course. Edmund the second. And you should know that we have three rules in my house: no eating in the parlor, no guests past seven, and no horseplay."

What about arse play? came back Baron's wicked inner voice, but he just twisted his smile down and tried to look angelic.

"Yes, sir."

"Go 'ed, that's a good lad. Get on upstairs, then." And Edmund II (the fuckfart) let the gate swing open for Baron, who traipsed up the stone stairs and went rattling right into young Eddie's house like he belonged there.

He had been invited, after all. By two editions of Edmund.

"Allo?" he called into the parlor. The space wasn't quiet or empty by any means, though it looked like it could use a good dusting. Aunt Deedz always kept his house clean of the dust, at least, and he didn't want to say that the woman of the house had been remiss, but that's how it felt, like a museum, but worse, and more stale-tasting. There was a fur over the radio and the chairs beside it had ratty upholstery and the roses on the wallpaper were peeling off a little. And yet the whole place felt incredibly lived in, too. There was music thumping through the walls, and footsteps, and a boy a little older than Baron who wasn't Eddie at all came thudding down the stairwell.

"You're not Diana," the boy said, like it was an accusation, so Baron did the only thing that felt natural, which was to stick his tongue in the corner of his cheek and stretch it out a little.

"I can pretend for you if you'd like."

The boy, who also had a variation of Eddie's face though his hair was a shade darker and his nose a touch more bulbous, looked like he was ready to sock Baron. But then another face appeared over the rail, Eddie, and Eddie fluttered his thin pale eyelashes and said, "It's just Baron. Don't mind him. He's the one I was telling you about."

"Oh," said the older one. Half-Eddie or something, "Your twirling partner."

"We're not twirling anywhere," said real-Eddie, though he blushed a little to say it. The older one rolled his eyes and went pushing past them down the stairs, letting his shoulder hit Baron's on the way down. Which is something Baron usually would have socked a guy for, but you know. Family. So he didn't.

"Tell me when Diana gets here," half-Eddie groused. Whole-Eddie rolled his eyes.

"She's gonna stand you up again. She always stands you up."

"What can I say?" said half-Eddie, "I'm a glutton for punishment."

"You're something," Eddie said as his brother disappeared into the bowels of the house, toward the kitchen or something, and leaving Baron and Eddie standing there on the stairwell, silence all pregnant and throbbing.

"Well," said Eddie, "Are you coming upstairs or not?"

Baron stuck his hands in his pockets. It seemed like the only rational thing to do. Then, with a slight nod of his head, he followed Eddie up the stairwell, past dozens of black and whites of the Hammond family. Old fucking father, pretty sainted mother, and about four or five sons too many, if Baron was counting right, but he really couldn't be arsed to check.

* * *

Eddie's room had three beds, or two, depending on how you counted it—a single under the window and two mattresses bunked behind the door. Eddie's was the bottom bunk, and they had to keep their voices low because there was a brother snoozing over them.

"Jamie needs his beauty sleep," he said, rolling his eyes. Baron glanced at the sagging mattress above them, wondering what it was like to grow up wedged between two other brothers like a bunch of cats crowded around a heating vent. If there was one thing he could say for his childhood at Aunt Deedzs', no matter how solemn or lonely it had been, it was that he had been allowed his space. Over them, Jamie snorted himself briefly awake and then went right on sleeping.

"How are we supposed to listen to records if we have to keep our voices quiet?" Baron asked, pulling the LPs out of his school bag. They were his favorites, American bands, Little Richard howling his guts out, Elvis shaking his…well, everything. Eddie seemed to hear the annoyance in Baron's voice. In a gentle one, he said, simply, "It's all right."

Then he took the records out of Baron's hands and started looking at them, really studying them, as though they could unlock some sort of Cyclopean horror if only you read them in the right way. Right to left, or backwards in a mirror, or something like that.

"I'll borrow them," Eddie said, then licked his pink lips and added, "If it's okay with you?"

The idea made Baron's fingers twitch. He'd earned those records—half stolen, half bought with the money he made at his job, which was sweeping other people's disgusting hair off the floor in a barbershop whose spinning pole made him think of murdering himself. Of course, he didn't want to part with them. But it was for the band . . .

"You can borrow some of mine," Eddie offered gently. He went and got his milk crate out from under the bed, then set it in front of Baron like a sacrifice. Baron's eyes bugged out a little at what he saw there, but he worked to keep his disaffected facade intact, plucking only one single—That'll Be the Day by the Crickets—out of the box.

"This one," he said greedily. Eddie looked at him, arched and eyebrow, shrugged.

"That's all right. I know how to play that one already. I can show you if you'd like."

It was like he was a starving hound and Eddie had just dangled a raw, bloody cut of steak over his head. The only songs that Baron knew how to play were the ones Eddie had already heard at the church fete, and half of those chords had to be faked to get the band through their set. But he didn't want Eddie to know how hungry he was for it. He reminded himself that he was the one with the band, the one with all the charisma. Older, funnier, and in the right light, more handsome, too.

"Alright," he squeaked out. And then his cheeks got hot. Good thing the light under Eddie's brother's bed was poor, and that Baron was dark, like his dad. Good thing. Imagine. Him. Baron. Blushing like a girl.

He stood up fast, throwing the single down on the bed.

"I need to piss," he said fast, "Where's the bog?"

There was a secret under Eddie's lips, a smile that he only half-smiled, a thought that he didn't speak. Instead, he nodded, put the records down on his tautly-made covers, and headed toward the hall. Baron followed him, stepping slowly now. It felt like he was walking into the belly of a great whale, that at any moment he might uncover a heart.

"That's Paulie and Tom's room. You met Tom. Thinks he's a Lothario. And that . . ." A pause, just a moment, at a half-open doorway that revealed a four-posted full bed with a floral bed skirt. "Dad's room."

Dad's room. Baron was still thinking about it as they made their way to the solitary bathroom. He was searching his mind for some scrap of a memory, something that Bongo had said before the fete. *Eddie hasn't been the same since last year. I think you blokes would get along. Cheer him up a little . . .*

The difference, then, between Eddie Hammond Three and other boys. No women here. The house, shabby, but loved, a dusty museum to the one piece that was missing. A mum.

Baron swallowed, his throat tight. The difference between Eddie Hammond Three and other boys—except for Baron. Because when had he ever had a proper mum, either?

Eddie opened the door for him.

"The khazi," Eddie said, as Baron squeezed by. "You know, it's the only place I can go to write my songs. Because of my brothers, yeh? But also the pipes mean the acoustics are fantastic."

Baron lifted the seat, swaying a little over the loo.

"A little privacy?" he asked, then made himself smile a wicked smile, "Or are you going to give me a hand?"

It was Eddie's turn to blush. He high-tailed it out, letting the door gently close behind him. Funny, in this house of overgrown colts, of heavy hoof beats on the stairs and snores that could shake the barn rafters, how quietly

Eddie moved, with deliberation, like every creaking bone mattered. Baron aimed, pissed, thinking about it. He wondered if Eddie ever said a word at dinner or if his brothers just talked over him. Maybe he needed music, then, to be heard.

He pulled the cord, watched the yellow water swirl away. Gave himself a glance in the mirror, touching his own oiled curls. And then stopped, looking at himself for a long time. What was it that Eddie had said?

There was only one way to know. When he swung open the door, Eddie was standing there in the hallway, one foot up on the wainscoting, waiting.

"Ey," said Baron, "Did you say something about writing songs?"

4 - 1997

Cymbeline had known coming into it that there would be no door in the counselor's rooms at Camp Kaaterskill. This had been emphasized to her in the brochure and on the training weekend, just four weeks before. Confronting the narrow space, the open doorway, the curtainless windows that looked out into a boggy lake and also directly into the window of the next cabin over, was, however, another thing entirely. On this, the first day of the summer, just twenty hours or so before her campers would arrive, she stood on the threshold of what would be her quarters for the next twelve weeks, and sighed. Heavily. The sound seemed to rattle and echo against the cobwebbed ceiling beams but did not shake a single mote of dust from them.

"You okay, Perky?" asked Alana, a junior counselor from South Carolina who would inhabit a bed surrounded by campers in the open main room of the cabin. Cymbeline didn't even turn her head at first to the name that meant nothing to her, not yet. It had been gifted to her on the last night of the training weekend, ironically, supposedly because of her particularly mumbling and depressive karaoke performance of "Call Me Al," though Cymbeline suspected that Mr. Kreizkin, the camp founder, had other talents in mind.

"Oh," Cymbeline said belatedly, "Yes. I'm just used to having more privacy, is all."

Her knapsack still in hand, she turned to look over one shoulder at Alana as the teenager folded her camp shirts into the cubby beneath her bed.

"Why would you come to camp, then?" Alana asked. She was a sun-kissed youth, what the counselors called a "lifer," whose parents had abandoned her here every year since she was six. Alana already knew all of the camp songs. Though she was four years younger than Cymbeline, the senior counselor could sense an eagerness there. Alana would gladly inculcate Cymbeline into the Ways of Camp, if only Cymbeline would allow her.

But that was not Cymbeline's way. "Perky" just shrugged her shoulders and slipped into the tiny counselor's room, dumping her heavy bag on the mattress, letting the contents all spill out.

"I needed an adventure," she said glumly, and Alana seemed to leave it there, at that, though the truth was darker and more bland, both.

I have nowhere else to go, Cymbeline thought. She shoved her clothes into the wooden dresser, not bothering folding them. A splinter lodged itself in her knuckle on the way, but Cymbeline didn't cry. She only squinted at her hand like it was a foreign creature, outside of her, and expertly fished the needle of cedar out.Camp Kaaterskill, as well as her brother camp for boys across the lake, Camp Berean, was supposed to be a dry camp. The lack of alcohol, marijuana, and harder substances had been made abundantly clear during training weekend. Why, then, Cymbeline wondered, did Alana take a soda bottle filled with vodka and tonic out of her overnight bag, tighten the lid, then tuck it into the pocket of her Baja poncho? Cymbeline supposed that as the senior counselor, she should have been the one to scold Alana, but she didn't feel up to it as they made their way across their darkening unit of cabins and toward the pitch-black path that ribboned through the camp.

* * *

She didn't feel up for a lot, lately. School or work. Dating. Books. Music. Anything. The summer job here had been a matter of absolute necessity. She couldn't stay with her Gram a moment longer, and her roommates had already sublet her room to someone else. Now it wasn't as though she'd been anticipating a *fun* summer. Miserable, in fact, as she had planned to spend it tending to her mother, whose body was by then riddled with cancer. But when Mom died suddenly in early April, she was left with a gap. An emptiness. An aimlessness. What purpose was there in anything, drinking or partying or studying or boys?

Maybe, she thought, breathing in the cool night air, this place could offer her that. Not just a bed. But a definition.

"Give it," she said, holding out her hand to Alana, who eyed the older counselor warily for a moment before passing the bottle of "Seven-Up" over. Alana watched as Cymbeline took a long swig.

"Easy there, Perky," Alana said, snatching the bottle back. Cymbeline coughed and sputtered, but her tongue felt prickly and that was something, at least, as they made their way toward the smoky glen.

Not all the counselors had gathered in the wooded spot—there were maybe twenty or two dozen of them, milling about with forbidden bottles and flasks and pipes. There was a group of boys prodding the fire, which had not yet caught in earnest, and a cluster of girls who had gathered around another boy with a guitar. Some of the silhouettes danced and gamboled; a boy with shaggy hair juggled a trio of hacky sacks before the fire. But most simply wandered in that way that young people do, talking to each other or trying to muster the courage to talk. As soon as they stepped into the clearing, Alana called to someone—"Alf! Alf!"—and then abandoned Cymbeline in the darkness.

So Cymbeline did what came naturally. She followed the strains of music.

The boy who played guitar did it well, his hands curling delicately around its neck. It made Cymbeline think of her mother, try as she might to stuff that memory down. She hadn't touched the guitar she'd received as a gift for her ninth birthday since before her mother got sick again. She wasn't even sure why she'd brought it to camp, except she didn't entirely trust her grandmother not to sell it behind her back. The thought of playing it made her feel queasy, like she was insulting her mother's memory. But part of her wondered, as she watched the boy's hands, if her mother wouldn't mind. Maybe she could ask the boy for *his* guitar. Maybe she could strum out a song or two. Maybe the chords would come back to her like old friends. Or maybe the boy would take the question the wrong way. Perhaps he'd be defensive, or ask if she really knew how to play. Boys got like that sometimes—prickly, ugly. Already, there were girlish eyes upon his pretty face. His eyelashes curled like spider's legs. His cheeks were mottled pink from the heat of the fire. *He* was the center here. She was an outsider.

He was cute, but cute didn't do much for Cymbeline. Not now, in the wake of her mother's death. She sat down in the cluster of other girls. Watching, too.

The boy's song tumbled from one ("Dust in the Wind") to the next. A familiar song, too-often played on the radio and in supermarket muzak. Still, there was something there, wasn't there? Cymbeline found herself drumming her fingers on the mossy log beneath her, gently nodding her head.

"Oh man," someone said behind her, "I *hate* this one."

There were lanky legs stepping over her, and a pair of eyes—black as spent coals—flitted toward her, too. She saw then that what she had thought had been a boy, juggling by the fire, was actually a girl, or a woman, nearly. Her age or just a little bit older. Dressed in baggy shorts and a tank top, hardly any breasts to speak of, dark brownish hair overgrown. The boy with the guitar looked up at the girl, scowling, his song momentarily broken.

"What are you talking about? The Ruffians are the voice of our generation."

The girl plopped herself down on the log next to Cymbeline. "It's hackneyed top 40s trash," she said. Her grin was broad, like she was hungry for something. Spoiling, Cymbeline thought, for a fight. The boy looked rattled. His fingers tensed awkwardly over the neck of his guitar, jerkily twanging.

"So it's popular. Not everything can be super obscure C-86 and John Peel and all that crap."

The girl snorted, but Cymbeline could see a conflicted look on her face hidden beneath the bravado. Like she'd been called to the mat. The girl tucked her head against her hands, watching the boy, apparently chastised.

Shedding their argument, he began to play again, more carefully this time. Cymbeline listened. The song wasn't bad, really, even if it *was* top

40s tripe. It had a spark. She glanced at the girl, seeing her deep-set eyes, the unrest in them. And suddenly felt spurred to prove something to her. To prove her wrong.

When the boy picked up the chorus again—*And if, after all this time, I find that I never find you*—Cymbeline sang along. She might have hated her voice—a bit too low and gravelly for her own tastes—but she knew that it had an impact on others. When she managed to raise it above the fog of her own anxiety, people listened. Always. Now, the girl turned to her, both eyebrows lifted in surprise. Before that moment, it was as though Cymbeline had been invisible. But now she was there, undressed within the girl's gaze. She felt herself trail off. She felt her cheeks heat.

"Not half bad," the girl said, when Cymbeline's voice had faded. The smile that lifted the corner of her mouth was still skeptical. But there was a hint of amusement, of pleasure, too, now, beneath that skepticism. "Even if that track is teenybopper bullshit. I'm Sid, here at camp."

The girl didn't say what her name was outside of camp. Cymbeline sensed that she wasn't meant to ask.

"Cymbeline," she answered, and held out a hand, which Sid took and shook firmly, like a businessman's handshake.

"Cymbeline, like Shakespeare? That's a mouthful for a camp name."

"No, no. I guess my camp name is Perky," Cymbeline said, and she couldn't help but grimace to say it. Sid grimaced too, then laughed. Without hesitation, her eyes went right to Cymbeline's chest.

"Oh man," she said, her gaze unmoving. "That's terrible."

"Yeah . . ." Cymbeline replied, feeling herself blush, or maybe it was the vodka, or the heat of the fire. "But it's funny. Most people know my name from the song. The Saffron one?"

Sid's eyes darted toward the stars. "Not my favorite track by them. I've always been more of a Templeton fan."

"Yeah," cut in the boy with the guitar, losing the music again. "You would be."

"Shut up, Neil," Sid said. "You wouldn't know good music if it bit you in the ass."

"Like you do," Neil said. Sid rolled her eyes.

"Yeah. I do. I'd make you a mix CD, if I gave a damn what you thought. Look, you just keep playing. Provide the soundtrack." Her shining eyes challenged Neil, who was male, and older, too, by at least a couple years. And yet he broke under their pressure. He bowed his head, fingers curling strings. More music, a new song. Not the Ruffians. Something older. Fuck. Saffron. "Cymbeline."

She winced. It was her mother's favorite song, the one she'd sung before bedtime and nap time and on long car rides too. Cymbeline recalled how it felt to tuck in her body next to her mother when she was three or four years old, too old for a nap, really, but still needing one. How her mother held her. She remembered putting her hands on her mother's face, cradling those powder-soft cheeks between them. She remembered how their heartbeats would seem to sync as they drifted toward sleep, her double-timed child's heart tripping along to her mother's slower pulse. Her mother, singing, but slower and slower still.

My Cymbeline, child of the darkest ocean . . .

"My real passion's music. My dad owned a record store when I was a kid. But of course I know Shakespeare," Sid was saying to her. "Marlowe. Thomas. I'm the most well-read mechanic-cum-camp counselor you'll ever meet."

"You're a mechanic?" Cymbeline asked, doing her best to shake the music out of her hair. This camp was mostly filled with campers and counselors far richer than she was. Legacy kids whose fathers could be seen on the lodge walls in Camp Berean, dressed in starchy and vaguely fascist uniforms. Sid only shrugged.

"Something like that," she said vaguely. "When I'm not doing this. My mom wanted me to go to a Seven Sisters school like she did. But I've had enough sisters just coming *here* to last me for the rest of my life."

A teenage rebellion, then. Sid was probably a rich kid, too. Cymbeline wanted to ask more, but the chords of Neil's song were plodding onward and onward. *Cymbeline, I am undressed before you, distressed before you, none comes before you . . .* The images were coming fast and thick now. Mom, nap time. Mom, during chemo. Or else Mom tying her hair up in the rear view mirror after an endless afternoon at the county pool. Or else dying, her breath prattling out to nothing.

Then she remembered what Sid had said. *I've always been more of a Templeton fan.* Those words sparked something inside her, setting a switch off in her brain.

"Hey," Cymbeline said at last, and when she spoke, Sid lifted both eyebrows, "Do you want to get out of here?"

"Perky," said Sid, grinning so big that Cymbeline could see the permanent retainer glued to her lower teeth, "I thought you'd never ask.

5 - 1957

On a Thursday, Baron sacked off from his art class, pinched a bottle of gin from his uncle's cabinet, and hoofed it down to Speke. The term had just started and the weather was warmish still. He wore a jumper but no coat, had no need for it, but it meant that the bottle looked obscene in the pocket of his trousers. When he passed by ladies he noticed them looking, giggling greenishly, and hoped they didn't know his aunt, and hoped that if they did they wouldn't say a word. And yet he couldn't resist a joke, not Baron, not then.

"You can touch it if ya'd like." Then the shriek and the run. Almost as satisfying as a kiss.

It was always like that for him, the dueling impulses. Sometimes he wanted a wank in the middle of a church and sometimes he wanted to be looked at like a saint in the middle of a hovel. Despite his aunt's Christian leanings, Baron figured she knew next to nothing about godhood. Christ had been a man, hadn't he? Probably got throbbers too, and pointed them around at Mary Magdalene. And here Baron was, and he hadn't even stuck it in a woman yet. Wasn't that godly? Jesus. Even thinking about it made him want a wank.

But there was no time for that, not now. He was skulking around the schoolyard, hooking and unhooking his fingers into the chain fence until he saw the boys tumble from the bus, his eyes searching out just one boy, that beautiful towhead with all its beautiful thoughts and even more beautiful songs just under it.

"Hey!" he called out, seeing the golden shine under the gray gray morning.

"Eddie!"

Eddie turned, warm air making those roses bloom on his cheeks again, and then when his eyes hit on Baron a grin lit up his whitish teeth. He said something to a friend beside him—brown-haired, ordinary—then hustled up to the fence.

"Baron," Eddie said simply, the simple smile beautiful on those simple lips. Maybe it was the devil in him, but Baron didn't dare to smile back. Just angled his head back, chin up, truly tough and untouchable.

"Thought you'd fancy a walk and a sip with me, Hammy," he said, the nickname falling into place at just that moment. Surely, he hadn't been the first to think of the name, and Eddie winced at Baron's words, then glanced toward the schoolyard, and to his friend, the brown-haired and the ordinary, waiting for him.

"A date then?" Eddie teased, but didn't meet Baron's eyes when he said it. "Well, I suppose I *would* fancy *that*. But can Liam come?"

"Can Liam come?" Baron echoed dumbly back but Eddie's brow was low and furrowed despite his invisibly pale eyebrows.

"Yeah, you heard me, can he come?"

"I won't be your mistress," Baron said mockingly, then pursed his lips down to the size of an arsehole and pushed his tongue against his cheek. Eddie rolled his eyes.

"It's not like that, Baron. You'll like Liam. He plays guitar, you know. Better'n you."

"Yeah," Baron said, "*That's* what I like." But he might as well have said it to himself because Eddie was running back into the throng of boys to fetch Liam. As he waited, Baron did his best to put a real, proper sulk on his face, scowling down at the scuffed up toes of his shoes.

"All right," he heard shortly after, and looking up, was faced with Eddie, and Liam, apparently, too. Up close he could see that Liam was hardly anything more than a baby. Thirteen or fourteen at most. Awful teeth. All mossy, like he hardly brushed.

"Baron," Eddie said, "This is Liam Waller, me best mate. Liam, this is—"

"Yeh, I heard," said Liam, buttoning up his coat. "Baron. Hi. Hammy said you got us booze then?"

Baron stuffed his hand in his pocket, wrapping his grip around the bottle, feeling it cold and hard. He considered the poppet, and Eddie's face. Even. Sweet. Unreadable.

"Okay, fine," Baron said, pulling the bottle out. "Yeah. But are you going to climb that fence or not?"

Eddie glanced at Liam, who grinned with those terrible teeth back. Then they both scrambled up and over.

* * *

Baron had had in his head a certain kind of day, that while his aunt was off doing the shopping and going round to his mother's house for tea, he would sneak Eddie into his bedroom and the two would sit there alone, the heads of their guitars knocking, and work on some songs. He'd been wanting to tell Eddie how that song had gotten inside his head. "My Little Bird," Ed had called it, playing it over at his house with his brother snoozing under the covers above. It had been cracking, but still not *done*, not *perfect*, which is how Eddie had put it and Baron had agreed. For two weeks now he'd sat through painting class, mushing up turpentine into paint, humming, half-drunk from the fumes, puzzling over it. Now he had an idea, the key to make it all work. Open with the chorus, yeah? Then come back to it again at the end, only with a tweak of the lyrics. "*His* little bird," and that would make the song mean something else, something bigger than a boy and a girl. The whole world. A story. A story in a song. Baron knew how to do it, even if he didn't know the chords yet, even if he needed Eddie to show him. And for Eddie to show him, he needed to get him alone, just the two of them, knocking their heads together over their guitars.

But instead they were sitting in the boggy woods outside the Seaman's Orphanage, taking turns pressing their lips up against the bottle.

Eddie and Baron listened as Liam complained about his father, first, and then his little sister, and then, finally, and with a flourish, his mother, whom he compared to Eva Braun. "She's obsessed with keeping the trains running on time," he said, loosening his schoolboy's tie. Baron didn't bother telling Liam that Eva Braun had nothing to do with the trains. He sensed in the younger boy the desire to be brash and shocking—to be what Baron was, more or less—but also sensed that Liam lacked the fundamental spark and fire that it would take to make that happen. Just wasn't bright enough. Sharp enough. Perhaps he was meant to be another sort of boy. Soulful or peaceful. Sweet like a girl, like Eddie was. But Liam hadn't realized that, not yet. Baron wondered if such a creature, lumpy and unformed, could *really* be better at him than guitar, and figured his Council-house dwelling, fully nuclear family (they even had a dog, Liam said!) must have scrimped and saved for guitar lessons for him. *Why, with lessons, even I could be a brilliant musician!* Baron told himself, but he'd been making do with those banjo chords from his dear sweet mostly-absent Mummy, and would make do awhile longer. His Aunt Deedz—who only kept cats, too many of them—thought that music was for scoundrels and sailors.

Anyway, eventually Liam had run his tongue out. By then he'd noticed how Eddie had kept his head bowed through the entire speech and he passed him the bottle and watched Eddie swig.

"Sorry, Hammy," he said. "I forget how lucky I am, you know, to have Mother at all."

"Yeh," was all Eddie said, no forgiveness in his voice.

"What happened to her, then?" Baron asked, a bit bolder than he'd meant to sound. But then, by way of an apology, he went fishing through his pockets for a pair of fags, lit both, and handed one to Eddie. Eddie took it, puffing and drinking away. When he looked up at Baron, his eyes seemed shadowed even under his pale, pale, powder pale eyelashes.

"Cancer. At the end, her whole body was just . . . littered with it."

"Sorry," Baron said. But he had that tone again, the one he sometimes couldn't help, like everything was a spoil for a fight. Actually, now that the gin was working good in him, he wouldn't have minded hitting someone. But neither of these boy children were worth a fist right now, not Liam and not the sad sorry Eddie, neither.

"Yeh," Eddie said again and then lifted his eyes up swiftly so that they settled in on Baron like a pair of science fictional laser beams. "What of *your* mother then? Sainted dead, or a whore?"

The corner of Baron's mouth squiggled up. This boy. This beautiful boy. All quiet until something brilliant hit him. Baron could relate to that, except the quiet parts.

"Bit of both. Sainted whore. Me father left when I was a whelp, and me mum used to have me share a bed with her and her boyfriend while they were fucking all night. I made the crucial error of telling my Aunt Deedz about the moans I heard when mummy and Uncle Timmy were scratching each others' backs so she had the police in to get me."

The faces of the other two boys were blank. Shocked. Which was how Baron liked it. It made the tender truth, squashed deep inside him, easier to swallow. *Dada left and Deedz practically kidnapped me since she couldn't have a baby of her own.*

"Sorry," Eddie said, too softly, too genuinely. Baron sucked at his fag, exhaled through flared nostrils.

"Yeh," Baron replied. "Well, I live with Aunt Deedz and me Uncle Fred, now. And two dozen cats." Lies. There were only four cats, maybe six if you counted the ones she left milk for on the step. "Me mum comes by for tea now and then. Plays the banjo, you know."

"Banjo!" Liam said, grinning suddenly, maniacally. That was when Baron decided that if he was going to hit one of them, it would definitely be Liam.

"Bought me that guitar, too," Baron went on, not entirely sure why he was still talking except the quiet, concerned way Eddie was still looking at him. "The one I played at the fete. She's an alright bloke, me mum."

"Heh," Liam said. "You know, Hammy told me you had a band."

"Have a band," Baron said evenly, eyeing Eddie, who'd gone quiet again. Christ, why was this boy so like an egg that had to be cracked open again and again before being ate? "The Bartlebys. Eddie's joining."

"Well, you should let me in, too," Liam said. Baron guffawed, his eyes going to Eddie like it should have been a secret between them, but Eddie only shrugged.

"Yeh," he said. "Liam's good. I told you—"

"Three guitars?" Baron sputtered. "Absurd."

"Not if the three know what they're doing. This one does." Eddie gestured with the bottle toward Liam, who wrestled it from his hands and took a swig. Baron watched him, his own nostrils going all wide and flarey again. He was becoming really, truly angry now, like he could feel his fists a-curling and uncurling. Pouncey.

"Besides, that'd be six of us altogether—"

"Five," said Eddie.

"What?" said Baron.

"Five. You kicked Dickie Ashby out, yeah?"

Baron's eyes went wider, his face red with the heat. "Yeah, yeah," he said, lying through his teeth as he stamped his cigarette out. The anger suddenly gone and leaving a naked kind of embarrassment in its wake. "Fine. Well, maybe. I'll have to see you play first."

Liam looked at Eddie, and let out the world's most mortifying sound in the history of sounds: "Hurrah!"

They couldn't go to anybody's home. It was late enough now that their mothers might have been there, or fathers, or brothers, or sisters, or aunts, or uncles, or cats, or dogs—anyone who might have known they'd skived off of school. So they went to Black's Music instead, slipping into the dusty space, the bell twinkling behind them. A few months ago this had been Baron's secret spot, where he'd wander around and look at guitars alone, feeling Byronic and fated. Strange, then, to be sharing it with somebody else. Two somebodies. He looked sourly at Liam's back, wondered how and why Eddie was wrapped so tight around his finger. It was a coward's back, not even the broadness of a man, yet. Slumpy shoulders. Probably had never even been in a fist fight. Probably had never had a proper wank.

They wandered about, their hands touching the glossy finishes of the axes there. Eddie lifted up a bass and diddled it a little. Looked good with it. Looked right. Gave Baron a thought so fleeting that he'd forget it for a year or three.

Meanwhile, Liam was holding the most expensive guitar in the shop. A custom Les Paul black beauty with a tune-a-matic bridge that flashed and shone in his hands like a comet. The shopkeeper called out to him—"Careful with that," but Liam only smirked as he slung the strap over his shoulder, plugged the guitar in to a nearby amplifier, and started playing.

Flash and bang. Drip drop. Explosion. Those hands flew through scales with a speed and ease that looked almost demonic to our young Baron, then broke away into the thrumming chord progression of "Be-bop a Lua" and then back to scales again, and then a solo, something familiar, one that Baron couldn't quite place. And he was struck in that moment by how good Liam was, yes, so unexpected in such a small, shitty body, but also by a peculiar notion of covetousness over this boy he'd only just met and didn't much like. Yes, yes, he'd have him in his band. Baron certainly couldn't let him go be in any other. Yes, it was a marriage of sorts, with Eddie standing between them as officiant, bopping his head in a way that wasn't cool at all and yet *yes*.

Over as soon as it began. Liam unplugged, hung the Gibson back up on the wall and then kissed his fingertips and let them linger over the shiny black like someone worshipful might kiss a holy ring or text.

"Right, then?" Liam asked. Baron felt how this child was waiting, really waiting for his approval, for his *permission*, felt a swell of power so sure it was basically erotic. Baron shrugged.

"Fuck," he said, and then laughed: "Yes."

* * *

They walked together into the twilight, the three of them, drunk and jagged with nicotine from Baron's stolen cigarettes. Baron and Eddie escorted Liam home, and as he turned up the path, Baron thumped him on the shoulder, brotherly, though he knew not what it was to have nor be a brother.

"Welcome," he said, "To the Bartlebys."

Liam only ugly-grinned.

After, without the frenetic Liam between them, the evening was almost mummified. Eddie and Baron spoke in low tones about records, the ones they'd traded and the ones they'd soon steal, and it felt like an intimate secret to talk about it. And then Baron brought Eddie to the path of the Hammond council house, the raucous den of a half dozen little and not-so-little boys.

"Practice soon then, yeah?" Eddie asked at last, hopeful, but in no way desperate. Baron nodded.

"Yeh, but . . ." His words faded. Christ, how he hated to ask for help. "We'll have to get together first so you can show me a few more chords. I won't be the worst one in me band."

"Fine," said Eddie, with an easy shrug. "I'll do that."

"Yeh," Baron said. "Thanks."

He could have gone up his path, but Eddie was lingering there, standing around, a question in his eyes.

"What?" Baron demanded.

"Dickie Ashby," Eddie spat back, and Baron was surprised by how firm and hot Eddie sounded, angry, truly. Which was a laugh, because hadn't Eddie just invited his own friend into the Bartlebys, too?

"Look, I don't see—"

"It's not just that there are too many of us," Eddie went on, talking right over Baron. "Dickie was *awful*. That boy on the jug could at least keep time. But Dickie kept getting you off the beat! And do we even need a jug or a washboard if we're going to be a rock 'n' roll band? We need a drummer. A *proper* drummer. Not him."

Baron was stunned. Eddie had been thinking about this, truly thinking about this, as though the band were as important to him as it was to Baron.

"Yeah," Baron said. "Well . . ."

"'Well' nothing," Eddie shook his head. "I'm serious about this, Baron. I thought you were too."

Baron stuffed his hands down in his pockets. "Hammy, I am," he said.

Eddie shook his head.

"Don't call me Hammy."

"Okay," was all Baron could say. Eddie started up the path to his home. Baron felt his stomach twist and clench. Maybe it was all the gin, but mostly, he thought, the day wasn't ending up how he wanted it to. He had wanted to make something special with Eddie. Something exquisite. A song that had been bubbling up inside him all this time.

"Eddie?" Baron called out. Eddie turned, looking. Not hopefully. A little hatefully, even. Until Baron spoke. "Dickie isn't a problem. He's gone. I promise you that."

"Yeah," said Eddie darkly, "We'll see."

He went inside his house and slammed the door behind him.

6 - 2017

The hired car wheezed up the narrow road, creaking upward and upward toward a sky that was gray as slate in this late winter. In fact, everything was gray: a mattress of snow against the mountain, the shiftless trees, the houses, mid-century, spare, tucked in against the Earth. It was not a promising season.

Matthew Hammond clutched his phone to his cheek. The reception here was spotty, in the mountains, in the woods, in the middle of nowhere New York State, and the sound of the tires against rocks and ice was enough to obliterate most of whatever remaining sound he might have heard sparking on some distant end.

"Sorry?" he shouted into the receiver, "Edelman?"

A spurt of fuzz crackled back at him. And then nothing. The driver's eyes briefly went to the rear view mirror, intercepting Matthew's pale blue eyes—and then away. Pretending to be as anonymous he was paid to be. Matthew hung up his phone and tucked it back into his pocket.

"Yeah?" he said to the driver, sounding tired already. The guy had been eyeing him all the way from the airport, dancing around it. Waiting to lunge in for the kill. Well, might as well get it over with. "What is it, then?"

"It's just . . ." the driver started. He laughed a little, dry, creaky laughter even though Matthew suspected that neither of them found it funny. It was all nerves for the old man, probably. "I've met plenty of celebrities in my line of work, you know?"

"Yeah?" Matthew said again.

"Ace Frehley once puked back there."

"Charming," Matthew said, glancing at the upholstery, which seemed clean enough, now, but now he would always know that it had once contained remnants of Ace Frehley's stomach.

"But," the driver began again, "It's still really remarkable."

The awe in his voice. It was stomach turning. Like the wonder of a child at meeting Santa Claus, even though Santa Claus was nothing but an old drunk in a fake beard. Matthew said nothing, his eyes going back out the window at the spider veins of tree limbs beyond the road. Pretending not to be here. Pretending not to be anywhere, or anyone.

"You really do look so much like your father," he said. Ah, there it was. The bullet. The arrow. The poison dart. Matthew resisted the urge to roll his eyes.

"Yes," he said dryly, "That's what I'm told."

It was true. Since he was a baby, really. Barely walking, the pale hair new on his head. *Oh, don't you look like Daddy!* And *Going to be a rock star someday?* Was it even true anymore? Forty two years old and that blond hair was thinning whereas daddy dear had gotten hair transplants in his thirties. Plus the eye lift. The Botox. Matthew had done none of it, and now his face had a certain disconcerting fleshiness to it. Once he'd told himself that this was a show of how *authentic* he was, unlike his father. How he could be real even when he had the money and the positioning to be just as plastic as dear old Dad.

But it had cleaved them, hadn't it? They no longer wore the same face, even if strangers claimed it wasn't true. Matthew glanced in the rear view mirror, his gaze catching the driver's.

"It's in the eyes," the driver said. "I had a poster of Hammond up in my bedroom when I was a boy. I wasn't a fag. I don't want you to think I was a fag. But I thought that maybe if I could learn to curl my lip like him or play bass like him the ladies would line up, you know? I'd study that poster for hours. And those eyes. Christ. Just like your eyes. It's uncanny. Like seeing a ghost."

"My dad's not dead," Matthew said quickly. The driver grunted in agreement, as the car slogged further and further up the mountain.

The phone rang again then. Matthew answered it, grateful for the respite from this interminable interrogation.

"Edelman," he said, not a question, but an imperative: *yes, go.*

"Matty," Edelman began. His manager often sounded like a manager on TV might, the lilting Brooklyn accent spilling through . The nicknames. The fluffing. The preening. "The house will be all ready for you when you arrive. You have the code, baby, yeah?"

"Yeah, baby," Matthew muttered in return. Sour at being patronized like this. Sour that this pilgrimage upstate was necessary at all.

"Good," Edelman said, unruffled. "I've taken care of everything. Fridge is stocked. Plenty of booze for you. Everything's gluten free, just like you like it. Cleaning woman comes on Tuesdays. Now remember: I've shut down the WiFi. You're up there to work, Matty, baby. I want you to focus. Recording studio's all yours, and the piano. You brought your guitar, yes? The missus'll be pissed if you touch any of hers."

"Yeah." Matthew licked his lips, feeling suddenly hungry for a cigarette even though he had mostly quit two years ago, except when he was drunk. He felt hungry for a drink, then, too, and fumbled for the flask in his pocket. He knew he should have been grateful for all of this—his manager's generosity, when the album was two years past due, when none of it was *clicking*, okay? And definitely not in a way that would have satisfied the label. But it felt wrong, also, to be dependent on his manager's wife's gear and space. He was the son of a megastar, after all. And she was only a mediocre shoe gazer musician from the turn of the century.

Still, it had been ages since he'd had a hit. And Edelman had promised him . . .

"I'm telling you, Matty. This place is magic. It's what you need. A week up there will get your head straight."

"Okay, okay," Matthew said, and laughed a little grimly as he took a dry swig of gin. The driver was watching him in the rear view mirror again. Matthew pretended that he wasn't.

"Oh, and one last thing," Edelman went on. "I've got a girl there who's going to be stopping by, in case you need a hand with anything."

"An intern?" Matthew asked, letting out a slight groan. That was the last thing he needed—some college kid hanging around, eyes haunted, as they always were, waiting for him to drop some scrap about the great Edmund Hammond. But Edelman clucked his tongue.

"Nah. A friend of the wife's. She's brilliant. We figured she could help you take down the music, whatever. Be your girl Friday."

"Edelman, I don't need—"

"Trust me on this one. You do." Suddenly, all lilt and accent was gone from Edelman's voice. Maybe a weaker man would have stuttered to explain himself to Matthew, but that wasn't the sort of guy that Edelman was. He knew how to be wheedly when he needed to be and when to be firm. Matthew respected that, mostly. In an industry full of pleasers and suck-ups, Edelman knew when to have a backbone. And his backbone hadn't steered Matthew wrong, not yet.

"Okay, fine. You're the boss," Matthew said, but by the time he answered, the reception had cut out again, and the hired car had reached the top of the mountain.

* * *

The limo driver dumped his luggage in the driveway, jostling Matthew's guitar more than he liked. He could have sworn he heard a faint ringing of strings when the case hit gravel. Then the guy had the gall to stand around with his hands in his pockets, waiting for a tip.

Always tip well, Matt, his father had told him, over and over again. *Better than they expect. Lets them know you appreciate them.*

The problem with that, Matthew thought, as he got out his wallet, was that once you slipped someone a hundred, they told all their friends about it. About your *generosity*. Once you gave someone an autograph, or a selfie in the middle of a Safeway aisle, people noticed when you had the nerve to try to go on with your own life like an ordinary person. They'd tweet about it or tell the gossip rags. Then the mythology would start: *Matthew Hammond, a real dick. I met him once, you know. Should have gotten hair plugs*

34

like his dad. So Matthew pulled out a crisp hundred and greased the guy's palms with it.

"Thanks so much, sir," the guy said, like he barely even meant it, and finally bent over to grunt and wheeze and carry Matthew's luggage up the steps.

"That's all right," Matthew tried to excuse him from having a heart attack, but the guy went up the stairs anyway, blocking them for a minute while Matthew scrambled up behind him and entered the code Edelman had given him for the front door.

"Want me to carry them in?" the guy asked. His middle-aged cheeks had burst into red poppy blossoms. Matthew couldn't help himself. He let out a barky laugh.

"God, no," he said, then blushed, himself, like a little boy might. "I mean, I'm sorry. That'll be fine."

Then he took his own bags and pulled the door closed behind him.

* * *

Edelman's wife was C-list at best. She had one album in the early aughts that had hit it big with college girls and secret lesbians, and if she had followed that up with something solid, then maybe she would have been something more than a trivia factoid at the suburban bar. But her next release flopped, and then she disappeared from the world. Matthew couldn't entirely blame her.

Sure, he'd had three albums that were well known, but none for nearly a decade and the last two had faded into obscurity. Edelman had told him that it was time to break out again. Once Matthew could have coasted on the strength of his father's name, but the kids today didn't care about Saffron, didn't care about the nostalgia trips of their grandparents. They listened to other kids on YouTube. They listened to SoundCloud rappers. Matthew would never be one of those, but he could write a solid pop song. A summertime hit, Edelman had said. That's what they needed to break out. Baby.

Matthew meandered through the spacious mid-century home, eyes scanning the polished surfaces. The living room was banked with glass windows and understuffed with Swedish wood and leather. On the shipboard walls hung the type of photos you'd see at any family house: snapshots of girls at summer camp, wedding photos with Edelman looking like a gawky teenage boy in his suit. Then there was the gold record, the pair of framed album covers. Beside them was a black and white photo of a woman at a piano, still looking more like a girl than a woman. Both Edelman and his wife possessed a sort of preternatural youthfulness. *Had probably gotten fat off the blood of young musicians,* Matthew joked to himself wryly as he sat down at the baby grand that took up the space in this home where a dining room table would have normally been. He lifted the fallboard, let his fingers glide over the white keys, not pressing any yet. Felt the stillness of the air.

Edelman's wife was a better musician than Matthew. A better musician than most, really. But while her husband had tucked more young musicians under his wing after that, the wifey had essentially disappeared. Now nearly fifteen years had passed without another song and no one knew why. Matthew felt the cool ivory, wondered what songs this piano had sung, or hadn't. He played the first few notes of Cymbeline's song "Absent Friends," and then stopped. It felt like the wrong magic for the moment, with the snow drifting hazily past the windows and the mountains and the lake out there looking so empty, so lonely, so gray. He stopped a moment, thought on it. Then let his fingers traipse in old, familiar patterns.

"Dear old boy," he sang. "Bonny boy, when you feel you've lost the path . . ."

It was Dad's song. Dad's song for an only son. There had been a time when he couldn't stand it, during adolescence, when the other boys at his private school had called him *bonny* and *precious* and worse. But it had been long enough, now, that he had almost forgotten the sweet, awful pain of it. Now he played and sang with his eyes closed, sounding as much like his Dad as he ever had. Voice getting more worn now, tender with age. Nothing that the surgeons could have done about that, even thirty years ago. Matthew found himself suddenly glad for it. With his eyes closed, he played, and his hands made the same pattern his Dad's hands once had, on a cold winter morning in Scotland, the wood fire that Ma had stoked dying out all because Dad hadn't been able to resist sitting cold-handed at the keys, pounding and pounding this song out all morning long. His song. "Matthew's Song."

It was only when the chords faded away to nothing, the memory to nothing, too, that he heard the buzzer ringing. Could have been ringing for ten minutes for all he'd known. He'd been too far off, in Scotland, age four, lying on the floorboards, watching his daddy's foot working the pedals. Matthew shook away the memory. He stood up, closing the keys, and went to the door, where he had to step around the bags still waiting for him there, the guitar case he had not yet bothered putting away.

Momentary confusion when he opened up the door because he'd mostly expected to find the limo driver, waiting with a bag he'd purposefully forgotten and a palm to be greased again. But this wasn't that filmy old man. This was a girl. No, a woman. But a young one. Willow limbed, with her natural hair combed back into a dark halo, wearing a peacoat and a sweater two sizes too big and leggings that clung to her skinny knees, her slender thighs.

There was some kind of stone at her throat. Jade green, a go light. She smiled, like she was relieved to see him, like she'd been waiting her whole life to see him, and he felt something light up inside of himself. A strange feeling. Twisty and instinctive and wrong.

"You must be Matt," she said, and stuck out a hand. "I'm Naomi. Cymbeline's friend."

He took her hand, shook, but the look of puzzlement hadn't left his face as he felt her bird bones clutched in his firmer hand.

"Who?"

"Oh, didn't Edelman tell you?" Naomi stepped over the threshold, not waiting for an invitation. He stepped back to make room, nearly tripping over the guitar case. She put her hand on his arm to steady him. "I'm the amanuensis. The intern. Your girl Friday?"

Matthew's frown deepened. He nodded dully, wondering to himself what Edelman had been thinking, sending him a creature so lovely. It could only mean one thing here, really. Not inspiration. Distraction. Already, Matthew imagined sinking himself into her, the shuddering release that would come for both of them, the catharsis. Edelman knew—had to know—that Matthew was not his father, the born monogamist, that Matthew had always had a soft spot for lovely girls. Maybe that's why he fixed his smile, quick, and did what his dad would never have done. Put one hand over hers, holding her there a moment longer than he should have.

"Naomi," he said, as if he'd expected this, had expected *her*, "Of course. Yes. Hello."

7 - 1957

Baron thundered through the door of his mother's house like a bull mastiff squeezing through a fox's den. Which is to say, Baron's mother's house was too small for him. Upstairs, there were just two bedrooms, and one belonged to his mum and Uncle Timmy and the other to his little sister, Bess—but neither of the beds belonged to Baron. When he stayed overnight—more and more frequently of late—he slept in Bess's bed, under the lace sheets and floral covers, and she snuggled between her parents, safe there, even though once that same place in that same bed had led Baron to a mess of trouble. No matter. His mum was always telling him he was welcome here, was family, so he came right into the bright front parlor, letting the door slam shut behind him, and then went back toward the kitchen. Bess was doing her schoolwork at the Formica table, her fat legs swinging under the hem of her dress, and his mum was there, too, doing the wash. The steam was in her face and her hair—unfashionably long for a woman her age—fell in limp ringlets over her collarbones. Her dress was tight over tight curves. Baron's stomach clenched, and he told the thought, the feeling to be gone—it was his *mum* after all.

"Allo," he said, and kissed Bess and kissed his mum, and that's when he saw the problem.

"Your buttons are all wrong," he said to her. His mum laughed at herself, looking down at the gap between those buttons and the beige fabric that shone through like a secret, buried heart.

"I don't know where me head is today," she said easily. Then she began unbuttoning, right there. Baron felt his dark cheeks blush, but that didn't stop her. So he sat down beside his sister to hide what the whole thing was doing to him, looking pointedly out the window over the stove, whistling and pretending to be anywhere else as his mother's girdle and brassiere were revealed and then covered again.

"There," she said. "Decent, now."

Baron looked. And lo, she certainly *was*. That dress, nipped in at the waist over child-bearing hips which had beared him. Those tits, pointy in their pointy brassiere. Her white white flesh just above where the buttons met, fixed now, though not much improved.

"Yeh," he said nervously. Then he grabbed Bess's pencil from her hand, dying for a distraction. She whined at him, like a ten year old would, which she was, but he didn't care.

"I'm just drawing you a picture," he said, and doodled a cartoon of her, fat calves and all, on the back of her maths worksheet. Darkened in every ringlet. Easier to focus on that than on his mum.

But it gnawed at him, as he drew and his mum went back to washing. Because she wasn't like other mums. She didn't wear her hair like them or her clothes like them and she didn't act like a mum to him at all, more like a sister. He loved her—Christ, of course he did. Always thinking about a way to get back there when he was stuck at Aunt Deedz', with the boring news radio and the no-guitars-downstairs and feet off the furniture and all of that. But his mum hadn't so much as paid him a visit between ages seven and twelve, and then, after that, it had gotten . . . wrong. His mind went back, as it so often did, to that afternoon this past summer, when she was showing him a new Elvis record and they started dancing and then laughing and then fell on the bed she shared with Timothy, just the two of them, Baron and Mum, in the crisp sheets. Then, breathless, she'd picked up his hand like it was nothing, like it was normal, and put it down on her tit.

"You used to suck on them all day," she'd said. "They told me I didn't have the milk, but I knew better. You got fat on them. You did."

He felt her heart beating wildly and the fuzzy threads of angora beneath his palm and he'd wondered if he was supposed to do something else, like he would to another girl, and for a moment, he *wanted* to, even knowing the wrongness.

But then Timothy had come home and shouted up to them and they were up from the bed in a flash.

Now he had a throbber thinking about it. Sitting at the table with his sister, shifting in his seat. If his mum noticed the way the blood had drained from his cheeks to go other places, she didn't say anything about it. He was coloring so hard the lines went through the paper.

"Hey!" Bess said, and at last snatched it back. Baron put down the pencil, and looked up at his mum.

"Well," she said, smirking back over her shoulder at him, "I saw Sue Grasso's mum at the market today."

Sue. Sweet, simple Sue. Hmm. Baron's tumescence was finally subsiding. He sat back in his chair.

"Did you send her my infinite love and affections?" he asked. His mum laughed a little too hard even though it wasn't all that funny.

"To her mother or to Sue?"

"Both, if it would suit them," Baron said, giving his eyebrows a wiggle. His mother giggled, girlishly.

"It might. Anyway," Baron's mother paused, taking a cigarette pack out of her apron and shaking one out. She stood there, waiting for him to light it, until he got out his lighter and did. "She said that Sue's been waiting for you to ask her to go steady."

"Aw," was all Baron said at first. He slipped the lighter back into his pocket, then pawed at the back of his neck. "I like Sue . . ."

"But?" his mum asked, inhaling.

"But I can't see much future in it."

His mother was smoking, watching him. Bess, beside him, was watching too.

"She's dull!" Baron finally blurted. It was true. Her sleepy little eyes and arse might have been right sexy, but she had barely a thought in her head besides how to comb her hair. She didn't even like music. What kind of a girl was that? "Besides that, I'm busy. I've got art school—"

"Which you barely ever go to," his mum said. Baron shrugged.

"And me band!"

"Ah," said his mother. She got the ashtray down from the shelf next to the flour and shed a long tower of ash into it. "The band."

"What?"

"You know I love the band. Watching you play up there at the fete . . ." His mother shivered. But it was fake, exaggerated. "Still, man cannot live on rock 'n' roll alone, Baron. You have a *chance*. You could really make it with her! You should take Sue up on it."

"Who are you," Baron sneered, standing up, "Aunt Deedz?" How he hated being lectured. Though of course, Aunt Deedz wanted him to stay a virgin until he was at least forty.

"Sorry." His mother held up her hands in that defensive gesture, the one meant to deflect all fault. "Far be it from me to tell you what to do."

"Yes," Baron said. "It's not as if you're me mother."

They both grinned at that, at his cleverness.

"No," she said. "It's not as if I birthed you from my own body."

"It's not as if you fed me from your tits," Baron said, his grin growing more jagged. A bit of a flirt, sure, but it felt good to be openly crass sometimes, and with the one person who truly understood him. That's when Bess threw her hands up over her ears.

"*Stop*, you two," she said. That's when Baron's mum—Bess's mum—bent over to kiss Bess on the head. Baron set his hands on the back of his chair, feeling warm at the sight. It was a real family moment, as if he was part of a real family.

"Fine," Baron said. "Besides, I didn't come here for fighting. I came here because Dickie Ashby is coming over."

Aunt Deedz hated Dickie ever since he broke one of her Royal Doulton collector's plates playing ball with Baron in the house. It had been Baron who'd thrown it, of course. But Dickie had taken the blame, noble mate that he was.

"Ashby," his mum said, giving her cigarette a drag. Rolling her eyes a little. She'd never really liked Dickie, either. Baron supposed that nobody did, except for him, of course. "Tell him to keep his eyes up this time. On *my* eyes."

"Promise you," Baron said, though he knew he couldn't really promise, "that he'll be a gentleman."

* * *

Twenty minutes later, they were lying on his mother's bed, listening to Carl Perkins on Radio Luxembourg. Baron had rehearsed what he was going to say all morning—*Dickie, you've got to go* and *this band stuff is getting more serious, we aren't just tossing off anymore, and I think there's a chance we'll really go somewhere with Eddie and Liam*—but he couldn't make his mouth say it, with Dickie right here beside him, breathing with his mouth open, jangling his feet off-beat to the music, like he always did.

He'd known Dickie since he'd been practically a baby. First day of primary, both boys in their short pants and striped socks and caps. Whereas Baron had been all tan and darkness small, Dickie was a lanky ginger. But he'd seemed funny back then. Bold. Pulling girls' pigtails and chewing gum off the bottoms of desks and things, and Baron had admired that, since back then he hadn't been funny yet, only a little haunted and damaged ever since Dada had left and he'd been taken away from Mummy. Dickie had showed him how to fold a paper airplane. Dickie had showed him how to shoot a rubber band. Dickie had shown him how to pull a thousand funny faces. Dickie had taught him how to laugh again, if he'd even known before.

Now, Dickie looked over to Baron, barking out a laugh as though he was determined to fill the silence. "Your mum's tits, mate," he said.

Baron groaned into his hands. "Feck off, Dickie," he said. "Look at yer own mum's tits."

"Hard to look past them," Dickie said with another bark, which was true. Dickie's mother was about sixty, an old Irish women with tits down around her ankles after whelping a million pups. "Besides, it's not as if *you* don't look at your mum's tits."

"They're more mine than yours," Baron said, grinning a little, because it was true. Dickie was laughing still, shaking his head.

"Cor! To have a mum like that."

"Yeah," Baron agreed. "You wish."

"I do."

"Wanna trade places then?" Baron asked. Dickie shrugged.

"It's not like yours isn't enviable, mate. Two whole houses to yourself? A mum stacked high as Brigitte Bardot?"

"One shit stain father and a partridge in a pear tree!" Baron sang. Dickie snickered.

"I could use a partridge," he said.

Baron looked over at him, at Dick's bucktoothed mouth and thin, chapped lips. He giggled, and Dickie giggled back. It was nice like this, here with Dickie. It was easy. They knew everything about each other, or nearly, but never had to talk about it because what they had was beyond words. Love, sure, in a way. Not a hungry love. A comfortable love.

And now he was going to have to go and break Dickie's heart. The boy loved the Bartlebys as much as any of them. Hadn't been his idea, but he'd been the one to fold the other mates at school into it, because Baron didn't have other friends, not exactly. Admirers, maybe. Enemies, definitely. But friends? No. Well, he'd told himself, plenty of times, famous artists didn't need friends. When had Van Gogh ever had a friend? Still, he hated to forsake his only one. No way Dickie would forgive him.

But right now, Dickie was looking at him with those beady little eyes, thin as an English sunrise, chewing on a piece of skin dead on his lip, and in the moment they were still mates. If Baron didn't know from the way that Dickie looked at him, he knew from the way that Dickie's hand went from the bed to the hardness that was already half-grown in Baron's trousers.

"That a partridge?" Baron asked.

"Some kind of waterfowl, I think. Maybe a goose," Dickie answered, grinning, and in a moment they were on top of each other, touching, grinding.

It always happened like this with the two of them. One moment, joking, normal. The next, all tightness and fists and bitten-down lips. Sometimes they'd do it together every day. Sometimes months would pass, and he'd think that he was over the habit, until he got Dickie alone and they started up all over again.

There were rules, Baron thought, as he pulled Dickie's hard prick out of his trouser, feeling the bead of wetness at the tip and the wrinkled warmth of his skin. They didn't kiss, and if their mouths made contact at all, it had to be plausibly deniable. Sometimes Baron's lips would grace an ear, or the base of Dickie's throat, or his chest, if they managed to get their shirts off, which usually they didn't. Dickie's lips mostly didn't touch anything. He was all hands and cock, but his hands went everywhere, right now wriggling their way under Baron's belt to touch Baron's small, muscular arse. Hadn't even touched Baron's prick yet but already Baron felt the pressure building inside him. Christ, he needed a release. And here it had been only hours since he'd wanked, and twice today in the shower, too.

"Unf," Baron said, biting his lip, because he wanted to kiss Dickie but he knew how that would go so he only panted out, "Touch it. Touch it." Dickie's hands went to the seam in the center of Baron's body, that bundle of nerves and electricity that sometimes felt like it was the source for all ecstasy and every ounce of pain. As Baron squirmed, he got his own cock out, touching his head to Dickie's head. Heat. And stroking, both. Until Dickie's hand went inside him and their bodies both went off, spilling across the covers and the inside of Baron's shirt.

"Christ," Baron said, panting still, waiting for his heart to stop pulsing in every part of him. Even his toes were twitching. Dickie had pulled away even before Baron's body was done, getting out a hanky, wiping himself clean, stuffing himself back into his pants.

"You think your mum minds washing us off her sheets?" Dickie asked, looking down at the puddle there. Baron still didn't want to move, wanted to stay a moment longer in this all-too-temporary place of calm. It was so rare that he wasn't wound up. Bollocks aching all the time.

"She's never said anything," he said, at last sitting up. He peeled off his sweater, using the already damp cotton of his shirt beneath to wipe himself clean.

"Well anyway," Dickie said with a grin, "It's her tits that got us all randy, right?"

Baron looked at him, squinting for a moment. He imagined another universe, another time. When he might kiss Dickie and say that tits had nothing to do with it. But was it even true? Wasn't as though Dickie were beautiful. Not like Sue Grasso or Eddie or even his Mum. *It's just a comfort, he told himself. Nothing else.*

"Right," Baron said, popped up from the bed, and began pulling the covers away. When he shoved them, and his shirt, back down into the hamper, he told himself he'd forgotten all about firing Dickie. Told himself it wasn't necessary. Certainly not yet.

8 - 1977

Two teenage boys sharing one bed. Maybe it was unavoidable. At first, furtive and mostly silent, they took turns twitching under the covers. Then later, over time, they began to coordinate. Mom would say goodnight, blow them kisses from the door, and Zachy would chirp "Goodnight" back, all sweet and innocent and then as the silence set in, he'd slink under the covers to wait for it to happen. His brother's movements. Rhythmic. Jerking. And rhythmically jerk himself, too.

Their motions matched. Their spines fused together like some kind of freak born of the wasteland of a nuclear disaster, leading to one pulse, one brain stem. *Sex*, Zachy thought. *Sex*. He wasn't having sex with his brother, but sometimes he felt like he was living in a miasma of it. The smell of armpits, of pubic hair, of cum all around them, on their bare mattress and laced up in their unwashed hair. He would go to school and scowl at girls and feel rage at them for being so distant and inaccessible, the secrets lands between their legs forever closed to him. He'd come from a woman's body, right? It felt absurd that he'd never touched one since, that he didn't know how a woman smelled but was so intimately familiar with his brother's odor, trapped under the same thin sheet.

"Farrah," Richard Charles purred one night as he stroked it. "Farrah fucking Fawcett."

Zach closed his eyes. Imagined billowing hair, tan collarbones—an image he'd seen in a magazine somewhere, her shirt unbuttoned and showing a peek of the space between her breasts, the crease. He imagined cramming his dick in that space. And then what? It almost didn't matter. The image was enough for him. He sped up, back arching.

"Lynda Carter," Richard Charles added, a wicked smile in his voice. Zach's eyes squeezed, and his hand did, too. Marigold loved Wonder Woman and usually they all watched it together on the kitchen TV, pretending that Lynda Carter's outfit didn't hug her fat hips and tiny waist in a way that was downright erotic. Pretending that it was family-friendly fare. Now Zachy's mind's eye was focused squarely on the image of blue fabric that was between her legs. He imagined smelling it. Tasting it.

"Unf," was all Zachy managed to say as he pumped and pumped beside his brother.

"Suzanne Somers," Richard Charles said, and it was almost too much, because all Zachy could think was *blonde* and *tits*, and he was getting close now, toes curling, his mind so full of the thoughts of skin tanned orange and pigtails and pink inside that he was all impulse. Close. And full.

He hadn't noticed that Richard Charles had writhed to a stop, finished already. *Crissy*, Zach thought, and he was imagining parting her yellow curtains with his prick when his brother, grinning wickedly beside him, called out, "Mr. Roper!"

The image of the balding landlord flashed in his head just as his pleasure came spilling out and over the mattress and as soon as it subsided he let out a howl of anger, kicking his brother hard. But Richard Charles was doubled over with laughter, choking on it, so bad that soon, their mother knocked on the door.

"Keep it down in there, boys," she said. "I have work in the morning."

"We will, mom! We will!" Zachy said, giving Richard Charles one last kick, but his brother wouldn't stop laughing, like it was the funniest thing he'd ever done.

* * *

The bell on the record shop door jangled as they stepped inside. Richard Charles glanced nervously around for a moment—he'd been banned from the store by the owner, Mr. Edelman—but when he saw that there was a black-haired girl behind the counter, idly doing her homework, he relaxed instantly. Zachary followed his brother, running a finger along the tops of the albums. It smelled like a library in here, like damp carpet squares and a certain kind of mildew, but there was a magic that didn't even exist in libraries. *Music.*

They wound through the rows and rows of disco and glam rock and heavy metal to the space in the back that said *Classic Rock.* Someone had drawn out all the artist names on the cards between the LPs, each in a different color and font. Meatloaf and Fleetwood Mac and Elvis Costello. Richard Charles loved all of it, every single note, and on rare occasions when they got together with their dad he could rattle off rock biographies like they were the models of cars or motorcycles, a habit which had previously made Zachy feel like another sort of alien entirely. Even now, Zach felt like there was no room in his head for so much music. He was single-minded, focused.

"Do you have any Saffron?" he asked the girl behind the counter. She looked at him. Wide-eyed. Blank.

"It's under S," she said, and he thought he could hear sarcasm buried under the surface of her voice, and it made him want to *murder* her for a moment. But before his anger boiled over into something tangible and real, Richard Charles called out, "Zachy! Here it is!"

Zach went to his brother, standing beside him in front of the rows and rows of vinyl. Richard Charles had taken out a record that bore the image of four leather-jacket clad boys on the front. They were holding their instruments at killer angles, except the drummer, who had his arms crossed over his chest. He looked like trouble. They all did, actually. Zachary reached out a hand and touched the image, the sharp shadows cast by the camera's flash.

"It's a fucking waste of our money," Richard Charles said. "I mean, dad *has* this. He has all of these."

They both fell silent for a moment, thinking about everything dad had that they didn't—all the things they would probably never inherit now. It had been months since even a phone call. If Zachary thought about it too much, he started feeling like a really angry ghost, hot and ugly and empty inside. He didn't want to feel that, didn't want to feel anything. He snatched the record from his brother's hand.

"Hey!" Richard Charles said, going to sock Zach on the arm, but he didn't. Instead he followed, like he was the younger brother and Zach the older one. Zach slipped into one of the listening booths, and held the curtain open for his brother.

When the fabric fell closed behind him, Richard Charles looked around. "I think I fucked Debbie Alspaugh in here," he said, in a matter-of-fact way that made Zach feel sure that it was a lie. Zach ignored him, pulling the record out of the sleeve and putting it down on the turntable. The two boys hunkered down, holding the head phones between them, and breathlessly listened.

I've searched high and low. Searched for you everywhere I go . . .

There it was. The softness of their voices. The sweetness of their harmonies. The rising guitar, distorted and rough and strange against the smooth shores of their sounds. Double baritone. Matched perfectly. Zach looked down at the album cover. It was funny how young and wild they looked. Unwashed teenage boys, just like them. And then the curling font up above them, like something out of an illuminated manuscript:

SAFFRON - THE RUFFIANS

"It's kind of gay, isn't it?" Richard Charles said, pressing the cup of the headphone against his ear, wrinkling his nose. But he didn't sound angry about it, like when he called Zachy a "faggot." He actually sounded kind of excited. "But not gay like Bowie. A different kind of gay. Not showy. Soft."

Zach put his hand down over the album cover, concealing the font, the fey name. He listened to the tender voices crashing toward the chorus.

Or else I'm dead or else I'm dead . . .

Doom and love. Zachy didn't see what was so gay about either of those things. Men could be soft, couldn't they? Straight men. Real men. He drummed his fingers against their shadows, their angularity.

Soon enough, the song turned over to the next one, but they stayed in there for a while, the two brothers, their knees touching.

"We need to get ourselves some guitars," Richard Charles said. "Or you can play the bass, maybe. It's so fucking retarded. Dad has more guitars than he knows what to do with. But we can ask grandma and grandpa for Christmas. They owe us. They paid for Tim to go to Disney when he was a kid. And if they won't do it, we can steal them. We'll find a fucking way." He wiggled his eyebrows.

Zach found himself nodding. Yes, this seemed like a logical next move in their adolescent lives. A guitar. A bass. Stolen, maybe. Probably. They'd be like Saffron, make music like Saffron. Zach looked down at the album cover, at the faces rendered in black and white. Three pale faces, one a few shades darker. He couldn't tell them apart, and yet still, he wanted to climb inside their leather skins and practice walking around like that for a while. Like someone who would matter, who could *transcend*. Transcend what? All this bullshit. Their fucking father and one shared bed to jack off in. School. Girls. Everything.

When the A side was over, they finally tumbled out of the booth, filled with a sort of quiet awe, both of them. Richard Charles carried the record up to the register, and Zachy only noted briefly the fat wad of bills he pulled out of his pocket and used to pay.

"This is a great album," said the girl behind the register, but in a mild way, like she didn't really care. Still, Zach noticed how Richard Charles puffed out his chest at not only female attention but female *validation*. "You know, we have the new Hammond album."

She gestured to a record on the wall behind them. It bore the mortifying image of a bunch of middle aged rockers, their hair feathered and wind-blown, wearing blue jeans that were too tight for them. *Hammond III* the cover said.

"God, no," Richard Charles said, so quick it was clear he hadn't even thought about it first. His gaze went quickly to the girl, doubting himself. But she just shoved a lock of hair behind her ear.

"Right? I can't stand that arena crap."

The corner of Richard Charles' mouth ticked up. Zachy thought it was funny to see his brother like this, doubting himself even momentarily. But now he was bolstered. Clearly Richard Charles and this girl were soulmates, or at least on the same page musically, which was nearly as good. Zach put his hands in his pockets, watching his older brother work.

"I wish Templeton were still making music," he said, angling his chin up, sounding confident now. Smooth.

"Right?" the record store girl said again. She slid the Saffron record into a paper sleeve. "It's an injustice. Those three protest albums and then nothing."

"I've heard he's a total recluse now." It was possible Richard Charles *had* heard this. After all, he was always stealing music magazines from the news stand on the corner. Music magazines and porno. Kept both between their mattresses like the contraband they were.

"Nah, that's not what I heard," said the girl, though her eyes shone a little bit after she said it, like it was a mistake to say anything at all, like it was a secret she was meant to keep, especially from zitty teenage boys with a boner for her.

"What," Richard Charles said. He tucked the record under his arm. It wasn't really a question. "Spill it. Don't be a tease."

The girl smirked. "I've heard he's in New York City. He took up with some radicals. You know he spent half his fortune trying to bust some terrorist out of jail in the UK? That's what my boss said."

"Edelman," Richard Charles grunted. "He's an asshole."

A miscalculation. The girl's nostrils flared. "Fuck you. He's not."

"Well, *I* think he's an asshole."

"He's better than you," she said. "He's got connections, you know."

"Yeah? Then why's he own a record store in fucking Poughkeepsie?"

"Fuck you," the girl said again, as though they hadn't heard her the first time. "Get out of here."

Zach watched the two of them glowering at each other, which was another kind of flirting, he thought, though maybe with more murderous intent. Anyway, sometimes it seemed to him like the line between hating someone and wanting to screw someone was barely more than a record groove and right now his brother and this chick were straddling it together, a foot in either song, both of them. Zach didn't want to wait around to see if the knives came out or the clothes came off. Instead, he put his hand on his brother's arm.

"Come on, Richie," he said, forgetting himself in the moment. Richard Charles pulled his arm away, clutching the record to his chest like a shield.

"Don't fucking call me that, you little cunt," he said, and went huffing out of the store. Zachy followed him, half waving to the girl behind the counter as he went.

"Bye," he said to her. "I guess."

"Have a nice day," she replied icily.

Outside, his cheeks still mottled red from anger, Richard Charles went fishing through his pocket for a crumpled pack of Parliaments.

"I fucking told you not to call me that," he said to Zachy as he lit one. Zach grabbed the pack from him, hoping for a cigarette of his own—not that he smoked, not usually, but standing outside a record store with his brother, it felt like the thing to do. It was empty, though. He balled up the plastic and foil and tossed it into the gutter.

"I know," Zach said. "I forgot."

"You're my brother," Richard Charles said, lighting up, sucking down mouthfuls of putrid smoke. "You're not just some asshole. If you don't respect me, they're never going to."

"'Richard Charles' is too long."

"Fuck you," Richard Charles said. "It's fucking distinguished. *Zachy.*"

"What's wrong with Zachy?"

"It's a baby name."

"Fuck you."

"Fuck you, too."

Zach half expected his brother to go storming off, then. But he didn't. He just stood there smoking, their invectives the last word in the argument. In a way, it didn't bother Zach as much as it should have. Unlike Richard Charles, he didn't care what people called him or whether they thought he was cool. He *knew* he was cool. He knew better than some gangly college girl in a record store and better than Mom, who was always saying stuff like *Of course you're cool, sweetie* in a simpering way that made you *less* cool, by default. For Zach, it wasn't really a question of *if* he'd someday be recognized for what he was—set apart, an artist, special, gifted—but when, and how.

Zach grabbed the paper bag out from under his brother's arm and slid the record out, staring down at it again. The four lads in leather jackets. The coolest people ever, and they knew it, too.

"Which one is Templeton?" Zach demanded. His brother hesitated a moment. Then he waved his hand in front of the record sleeve, shedding ash everywhere.

"That one," he said.

Zach looked. It was the band member who black-eyed and black-haired, a wounded look in his eyes. The other three were smiling, vaguely, despite the shadows and the leather and the guitars. Zach found the words *good boys* going through his head, but no such words came to mind when he looked at Templeton. What was it that the record store chick had said? That Templeton was a radical, or had fallen in with radicals? Templeton wasn't smiling. Templeton was scowling right into the camera. What did they call that kind of look in animals? Zachy tried to remember what they'd taught him in biology class. Ah, a *threat display*. That was the phrase.

"What's his first name?" Zach asked. His brother shrugged, stomping out his cigarette with the toe of his Jack Purcell.

"Baron." And then he added, in a faux-German accent. "De Baron Von Templeton."

"Baron." Zach looked down at the image again, studying it. He noted the way that Baron's hands played silently at the strings of his strange guitar—shiny and black in the black-and-white photo—like he hardly cared about the picture that was being taken of him, like all that mattered was being alone with his music.

"I don't want to play bass," Zachy said. "I want to play guitar."

"Fine," answered Richard Charles. "Whatever. Can we go?"

But they remained frozen on the sidewalk for a moment longer, Zach staring down at the image of the rock star like there might be an answer in there for him if only he looked at it long enough. He hadn't even asked a *question*. But he was sure, if he searched hard enough, he would find a solution there.

9 - 1957

Baron Templeton's bedroom was hardly any bigger than the long single bed. He couldn't even fit a dresser inside, just a trunk underneath it where he kept his trousers and his jumpers, all neatly folded by his aunt. Once, it had seemed big enough, when he'd been a small boy, coming from a place without a room of his own. Back then, he'd taped up the postcards that he'd get from his Dad—once, maybe twice a year—and lie himself down in the middle of the mattress and stare out at them, dreaming of foreign lands. Hamburg and Paulsboro, strange locales that left strange odors in his mind.

That was the era where he'd dreamed mostly of his father. *I miss you I miss you,* his Dad had written and Baron, back when he couldn't even write words himself, had etched the letters in his mind: *Take me with you. I miss you, too.* Maybe they would be sailors together someday, carrying their trunks on their backs over wood planks, jumping from ship to ship, the scent of the sea all around them, their hands hard from the pass of the rope. But eventually, the small boy grew; the postcards stopped. Baron was left lanky-legged and he pasted up photos from girly mags right over the postcards, and he told himself he didn't notice the way the ink faded unevenly over them. Ghostly rectangles for ghostly dreams.

Now he just wanted out of here. Even a closed door offered no respite. Even a radio clutched against his cheek as he tried to spread out across the bed. His Aunt Deedz vacuumed endless lines up and down the hall, purposefully intruding on his tiny world, and then at last, she pounded her fist against the door.

"Baron! Baron!" She easily drowned out the soft sound of Buddy Holly, that faint cricket's chirp.

"Yeh!" he bellowed back. "What do you want?"

The door burst open, and out of the corner of his eye he saw a pale shadow flying toward him. He had to act fast in Deedz' house, think fast, for his instinct was often to duck down and hide. But now, instead, well trained, his hands caught the heavy object. His guitar, a sunburst Antoria archtop with curling F holes, second-hand, but the most expensive thing he owned. The guitar his mum had given him, as an apology of sorts, for leaving him so sad and motherless for all these years.

"Ey!" he cried out, as he'd almost tumbled to the floor in catching it. "What are you doing?"

"I told you not to leave that in the sitting room!" Aunt Deedz sneered. "My house a mess, and always because of you, child! And what are you doing in here? Wasting time! Don't you have schoolwork to do, or money to make?"

Money and school. Those had always been Aunt Deedz' primary preoccupations for him. If he wasn't going to be something truly *useful*—a barrister or a doctor would have been her preference—then at least he wouldn't be a *burden*. She hadn't been the one to get him the job at the barbershop—that had been Uncle Fred, to get Deedz out of Baron's hair—but it had been her idea for him to get *some* kind of job to keep him in pocket money and so he could contribute to the household in some sort of way, even if it was to pay the dairyman every week. And art school had been her idea, too. She didn't have it in her head that he would be any kind of *artist*, mind you. There would be no turtlenecks and Beat poetry and eating paint like batty old Van Gogh for young Baron. But she thought he might someday become an art *professor*. He used to listen to her cooing to her ladies at tea about it. How he might wear leather elbow patches and mold young minds and Make Something of Himself. Never mind that he rarely could be arsed to go to class, much less in some distant future ever *teach* it.

"I'm not wasting time!" he yelped, and hated how he yelped it. Something about Aunt Deedz always got to him, got under his skin and nails and brain stem to the parts where he was the most gooey and vulnerable. "I'm trying to take down the chords!"

He picked up the notebook that he'd had tucked in next to him in bed and hurled it at her. It spun uselessly in the air like a whirligig and landed beside her house slippers. She bent down and picked it up.

"This again?" she said, letting out a sigh. "Baron, there isn't any money in rock and roll music. An' your handwriting is rubbish, too." She tossed the book back on the bed, tired, like it was a piece of trash she was throwing in the bin.

"Now I ask you again," she said, more evenly this time. "Don't you have something *useful* to do on a Saturday? Hasn't Mr. Conway had work for you?" Mr. Conway was the barber, and Baron wasn't sure, because he'd stopped asking for work weeks ago. Hated that job, anyway, the hair that was always getting everywhere and the jokes Conway would make at Baron about the way that he walked.

"No. I told you, Deedz," Baron said, scrambling forward to grab the book. He held his guitar by the neck in one hand, the book in the other. He might as well have been a Renaissance portrait or something. Pope Baron the First, Destroyer of his Auntie's Grand Schemes. "I'm having me mates over to practice today."

She stared at him. There was a beat of excruciating silence, and then her lip curled and her voice cracked. "Practice? Practice *what*?"

"Music, Deedz!" He shook his hands, his guitar and book. "Me band, the Bartlebys! I told you last night!"

He *had* told her last night, but she'd been too busy arguing over him with Fred about the grocery bills and the program Fred wanted to play on the radio over dinner. She hadn't even heard him, which was nothing new.

"You can't have your band play *here*!" she said, mouth dropping open, aghast. "Now, really, Baron, be sensible. What will the neighbors think if you have those ruffians in their drainpipe trousers over *here*?"

"That I'm a perfectly normal bloke, with *mates*, like a bloke has."

"Normal. Baron. Honestly." Those three words held the weight of the world for Baron and his Auntie. Because they both knew, way down deep, that he had never been normal—would never be normal. They'd just come up with different ways of hiding it was all.

The thing was, Baron thought, as he began to set his lips, his jaw, his shoulders, all firm and immovable, that he didn't want to even be normal anymore. If he only ever endeavored to be an acceptable sort of lad, the way that Deedz wanted him to be, then he'd never be more than her small ambitions. If he could stay sober and stay out of fights and stop wanking Dickie Ashby and stop wanting the whole world to look at him, if he could go to school and become an art teacher and get himself a pretty little wife? What then? Stuck here, still. Maybe not in this room, teeny as a thimble. But in this city. Which in its own way was even tinier than a thimble.

Aunt Deedz had settled for that. His mum had, too. But Baron? He had too much of his dark-skinned father in him. A sailor. An itinerant. A wanderer. Seduced by wine and song and the promise of the sea.

Besides, he told himself, it's not like they could go to Ashby's to practice anymore, not if he wanted Eddie to come along. It had to be Aunt Deedz' house or nothing.

Baron stood up from the bed, took two steps forward. Guitar in one hand, notebook in the next. He was a full head taller than Deedz now, and while he'd never hit her back and though when she struck him he inevitably cowered, there were moments when he was able to use his body, his sheer masculinity to his own advantage. Towering over her now. Lip curling.

"We're practicing here today, Deedz. And that's final."

A flash of fear in Deedz' eyes. How satisfying. But momentary, fleeting, passing, gone. She scoffed at him, stepped back.

"Too much of your father in you," she said to him, which he knew he was meant to take as the ultimate insult. She rolled her eyes, started up the vacuum again, and spoke to him over it. "They'll come in through the back door. And they can play in the sun room. I won't be having their cigarettes fouling up my sitting room."

Baron watched her scurry down the hall. It was a victory, but it didn't feel like one. With Aunt Deedz, it never did.

* * *

To be fair, filled to the brim with boys, the sun room's glass walls quickly began to steam. Or maybe it was the cigarettes they passed around between them, lighting them and coughing as they fiddled with their guitar tuners. Liam Waller had shown up first, guitar case in hand, and was the kind of polite toward Deedz that made her hum and flutter a little and offer him up a few scones even though she usually told Baron that the baked goods were for her ladies. He wondered what it was like to be able to turn it on and off like that—charm. Because when Liam sat down in the sun room and opened up his ax case and bent over it, he let out a scone-stinky belch and laughed at his own crassness like Baron should have been laughing, too.

He did laugh a little. After all, he thought, watching as Waller tuned up his guitar, he knew how well Liam played.

Next came Dickie, washboard in hand, and Baron made the introductions and the two lads shook on it. Liam immediately bent over his slender necked Hagstrom and played the opening of "Miserlou." Dickie's eyes went wide in admiration, and Baron stuffed down the seeds of jealousy, told himself it was nothing. They were all in this together, anyway.

"Where'd you get this one, Baron?" he asked. Baron gave a shrug, like it was easy.

"Seaman's Orphanage, Dick," he said and grinned. "Paid for him with pencil shavings. He'll give his arse to you if you'd like."

Felt good to be shocking. Reminded them who was on top here. Dickie just choked back some laughter, even as Liam began to turn bright pink.

"Ey!" he said. "Wot?"

"Oh, wet yerself," Baron said.

Then came Alfie Duggan, who played the bass, because no one else had wanted to and Alfie'd figured it was easier than the drums, anyway. It had been easier to nick one, at least. He dragged along a boy named Ivan Smith, who played a half-filled whiskey jug, who would drift away from the band soon enough when it was clear their rock band stylings would stay. Still, for now, there were five in that foggy sun room, and they were still nominally a skiffle band. The Bartlebys, after Baron's favorite short story from school a few years back. Baron's idea. Baron's band. There were more handshakes. Cigarettes. Tuning. Teasing. Baron was almost starting to feel comfortable there, with all these lads, the hums of their music and the smell of their armpits all around him. He put his notebook down on the wicker coffee table, then set his guitar on his knee.

"'Ey, Liam?" he called. "You think these chords are right?"

Liam shuffled closer. He strummed out a few, shook his head.

"No, that's not an E. E7, maybe? Christ, I know Hammy knows this one. Where is he, anyway?"

"I'm right here." They all turned, looked up. There was pretty little Edmund. Pink-cheeked, still, from the cool air. But he was hardly looking at Baron and Liam. Instead, his gaze was in the corner on Dickie, who was fumbling to get his thimbles on his hand.

"What's this, son?" Eddie asked.

Baron blinked once. Stood. Tried to summon up who he had been an hour earlier with Aunt Deedz. His father, strong and firm and terrifying, or so the stories went. The boss of the world.

"Dickie Ashby, son. Dick, this is Edmund Hammond III."

"Call him Hammy," Liam said, smirking. Eddie shook his head.

"Don't call me Hammy. Baron—"

But before Eddie could say anything, Dickie shot out his hand.

"Eddie, yeh?" Dickie offered, words firm enough that they could not be denied. Eddie sighed, a thin, simpering sound. He shook Dickie's hand, but his expression, all worn out, was aimed directly at Baron.

"Yeh," was all Eddie said.

10 - 1997

It wasn't the first time Cymbeline had ever made love to a woman, though those early experiences felt like ancient history. High school. Fumbling with a girl she'd met in debate club for a few weeks before her partner had gotten tired of clandestine "dates" with the doors closed. Back then, Cymbeline had worried about making too much noise, about her friends finding out the truth—about telling her mother. Her mother had been sick, on and off, through most of her childhood, and it seemed wrong to burden her with one more thing. With anything, really. "You're so easy," is what her mother had told her, over and over again, and she had wanted to remain easy. Bisexuality was not easy to explain, even to kids her own age. Much less her old hippie mother, who pretended to be progressive and liberal but who had still grown up with certain ideas about what a man and a woman should be.

"I wish I had a man to put this furniture together," her mother had told her once after a trip to IKEA, and then later: "You can't change your own tires. You might hurt yourself. We'll get you AAA."

"What do lesbians even *do* to each other?" her mother had asked one time when a lesbian couple had appeared on *Oprah* and, in the days before Pamela, Cymbeline's first girlfriend, Cymbeline had shrugged and said, "I don't know. Oral, I guess."

Now that guess seemed quaint. As though sexual acts between women were so limited. Now, with more experience under her belt—not just with Pamela but with three interchangeable college boyfriends in a row, it seemed that it was *heterosexual* sex that was limited. A drab progression:

kissing, tits, jerking, sucking, fucking, done. Sex without a cock was *different* though. A non-linear story. Climaxes tumbling into one another, acts in parallel and perpendicular, both. Giving and receiving, a sort of woven cloth of bodies and parts. In Sid's empty cabin, Cymbeline practically trembled with anticipation of what was to come. It had been so long since she'd touched a body like her own.

Funny, though, because Sid kissed like a boy. Pressing her up against the splintery wood planks, grinding her knee into Cymbeline's crotch, hard. Cymbeline heard herself squeal with unburied, almost painful pleasure. Her hands slipped up Sid's tank top, feeling the fat of hip leading to the soft fur of belly and the knot of a navel. Her hands drifted up, toward Sid's sports bra, but Sid's hand stopped her.

"Not there," Sid growled, her voice low and full of gravel. "Here." She led Cymbeline's fingers downward into the waistband of her shorts, to the warm thatch of hair and the slippery wetness inside her cunt. Cymbeline found the bundle of nerves and began to rub. Sid, her weight on Cymbeline, moaned, her hips bucking.

"Damn, Perky," she said, her hot breath falling against Cymbeline's neck as she laughed. Cymbeline laughed too.

"Where's your junior counselor?" Cymbeline asked suddenly, casting her gaze back toward the darkness. Sid shrugged.

"Off with her boyfriend on the other side of the lake. No worries."

So Cymbeline didn't.

In that last night before the campers arrived, they had their choice of a dozen different plastic-wrapped beds, an entire dark cabin, a universe that felt uninhabited except for the heat of their bodies. Cymbeline hadn't been much for one night stands before, but now she could see their utility. They had no preconceptions about one another or their bodies. Everything was new and there was no self-consciousness, no history of shame or conflict. Their clothes were discarded on the floor save for Sid's sports bra, which she kept on throughout, as their bodies crested and came together and then grew once more aroused and spent again and again.

"Damn, Perky," Sid said again when finally, through mutual exhaustion, it seemed their tryst had ended. By then, the sunlight was starting to turn gray through the uncurtained windows. It was hours from morning, but still, too soon.

"Are you going to keep calling me that?" Cymbeline asked. Sid grinned.

"I can't call you Cymbeline," she said. "That's a boy's name." Tucked under Sid's naked arm, Cymbeline frowned.

"So is Sid," she said. Sid laughed.

"Well, maybe I'm a boy."

Cymbeline looked at her, at Sid's strong nose and youthful features, her shaggy, unkempt hair.

"Aren't you on the wrong side of the lake, then?" Cymbeline asked. Sid let out a snort, and didn't answer, though there was something in her eyes like a memory of an ancient pain. She fumbled through her little bedside cubby until she came up with two smooth brown clove cigarettes. Sid lit one. Offered the other to Cymbeline.

Cymbeline hesitated. Smoking had done her mother in, and she'd sworn that she never would. But this night was different. One where either girl was pretending they came into this exchange without baggage. So Cymbeline took one, and, as Sid lit the tip, inhaled a mouthful of the sweetest smoke.

* * *

Everything looked different by the light of morning. Their clothes strewn out across the dusty floor, forming a pattern that was now more haphazard than romantic. The windows, which she could now see were dirty and laced with cobwebs. Cymbeline got dressed, still smelling the smoke and sex on her own body. She glanced at Sid's head, barely visible at the lip of her sleeping bag. She considered leaving without a word, but it didn't feel right. For Cymbeline, sex had always been more than just a passing interest. She couldn't touch someone without falling halfway in love with them, and the curve of Sid's freckly shoulder just peeking out over the fabric seemed incredibly vulnerable and sweet. She bent down and kissed it. Sid stirred. Turned over. Looked at her, smiling.

"A summer romance," Sid said. "Been coming to camp since I was six and I've never yet had one of those."

Cymbeline kissed her again. "There's a first time for everything," she said.

Drawing away from the kiss, Sid crawled out of her sleeping bag. She dressed herself in athletic shorts and another tank top, not bothering to change her bra. Then, with one bare foot, she nudged her clothes around the floor until they settled safely within the threshold of her senior counselor's bedroom. Cymbeline watched, eyebrows wrinkled up, amused.

"What?" Sid said. "It makes the brats feel more at home. They're always fucking slobs, too."

"Aren't we supposed to set a good example?" Cymbeline asked, trying to remember the camp mottoes they'd been forced to memorize on their training weekend. Failing. She was sure there was one about tidiness, though. The boys at Camp Berean all made vows about being a true friend and helping their fellows. The girls at Camp Kaaterskill had to promise to keep their cabins clean. Sid shrugged.

"I only know how to be myself," she said. Cymbeline watched her, head cocked to her side. She wondered what that was like. Most of her life, she'd been setting a part of herself in reserve, back behind everyone else's needs. Her mom's. Her grandmother's. Pamela's. Her entire personality was based on artifice. Sid had none.h

"Come on, Perky," Sid said, holding the cabin door open. "You don't want to miss breakfast. It's our last chance to eat in peace before the brats get here."

Cymbeline looked at her for a moment, wondering if this meant that they were an item, truly. If they would sit together at breakfast, holding hands under the table. The way that Sid spoke to her didn't feel like a romantic partner, not exactly. Not like the sweet boyfriends she'd had or the secret girlfriend, either. Sid wasn't nervous or fawning. Sid was something else.

"Come *on*," Sid said again, grinning, waving her hand. Cymbeline let Sid hold the door open for her as she streamed on through.

* * *

A continental breakfast buffet of overcooked eggs and rubbery waffles. No hands held beneath the table. Cymbeline sat with Sid and some other girls, who were all caught in the same strange phase between late adolescence and early adulthood. The other girls had smooth hair and wore their camp clothes like they'd been born into them. Sid, it was clear, did not belong. And yet the other young women did more than merely tolerate Sid's presence. They laughed with her, trading jokes about camp summers that had passed. When Sid commented that Mr. Kreizken should "Eat my cunt" for some imagined slight, the other girls just blinked, then giggled politely.

It seemed to Cymbeline that there was space in their lives—wealthy, privileged, and generally very straight—for Sid's brand of queerness, but only so long as they were able to frame it as familial eccentricity rather than something outside of their sphere. When the camp director announced that the busses were now arriving with the campers, the other girls all cheered. Sid looped one finger in the air and sarcastically let out a "Woo!" One of the girls laughed at her, and one clapped Sid on the back. Cymbeline felt no jealousy. This was a toothless world, she thought. Deathless. If there was something she'd recognized in Sid in their tryst the night before, it was a certain familiarity with the wild dark.

They didn't hold hands over breakfast, but as they left the mess hall, Sid put her palm on Cymbeline's back. A gesture that the other young woman would have seen as simply cordial. But there would have been no explanation for the way that Sid leaned in then, and whispered right in Cymbeline's ear: "I can't get the taste of pussy out of my head."

She had never been spoke to this way—with such crassness. Though, blushing, she was surprised to find that she truly didn't mind it, not at all. Before she could muster the courage to tell Sid that *she* had enjoyed the taste of Sid's pussy, too, the busses rolled up, and Sid broke away from her to run toward them, wooing again, but with genuine enthusiasm this time. The children were shuffled off the busses, some crying, some laughing, all with the same wary looks on their faces. As the camp director called out the unit placements, Cymbeline watched Sid joke and gambol for her new charges. She'd gotten out those hacky sacks again, was throwing them in the air, purposefully dropping them until, at last, on the third try, she got it right. Her kids were older, ten and eleven, just past that first era of cool disaffection. And yet still they laughed at Sid. How could they not?

There's power in being the court jester, Cymbeline thought idly. *Safety.*

"Excuse me? Are you Perky?" Remembering that she was, Cymbeline turned. That's when she saw a sea of eight and nine year old eyes, staring back at her, full of expectation and yearning. She forced a smile.

"Yeah," she said. "I guess I am."

11 - 1957

To be alone with Eddie. Yes, yes, Baron realized, as they crossed the docks at midday, a pair together, a pair alone. This is what Baron had wanted all along.

They'd skived off school again. This time, though, no Liam Waller. Little Liam had a test. So today Baron and Eddie walked alone together, sharing Baron's uncle's stolen flask filled with his uncle's stolen gin. They whistled at old women as though they were young women and paused to flirt with young women over their baby carriages. Useful, Baron thought, to have a boy who looked like Eddie around. His golden angelic curls and sweet blushing face meant that every single bird blushed back at him, giggled, stroked his arm. A few even flashed their teeth at Baron.

"Cor," grinned Eddie, as they walked away from their third pram of the day. His cheeks were blossoming like poppy flowers, and he seemed looser from the booze, "I can't believe that girl is a mother. Can you imagine being her husband, sticking it in her? I wish I could, mate."

"Yeh," said Baron, hands down in his pockets, grinning at Eddie. "Wish I could, too."

"Have you ever done it?" asked Eddie suddenly, his pale eyes going to Baron. "I haven't. Not yet. I can't wait till I can."

"Not with a bird like that," Baron said, glancing back over his shoulder. It was his standard answer to the question, because it wasn't a lie, not exactly, and because sometimes the true answer felt more complicated than he liked to admit. He and Dickie didn't have sex with each other, did they? Just wanking. What was a wank between friends?

(Except somehow in the back of his head he felt like it *was* different. Not like wanking alone at least. There was the rhythm and the excitement of it, the feeling that, together, their individual desires were somehow squared. Not that he was ever going to tell Eddie that. Eddie seemed like a bloke who wouldn't even have a wank in the same room as his brothers so he could act all superior to them during Sunday dinner.)

"I haven't even touched a tit yet, you know," Eddie said. He seemed all excited to admit that, like he'd been aching to let out this news. "Have you?"

"Yes. Yes I have touched these mortal hands to a mortal tit," Baron said, and he reached his one hand out in the shape of a tit-grabbing claw and Eddie howled laughter.

"I knew it," he said. "What was it like?"

Christ. Of course, Baron thought of his mum first and not Sue Grasso. But Baron shoved down thoughts of dear old mum, whose tits had been kind of pointy and small in all that fabric anyway.

"Squishy. Like custard in a sock."

"You're revolting." Eddie said, but he was grinning at Baron. But then he started singing, in his high, strong boy's voice, the voice that had barely cracked yet and hardly ever would. "My true love's tits are soft and jiggly like a stocking full of Chiver's jelly."

Baron looked at him, grinned back. "When I feel her up," he sang, "My hand gets stuck. I can't get free till I'm on my knees."

Eddie didn't wait even a beat. The absurd song went on and on, loud enough that some of the passing missuses turned, raising eyebrows. "I eat her out. I lick those tits. I'm a good boy, mum. I finish it."

With that, a gesture. A wank off. An explosion. With the sound effect to match. Eddie and Baron both burst into giggles.

"Disgusting," Baron said. Eddie, still giggling, agreed.

"We should be ashamed of ourselves."

By then, they'd reached Otterspool Park. The path was dappled by leaves, which were all dressed up in their autumn shades. Nearly empty this time of day, no children either loitering or littering about. They slumped themselves down on a park bench just a little ways off from the path and started passing the flask back and forth between them.

"I shouldn't joke about me mum, though," Eddie said, taking a deep swig and wincing. Baron ticked up an eyebrow.

"Why not? Can't hurt her now."

"Yeh. Dunno," Eddie said. He handed the flask back. Baron drank. "You know, I saw her tits once. Was ten, maybe eleven."

Baron swallowed the gin, feeling the bite at his throat as he lifted his eyebrows. He pretended to be unaffected, merely curious, perhaps. But there was a strange warmth spreading through his belly. Eddie had a pain down inside him, a guilt, a twisting. Just like Baron's.

"How were they?" Baron asked, the mouth of the flask resting against his lip. Eddie laughed, a tittering, chipmunk sound. Heh heh. Heh heh.

"They were all right, you know? I got a throbber and I thought, oh, this is okay. Not every bloke's mum can do something like that. I was almost proud of it."

"Yeh," Baron said, snorting. "Yeh. Me mum's got a pair, too." He gestured with his hands. Two grapefruit, ripe for squeezing. "I know what you mean."

"Yes, but . . ." Eddie trailed off for a moment. He paused to grab the flask from Baron, drank deep, coughed. "All that time wanking off to the thought of me mum's tits. When she got cancer in them, my first thought was, that's it. I'd done it. Poisoned her somehow."

"Christ," Baron said, wincing. "Christ, Hammy, that's not how it works."

For once, Eddie didn't object to the nickname. He just studied Baron's face, then looked down at his shiny school shoes. At a full year older, Barron could be an authority on plenty of things. Including wanking. Including death. "Yeh, I know, Baron. I know."

"Christ," Baron said again, and laughed even though there was little humor in it, "If wanking could give someone cancer I'd have murdered my whole family and half the population of Liverpool by now."

"Yeh, Baron," Eddie said. He was hanging his head down practically between his knees, and for a second he made a sound that sounded like a laugh. But then Baron realized it wasn't a laugh. It was a sniffle. Fuck, the boy was crying. The beautiful, soft, soft boy. Made Baron want to murder himself, or maybe Eddie—he wasn't sure.

"Hey, Hammy," Baron said, giving the other boy's shoulder a little shove. "Don't go turning soft on me. Crying about your mummy like some kind of queer."

Eddie laughed again, sucking in a deep breath of tears and snot. "A queer," he said, still staring down at his shoes. He then lifted his head, wiped his face clean with his coat sleeve, drank again, laughed again. "I'm no queer. Grew up with enough pricks in the house to know I never wanna suck one."

Then, of all absurdities, he leaned back against Baron, putting his head on Baron's shoulder. Christ. This boy. And the stabbing, disappointed feeling Baron felt in his chest. Was no surprise, of course. Just strange to hear it, and stranger, even, to feel sad about it. He'd known it wasn't a romance between the two of them. But still. He looked at Eddie out of the corner of his eye, at the pale feathers of hair curling from his head. Did he have to be such a soft, pretty tease?

"If you don't want to suck it you could stick it in your arsehole," Baron said, wrestled the flask from Eddie's hands, and drank it down. Drained it.

"You're disgusting," Eddie said.

"Rude," shot back Baron.

"Sorry," Eddie said.

"What I meant to say was 'no, thank you,'" Eddie said.

"That's better," Baron said with a grunt. "Mind your manners, son."

Eddie grinned through his snotty crying. Then (more horrors, more absurdities) Eddie pressed a quick kiss to Baron's cheek and hopped to his feet, tears gone, tension gone—everything, gone.

"Me dad's at work today. We could go back to my house if you'd like, jam a bit."

Baron squinted at the sunny-haired boy standing above him, practically haloed by the feeble English sunlight. "Yeh," Baron said, making a point to wipe the kiss off. "I would."

"Well, come on, then," said Eddie, and ran off down the path.

* * *

Empty of boys and men, the Hammond household echoed like an empty chapel. Baron could hear even the floor groan and creak under his weight, which was not significant. He felt almost obligated to whisper so as to not offend the ghosts. But Eddie held nonesuch superstitions. He tromped around like he owned the place, which Baron supposed he did. Disappeared for a few minutes, leaving Baron standing there with his hands in his pockets in the haunted living room, then returned with a guitar.

"Here," he said, handing it over. "I'll play the piano. You play this."

Baron sat on the edge of a dusty chair, tuning the instrument. It was nicer than his guitar, a red Hofner 520, newer (though not *new*), with a pearly white pickguard and with none of the buzzy fret sound that Baron's Antoria had. He watched as Eddie opened the piano, began caressing it, letting his fingers trip and dance over every key.

"Is there anything you can't play?" Baron asked, a note of nasty jealousy in his voice, but he didn't care, not now, not today. With Eddie playing with his heart, as always, and the gin still churning in his guts.

"The oboe," Eddie responded smoothly. "Never could manage an oboe. Anyway—" He pounded out a few chords. "—me dad plays the piano. Bought me a trumpet when I was, what? Four? Five? Used to sit in with me uncles and me brothers. Everybody playing. It's in me blood. Some families make babies. Ours makes music."

"Yours makes babies too," Baron said, pointing with his pick to one of the crowded family portraits. Eddie laughed.

"Yeh, that too. But mostly music. See how this goes? G, then an E7, then a D."

Baron bent forward, strummed. Eddie was showing him how with his mouth, going "Doo, doo, *doo*." In a moment, they were playing together, making a song together like it was nothing. It always felt like that with the two of them. Everything else had some difficulty to it—and with other people, even music could go wrong. But Eddie was here to help him, to guide him. Why?

"If your family is so full of music, why don't you just play with them, then?" Baron asked over his own strumming. Eddie's hands stilled, the last chord still ringing out. He looked at Baron, smirking.

"Because you're not dead yet, son," Eddie said. Baron leaned back, curling his lip.

"What?"

"That's what me dad said after me mum died. She wasn't like other mums, you know. The ones who stay home with their babies. She was a teacher. When she got sick, we were in a tight spot. Dad working all the time, and Jamie and Paulie and me helping to keep house. At first we thought it was only temporary, only for awhile. But then mum died and—well. I saw how tired me dad was all the time and I said to him one night, *I wish I could help you out. Get a real job or something.* And me dad says to me, *Eddie, you might be only fourteen, but you're not dead yet.*"

Baron lifted just one eyebrow. "So it's not rock 'n' roll to you. It's money, mate."

"Nahhh . . ." Eddie let his hands go down the keys. "It's not just money. I know I'm good, Baron. I might not be lucky, but I'm good. Like Liam, but more than that. The way girls look at me, and their sisters and even their mothers. The way I can sit down with me uncles and pick up a guitar and pick up a song just like that." One hand paused to snap. But then quickly returned to the music. "I listen to rock 'n' roll music and it's better than wanking. I turn the music around in me head and it becomes something else. It's not just money, Barry. It's piles and piles of money. So much that me dad and me brothers will never have to work again. And not just money. Girls. Dozens of them. Fame. Even the boys will love me. It's all mine. And I can taste it."

Baron had stopped playing to watch Eddie. To watch, and to listen. His belly felt full and warm and not from the gin. Because he could taste it, too. He always had. Sitting in his school uniform, drawing all over the margins of his notebooks. Waiting for the whole wide world to recognize that he was brilliant. Smarter and better than anyone else in that tall brick prison. Fuck. But somehow, they never had. If anything, the world kept trying to file down his edges, to make him smaller, better able to fit inside their boxes.

But it never worked.

"You aren't the only one with a gift," Baron said sourly. Eddie laughed. Kept playing, but laughed.

"Yeh," he said. "I know. I saw it there at the St. Michael's fete. Bongo had been telling me I needed to meet you, and I thought, *Christ, I have friends. What need would I have for him?* But then I see you up there in your checkered shirt, and I thought, *Yeh, he's beautiful. He's got it too.* I could be successful on my own, but with you alongside me? It'd be something else."

"We'll be famous," Baron said. He was grinning in earnest now, and blushing from his ears to his toes. But Eddie shook his head. "Like Little Richard. Or Bill Haley. Like—like bloody Buddy Holly."

"Nah. More famous than *that.* Elvis, son. We'll be like Elvis."

The chords suddenly crashed and rattled on the old upright piano. Baron, the smile still stretched from ear to ear, leaned forward over his guitar and began strumming. Over and over again. The same chords. G and an E7 and a D. Then stopped.

"What if we don't do it like this?" he said. "What if we do, like . . . ehhh . . ." He strummed out a few chords, testing. An F. No. A C. No, certainly not.

"This one!" He said. "What's this one called, Ed?"

Eddie leaned forward.

"A minor, mate?"

"Yeah, look, then we can go somewhere else with it. But if we give them an A minor it'll surprise them. A door to somewhere new, you know?"

Eddie studied Baron's face for a moment. Then he pounded out the chords. G and an E7 and an A minor. A worrying sort of sound. Tension building. Not quite resolving, yet.

"It's good," Eddie said carefully. "You've got something."

"Fuck you," Baron replied, grinning. "I know I do."

"Yeah," said Eddie. "You do."

Grinning. Grinning. But then, that grinning faltering. A worrying sort of look.

"We still need to sack Dickie though," he said. Baron rolled his eyes.

"I won't," Baron said.

"You have to," Eddie pushed back easily, like it was nothing to push back against Baron. He wasn't used to that. Usually people were too scared of him to push, unless they were Aunt Deedz, and that was more like a battering. "He's your mate. I understand. I'll wait. But eventually you'll come to a point where you have to make a decision, Barry. Dickie Ashby, or the entire world."

He let his fingers linger on that A minor chord. Pressed the keys over and over again.

"I know you'll make the right choice," he said.

12 - 2017

Naomi made herself right at home in Edelman's castle. She grabbed Matthew's overnight bags and hefted them up the wide, railingless stairway. Matthew was still for a moment, watching her go. He thought about the last time he'd met a creature who had so immediately moved him.

It had been the night he met Kara. But it hadn't been Kara. It had been her sister, Pearl, with her bee stung mouth and small, lithe body, perched on that bar stool in Hell's Kitchen, twining her hair around her finger, grilling him for more and more gossip about his parents. Had they really been swingers in the '70s? Was it true they had a grow room in the basement of their farm house? Had his daddy cried when Baron Templeton died? He'd half wanted to shove her right off the bar stool, make her shut up, make her stop it. He'd half wanted to shove his tongue in her mouth. It wouldn't be until they were four drinks in that she mentioned the fiancé and somehow set her sister in front of him. Kara. 22 years old and just off a Broadway run of Hedwig where she'd played Yitzhak with a barely convincing, drawn-on beard. Pretty, in a highly cultivated, sculpted way, but with a set of lungs on her. Kara told him she could sing. Those were her first words to him. Matthew hadn't cared, not at the time. He'd wanted Pearl, who was obnoxious, a dynamo, a challenge, but by the time Pearl got up to use the bathroom he'd decided that Kara would do.

Maybe he would have decided differently that night if he'd known what a knot Kara would be. If he'd known that there was a girl like Naomi somewhere. He watched her, considered following her up the stairs, but decided against it. Took the flask out of his pocket, took a long swig, tucked it away. Then he grabbed his guitar case and brought it over to the Danish chair in the corner. It wasn't just that he was here to work, he thought, as he quickly took out the guitar and tuned it. Mostly he was motivated by a memory of high school. A time when all he had to do was play, and the girls would flock to him.

The family gift, his father had told him, but he said it almost like it was a warning. His father had never really appreciated the dagger side of what they both had. Beauty, and beautiful voices. Animal magnetism for a certain type of bird.

Not all birds. Not Pearl, for one. But it had worked on Kara, who always wanted to sit on his knee and sing while he strummed. She might have been second choice for him, but how could he say no? She leaned forward in her tight jeans, giving him a peek of the back of her red lace thong.

Maybe it would work on Naomi too. His music, that was. He strummed his guitar, began to hum a tune. Soon, he heard her light footsteps come down the stairs and toward him. She stood there in the almost-empty room watching him, one hand on her hip. When he looked her in the eye as he began to sing—"Mountains and Foothills," off his second album—her expression was closed, unreadable.

He tried not to deflate as he played, though he slowly realized the possibility that this new girl was, in fact, more of a Pearl than a Kara. Kept strumming for another bar, maybe two. But at last he broke his fingers away from the strings, the sound sputtering out like a musical version of an exclamation point.

"What?" he asked, maybe harder than he should have. Her expression softened a drop and she let her hands hang down close to the hem of that ridiculously large sweater.

"It's just that I've heard that one," she said, and let her lips part in an easy smile. "Aren't you supposed to be working on something new?"

She was teasing, he told himself. He could handle teasing. He let himself grin.

"Quite the taskmaster, I see," he said. She shrugged, but didn't laugh.

Maybe not teasing, then. The lack of laughter disarmed him, and he frowned.

"I'm not. I'm just here to help you," she said. "C'mon. You must have something new in your pocket."

Now he hesitated. Of course he did, snippets. Rough. "I don't like to play them until they're done. It's part of my process."

"Is that what your father taught you?" she asked, and somehow, it surprised him, coming now, in what he'd *almost* momentarily convinced himself was mid-flirt. Mention of his dad. Usually it came up first thing, like it had with the limo driver. Or not at all.

"He didn't teach me," Matthew said, and cringed inwardly at how defensive he sounded. How defensive he always sounded. At the implication that his talent was something imparted and not spontaneously occurring. But she had no idea what it was like, the assumption that what you had was somehow unfairly given. That it was the result of privilege, and not talent.

"That can't be true," she said to him. "I bet there was music in your house—"

"Well, music, yes, but he was touring, half the time. I had no more than anyone else has as a kid—"

"I don't believe you," she said simply. Matthew stared at her. *Her* eyes were wide and open back, not particularly challenging, but confident, as if she could read the real truth that he held inside him. Those early days, face pressed to the floorboards, feeling the vibrations of his father's music hum through each and every cell. Those were private moments, private memories. He'd never put them in press releases or interviews and yet somehow he felt certain that she could read them on him, now. Well, perhaps she'd seen something on some website or in one of the dozens of biographies he'd chosen to go his whole life ignoring. Perhaps she was a *fan*.

"Are you an expert, then?" he asked sharply. "A Saffron freak? Is that why Edelman hired you?"

"It was a favor to Cymbeline," she said. "Anyway, you can just tell when someone grows up around music. It's in the way that they walk. The way that they jiggle their knees when they're nervous, like there's a beat behind it, a song."

Matthew stopped jiggling his leg.

"Anyway," Naomi said—she had a broad, unpolished way of speaking, like she was less educated than he was and didn't realize it. Like she wasn't used to speaking to celebrities. He found it fairly insulting and incredibly appealing, all at once. She was, in fact, dead sexy, he thought, as she began to walk closer to him. "From what I *do* know of Saffron, all of their best songs were collaborations, weren't they? Templeton and Hammond."

"Hammond and Templeton," Matthew corrected her, quickly, barely thinking. She smirked.

"What's the difference?" she asked.

"For one thing," he said, "It scans better. And they worked it out with the lawyers, you know. It was Hammond and Templeton *officially*. Legally."

"I don't think it matters," she told him, "Though you clearly think it does. Fine. Hammond and Templeton. Your dad and his best buddy, writing music together. Everything he did solo sucked, you know. Your dad, I mean. Templeton didn't really do anything solo either way, but maybe that was better."

Matthew's frown was immediate and deep.

"You're bold," he said at last. She shrugged.

"I'm just telling you the truth. Your dad might be a millionaire, but he hasn't made real art since Templeton died. Since maybe even before that. And I don't know if you have either, yet. But you will."

Christ, he was itching for a cigarette, for a stiffer drink than what was in his flask. This girl and her swagger. Who was she, anyway?

"Is that right?" he asked.

"Yes," she said. "Because I'm going to help you."

"You." It wasn't even a question. Matthew's eyebrows stayed lifted when he said it, the disbelief clear.

"Me," she agreed. "We're going to write songs together. That's what Cymbeline wanted me to do. I'm going to help you make *real*, actual art.

Not this 'Mountains and Foothills' tripe."

Silence, for a long time. And Matthew scowling hatefully at her.

"What about 'Matthew's Song'?" he said at last. Her brow furrowed, and she suddenly looked much older than he'd assumed. 30, at least.

"What?"

"'Matthew's Song.' The one my dad wrote for me when I was a baby. Have you heard of it? Went triple platinum in four territories."

He saw that same flash then. Himself at age four on the floorboards, the music shaking through him. The beautiful poetry of it, and then later, how the boys had sunk their fists into his flesh, calling him *precious* and *bonny* and worse.

It was good, though. Beautiful. He'd always known that, no matter what those boys had said. Even though one of his front teeth was false for it—even though he'd caught all manner of hell. They hadn't been able to take it away from him. "Matthew's Song." Matthew's transcendent *fucking* song.

But Naomi just turned on her heels and went over to the piano. As she opened it up, she shrugged.

"Never cared for it," she said.

* * *

Matthew stared himself down from the bathroom mirror. The water he'd splashed over his face in an attempt to calm himself seemed to do nothing but settle into the fine lines, accentuating the freckles and the age spots and the age spots he normally tried to tell himself were freckles but could not, right now, in his condition. He shouldn't have been so rattled by this stranger; he shouldn't have been so ill at ease. He was Edmund Matthew Hammond IV, and he had been inculcated with a familial belief in his own inherent self-worth. That he could be treated well, and succeed, and gain even more respect as a result. That the fruits of his labor would be ripe and sweet. That all manners of pleasant things awaited him.

Why, then, was he so unmoored? He looked around the clean, white bathroom for a hand towel, and found only a thin striped length of Turkish cloth on which he could press his face. For a moment he groaned into the ensuing darkness. Then he sat down on the toilet, the water still running. He'd hoped Naomi, half a house away, would not be able to hear what came next.

He took out his flask, drank down the remainder of his gin. Then he pulled out his phone, which had a single thin bar of reception. As he waited for Kara to pick up, he sat with his knees angled, and his elbows on his knees, propping himself up.

"Sweetie," she said, by way of greeting, "I was hoping you'd call today. How's the sojourn?"

He'd left her at the elevator of the New York penthouse only three, maybe four hours before. She'd looked pale and fretful, her bathrobe half open and showing the small bulge of her belly above the dark thatch of hair she left ungroomed, now, that they'd been together so long and had a baby on the way. She'd reminded him of a Victorian widow, wanly circling a widow's walk, waiting for her sailor to return from sea. In that moment, he'd thought he would never love anyone more. Now, too, his heart ached for her, but it was a reactionary ache. He only wanted one woman's presence, instead of another's. Someone who would heal him rather than challenge him.

"It's, ah—" he hesitated, his gaze drifting to the closed door. "Well, Edelman's house is beautiful."

"His wife told me all about it last time they were over for dinner. Do you remember, how she was trying to get us to buy a place up here?"

Matthew grunted. He didn't remember, rarely listened to the women and their chatter, but that wasn't entirely his fault. When Edelman was there, he demanded every single ounce of his time and attention. He'd talk right over the women, a right he'd earned by his gender and a right that Matthew, sharing in it, wasn't about to challenge.

"Apparently she went to camp across the lake," she said, "As a girl. I always wanted to go to camp. Do you think we'll send Everleigh to camp someday?"

He imagined Kara still only half-dressed, touching a hand to her naked belly. They didn't know for certain whether the child was a girl or boy yet, but no boy's name had become apparent to them, and so they were calling the child Everleigh. So far.

"If she wants. Of course." He felt very young in that moment, considering it. He hadn't considered much about the child to come, though Kara talked about it all the time. What schools they would send Everleigh to, the specific brand of sound machine they would buy for her room, how they would talk to her about sex someday, early, so that there would be no nasty surprises like there had been for Kara. "I always thought she could spend the summers at Kingcausie."

"Kingcausie?" Kara asked, the disbelief cracking her voice, "Really? I don't know—"

Matthew squared his shoulders. He remembered their single visit there, right after they met—how Kara hadn't wanted to sleep in his unheated childhood bedroom even with the fire going, how they'd ended up in a hotel in Aberdeen where they'd fought all night instead.

"It's where I grew up, Kara," he said. "It's where I spent the first four years of my life. If you're saying it's not good enough for our daughter—"

"No, no, Matt," she said soothingly. He could hear the weariness in her voice, a general unwillingness to fight. Again. "It's fine. Summers in Kingcausie it is. I'm sure she'll like the animals on the estate."

Estate. That was a laugh. It was a *farm*. His Dad hadn't even hired anyone to help work it until the '90s. Still, the notion brought back fond memories.

"Yeah," Matthew said. He was thinking of Snicker, the spotted pony he loved as a boy. Dead now, like all those cats his dad had loved in succession. The memory made Matthew itch, once again, for a cigarette. "I'm sure she will."

After a long pause, too long, Kara let out a sigh. "Okay, sweetie. I need to go. Pearl's coming by for dinner."

"Wait," he said. "I called you for a reason—" He felt as if he were reaching ineffectually out to her, about to grip her filamentous robe in his hand but the fabric kept slipping away.

"What is it?" she asked. He couldn't be sure, but he thought perhaps she was forcing her voice to be patient, gentle, when she really wanted to be anything but. She hated fighting now, though she loved it once. Hated the idea of stressing the baby.

"There's a woman here," he said. "A friend of Cymbeline's. Edelman said she was supposed to be my assistant for the visit, but—"

"A woman?" There was curiosity brightening Kara's voice, as there always was, at moments like these. Oh, they had their arrangement. She wasn't supposed to ask, or get angry, but he always felt as though she were filing any little scrap she could get from him about any woman he mentioned for later.

"Not like that," he said. "It's not like that. She showed up, and says she wants to collaborate with me. We're supposed to write songs together. Like my Dad and—and Baron Fucking Templeton."

A long pause. A thin, gentle laugh at the other end of the receiver.

"Well, she must not know you very well," Kara said. "You're *not* your father, Matt. You can write songs just fine all on your own."

He closed his eyes. Heard her praise. Didn't feel it. Sighed, and said anyway, "Thanks, babe."

"Of course, sweetie. I'll call you tomorrow morning, okay?"

"First thing?"

"First thing. Now I really do have to go—"

"Yeah," he said. "Love you."

"Love you, too."

Kara hung up. Matthew held the phone for one more moment, feeling how it had grown warm against his cheek. He put it back in his pocket, took one last look at the fleshy face in the mirror, turned to leave, left. He heard Kara's words echoing in his head with every footstep down the hallway.

You're not your father. You're not your father.

But after just a few steps, the thought was drowned out by another sound. Hands against the piano. Incessant. Pounding. He came to stand in the big, empty living room, where he watched Naomi play those piano keys, where he watched her body bent over the instrument and silhouetted against a tangerine sunset. There was something about the sight of it, about the sound. He felt a lump rise like a fist lodged in his throat.

"Remarkable," he said softly, when the notes had finally died. Naomi looked up at him, grinning, and when she did he realized he wasn't certain if he meant her music—or Naomi herself.

13 - 1957

Their first show together. The light pouring in through the windows of the veteran's hall, lighting every single mote of dust. The boys—his boys, his band—taking out their instruments, tuning up. Ivan had already packed it in three days before. Said he had a crack in his jug, that he was too busy with his mechanic's apprenticeship, anyway. Made it easier. But not *easy*. Baron's hands shook as he took his guitar out of his case. He'd played in public twice before—once early in the summer, a street parade where a rickety lorry pulled the boys along as they strummed drunkenly and tried to keep time and not fall off, and the St. Michael's Fete, which went better, but even so, he hadn't been able to remember any of the words.

Still, that had been before Eddie had had his way with him, teaching him the proper shape for the chords and making him sing the words right until they were practically imprinted on his brain. There was no fucking it up now, was there? He cast his gaze sidelong to Ed, who wore a white sports coat with a pink carnation stuck through the lapel. If Baron had dressed that way, he'd have never heard the end of it. But not Eddie. Already, a small crowd of girls from Eddie's school had gathered around him to watch as he slung his guitar over his back and tuned it, offhandedly.

"Birds always go for the girly ones," Dickie said, standing beside Baron. Baron watched and scowled. He couldn't deny it was true. Eddie was beautiful and harmless in a way he would never be, with his dark eyes and darker gaze.

But that wasn't why he was scowling.

"Leave Hammy alone then," he said, swinging his look decisively to Dickie. "He's had a hard enough time of it without hearing any shite from you."

Dickie's eyes widened. He held his hands up, a wall between the two of them. "All right, Baron. I didn't mean anything by it."

"Yeh," said Baron. "You never do." He waited a beat to punctuate his words better. "Prick." Without waiting for an answer, Baron hustled off toward Eddie, pushing through the throng of girls to get there.

He stood there for a moment, still angry in the sweet haze of perfume and setting spray, eyes smoldering like he imagined Elvis' eyes might smolder in a moment like that. Then he reached into his leather jacket and pulled out a flask.

"To take the edge off before the show," he said, offering it to Eddie first. Baron hadn't even drunk from it yet, much less Dickie, much less Liam and the rest of them. Ed had to know what a gesture it was, to be offered a drink first. But the boy just shrugged. Cool. Maddening.

"Nah, I need me edge," he said. The girls around them giggled, whispered. So Baron took the first swig.

"You gonna share that?" Liam asked, appearing out of nowhere to wrestle the flask away. After he drank down a slag, he winced.

"Yuck. Do you always drink gin?"

"No," Baron said. He grabbed the flask from Liam, put it away before the old vets at the bar in the back of the hall could see them. "But me uncle does."

"Disgusting," Liam said, as though Baron hadn't gotten the message in the first place. "You know what I like to drink?"

"No, and I don't care," Baron said. Eddie was watching them in silence, an amused smile on his sweet lips, but Liam just went on anyway.

"Scotch. That's a man's drink."

"Sure, Liam," Baron said. "Look, we need to be getting on stage soon. We're supposed to start at two."

"Hardly anyone's here, Baron," Dickie called from behind him. Acting like he was still a part of the conversation. Which he wasn't.

"I don't think that's true," Baron said. He looked at the closest bird, a blonde little thing in pedal pushers, glasses making her eyes look like a pair of ripe round cocktail olives floating near the bottom of a tumbler. It felt absurd if he thought about it, about what he was about to do, but if he were Eddie or a guy who liked himself better half the time then it would have seemed normal. So he did it anyway. Winked at her. She looked down at the points of her shoes, blushing. "I think these girls will give us a show if we give them one. Right, girls?"

Giggles. Approval. And somehow, best of all, triumphing over Dickie, who was made to look like a mother hen, fretting and restless. Out of the corner of his eye, Baron saw Eddie smirk.

"Right then," Eddie said. "Let's go."

* * *

It was easier on stage this time, with Ed beside him. When the music flowed through them, when they were bending the strings together, when their hearts were beating out a stuttered rhythm that pulsed from their cocks down to the tips of their toes and up again, into their strumming hands, it felt like it all finally meant something. All this strife. Like he just had to lift a lip in a jagged grin, lean into the microphone, ignore the feedback, and *sing*, together, with Ed. Culmination. And ease. Nothing was easy for Baron Templeton, not even wanking, not even home. But this. This was all right.

The veteran's hall, nearly empty at first, was filling up with girls and their boys. He saw now that it was the girls who led the way, packs of them, hungry for something. For him? Nah. For dancing. They'd shimmy out to the dance floor together, just the girls and their girlfriends, because the boys were gangly, smelly, self-conscious, and together the girls would wiggle their asses and their feet, squealing together, turning round and round. Baron understood the way the boys stood back, only nodding their heads, arms crossed tight over their teddy boy button-ups. It was embarrassing to dance. Queer. A man should be ashamed that he had a body, that he felt anything, even lust. As Baron leaned toward the microphone, harmonizing with Eddie, he thought that in the next life he might want to come back as a girl. Easier to be fine and feel things. Easier to let the music flow through.

But, well, then, he'd found this, hadn't he? Eddie grinned at Baron from across the microphone's patterned metal head and Baron grinned back. It wasn't a queer kind of smile at all. He knew it wasn't. It was about this song, nicked from Little Richard, and this beat, ripped from his own chest, and being able to move to it for once—not quite dancing, but bending his knees a bit as he strummed, up and down. Up and down.

The song burst toward its conclusion. The boys looked at one another, sweaty, grinning, slick. Baron could hear the small explosion of applause from out in the distance. Not just girls, but their boys, too. Couple a low whistles. Couple a almost-reluctant hand claps. He knew, because he was one of them, what a triumph it was to receive even this scant approval. And so he leaned into the microphone again.

"Thank you, thank you, ladies and germs." A groan in the audience. A grin from Baron, at the old terrible joke. "We're the Bartlebys. Because we'd prefer not to. But here we are, eh? That's Liam Walker, on guitar over there. Promise you he's toilet trained."

Baron glanced back. He'd half expected Liam to let out a whine at the teasing. But for once, Liam was cool. He just bent his strings back, letting out a little trickle of notes, and a little bird out in the audience let a squeal out back. Liam smirked. A girlfriend, then? Right.

"And this is Alf Duggan, on the bass. Play it, Alf."

"No," Alf said into the microphone, and smiled sweetly. Baron licked his lips, went on.

"And here making his grand debut on this stage is Edmund Hammond the third. Son, do you have anything to say for yourself?"

"Christ, Baron," Eddie said, blushing, and Baron could have grabbed him and kissed him for it, in front of God and about thirty-nine horny teenagers and a few horny old veterans, too. But instead, he just leaned close to the microphone again.

"I'm de Baron von Templeton and you can shove it up your arse if you'd like." An appreciative guffaw from one of the old vets in back. "But if not, then you can listen to this next song, which we wrote. The two of us." He pointed to Eddie, who looked down, blushing still. "A brand new Templeton and Hammond original."

Eddie, abruptly, no longer blushing, craned his neck to the shared microphone. Was all cool, cool.

"Hammond and Templeton," he said. Baron gave a wicked grin.

"Whatever. And a one and a two and a three—"

The boys exploded out into music again, beautiful music, and this time, there was something even more beautiful about it. It was *theirs*. It had come from *them*. From their sweat and their brains and their fingers, and here it was, in this big hollow hall that usually was filled with only ghosts, now swollen with the force of their music, which they had somehow pushed out and past them, into the bodies of these pretty little girls and their boyfriends. Proving to the whole wide world that they were alive and they mattered. Proving that they were not dead. *Yet*.

Of course Baron had to ignore the dreadful scraping and rapping behind him. Dickie and his thimbles and the washboard, and how he knew, though he could not see, how Dickie scowled at the effort. There had been a reason Baron hadn't bothered to introduce him, after all.

* * *

After, they celebrated at Baron's mum's house, all five of them and a couple of birds who had followed them back from the veteran's hall and some blokes from school who had it in their heads that if they stayed close to Baron Templeton maybe some of his glitter would fall off him and they could sprinkle themselves and looked special for a moment, too. Baron did not mind. He was high as a kite, high as the Tower of London, high as the Empire State Building, even, though he was mostly, actually, sober. Sitting on his mum's settee and eating her scones.

"Oh, Baron!" his mum was enthusing. "That was just *wonderful!*"

She'd come out for the end of the show, caught the last three numbers—the tail end of he and Ed's new song among them. And he could tell by the full, warm quality of her eyes that she truly meant it. It was the same kind of way she'd gushed and creamed a few weeks back when they'd gone to see *Jailhouse Rock* together. A real breathless, disembodied sort of exclamation. The other fellows just kind of tittered.

"And you wrote that song *yourself*?" she was saying. "I had no idea you were a *songwriter*."

"Yeah, well," Baron said, feeling his cheeks heat and ignoring it. "Eddie helped too."

"'Helped,'" Eddie said, giving his eyes a high roll. "Baron, it was half-written by the time you got to it."

"Yeh, but I made it *good*. No lying."

Eddie, mild, lifted one eyebrow, even as he took a sip of Baron's mum's tea. "Yeh, I suppose there's some truth to that."

"Come off it. You'd be lost without me. Now give us a kiss." Baron made some kissy sounds, and all the boys howled, and even Eddie laughed, losing it a little. But weren't they all losing it there, in Baron's mum's living room? High on the adrenaline of the stage, still, and the smell of the birds in the corner, sweet perfume covering up their musk. There was a knock on the door. Baron's mother let out a stream of cigarette smoke from her pretty painted mouth and rushed to get it.

"Oh, Sue!" Baron heard her say, voice full of cheer, and soon she pushed Sue Grasso through the doorway. Baron flitted his eyes up. There she was, twisting a strand of yellow hair around her finger, standing back with the other birds. Among them she didn't look so special, though she did have that cute little gap to her teeth. He couldn't see it without thinking of kissing her, just for a moment, throbbing and true.

"Hi," she said shyly to the others, though they must have known each other from school. Then she looked over to Baron, fluttering her mascara coated eyelashes. "Sorry I missed your show. Me gran was visiting, Baron."

"It's all right," Baron said, feeling his jaw tighten. He didn't want to forgive or begrudge Sue Grasso. Didn't really want anything at all to do with her anymore. So instead he looked over to Eddie and started to say something to him, but before he could speak, there was a ukulele being passed to him.

His mother, smoking frantically, grinning like a desperate maniac. Pushing the little shrunken guitar into his hand.

"Since she missed it I thought you could play her the song you boys wrote," Baron's mum was saying. Baron just let her stand there, dangling the instrument over him.

"I would prefer not to," he said.

"Baron, come on."

"I'll do it . . ." Eddie began, reaching for it. But Baron's mum just snatched it back, pressing it toward Baron until it was fully in his hands.

"No, no, Baron should."

Anger. Yeah. And humiliation. He took the stinking little ukulele and held it to his knee. The chords were different than guitar or even banjo. The chords were all wrong, though he could have guessed them, he supposed. Or felt out the shape of them. Maybe. Or just *pretended* he knew fuck-all what he was doing. Wouldn't have been the first time. For a split second, he looked grimly at Eddie, thinking about how Ed could have probably played it perfectly. In a flash Baron was imaging Eddie crooning at Sue Grasso, then maybe dancing later, then maybe Ed finally touching a tit. Killing two birds with one stone, as it were. But Baron's mother was standing in front of him, her hands on her fat little hips, her head cocked, the ciggie that was rapidly burning away dangling from unmoving lips.

"*Play*, Baron!" And for a moment he could see how she and Deedz were, in fact, sisters, how the world for them revolved around them and their wants. He'd never really seen his mum get mad, though he'd heard her arguing with Timmy about Baron spending the night once or twice. Anyway, an argument didn't seem to be an option here in her living room with so many eyes watching. Even little Bessie contemplated him from the corner of the room, waiting to see what he would do next.

"Right, then," Baron said at last. He set the little instrument on his knee, began hazily strumming out the chords. Stopping. Starting again. Waiting to catch the look of Eddie cringing from the corner of his eye at the chords that were not right, at the strings that were not even properly tuned, but that wasn't the sort of bloke Ed was. Instead, Eddie just leaned forward over his own plate of scones and began singing the words, loud enough that any mistakes Baron might have made were all covered and gone. And it worked, after a verse or two. Mum started shimmying her hips along with the music, then held out her hand for Sue to join her. The two of them, their hips bumping into each other over Baron's bumbling song. The two of them sweating together. Almost like fucking. And Baron and every other boy in the room growing a throbber over it, until, not to be outdone and ignored, the other girls began to join in, too.

The Bartlebys were left alone on the sofa and chairs, singing, strumming, watching. After a moment, Dickie Ashby started to thump his hands against the coffee table in a perverse attempt to keep the beat. If Baron's music was wrong and strange, then this was some sort of travesty. Dickie had no rhythm at all, no real talent. Baron knew that now. Knew what had to be done. But as Dickie played, he pressed his beery mouth up against Baron's ear and said to him, grinning, "I just fucking love being in a band."

14 - 1977

That autumn and all into the darkening winter, Zachary ate, drank, and slept Baron Templeton. He got an old, taped-up biography on him from the school library and took to carrying it with him wherever he went, long past the day when it should have been returned. He sketched pictures of him in his notebooks, terrible pictures. Baron's greasy, Teddy Boy flop of hair lank over one eye, concealing how Zachy had not drawn the sockets straight. Baron's smile, jagged and cutting and full of Chiclet teeth. Baron's hands, which seemed to contain too many joints no matter how many times he erased and redrew them, working the frets of his infamous Rickenbacker Combo.

Zach drew all of Baron's guitars—his ancient Antoria and the Les Paul he allegedly smashed after their final-ever show. But he especially drew the Rickenbacker. It was a strange Frankenguitar Baron had once told the press was named Eddie, a joke that made the *real* Eddie glower during the interview, the Frankenguitar whose providence was unknown until, in the late '60s, the finish started wearing down, revealing pink beneath, and the owner of the Steinway Music Shop in Hamburg came out of hiding to tell how a pair of boys had nicked his last Rickenbacker Combo 800, a pink one, and he'd never known where it had gotten to because the new owner had coated it with a bright green sparkly car paint as though to declare his masculine possession over it. *That* guitar. Zachy drew that. Zach drew every detail: the strange pick-ups and a tremolo Baron had bought on tour in Japan after the bridge snapped off, Zach drew it because guitars were easier to draw than people, and he drew it everywhere, on the back of every test and on the hard scratched surface of his desk until Mr. Conway caught him and told him he'd have to stay after to erase his work.

Obsession was nothing new. The year before it had been airplanes. A few years before that, chess. Zachy had once gotten it into his head that he'd be a chess champion, just like Bobby Fischer, had read biographies of him and magazine profiles, had brought his chess board to dinner, which had pissed Richard Charles off but mom had been tickled by the thought of him becoming a certifiable famous genius and so she had tolerated his rattling off of factoids about Fischer's biography when she was trying to listen to the news.

Now, at nearly fourteen, Zachy could remember in a factual way that he had once loved Bobby Fischer. But he could no longer *feel* it, or really even see the appeal. Baron Templeton was much more interesting. Impenetrably hard. Powerful. Zach found one of his dad's leather jackets at the back of his mother's closet, and, without bothering to ask his mother for permission, he started to wear it everywhere, even though the lining was disintegrating to pieces after twenty years stored. Actually, maybe that made it even more appealing. His father had been born in England, too—in Liverpool, actually, just like Saffron. Just like Templeton. And sometimes, shrugging into his coat, Zachy would imagine that his dad and Templeton had been friends together. Shoplifting—no, *nicking*—coats. Smoking fags. Being wild.

It wasn't a total fiction. Templeton hadn't been poor as a kid, but he hadn't been rich, either. There were stories in the biography about the band's Hamburg days, about how they'd stolen their clothes off visiting sailors because they could not afford their own. There was something romantic now about being decrepit, impoverished, about filching dad's clothes in his absence. Maybe if he'd been a Hammond kind of boy he would have gotten a job and saved up his own money for a brand new leather jacket. But, now that he could tell the difference between Templeton and the others, he knew that criminality and daring and begging forgiveness rather than asking permission were the way to go. Templeton was *bad*. Now *bad* was aspirational.

Normally, Richard Charles would have given Zach a hard time about his interests. He had in the past—it had been a source of endless amusement that, for all the chess books Zachy read, he remained terrible at the game, and that he especially had never once managed to beat his big brother. The plane obsession had, meanwhile, elicited endless eye rolling, and once when he left his best compendium on World War II planes in the bathroom, he'd returned to find the words "DWEEB" and "REJECT" drawn across the cover, and cartoonish faces and an exploding penis etched over the nose of nearly every plane. But this interest in Saffron was different for both of them—it was something new. It was, if not precisely cool, then cool*ish* at least, tangential to Richard Charles' innate musical interests and talents rather than wholly outside it. It was, for once, something they shared.

Zach's fourteenth birthday arrived, and a second-hand powder blue Fender telecaster from grandma with it, and Richard Charles had managed to acquire a dented Teisco bass from unknown sources. From that day forward, they spent almost every minute in their room together, puzzling out songs. It was the first time they were united in something, and for once, that union didn't mean squabbling or competition but rather true friendship. After all, Zach needed Richard Charles. He knew he did. Richard Charles understood music. Chord structure and theory and key. Zach didn't know where he'd picked this stuff up, but suddenly Richard Charles would start talking about the circle of fifths, about countermelody, and Zach would sit up a little straighter. And his older brother, in turn, was for the first time willing to be patient and teach. Gently, he'd take Zachy's hands and form the proper chords with them, holding fingers against strings until they felt so raw they could have been bleeding. When Zach winced, Richard Charles didn't tease or mock him. Instead, gently, he held his hands in place. "If you don't build up calluses it will hurt worse. Remember what you were telling me about Templeton?"

"After his mom taught him to play the Antoria, his fingers bled," Zach replied, grimacing. If he were a softer boy, maybe he would have cried at the pain. But no matter how patient in the moment, he knew he couldn't cry in front of Richard Charles. To do so would have meant endless mockery. To feel would have been to lose.

"That's right," his brother said. "It's just part of the process. The transformation."

"Transformation into *what*?" he asked, the third or fourth time Richard Charles had said the phrase over the course of a week. His brother was like that sometimes, falling so in love with one of his own thoughts that he couldn't stop himself from repeating it over and over again.

His brother, leaning in close, his breath a little yeasty from the beer he'd been drinking all day while playing hooky from school, broke out into the world's sweetest grin. "Into a rock star," was what he said.

* * *

In early November, the eighth graders were bused to the high school for an orientation, meant to prepare them for the next phase of their lives. Zach took his Templeton biography with him, though if a stranger asked, he would be hard pressed to give an answer as to why. He'd already read it, more than once. But sometimes, a slip of conversation would remind him of something, and he liked to page back through it, just to be extra certain that he had his facts straight.

He sat on the bus alone, even though he was surrounded by people. That was nothing new. Last year, he'd had one friend: Mikey Alspaugh. But Alspaugh had decided to join the football team and had left Zach behind to go be one of the popular kids. They hadn't fought about it. The friendship hadn't really been worth either of their time, or effort. Most days, Zach felt like he lived outside of other people. The things they cared about, he didn't. Couldn't. School dances. The fights in the hallway that other boys sometimes had over who had stolen what from whom. Until now, music. And actual girls, the ones who occupied the same physical space as him, who always seemed ordinary and a little dull despite the way they looked sometimes, long hair and lips sticky from those strawberry lip smackers. The girls on TV never had a crust of boogers on the edge of their nostrils in the winter, never scratched their bra straps when they thought someone wasn't looking, never got BO, even in gym. Without even making a conscious decision about it, he'd decided that girls were better kept under glass.

Still, he thought, thumbing through *Templeton: A Life in Exile* for the four thousandth time as the gray landscape streamed by him, it would have been nice to have been . . . recognized. In the back of his head he kept a fantasy which he wouldn't have shared with anyone, which he wouldn't have even been able to find words for, where he carried that book into the high school and a girl—older, almost a woman, a senior, maybe—would have seen it in his hands and in the crowded hallway, the other students would fade away to nothingness and she would have approached him, tucking a strand of hair behind her ear, and said, "I love Baron Templeton. Are you a musician?"

In his head, he had the whole romance plotted out. She'd be a child of divorce, with a rich father who lived up in Hyde Park. They'd spend their weekends together in her bedroom there, which would be all girlish pink and lace, and she'd listen to him play guitar for hours, and then her dad would come in, and he wouldn't be mad, he'd only tell him about a friend who worked at a record company down in the city, and one weekend, they'd drive down together in his Town Car, her in the backseat with him, her perfect dream body pressed up against his arm. And he would record a song for her, his dream girl, and all that fame and fortune and notoriety that he knew he was owed would flow to him like water flows downstream.

He could see the girl's face in his mind, bright and shining. It wasn't about sex for him, not really. It was about escape. Escape and recognition. Escape and recognition and okay, he thought, pushing the thick book down against his boner, willing it away, sex, too.

The bus let them off outside the school. Mrs. Strouther bellowed at them to walk in a straight line back toward the auditorium, and, in the jostling crowd, Zach did. But just at the auditorium door, he felt a hand fix itself around the elbow of his leather jacket and wrench him away.

"Hey!" he belched out, his voice cracking as he spoke, but he didn't need to worry about anyone hearing, because it was just Richard Charles. His surly brother, in shorts despite the season, and a stained t-shirt with an old shearling coat on top, one he'd stolen from the Goodwill on 9W.

"We're cutting today," he said, and in the moment, Zach was surprised by how brave—or how stupid—his brother was about the whole thing. He didn't bother whispering. He didn't even bother lowering his voice.

"They're making us sign in," Zach said. Richard Charles rolled his eyes.

"So you go and you sign in and you wait about two and a half minutes, then you raise your hand and ask if you can take a leak. But instead of going to the bathroom you come and meet me by the south entrance."

"Where's that?" Zach asked. More eye rolling.

"Around the corner, third door to the left."

"Are you sure we won't get busted?"

Richard Charles shrugged. "I don't know. Who cares?"

And then his brother was gone.

Zach's whole body tightened, tensed as he walked through the auditorium doors with his classmates, his book clutched against his hip with an increasingly sweaty hand. He was a good kid—*the* good kid—of his family, a real unapologetic apple shiner, as Baron Templeton used to say about Edmund Hammond. He'd never cut class before, and Mr. Mollar the principal was going on and on about how *important* this assembly was, the beginning of their adult lives.

But what kind of life? Zach found himself thinking. Once he'd wanted to be a US Air Force pilot. Before that, a worldwide ranked chess champion. And maybe you needed a high school diploma for that. Maybe you needed to be somehow upstanding. *Professional.*

But sitting there, sweating into his leather coat, which he had not bothered removing, it all seemed suddenly pointless to him. Baron Templeton had never graduated from art school, had he? Baron Templeton cut class *all the god damned time*, starting when he was a schoolboy, starting at six or seven. And it hadn't hurt him any. Baron Templeton had, until recently, been one of the richest and most infamous men in the world. A hero to millions. His fingers shaking slightly, Zach raised his hand, and Mrs. Strouther came over and bent low.

"Can I use the bathroom?" Zach whispered. Mrs. Strouther frowned.

"You should have gone before you left," she said. "I don't want you to miss anything."

Zach pulled down the corners of his mouth, and then squirmed in his seat. "I'll be right back. I have to go!"

"Fine. Fine." She cocked a thumb to the side door of the auditorium. Suddenly, it felt like every single one of Zach's movements were ungainly, awkward, obvious. He stepped on toes as he squeezed his way down the aisle. Girls glared at him. He tripped up the steps, and through the door, and into the strange buzzing silence of the high school hallway.

And then, to his own surprise, he went straight into the boy's room. He *did* have to take a leak, he decided, standing at the urinal, letting it all hang out. He kept the Templeton book under his armpit as he pissed, trying to ignore how hard his heart was pounding. There was graffiti all over the place, but he couldn't make it out. That's how scared he was. Zipping up. Washing his hands for too long, finding the towel dispenser empty, turning to leave. Doing what his brother told him, which was another kind of obedience. Walking out into the freezing cold parking lot, where Richard Charles was waiting.

"I thought you'd wuss out," Richard Charles said. Zach narrowed his eyes.

"No," he replied, as he felt his big brother's palm fall in between his shoulder blades, slapping against the leather skin.

* * *

The two of them walked together down past the convenience store by the high school, then back to a wooded area behind it. The sunlight was bright overhead, and sparkling off a little river. It almost felt like autumn still, almost felt okay. Zach filled his lungs up with warm smoke from one of his brother's stolen Marlboros. He'd only had a few cigarettes before, but it seemed important to look like he knew what he was doing with it, so he was careful not to suck the smoke in too deep, not to cough, not to give himself away like a baby.

They finally reached an appointed spot, under a little bridge that rattled every few minutes from a car passing over. There was garbage everywhere pressed into the brown mud and dead grass, and graffiti. Pentacles, mostly. A swastika. An Illuminati eye. And of course, cocks. Beneath a particularly veiny one, framed by large tear-drops of jizz, sat two girls. They were unbelievably skinny, both of them. One had brown feathered hair. The other was a dishwater blonde. Otherwise, they could have been the same person. For all intents and purposes, Zach thought, they were.

He watched his brother sit beside the blonde and press a revolting kiss to her neck.

"Jennifer," he said. "This is Zachy."

"Oh, your brother," she said, sounding particularly disinterested. She put out her cigarette on the cement wall, then offered Zach her hand.

"I'm Jennifer," she said. Zach took it. Shook. Her bones felt like they were a bird's bones, hollow, ready to break. He studied her face. Sunken cheeks. Plucked eyebrows. Obvious, caked-on makeup. It was kind of disappointing. Zach had figured that if his brother were going to have a girlfriend, she'd be better than reality. Like something off a poster.

"You're the guitarist, right?" the other girl asked. Her voice was low and thick, almost like a boy's voice. "In his band?"

Band? Zach looked at his brother in surprise, but Richard Charles' expression was mild and inscrutable. He wondered what his brother had been telling his friends, what he'd been telling these girls. That the two of them were in a band. Apparently.

"Yeah," Zach said.

"I want to call ourselves the Dervishes," Richard Charles said. "Zach thinks the Ruffians is a better name."

"I think they're both terrible," Jennifer said with a grin. Richard Charles kind of pummeled her in the arm, but gently. Zachy was glad. She was so skinny under her huge army coat that he suspected she'd bruise in an instant.

"The Dervishes, like the Saffron Dervishes?" the other girl asked. Zach's eyes went to her in a flash. He resisted the urge to reach for his Templeton book, which he'd tucked into the back of the waistband of his jeans. The Saffron Dervishes had been a name that the band had gone by for two shows in 1958, after they'd discovered that another band was using the name the Bartlebys but before they'd become simply Saffron. He wondered who this creature was who also knew Saffron.

"Yeah," Richard Charles answered. "My brother has a boner for Baron Templeton."

"I do not," Zach said.

"Do too. I hear him at night, you know," Richard Charles pressed on, acting like he was only talking to Jennifer, "Having wet dreams." And then he added, in a girlish voice, "Oh, Baron, stick it up my asshole. You're so sexy. I want to lick you."

"Fuck you," Zach said, his cheeks burning, his gaze burning, too. Richard Charles and Jennifer were laughing. But the dark-haired girl just leaned forward, holding her cigarette against her mouth without inhaling.

"I can't say I disagree with your brother," she said. "I'd let him fuck me in a heartbeat."

"What?" Richard Charles stopped laughing. "You'd fuck little Zachy?"

The brunette smirked. "No way. Templeton."

Elated and crushed in the thin margin it took the girl to take another breath and exhale a cloud of smoke. Still, there was something there. He turned to look at her for the first time. Maybe not *so* ugly. She had a big square jaw, smooth hair. He felt a spark. Just from the expression in her murky eyes, he knew that *she* liked Baron Templeton, too.

"I like the name the Ruffians because it was the name of their first album," Zachy said. "You know, like Baron's Aunt Deedz always said. *I won't let those ruffians in their drainpipe trousers be seen coming in through my front door.*"

"Yeah, yeah," the girl said coolly. "I've read all the bios."

"You have?" Zachy asked. He could hear how there was too much eagerness in his voice—too much desperation. But somehow, he couldn't keep it out. He'd wanted to meet a girl like him for *so long*. Someone who carried the same rhythm he did tucked inside his veins. It made him think of his brother and that girl in the record store. Doomed soulmates, clearly. "Have you read this one?"

His hand was shaking as he pulled the book out of the waistband of his jeans. She hesitated a moment, shed ash, one eyebrow lifted. Then she took it from him.

"This one's expurgated," she said. He didn't know what that meant. He didn't want to ask her.

"Oh, yeah?" he said, lifting his eyebrows in return. She sucked in a breath of cigarette smoke, exhaled, taking her time with him.

"Yeah. The biographer doesn't talk about any of the juicy stuff." She handed his book back to him. He took it, folding the worn stack of paperback pages between his hands.

"What do you mean?" Richard Charles asked from where he sat with Jennifer. There was a funny look on his face, coy beneath his acne. Like he was trying to keep control of this conversation, but knew he was losing it. Before the brunette could answer, Richard Charles had turned back to Jennifer and begun to kiss her, pretending like he didn't *really* care.

But Zach knew better.

"He's a total fag," the brunette said, and the words sank into Zach like a fist into Silly Putty. He tried to keep his expression straight, but couldn't. Even Richard Charles had coughed up a spitty wad of laughter as he pulled his lips away from Jennifer's.

"Seriously?"

"Yeah, man," she said, in her boy's voice, firm and sure, and Zach felt it was wrong, all wrong, for this conversation.

He could feel his face burning bright, bright red, as though his veins were dipped in hot pepper, as if his skin had been scoured by the surface of the sun. It wasn't possible. He would know if it was true. He'd read every page in *Templeton: A Life in Exile* four times, maybe five. Baron's life was like Zach's life. Fatherless. Touched. If Baron was a fag . . .

"Oh, god," he heard Jennifer say, but it sounded like her voice was coming from far, far away, "Shay is just fucking with you, Zachy. Don't have a heart attack."

"I'm not," Shay said sourly. Richard Charles was laughing. Zach shook his head, like he was trying to rattle the thought out of it. Forced a smile. Laughed, too.

"You got me, there," Zach said. Shay's frown deepened even more.

"I wasn't joking," she said. Glowering like she was, he decided she was even uglier than he initially thought. Improperly formed. Like she'd missed some kind of important lesson in being a girl. "You know what? I'll prove it to you."

Richard Charles snorted. Jennifer laughed, too. But Zach only looked at her, wrinkling his brow.

"How?"

"He's in New York City, right?" Shay said. "At the Chelsea Hotel. That's what I've heard."

"Yeah?" said Zach. "So?"

"So we'll take the train in next weekend, and we'll ask him."

At that, Richard Charles howled. "What, we walk right up to this reclusive millionaire and say, 'Baron Templeton, are thee a faggot?'" Jennifer was laughing, too, high and giggly, like an idiot. The both of them, too loud

"Yeah," Shay said, stomping her cigarette out on the ground. "That's exactly what we do."

More laughter from his brother and his girlfriend. But Zach only looked at Shay. Zach only stared.

15 - 1957

It was autumn in earnest now, autumn tucking its head into winter almost, and Baron started to go around in one of his uncle's old jumpers and his pea coat from the war, imagining it to be his father's pea coat. His father, the sailor, gone and disappeared forever and forever unseen. Baron was on the verge of disappearing together himself—of dropping out. He should have been sticking with it. He knew that, really. A bloke who had any sense would have been doing what Aunt Deedz wanted, which was finishing school and then off to be a teacher or something else of Useful Note. And after a fashion, every morning, he *meant* to go to school. But then Liam or Eddie would show up and spirit him away like a pied piper, only they had guitars instead of flutes.

A club had opened on Slater Street, the Delphinium, or the Delph as the boys all called it. It wasn't much, but it had an espresso machine and a few tables and a thin stage with hammered boards in the center of it all. It was run by a Black man, Lord Jessamine, they all called him, and he had mostly calypso bands playing when the juke wasn't going. Baron didn't feel about these bands quite the same way he felt about Elvis, for what he felt when he looked at Elvis seemed somehow attainable. He could be a white boy shaking his hips to someone else's songs, or even the songs he wrote with Eddie. But he could not ever inhabit the sound the way these men did.

The truth was these blokes were better at music at him. Still, sometimes, if he let himself admit it, he felt a kinship. Wasn't he so dark in the summer that people would mistake him for a Negro? It happened, sometimes, and here he felt in a way a comfortable sort of invisibility never felt anywhere else.

Plus the *music*, man, the music.

He and Liam and Eddie would sit at the front table from morning to afternoon, soaking up the new chords, the new sounds. Then go off to Liam or Eddie's house to smash those chords into new songs. A few years ago, Baron had been obsessed with wanking. Had done it so much that he thought his prick might fall off, whenever Deedz was out of the house and sometimes, if he dared, if he couldn't stop himself, when she was at home. Now it was all music, all the time, and fuckitall what Deedz said about it—threatening to throw out his guitar whenever he came in late. He'd stash it at Eddie's if he needed to, because what was one more guitar to a musical family? Soon, Eddie said, they'd be ready to tell Jessamine that *they* had written a song or two, and maybe they could go on stage to play it? The bands that played the Delph were *good*, and Eddie had a spark but said they weren't quite sparkling yet. Soon, soon, though—the rest of their lives would begin.

On that day in November, Baron and Eddie and Liam sat at the little front table, slurping down their filter coffee and listening to the jukebox play. There were a coupla older blokes at the next table over, but it was cold and vaguely snowy and the general slog of the weather had chased most of the regulars away. Eddie was showing Liam the solo to "Twenty Flight Rock," which he'd worked out the week before and was now jotting nearly illegibly on a paper napkin. Liam was nodding, pretending to understand, or maybe he actually did. Baron never felt sure. Baron himself was only half there, half elsewhere. Imagining another world, one fire warmed and ancient. In another life, he could have played a lute, he thought as he shed ash from his fag onto the floor. Could have worn tights and velvet. Could have been fine, in a way that wasn't possible in this coarse, coarse world. He was tugging at the itchy collar of his jumper, thinking on it. That's when the door opened and Dickie Ashby walked in.

"Hullo! Boys!" Dick shouted, not only entirely to Baron and the band but also to Jessamine and the decrepit coffee drinkers and the world at large. Eddie was still bent over his napkin, his head nearly touching Liam's, and from his angle, Baron could see how Eddie's eyes rolled, just imperceptibly enough to avoid Dickie spotting them.

"Dick," Baron said flatly, putting the cigarette between his lips and letting it dangle. The smoke felt like a good cover, a thin and hazy wall that could stand between the two of them. In fact, he let his whole body be a wall. He was spread all out in his chair, one arm draped over the back of Liam's chair, chin angled up. Not quite a threat, but not *not* a threat, either. Dickie, like a boundlessly energetic Scottish terrier, ignored him. Grabbed an empty chair from the old men's table, turned it around. And sat down.

"I realized you weren't in class today," Dickie said to Baron, "We was drawing naked ladies, and you weren't even there. So I said to myself, *where could Baron Templeton be?* And I just knew I'd find you here."

"You found me," Baron said, letting no light in. Dickie's smile was off kilter.

"Yeh," he said. And then he turned to Liam and Eddie.

"What are you pansies doing, then?"

"'Twenty Flight Rock,'" Liam said, with enthusiasm, because he was clueless, and because he and Dickie were sort of the same kind of boy—weaselly and beady eyed—and so they liked one another, after a fashion. Dickie only snorted.

"I can't stand Eddie Cochran. Give us a fag, Baron," he said, and held out his fingers, waiting for Baron to put a cigarette in his hand. Baron looked at him, grinding his rear teeth. He could see, too, how Eddie was also on edge. His eyes gone hard and flinty at Eddie Cochran—one of Eddie's gods, a primary god, even, what with them sharing a name and all—being dismissed.

"Baron," Eddie said slowly. Baron looked at him and felt the gears in his body begin to groan to a halt. Baron pulled out his pack of cigarettes and gave one to Dickie, slowly. But then he stood up. His own fag was still dangling between his lips when he set a heavy hand on Dickie's shoulder.

"Let's go for a walk, Dick," Baron said. He felt all eyes at him. Eddie, glowering. Liam's, full of questions. And Dickie's, which contained murky depths he could not make clear.

"Right," Dickie said. "See you, boys."

For a moment, Baron thought he detected a curious resignation in Dickie's voice, as if he knew that saying goodbye meant really, truly saying goodbye.

Maybe this'll be easy, Baron thought, as the two walked out into the gray, slop-edged morning. Their shoulders were nearly touching as they puffed at their cigarettes and walked side-by-side. Baron hitched his pea coat tighter around his body. He'd been getting taller lately, though he'd never be *tall*, and, as a side effect, growing leaner as well. It felt like he was always cold, but he didn't mind it. Kind of liked the Byronic edge the leanness had given him, the drama of it. For a moment, he punned in his head about Byron and Baron. Anything to avoid thinking about the words he was not saying.

"I know you want to get rid of me," Dickie said. Baron stopped, surprised, in his place.

"Oh?" he asked, squinting past the lazy snowflakes. Dickie let out a rough scoffing noise like he couldn't quite believe Baron.

"C'mon," Dickie said, and headed down into an alleyway behind two shops. Baron found himself dutifully following.

"I'm not as good at music as Eddie," Dickie said. He leaned against the wall, shedding ash everywhere, his breath making hot, nicotine-laced clouds all around. "I know it. You don't have to tell me."

"Yeh, but—" Baron began. Something about the way Dickie had brought it up, so plain and unavoidable, made Baron want to deny it. Still, he fell silent. Wasn't it true?

"But nothin'," said Dickie, taking a long drag. There was still a little stub of cigarette left, but he flicked it away down the alley, where Baron watched it smolder against wet brick until it went out. Baron, meanwhile, was smoking and smoking away. Standing awkward and weak there, while Dickie talked at him. "Doesn't matter that you were just as bad as I am, once. Not when you've got Eddie. He's got something, hasn't he?"

"You know he has," Baron said, angling his chin up. Nobody could deny it. Eddie Hammond had magic. *Was* magic. And he'd shared his magic with Baron, but not Dickie, and now Dickie was on the outs. Dick sneered.

"You sweet on him?"

A burst of smoke. A sputter. "Wot?" Baron asked, feeling his cheeks heat at the question.

"You know what I'm asking."

"We're just mates, Dick," Baron said. And then began, "Like you and I are mates—" But he broke off, because in a way Baron and Dickie weren't just mates. More than mates. It had been months since they'd last touched body to body, cock to cock, in his mother's bedroom. But it was there. Under everything else. The tension. The question of what they were. Who they were.

"Thought so," said Dickie, even though he was wrong, in a way, about Baron and Eddie. It was just music for Baron, wasn't it? Or mostly only music. Only it wasn't music. It was more, for both Eddie and Baron. It was the spark. The potential. It was being understood. Not sex. But something like sex. Something better than sex.

"Well, I want you to know something, Templeton," Dickie said. He took one step forward. For a brief whisper of a second, Baron felt the shared heat of their bodies, aligned, as they were, like two jagged exclamation points jammed right up next to each other. So Baron took one step back, then another. Strange, like a dance, how Dickie just followed him—until Baron's back was pressed to the far side of the wall, and Dickie's chest was nearly touching his.

"I ain't leavin' the band."

Baron's mouth was open, soft. "Oh, Dick," he said. "You have to. You know you have to."

"Don't have to," said Dickie. "Don't have to nothin'. You lot are gonna be famous. Gonna get girls. Gonna get money. Don't you think I want those things? Don't you think I deserve them?"

Even now, Dickie's hot breath against his face, and their hearts pounding hard together, all at once, Baron couldn't resist the joke.

"Well, I know you *want* them," said Baron, smirking at the absent implication: no, Dickie Ashby was deserving of neither girls nor money.

But it was a misstep. A miscalculation. Because Dickie's hand shot up and cradled Baron's jaw in its cup. Baron could feel the pressure against his Adam's apple, and in it the fragility of his own body, the force of Dickie's. Baron was thinner that winter than he'd ever been before. And Dickie, in his jumper, had that Irish solidity that he always had, inherited from his Mum. Muscles and veins curling all over. Whereas Baron was just all British and something else, and could easily be crushed, like a brown hen's egg in Dickie's white-carved hands.

"What do you want me to do?" Baron asked, his voice coming out faint. "You'll ruin us. You're awful, Dick. The band won't go *anywhere* with you."

Dickie. Squeezing his jaw. The black in his eyes shrinking down to pinpricks. "Won't be going anywhere without me."

"Dick—"

"No." His friend, his best friend, the one who had wanked him, the one who had defended him as a boy, now with his hot breath upon him and hands squeezing at his jaw like a pimple he meant to viciously pop and while everything from the waist up was anger, ugly and blue with heat, from the waist down, Baron was aware of how Dickie Ashby was grinding into him, his cock big and heavy in his trousers. A fear pricked at Baron, and his eyes went to the mouth of the alley. Always what had happened between them had happened behind closed doors, a mutual secret. This was daylight. This was dangerous. This was open. This was giving Baron a throbber, too, through the tender muck of terror.

"You kick me out of the band," Dickie said, "And I tell them all that you like this."

His free hand went down and grabbed at Baron's cock through his pants. Tight as an ox yoke. Gripping so hard that Baron's balls ached.

"You kick me out and I'll tell your aunt, and your mother, and your fat little sister. I'll tell them all, Baron. You think I'll stop there? I'll tell Liam. I'll tell Eddie. I'll tell Ed that you like a finger up your arsehole. I only let you wank me, but a right fairy, you are. And they'll all know it. Every single one."

Baron only made a thin, strangled noise. Both hands were free except for the cigarette, and Baron had an absurd thought that he could press it into Dickie's eyeball like a weapon. That he could fight him. The way they'd fought before, dozens of times, and Baron always winning—not because he was bigger, because he wasn't. Because he was wilier. And yet, still, Dickie's hand was on his cock, and Baron wanted it, and wanted him, and could not move. Dickie bent in even closer, which seemed impossible to Baron, and their throbbers touched through rough fabric, and Baron dropped his fag. Just as Dickie's mouth touched his, a savage kiss, stubble and tongue and teeth clashing, none of the softness or grace of kissing Sue Grasso, and yet somehow so much better.

Their first kiss. Baron's first kiss from a boy, and their cocks together, and the breath coming thin through Baron's body, so thin he was growing dizzy and the alley was seeming to dip and sway, and Dickie was stabbing his hips into him, and Baron's hips were rising to meet him. Ugly and incessant humping, in an alleyway strewn with garbage and gray snow, until Baron felt his body give shameful release and Dickie shuddered, too, the both of them trembling and trembling and trembling together—pleasure and hatred all mixed up together, fear and ecstasy.

The way that Dickie tore his body away could only be called violent. Cold seeping in where there had once been heat. Baron kept his head down, only peripherally aware of how Dickie wiped himself clean with a handkerchief, tossing it against a wall, leaving his mess for someone else to clean up, as usual. Baron hitched his own coat tight, closing the buttons, hoping it would conceal the stain on his pants. His face had blossomed red in his orgasm. Now, it felt a strange dappled mixture of hot and cold. He couldn't look at Dickie, not directly. Could certainly not speak to him as he followed him out of the alleyway and back into the Delph.

Dickie went over and sat back down with Liam and Eddie. Started talking to them, too loud, too eager. Telling them about some Lonnie Donegan song he'd heard, how he thought it was alright. Baron went up to the counter, angling his body away from them. Ordered an espresso from Lord Jessamine, hot slop in a tiny, dainty cup. Fit for a fairy, Baron thought to himself, though he found no humor in it.

After a minute, Eddie came and stood beside him. Draped an arm over Baron's shoulders, and Baron did his best to resist flinching away.

"There's still time," Eddie said gently. Baron hated him for it. Wanted to break his jaw for his gentleness. Stuffed those violent thoughts down deep. "There's still plenty of time."

Baron sipped his espresso. Said not a word. When he didn't, Eddie gave his shoulder a pat.

"Warm in here," Eddie said. "Innit? Aren't you going to take your coat off, Barry?"

Baron looked at him. At the blue eyes so bright they nearly burned. At the pink lips. At the skin, girlishly smooth, not a pimple on it.

"No," he simply said.

16 - 1997

Cymbeline had seen the lights before, though it had been a few months since they'd streaked across her vision. Before her mother had gotten sick, they had come with some regularity, appearing through the rain-speckled window of her grandfather's station wagon at night, reflecting off a rippling stream in the suburban woods on a golden afternoon. After the lights, the headaches would come—inescapable and debilitating. For a time, her mother had been determined to find a cause for the problem. She'd taken Cymbeline from doctor to doctor, where they'd run blood tests, put her in an enormous plastic tube, all to no avail. "Migraines," they said, though the migraine pills they prescribed did nothing but make her sleep. At least, then, sleep had been a balm. Until her mother's cancer came back and the lights stopped flashing, and they both forgot it had ever happened in their preoccupation with dying and with preparing for death.

Now, on this night, July's air still muggy even though it was nearly ten o'clock, Perky led her campers through the woods. They were whiny, tired, and bug bitten. They dragged their expensive hiking boots through the brush, mocking each other with more cruelty than was warranted, teasing Perky that she'd lost her way. She hadn't. She knew the way back from the playfield well, and if her flashlight bounced, then it was just because of the briskness of her own steps. Despite the darkness, she knew that soon, soon, she and Sid would tumble together on a blanket in the woods between their units. Her body ached for it like a song that desperately needed to be written.

She was thinking about songs, about Sid, about sex, when her flashlight's beam hit on something metallic buried in the path ahead. Some dropped coin or key, something small—something inconsequential. And yet the light seemed to fill up the entirety of the woods. It wasn't *just* light. It was never merely light. It was a pattern of faces *punctuated* by light. Thousands of faces, and screaming, hungry mouths, and sex, miasmic, all around her, but also fear. As it always was in those moments, she felt a sudden certain clamminess on her skin—like the face paint her mother had bought her for her fifth birthday. An inescapable greasiness. A sense that she was wearing many layers of uncomfortable clothing. Too many layers. The feeling of a hand at her throat, strangling her. She stumbled, and steadied herself on a tree.

"Whoa, Perky," Alana said, rushing up to her from the rear of the group of girls. Alana, whose camp name was Spruce, but whom the campers just as often called Bruce, as in Bruce Springsteen, as in The Boss. Alana, whose eyes were small round bowls of concern. Cymbeline felt abundantly glad for Alana in that moment, because Alana was experienced. She knew what she was doing at camp. She had been a child here once, a camper, and now knew how to be an adult even when adulthood failed Cymbeline. Spruce touched Perky's elbow, steadying her. "Are you okay?"

"Yeah," Cymbeline said, feeling waves of nausea as the faces receded into a black gap of nothing, leaving that headache in their wake. "I just . . . tripped."

It was a lame excuse that felt limp on her tongue, and she could see from Alana's expression that Alana found it unconvincing, too. But there was nothing either of them could do about that. Alana took the flashlight from Cymbeline and waved the girls forward, toward their unit.

"C'mon, kids. Chins up. Let's sing. This is a repeat after me song!"

The weary chorus of voices mumbled back at her. "This is a repeat after me song . . ."

"I can't hear you!"

More enthusiasm now: "I can't hear you!"

"The Princess Pat!"

"The Princess Pat"

"Lived in a tree!"

"Lived in a tree!"

The small army of girls marched off into the woods.

Cymbeline stayed there for a moment, steadying herself on the tree, doing her best to catch her breath. As the pack of children moved forward down the path, the world was darker for a moment, and then brighter. Cymbeline began to see the true shape of the world around her: shaggy, vine-wrapped trees, leaf litter, tents hulking silently in the distance. She took tentative steps forward through the headache haze, feeling for the path in front of her, uncertain it was there at all.

When she reached the spot where she'd been sure something had flashed at her like a diamond, she stopped, touching the dirt with the toe of her old tennis shoe. She'd been right. There had been something buried there. She bent over and fished it out, the packed, dry soil painful under her nails. It was a penknife, a small one, steel, perhaps. Some toy some child had brought with her to camp. Probably not recently, judging from the dirt. Probably a long time ago.

She tucked it into her pocket and followed her campers through the woods.

* * *

"What do you mean, you don't want to go out tonight?"

Three days later, Sid sat on the edge of Cymbeline's bed. It was evening, just before lights out. The girls were not *all* settling in for the night. They were playing cards and squealing at each other about their perceived vaginal odor and making lists of the cutest boys at the camp across the lake. But tonight, it wasn't Cymbeline's problem. It was Tuesday, the night all counselors were free for a few hours, and if Alana was supposed to corral the children into something resembling a bedtime routine, well, then Cymbeline was going to let her.

She was not, however, going to go out.

"I have a headache," Cymbeline mumbled, drawing the sleeping bag over her. She craved the fuzzy darkness that the night would offer, the silence, the anonymity. But it seemed that Sid would not allow that; she grabbed the covers back, tugging them down.

"C'mon, you said you had a headache yesterday."

"I did," Cymbeline said. She half-sat up, squinting. The eyes were there, swarming the edge of her vision. The mouths. They almost blotted out Sid's dark, sun-kissed face. Sometimes, at times like these, when she was raw and tired and aching, she felt a nearly uncontrollable urge to tell an inappropriate joke. *I was just trying to get out of sex before. I'm telling the truth, now.* But she squashed it. Her desperate gallows humor had never gone over well before. At her mother's funeral, she'd approached the coffin, and through the fog of grief, knocked on the wood top—then bent low like she was expecting an answer. Wasn't really sure then who she was *making* that joke for, except for herself. But others saw it. Cousins, snickering. Great aunts and uncles, quietly horrified. Her grandmother had taken her aside to some hallway lined with floral wallpaper and slapped her. If she hadn't learned when she was young the price of wry levity, she had learned it now.

"I told you," she said at last. "I get migraines—"

Sid shook her head a little too hard. There was something behind her eyes, something veiled. "Are you ashamed to be seen with me?"

"What?" said Cymbeline. It was too much—this conversation, right now, with those teeth gnashing at the corner of her vision, with the sensation of the ghostly hands tearing at her clothes. "I'm not ashamed—"

"Then take a Tylenol and come out with me," Sid said. She pouted her lower lip, but it was more a pantomime of a *real* pout, meant to cover up some very real, very deep pain. "If you're not ashamed, then what's the big deal?"

Cymbeline winced. Because she hadn't thought of that aspect of things, at all—but clearly Sid had.

"I care about you," she said softly. It made her feel vulnerable to say it. Corny. Naked. "I don't care what people say . . ." But her voice was so trembling and hoarse that it almost seemed like she wasn't speaking at all.

"Then come out with me," Sid said again. She pressed her lips together, waiting. And for a moment, Cymbeline thought she might just do it. Get up, out of bed, shake the headache off, or manage to ignore it, at least. Numb the pain with alcohol. She could almost see it. The two of them in a bar together, young and charming. Someone picking a song on an old fashioned jukebox. She could see how she would look with Sid's arms wrapped around her waist as she danced.

But—well, she couldn't deny that she *was* nervous, going out there for the very first time. *Publicly.* A couple. She and Pamela had never crossed that threshold. She'd been too scared then, too. It would have been a disappointment to her mother, more than she could bear. Her mother's judgment no longer weighed on her, but that didn't mean it was as easy as Sid made it out to be. They were in the middle of nowhere. What if someone said something? What if someone *threw* something, or worse?

There was a certain familiar comfort in hiding.

"Yeah that's what I thought," Sid said, before Cymbeline could even respond. She stood, heading for the door, but paused when she was just inside it. "I should know better than getting involved with you bisexual girls by now. You always take the easy way out."

Cymbeline reached out her hand, making a strangled noise of objection, but Sid didn't want to hear it.

"Nah," she said, her voice light with false breeze, "Don't worry about it, Perky. It's not like we mean anything to each other, anyway. Hell, I hardly even know who you are."

With that, she brushed aside the thin old floral sheet Cymbeline had hung up for a curtain, and left the way she came.

Cymbeline watched the curtain shiver. She felt her stomach twist, heard that familiar high pitched feedback in her left ear. And she pulled the sleeping bag up over her head and willed herself—despite the noise, despite her feelings, physical, and emotional—into a dreamless sleep.

* * *

At first, Cymbeline told herself it was okay. Eventually, the campers quieted down, and in the darkness, Cymbeline could hear nothing but crickets and katydids and cicadas, and her headache, for the first time in days, began to fade. Still, though, she couldn't sleep. She wanted to. Wanted to forget the lights, and her dead mother, and the fight she'd had with Sid, and the fact that she wanted nothing more than to drop out of school come September, to never return to any meaningful sort of life. To sleep, and sleep forever. To be no one. To be nothing.

But it was the guilt that brought her out of it. She'd let Sid down. Sid's face, in that moment—the worry creasing her unkempt brow—weighed on her. Who was she, anyway? Nineteen years so far, living like a shadow. Pretending she was less than a person. That she believed in nothing, had no talent, was no use. That she loved no one, now that her mother was dead, and she'd often worried when she was alive that she only ever loved her mother out of obligation. Sid's voice rang out in her mind: *I hardly even know who you are.* Who was she, anyway? Cymbeline tossed and turned in her sheets.

The sun had started to rise over the lake, coming in sweet and yellow through the window. The birds had started to sing, too incessantly to ignore. It was only five a.m.—two hours, still, before the girls would be pulled reluctantly from their beds for morning flag salute—when Cymbeline finally gave up on sleep. She dragged herself out of bed, put on her uniform t-shirt and shorts, tied her hair up into a simple ponytail, pulled her socks up along legs that were badly in need of a shave. She sat there for a moment, her head dull and quiet. Closed her eyes. Saw something. The shape of chords she'd never played before, but somehow instinctively knew.

She knelt in the dust and felt around for the guitar case under her bed. When she found it, she discovered it had an old familiar heft in her hand. Like it belonged there. Like this moment was meant to be. She left the cabin, the sound of sleeping girls ringing out behind her. Snores and little whimpering dreams that couldn't be comforted. Wouldn't. This wasn't about the children. This was about *her.* Not Cymbeline. It was about Sid.

She walked across camp, tracing a line through the trees. Sid's unit was only two away, her cabin, the first in the ring, just past the cinder block bathrooms that they called cindies on this side of the water and privies over on the boys'. The cabins were lifted up on risers for when the lake flooded in the spring. The window to Sid's room was right there, barely beyond reach, though she had to jump a few times to touch it, rapping her knuckle against it, hard.

When Sid didn't answer immediately, Cymbeline worried for a moment that she'd made a miscalculation. Maybe after drinking at the bar Sid had gone to bed with someone else—some other girl. Or (as absurd as it seemed, felt) maybe a boy. There was so much they didn't know about each other. They talked about camp and about books and about movies but never their pasts and never their identities and never their families and never their feelings. Those had been things they could ignore, up to now, in this hazy summerspace. But Cymbeline knew in this moment that it was time to make a decision. No, a declaration. This was no simple summer romance, had me a blast. This was different. This was serious. Despite her jangly nerves, Cymbeline found herself grinning as Sid, finally, opened the window up.

"Perky?" Sid shouted down in surprise, her eyes squinted from the hangover, her shaggy hair a mess. Cymbeline didn't say a word. She just sat down on a rock in the brush beside Sid's cabin, took out her guitar, and began tuning it.

"I didn't know you play," Sid called down again. Cymbeline was only smiling. She hadn't told Sid that she did play, because she hadn't been sure if she could anymore. It had been years, after all. But now, with the guitar in her hands, it felt obvious. Even if she hadn't known what to do, the guitar did. It knew everything. It always had. It was just a matter of coaxing the notes from the ether, of conquering her own nerves well enough to sing along.

Cymbeline began to strum out chords. Somehow, in her walk over, she'd already memorized the shape of the sound, the rhythm of it. That had been her special talent once. She could play just about anything. Only had to hear a song a few times, and it would just lodge itself in her head.

At first as she sang and strummed, her voice was soft. Tired and tremulous. She'd never liked her voice. Couldn't stand the sound of it, really. But she knew the effect it had on other people—that it had already had on Sid, once, and would have again. Soon it grew louder, and Sid started grinning. Cymbeline reached the chorus, and they both sang out to each other. Sid, half-off key, warbling back to her own, pitch-perfect voice.

"And if, after all this time, I find that I never find you, know that I'm here, that I'm waiting, where the sea rolls green and the grass is tumbled blue."

By the time the chords had faded, a few of Sid's campers had wandered out of the cabin to stand in the buggy grass, dressed in night gowns and boxer shorts and overgrown t-shirts, listening, watching. There was scattered applause when the song ended. Meanwhile, Sid was just grinning and grinning away.

"Aw, Perky," she said. "That's our song. The Ruffians."

"Voice of our generation," Cymbeline said, and the way that Sid smiled at her, Cymbeline wanted to kiss her. She wanted to hold her close. She wanted to never let go.

17 - 1957/1958

Liam's family was like no family Baron had ever known, not here. Perhaps on the telly or the radio, in America, he assumed, there was families like these, with a mum and a dad who loved one another, who encouraged their son and had a little sister all perfect and sweet and not the least bit fat, like Bess was. Liam's sister Eugenia was called Genie for short, and she had bright eyes and was just old enough to have tits, and seemed in love with all of them, but Eddie, especially, and Ed just took it in stride, humming tunes for her right over the dinner table.

When Ed was done humming, Liam's mother burst into applause and started crowing on about how the boys were going to have a show soon at the Delph and how soon after that—tomorrow, probably—the lot of them would be bigger than Elvis. And when Liam's dad grumbled back a response, it was with fondness, not annoyance, like Deedz might have grumbled. Like the lot of them actually *believed* it to be true. Liam, of course, found all of this utterly mortifying.

"Mum, it ain't all of that!" He was blushing like a ruby, charmed and charming, and his mother only cackled sweet laughter. Baron watched all of this quietly, with wide, quiet eyes. He'd gotten quiet that winter thanks to Dickie's threat hanging over him. With Dickie taking a place up at the Waller's dinner table, even now, where Baron knew he did not belong.

"I like the sound of that," Dickie said. "Bigger'n Elvis. Should be the name of our first LP, yeah, mates?"

Eddie chuckled. "Can you imagine the press we'd get." But it wasn't really a question, and his eyes flashed to Baron as he said it, so Baron knew that

Eddie really thought it was a terrible idea, and wasn't pushing, for Baron's sake. He had a good head on him, Ed did, about music and all of that. He was always talking about how they'd have to position themselves in the "industry." He was always talking about image. He was always talking like they were a real band already and worth taking seriously. Besides, Eddie loved Elvis and so did Baron, and why would they want to start off their careers insulting him, just because Ma Waller thought it a good idea? Sure, it had been something they'd whispered before. In private. But those had not been public thoughts.

Dickie Ashby missed all that subtext, though. Of course he did. "Yeh," he said. "It'd be great!"

"Oh, don't encourage her," Liam said, pushing his chair away from the table. "Mum, we're all done. Don't bother us upstairs, Genie."

And with that, he led the tromping troops up into his bedroom. His mother called out after him, just once, "Be sure to come down before midnight!" and Liam kind of grumbled to himself beneath his breath.

"Yeh, yeh."

They all wedged themselves into the tiny council house bedroom, where a different floral wallpaper greeted them on every wall. At least Liam didn't share his room like Eddie did, so when he flopped himself down on the bed, he spread out his whole body there like he owned the place, which he did. Eddie sat at the writing desk, picking up Liam's Hagstrom and strumming at it. Baron had noticed that this was Ed's habit whenever he was in a place with an instrument. Some people smoked fags. Some jiggled their knees. Ed Hammond hid himself behind the body of a guitar, tuning it, showing off, even when he had nothing to prove to no one with it. Dickie knelt on the floor by the record player, flipping through Liam's albums, scoffing at the titles. Baron, meanwhile, held up the wall.

He felt as though he were outside *everything* lately, like he was watching it all play out on telly, bracing himself as the world was ground down to some sort of awful and inevitable conclusion. He felt hyperaware of every single movement of his own body, too, and how it might give him away as a queer, and so it felt better to barely move and say nothing. "You're the quiet one," Eugenia had said to him earlier that night, and Dickie, beside him, had laughed out loud because Baron had never been known to be quiet. Once when they were boys, the headmaster had caned him while shouting "Shut up! Shut up!" and still Baron had been unable to stop laughing at him and cracking jokes, "But your mother likes it when I talk dirty to her!"

Now, finally, at last, the world had shut up Baron Templeton, only it hadn't been the world who had done it. It had been his best friend. He glared down at Dickie's back now, at the muscular shape of his shoulders. He hated them. Hated him. Even as he knew he wanted him. Back to wanking two, three times a day lately, and always thinking about that moment in the alley, how dirty and wrong and wonderful it had been.

"Cat got your tongue, Barry?" Liam asked, and he realized that Liam had been watching him this whole time, watching Baron shoot bullets through his eyes at Dickie, watching Baron chew over his own desires. Baron felt his cheeks heat, was glad for the dark tones of his face that would not give it away, but still—wondered if somehow Liam suspected. He was always wondering now, wondering if and what everybody knew.

"Cat gut," he said, "Yeh." It wasn't even a joke, though Liam laughed a little bit, eager, as he always was, to get in good with the older boys. But Dickie's head whipped back.

"Baron, that doesn't even make sense."

"Ask your mother to explain it to you," Baron said idly, which *also* didn't make sense, but it didn't matter. Liam laughed again. Under all this awkwardness was Eddie pricking at the strings. But he stopped for a moment, looking at all of them with serious eyes.

"I need to tell you lot something," he said. Baron looked over.

"What's that, then?"

Eddie was drawing in a big breath, taking his time over it. Baron's whole body was filled with stabbing knives of fear. *This is it, then*, he thought. *Eddie knows.* And he braced himself for the announcement that he was sure Eddie Hammond III was about to make, that Baron Templeton was a queer and a fairy who liked to get it up the arse, in alleys and with boys. Only one boy so far, but he couldn't deny how he'd dreamed of sailors nightly for years, and the things they must have done with each other, buried deep below the decks with not a woman in sight.

But Eddie didn't say that. He just licked his lips tentatively, then said, "Dylan Miranda's asked me to join his band."

Liam bolted upright in his bed. Dickie blinked several times, as if he wasn't sure he'd heard. And Baron, despite the new, quiet haze that had descended upon him these past weeks, stood up straight, flexing his fists.

"Wot?" he demanded, the anger and betrayal clear in his voice. Ed avoided his gaze, letting his eyes slide along the splintered wood floor instead.

"You know them, Barry. Dylan Miranda and the Tempests."

Of course Baron knew about Dylan Miranda and his band. They were older—in their twenties, already—and real professionals, with matching suits and high hair and creeper shoes. They'd gone on tour in Scotland last summer, and even had an EP. All the girls were crazy about them. In his head, Baron saw a flash, like a vision: by summer, Eddie would be combing his own pale hair high, greasing the sides down, wearing his own matching shoes. Bending chords and humming into a microphone. Without him.

"You can't! *We're* a band!" Baron said, and Liam and Dickie were both nodding and murmuring agreement to that, because the Bartlebys were important to all of them, and without Eddie as the glue to hold them all together and treat them like they *were* something, well—then it would all just fall apart. Baron knew. He felt it.

"I haven't said yes, yet," Eddie said. He finally put the guitar down, sitting with his arms crossed over his chest like a defensive shield. Baron's fists were still fisted, and he could feel his nails bite hard into his palm.

"But yer thinking about it?" sneered Baron.

"I don't know yet," Eddie said. He tilted his head, finally meeting Baron's eye. "Haven't decided. They're good. They've got something, Barry."

"You told me *we* had something, *Hammy*," Baron shot back. Eddie shrugged.

"We did. Do. Dylan doesn't write any songs, you know. Everything he plays is covers. That's alright for Scotland. But I don't think it's gonna get him very far."

"You gonna write songs for him?" Liam asked softly, and when Baron saw a dim light flash behind Ed's pale eyes, he almost wanted to sock Liam for giving him the idea.

"Dunno. I might. But I don't *want* to."

Dickie let out a laugh. Broad, nervous laughter, which made Baron want to sock him, too. "Why you getting us all worked up over it, then?"

Eddie's soft lips went tight for a moment. "Because I feel like *should*, Dick. Like I'd be a fool to let this chance go. Do you know they've got a weekly gig at the Star Theater? The four of them, making nearly £50 a week. And they want to share it with me. They think I could be an asset. I know I can."

"£50," Liam said. "That's more'n my dad gets paid."

"Split five ways," said Baron.

"It's more than making nothing," Eddie sneered back and Baron shook his head.

"You know we have a chance to make more'n that," Baron pressed, and part of him wanted to beg. *Please, Ed, please, don't take this all away from me.* But he liked himself too much. So he wouldn't.

"Do we?" Eddie asked. "What's the Bartlebys gotten me so far, Baron? One show and one song?"

"We're working on new songs," Baron said. "Didn't you say that the dance hall number might be our best yet?"

"Yeah but you haven't finished the chorus yet," Eddie said. "You told me yourself, the chorus isn't right yet."

"Give us a chance, Hammy." Nearly pleading now, close to it. Knowing it was humiliating and that it wouldn't win Eddie over, but so desperate he was doing it anyway.

"I *have* been, Baron. But we're not going anywhere, not yet. It's been six months, hasn't it? And we don't even have a drummer."

"I'm your rhythm section!" Dickie Ashby squeaked out from where he'd been almost forgotten on Liam's thin rug. Eddie looked at him. Angled his chin. Narrowed his eyes.

"Yeh, I know," he said disdainfully.

Silence fell, ugly and thick like the dirty snow that clogged the the gutters and the streets and Baron's heart. He was hurt, but not only hurt. A vein of panic ran under everything. If Eddie left, where would that leave him? Practically flunking out of art school already, and only halfway through his first year. Stuck in a band with Dickie Ashby and a ten-year-old. Sure, Liam Waller was talented, but he was a child, and talent wasn't all they needed. They needed flash and they needed spark and they needed Ed's vision, most of all. Why, Baron couldn't even write a song on his own. Had thought that what he'd had with Ed had been a sort of sympathetic magic, enough to carry them through. But he'd been failing Ed, failing all of them. All because of Dickie.

He glared at Dickie.

"What?" Dick said sharply. Baron licked his lips and was about to lay into him, about to really let him have it, dirty threats and back alleyway wanking be damned. But just as he opened his mouth, Ma Waller burst through the door.

"Boys! Boys!" she crooned. "It's nearly midnight! C'mon, Liam, up up."

Like sunlight through a crack in a wall, she came into Liam's room and yanked him up out of bed. Liam protested only a minute, ineffectually, before she gave his rear a tender slap and ushered him down the stairs. Dickie looked back over his shoulder at Baron and Eddie, saw the dark looks on both of their faces, and perhaps sensing how close he was to coming under Baron's knife, got out of there, making clucking noises with his tongue as he went.

Baron looked at Eddie for a long time. "Don't leave," he said. "Not yet."

"I haven't," Eddie said, then added, more sharply, "Yet."

Baron nodded. There was more that could be said, whole books of it, but Baron didn't know how to wrap his tongue around it. Maybe if he were more like Eddie, he could be calculating and seductive all at once. He could turn it into a poem, a song, a business plan. Instead, all he had were feelings, and feelings were dangerous. They told the world the truth about you, truths you'd tried so hard to conceal for seventeen years, a lifetime already.

"Let's go downstairs," Baron said, because he sensed then, in the moments before the next year began, a sort of stay of execution. They could pretend like everything was normal and it almost would be, for now. Eddie nodded.

"Sure, Barry," he said, and finally stood up from Liam's desk chair, sighing. Together, they went down the stairs.

The chimes on the radio had already rung out midnight. The Wallers and Dickie were all singing that Auld Lang Syne. When Eddie appeared, Genie threw her arms around him and pressed her lips against his. She was only thirteen, a child, really, but he kissed her like he meant it, like a grown-up might. Watching, Baron had the sense that Genie would remember that kiss for the rest of her life.

18 - 2017

For nearly two hours, until the sun had sunk low in the sky and Matthew had to go around, turning on every lamp in the place, he listened to Naomi play. Matthew had grown up around musicians. His dad could hardly be in a room with a guitar without picking it up and strumming at it, almost like a defensive shield. In a way, Matthew was used to tuning music out, even though he loved it. He'd often felt like if he didn't, then all that brilliance would overpower him, overpower his own songs. And he knew that he had something to say.

But tonight, he only listened.

Her songs had no words. She slammed into the keys in a manner that reminded him of Liberace. Of Billy Joel. Of Elton John. Of Ben Fucking Folds, who he'd never really enjoyed except grudgingly. The music moving him even though he hadn't wanted to be moved, even though it was all a little hip for him, a little twee. Naomi's music reminded him of that. Swaying him, against his own objections, like an erection that couldn't be trained down by any thought of his dead, saintly grandmother.

This music wasn't erotic, though, not precisely erotic, at least not erotic in any way he was accustomed to being aroused. He'd always preferred to be the dominant one, and though Naomi was fine-boned and lovely, it was clear, through her music, that she was the one on top. There was almost a violence to it, and it made him hunger for something he could not name, had not felt since he was very young, captivated by his father's music and not even knowing yet that the whole world loved his father, too.

And yet there were edges that he could see. Edges that were wrong. A violence, and yet a lack of tension. It was like she was setting a flamethrower to innocent children who were standing limp and ready to accept their fates. It wasn't an *interesting* violence, not yet. She needed her edges filed down just a little. Needed some gentleness, to push against her ferocity.

Christ, he thought. *I'm editing her. Already.*

Near the two hour mark, Naomi, grown soggy from sweat, her hair frizzed near her temples, her smile maniacal, finally drew her hands away from the keyboard.

"Well," she said, wiping her brow on the sleeve of her sweater. "Did I pass the audition?"

"Fuckin'," was all Matthew said. Not fuckin' hell or fuckin' a, just fucking, as though fucking were enough. He leaned forward in the bentwood chair, licked his lips. "Where'd you learn to play like that?"

"Where's anyone learn to play?" she asked. "I took a couple lessons. When I was . . . eight or nine years old? Mom wanted to start me earlier, but we never had the money. Anyway, I realized it was never going to happen unless I made it happen. Started selling candy on the subway, telling people it was for school. It wasn't a total lie."

The edges of her smile were sparkling, not the least bit embarrassed by the poverty she'd just admitted to, if she was even aware of it. How crass it was, to talk about money, about her family's finances, even so long ago. Matthew had been raised to never mention money, but of course, he'd also been raised in a world that was full of it. Money, that is. Among other things.

He shrugged, now, though. "I never took formal lessons," he said. "My dad taught me. He can't even read music, though I improved on that a little, over the years."

"I thought you said you were self-taught," she said. She pressed her hands together, leaning forward a little. Her body angling toward his, the sweater dangling low and showing the brown expanse of her slender chest. He grunted.

"Well, we all have to start somewhere, and if I started with me dad showing me a few chords, what's the harm in it?"

"You sound more British," she said, "When you talk about him."

Matthew shrugged.

As if that were the end of that conversation, Naomi closed the keyboard cover and stood. She went and got her coat from the tasteful Swedish coat rack by the door. "I hope I've convinced you," she said, buttoning up her pea coat, which looked ancient. Vintage piece, Matthew thought. "I'll be back in the morning. If you don't want to work together, it's fine. I'll take down notation for you, make you breakfast. Whatever. They're paying me either way. It would be much more fun, though, to make something meaningful together. Don't you think?"

It wasn't a question that she meant to have him answer. It was meant to dangle there like a mystery. Still, Matthew couldn't resist pulling at the thread.

"I'm not saying I've decided," he said, lying through his teeth, "But what do you want from this? I'm a solo artist. We've used studio musicians, but I've never been in a *band*."

"I don't want to perform," she said, shrugging. "I'm not in it for the tours or the fans. I just want to make music. A songwriting credit, that's all."

Matthew snorted. It was an ugly sound. "A songwriting credit? What, Hammond and—"

"No." Naomi spoke with surprising firmness. "Not Hammond first. That was your dad. Well, our dads."

Matthew felt his brow furrow. Trying to make the pieces fit of what she was saying. Failing.

"Templeton and Hammond, this time around," she said. "It's only fair. Anyway, I'll be back in the morning. Goodnight, Matt."

She was in and out of the door in a flash, before he could ask any questions, before he could let his mouth fall open in incredulity and disbelief. It was only when the door slammed shut behind her and silence fell over the echoing house that he realized what she was saying, what she was *really* saying.

That she was Baron Templeton's daughter. That the name of Templeton, long thought buried, had somehow returned.

* * *

He couldn't call Kara. Oh, that was the last person he could call. She didn't care a drop about Saffron, not in any significant way. Once he'd thought that was an admirable trait, how she only briefly, blushingly admitted a childhood crush on Liam Waller once, while drunk, and then pretended for the rest of their lives together,that those words had never been spoken, even when she met Uncle Liam later, at one of those dreadful charity events. She'd been polite, but not fawning. Mostly disinterested. No, Kara would never care, much less understand. Kara was not an option.

He rang Edelman once, got no answer, which he'd expected. His manager never answered after 6 pm, said his family time was sacred, a trait Matthew had once admired too, as someone who had been raised to believe in the sanctity of family. But he felt a flare of anger when he got Edelman's voicemail this time and almost hurled the phone across the empty kitchen. It had been Edelman who'd had this idea, Edelman who'd gotten him into the mess. Without warning him, without explaining. And there was no way that Edelman hadn't known. Of course he must have. It would be what the whole world was waiting for—a sort-of reunion of Saffron, miraculous and improbable. They'd make reams and reams of money, wouldn't they? Well, Matthew didn't *need* money. He'd been born into money, scads of it. He'd wanted to make something of his own, away from the tangled history, the family tree.

But Edelman—Edelman was only human. Of course he wanted money. He was a *manager*. He definitely hadn't bought this place, up in the isolated mountains, on a gorgeous lakefront, on his own family's coffers. From what Matthew knew, Edelman had no ancestors, had been born fully formed as though from the head of Zeus. He didn't care if Matthew made art, not really. Edelman was here for the wheeling and dealing. The cash of it.

Prick, Matthew thought.

But he steeled himself, and did not throw the phone. Instead, he looked down at the square of plastic and glass and rare earth metals and let out a sigh, low and long. And then began to do the calculations in his head. It was nearly nine here. So the middle of the night in London. But really, he could see no other choice. No alternative option. He dialed his Dad, and tucked the phone in against his face.

No answer, of course. He hadn't expected otherwise. His father was an early to bed kind of man, always had been, except when he was touring, in which case he napped prolifically on the sofa or a cozy chair or the old RV camper they'd converted into a family bus in the '70s. He wasn't touring now though. Between albums, and shacked up with a new wife who was less than half his own age but acted like a little old granny most of the time. Both of them, maybe fucking, but more likely asleep.

"Hi Dad, it's Matt. I—I need you to call me, okay? It's important. It's—" He paused, licked his dry lips. Thought of how often his dad had fretted over him, like a granny himself. "Everyone is fine. It's not an emergency. Kara is fine and the baby is fine and I'm fine. But call me as soon as you're up, okay? I'll answer."

Then he hung up. Put the phone down on the counter. Stared at it, as though waiting for it to ring. Even though he knew it was absurd.

* * *

Eventually Matthew found himself a half-full bottle of Grey Goose in the wet bar off the kitchen and trudged upstairs, phone in one hand, neck of the bottle in the other. He shed his clothes on the way, not caring where they landed, perched his phone at the edge of the bed stand, and brought the bottle into the upstairs shower. Edelman's bathroom was all slate and glass. Looked expensive, and it probably was. Matthew turned the shower on hot. Started drinking, though he hadn't really stopped all day, except for those few hours when he'd been captivated by Naomi. Something about the prospect of days and days of solitude had made him nervous from the start, and that anxiety hadn't been alleviated by Naomi's presence, certainly not. He felt the sludge of vodka work through him, scowled into the stream of water. It made no sense to him. She seemed too young to be Templeton's child. He'd been dead for, what, forty years now? Or nearly? And had never had any children that he'd ever heard about.

If children had even been possible for Templeton. There had been those rumors about him—ones that his father was always quick to evade. If asked, Eddie Hammond III would shrug, say, "I never saw him with a man, and we were close, in the early days. You share a bus—or a broken down van, which we did, back then—and you learn the truth about a person. Quickly." There had been a wife, for a short time, a boring one, and more exotic rumored girlfriends, the business with the radicals in Trinidad, who were supposedly into free love, but no children. Never any children. That Matthew had ever heard about.

And he would have heard. They were a family, the Saffron children. Charlie Peck's three and Matthew and his sisters, and Barry Waller, whom Matthew couldn't stand. They'd be paraded out at reunion shows and Hall of Fame inductions, were occasionally invited to one another's weddings. Treated, publicly and privately, like cousins. Sheila Peck had been a musician for awhile, playing a key-tar in a band of C-list celebrity kids that had been good enough for a few SNL appearances, and there had been talk about Sheila and Barry and Matthew doing an album together down the line, but it never turned into anything. Mostly because of Matthew, who pretended to be too busy for it. But they still stayed aware of each other, and once, after Templeton's turn in the Hall of Fame, with their dads all soppy and teary eyed, they'd escaped to get stoned in the green room, just the kids, who were adults by then, and they finally talked about the weirdness of it between spliff hits and giggles. That had been the only time he'd ever been able to fully articulate the strangeness of his life, of inheriting a family that belongs to the world. Kind of like being royalty, but infinitely shittier, because you only have an MBE, maybe, and none of the family jewels.

But Naomi. Hell. Well. She couldn't have been. Her age, her accent, her general uncouthness all made it seem impossible. She didn't look it, or was he wrong about that? He thought about the way the corners of her eyes had wrinkled just a little when she laughed.

Matthew chugged the vodka like it was beer. He'd never met Templeton, of course. The sainted snarker had dropped dead a few months after he was born. But in his dad's stories he always seemed almost beyond human. Well-read. Funny. Artistic. Driven. Destined for bigger things. Brilliant. You could see it, too, in the interviews they dragged out for documentaries, that sort of thing. Baron Templeton had been touched. And Naomi, well—

No, she had to be someone else. A pretender. A con. *Yes*, she was beautiful, and even his internal grudging acknowledgment of her beauty made his cock throb a little, suddenly heavy against his own thigh. But she was also crass and ordinary, a real no one.

Except. Except.

He remembered her music. The incessant pound of it. The anger. Like she knew she was owed something bigger than everything she'd ever gotten. Matthew finally put the bottle down on the wet slate, leaning against the shower wall. Naomi walked around like the world was indebted to her, and hell, if Matthew hadn't thought, for a moment, at least, that he was. He could have knelt at her feet as she played, begging her to let him fuck her right. The way she'd always meant to be fucked.

It wasn't her beauty. It wasn't *just* her beauty. The way that she played was something more than that, something beside that. He wanted to roll himself around in her music. Yes. To let it swallow him. He closed his eyes, remembering the way that the notes had slid through him. A familiar, ancient feeling, but different, because it was *her*. Those slender fingers. Those lush lips, just a little chapped. He thought of her music, and his hand drifted down. Matthew yanked it, leaning back against the shower wall, and it was almost no time at all before his cum spilled out in ropy streams. He let out a sound, small and strangled. Let the water wash it all away. Hated himself for a second, but not as much as he probably should have. Turned the shower off. And trudged off to bed.

It was early and he was drunk but it didn't matter. He buried himself in the reams of white bedding that made up the bed Edelman normally shared with his wife. It felt like a nest, safe and downy, and he was tired and cotton-headed from his orgasm and the shower and the booze. Before he knew it, he drifted away into dreamless sleep.

* * *

The phone rang too early, though Matthew would have been at a loss to say what time it was. In Edelman's bedroom, in Edelman's mountain house, the curtains were all pulled closed. Groggy, his throat parched, his ears pulsing painfully, Matthew pawed around the nightstand until his fingers found the phone. Without looking, he answered it.

"Dad, is that you?"

"It's me, baby," a voice purred back and Matthew winced. Kara.

"Hey. Sorry. I was waiting for a call."

"Your dad?"

Matthew swallowed, remembering the voicemail he'd left the night before.

"Mmf," he mumbled in agreement. There was light and laughter in Kara's voice.

"Oh, good, you know how I'm always telling you to call him more."

"Yeah," said Matthew, his head still tucked beneath the blankets. "I know."

"He's a nice dad. You're lucky, Matthew."

"Yes, nice. I know."

"We're both so lucky that Everleigh will have one grandfather, at least—" At this, her voice cracked in a show of painful emotion. Kara had no father; her mother was an infamous grunge rock groupie of the '90s, had even been in her own band for awhile. The paternity of both of her children was unknown, no matter how resolutely Kara had tried to pull this information out of her. Matthew winced, both because of the sound, and the sentiment. It was too early to have this conversation. He was too hungover, or drunk still. It was hard to tell.

"Yes," he said, more robotically than he intended, "We're very lucky."

But she ignored his tone. Instead, Kara launched into a discussion of everything she had planned for that day: a manicure, and an appointment with her midwife, whom Matthew hadn't met yet, much to Kara's chagrin. Later, dinner with her sister at this macrobiotic place. Kara had been considering giving up nightshades completely (in addition to already eschewing gluten and dairy), because she thought they were contributing to her digestive problems. Had he been more sober, Matthew's ears would have pricked up at the mention of Pearl, but the headache deflated every other emotion he might have had beside a sluggish, groggy confusion. As Kara chattered, he rose from the bed, opened his suitcase, and pulled out his thin flannel bathrobe—the one she hated, the one she was always telling him to throw away. Then, after donning it, he went to the bathroom and shoved his mouth under the expensive copper spigot of Edelman's sink. The water was salty from the water softener, a touch sweet. Matthew scowled. It was only then that Kara realized he wasn't listening.

"Should I call you later?" she asked, sounding wounded. Matthew sighed, more at himself than at her. He never meant to hurt her, but it seemed he always did.

"I'll call you tonight," he promised, then hung up without telling Kara that he loved her, without even saying goodbye. He spat out what was left of the water, wiped his mouth against the arm of his robe. He looked at himself for a long moment. He looked even older than he had the day before, as if he were progressing towards some skeletal state with each passing moment. Or maybe it was just the booze. No telling, he told himself, going to fetch the bottle from the floor of the shower to take one last swig from it. It was warm, but the bite helped wash away the taste of the water.

He was just about to head downstairs to find himself breakfast when the phone rang again. He sat on the edge of the bed, eyeing the vibrating square before picking it up. It was, indeed, his father—calling at 9 a.m. on the dot, or just past lunch in London. His father was always prompt, always courteous. Matthew braced himself, as he always did, before talking to him.

"Hey," he said, holding in a breath between syllables, "Dad."

"Matt! I was so pleased to get your call." There was a note of puppy-like desperation in his dad's voice, which his father didn't even bother to try and hide. Once, when he was a boy, Matthew's adoration of his father had been clear. But adolescence had changed that, made his father suddenly embarrassing, and though they were decades away from the rawness of that embarrassment, Matthew's regard for his father had never quite changed back from a state of pubescent wincing.

"Good to hear your voice, Dad," Matthew said, forcing warmth into his own. It shouldn't have been so hard to love his father. His own dad was the type to give his father kisses on the lips well into adulthood. He'd cried openly over his body when he died. All the Hammond men were like that, the whole gaggle of uncles, full of girlish affection and startling depths of feeling. Maybe it was living in America, the distance, the state-mandated machismo, but Matthew was different than other Hammond men. He had more walls.

"Tell me, how are Kara and the baby? Have you seen an ultrasound yet?"

"No, Dad, not yet. Twenty weeks. That's when they do it."

"Oh yeah? Well, are you hoping for a boy? Eddie the V?"

For some reason, the question surprised him. He hadn't considered it—a son. A son like *him*. With the same name and everything. It filled him with an emotion he couldn't name. Of course, he had no desire to reveal that to his father. It would have been akin to admitting they were alike after all.

"I'll be happy no matter what," he said, and then added, "Kara wants a girl."

"Oh, of course she does. And girls are lovely. You know I adore your sisters. Nothing like a baby girl."

"Yes, I know dad."

"But there's something about a *boy*."

Sitting there, Matthew felt his cheeks heat. Felt an indescribable urge to hang up the phone, launch himself off the balcony that was off Edelman's bedroom, and go tumbling right down the frozen mountain.

When Matthew's dad spoke again, his voice was sparkling with emotion. "You know, when you were born, I said to your mum—"

"Dad, I called you because I wanted to talk to you about something," Matthew cut in, before his father could tell him whatever mortifying sentiment it was that he so desperately needed to share. His father went quiet for a moment.

"Oh?"

"Yeah," Matthew said, but then he realized he didn't know how to start. One did not just *talk* about Saffron in his home growing up, and one certainly did not *talk* about *Baron Templeton*, whose death his father seemed to carry like a silent war wound. Anyway, Matthew had only learned of his father's fame and career through a certain strange osmosis. First there was the dim awareness that music was a part of father's life in a way that went beyond bedtime songs, then the grim reality of touring—of a *career*. It was only later, when Matthew joined his family on the bus, that he truly realized the scope of it. The screaming girls and women and even men. The way they all lifted up their voices to sing along with his father's oldest songs, lighting candles or matches or BIC lighters when his father sat down to play "Cymbeline." That was how Matthew had divined the meaning of all those gold records on the walls of his family's London flat. *Saffron* their covers said, a word that conjured foreign magic even though all four lads were working class kids from the UK. Baron himself had entered Matthew's awareness even later. It was mostly through Baron's absence that he was defined. He was dead, but he was also never mentioned.

"Well?" his father pressed, gentleness in his voice. Matthew found himself rolling his eyes. His dad was always so good, always so outwardly sweet, and Christ, did he find it exhausting most days.

"I—well, I wanted to ask you about Baron Templeton."

A long crackle of silence, like a betrayal. But when his father's old voice came back, it wasn't angry. Still infuriatingly gentle. "What about Baron, then?"

Matthew licked his lips. In that moment he realized that he had an opportunity. His father, so desperate for connection, might have told him *anything*. Might have addressed the rumors about Templeton's sexuality, or his ties to the Black Panthers—might have shared stories with him that no one had ever heard, not the fans, not the press. About their fights. Their break-up. The nearly ten years of terse public silence that followed. But to ask those things would have somehow *changed* Matthew. It would have been like admitting he was no better than everyone else, the whole world, who only wanted a piece of Edmund Hammond III's history and not the actual skin and flesh of him. Not the actual man. No, Matthew could not ask anything so pointed. It would have done him—and his father—no good.

He settled on the conversational. A simple question. About his father's feelings. "What was it like, writing songs with him?"

"Oh!" Laughter in Dad's voice. Not studied, like the laugh he used in interviews. Not hungry, like the way he usually spoke to his son. Easy. Comfortable. "Baron was a beautiful guy, you know? I saw that the first day I ever heard him play."

"The fete?" Matthew asked, because he'd heard his father repeat that story over and over again in interviews that he would have never admitted he watched. He father grunted a little.

"Well, that's the story I tell *them*. That's the one that Baron believed, too. But you want to know the truth?"

Matthew frowned. "Yeah?"

"I saw him play weeks before that. There was a parade that summer. Or maybe it was late that spring. They had the whole band up on the back of a lorry. Could hardly hear them over the engine. But I saw him in his pink checkered shirt, saw the way he grinned at the girls and the boys, both. Heard the lyrics he was making up for the songs. Oh, he was awful. Like some kind of hobo pansy. But you know, Matt? It was like falling in love with a bloke, as much as one can. I was sixteen. Had just lost me mum—"

"The cancer," Matthew murmured, still frowning. He'd heard parts of this story before, but never like this.

"Yeah," he said. "The cancer. And my dad was pressing me to stop going to school and get a real job, like me brothers, but then I saw Baron playing, and I just—I had it in my head then. I had to be in a band with *that* boy. He was magical. I don't know how else to say it. If he'd been a bird, I'd have married him. You look at someone, and you just know. I sold my trumpet that afternoon, picked myself up a guitar and for weeks straight did nothing but play it. Had Liam show me the way to play a few songs so I could impress Baron when I met him. When my friend Ted Turner said they was playing at the St. Michael's and All Angels Fete, I knew I had to be there. I had to have him."

"And you did."

"And I did," his father agreed. "And I had my moments of doubt. Baron was a right mess sometimes, but you know? But once we started writing songs together it was like nothing I ever did before. Sometimes I feel like it's like nothing I've done since. Better than fucking, I sometimes think. Better than getting drunk or dropping acid or smoking a spliff. Writing songs with Baron Templeton. Cor. What I wouldn't go back to that. To be sixteen and have all that inside you and to be going somewhere with your best mate."

Matthew's chest felt tight. He looked down at his knees. He had never felt anything like what his father described, not at sixteen, and not at forty-two. He'd had love. He'd fucked, and been fucked. He'd written a few songs, even. But what magic had his life held? None so far. Nothing like that. Matthew swallowed, and it felt like his mouth and his throat were full of needles.

"But it ended?" Matthew asked, because he knew it had. The band had broken up. The magic had fallen apart. By the time Matthew was born, it had been years since the two had seen each other. There had been public professions of hatred, the ugliest kind of divorce. And then, a truce. And nothing. Not until the murders. The funeral. The vigils every year, on the anniversary, and Eddie in his easy chair at home in London, napping through it.

"Well, sure," his father said. "But everything ends someday, doesn't it? When you're in it, though? There's no endings. Only beginnings. The start of something bigger than you."

"Art," Matthew said, and hated himself for it. It was so pretentious, the kind of thing Kara would joke with him about after a museum showing. *Aaaaht, dahlink.* But that's what it was.

"You're bloody right," said his dad.

Matthew was gazing down at the dark boards of the polished wood floor, thinking about it, trying to see it. His father and Baron Templeton, bent over mutual guitars. Little boys, really. Children. Laughing at each other.

Strumming. Making something bigger than both of them.

The doorbell rang. Matthew, in his bathrobe and still naked underneath, let out a curse.

"I have to go dad," Matthew said. His father chirruped back.

"Yeah, Matt. I love you, son."

That's when Matthew realized he hadn't asked the most important thing. If Baron Templeton had had a daughter that Eddie Hammond knew about. If Naomi could be trusted. If it was just a con—or magic, like the kind that Baron had made with Eddie, ages and ages ago. Some unlikely but perfect twist of fate.

But when Matthew said, "Dad?" into the phone, only silence crackled back. Matthew sighed, rose from the bed, and padded barefoot down the steps to let Naomi in.

19 - 1958

The house was empty, Uncle Fred away at work or maybe the pub and Aunt Deedz out with the ladies getting groceries or playing bridge or doing whatever Aunt Deedz did when she disappeared. Baron had pretended like he'd left for school and then looped right back around, in through the sun room, to grab his guitar from his room and go downstairs to sit with the cats in the sitting room full of cat hair to strum away on his own, in peace. He was determined now to work out the dance hall number, the one with the bad chorus, the one whose bridge—or was it the middle 8? He didn't really understand the difference between the two—had not yet locked into place. He sat there on the settee, strumming away, for hours and hours on end.

If you had asked his aunt what he was doing, sitting, then occasionally rising up to pace back and forth across the carpet, then sitting again to jot down the names of a few chords, she would have assured you that it was nothing, and certainly nothing good. He was a lolly-gagger, a layabout, no help to no one, sure to end up on the dole soon. Why, he hadn't even bothered to formally drop out of art college—that would have required going *in* to art college. Which he hadn't done in ages. Meanwhile, he ate *her* food, of course, slept in *her* bed, breathed *her* air and on weekends, luxuriated late beneath the sheets that *she* washed with two of *her* cats tucked up beneath him. Even now he could hear her voice pressing on him, listing his failures. There would be a point later, into adulthood, when he would realize that her voice had, in a way, become his own internal voice. He'd make a simple mistake, call someone by the wrong name, take a wrong turn in the studio and come in just a few minutes late. Then he would hear her echo back at him inside his head. Even stepping out onto a stage in front of thousands of people who loved him, who wanted to fuck him and hold his words in the conch shells of their ears—maybe even especially then, he heard her.

Worthless, worthless Baron, just like that worthless father of yours, never done a favor nor a kindness to anyone, a burden on the whole world.

He would never ever be rid of her or her voice, but right now he pushed himself through it. He had to. Persistence was necessary now, more than ever before in his life. He needed to finish the song. To win over Eddie, or to win him back, he wasn't sure which. Had Eddie even ever been particularly taken by Baron? In some prickly, sensitive part of his heart, he just wasn't sure. When they'd met, he'd assumed he'd been the one on top. He was older, of course. He was the one with the band. But they'd both known that Eddie was prettier, more talented, that girls liked him more. Sure, he wasn't funny like Baron was funny. But he wasn't exactly *unfunny*, either. He was charming. Firm. In a way that Baron fundamentally wasn't. Baron hadn't known it then, but he knew it now. Now, six months later, Baron half-wondered if it had all been charity on Eddie's part. Tolerating him. Agreeing to join his band. He half-wondered if the Bartlebys had been a matter of pity above all else, if he'd been mistaken about the whole thing.

He plinked out the chords, the solo, still not there, but closer. He gritted his teeth and snarled through them to no one in particular. He played and played.

It was sometime past lunch when he heard applause at his back and nearly jumped out of his skin.

"That's all right," Uncle Fred was saying from the doorway, a trilby hat set at a drunken angle on his head. Then he came out into the room and squeezed Baron on his shoulder.

"Mind if I have a listen?"

Uncle Fred smelled boozy. But then, Uncle Fred always did.

"Tolliver might," Baron said, angling his plectrum toward the fat old gray cat who occupied Uncle Fred's chair, Uncle Fred hooked a hand under the cat's belly. Tolliver yowled in return, but Uncle Fred simply told him to feck off and tossed his limber body down at the floor. Fred hated the cats, all four of them. They were Aunt Deedz' children but not his own.

"Tolliver can go lick himself," Uncle Fred said with a jagged grin. He got out his pipe and began packing it with tobacco, then lit it and puffed away.

"Well," he said. "Go on."

Baron hesitated. He felt suddenly very, very young, with his uncle staring at him, waiting for him to play. Funny how he didn't mind the idea of being up on stage. He wanted to be worshiped by girls and boys, the same way that Tommy Steele and Elvis were worshiped. He wanted his voice to snuggle into the basin of a stranger's ear. He wanted them to *all* want to fuck him. And yet he hated the idea of someone who knew him as well as his uncle did—someone who had wiped shit off his bollocks when he was in nappies—seeing him play, and, presumably, make a mistake. It was one thing to be an anonymous heartthrob. It was another to hide in the anonymity of his bedroom and to strum away. It was yet another still to actually *play* for his uncle, and a song he had mostly written himself, at that.

"Are you going to play or just finger it, now, Barry?" Uncle Fred pushed. Baron rolled his eyes.

"All right, all right," he said. And then, without bothering to count it off or crack a joke, he let his music fill the room.

There are some moments that change you. There are moments when you realize, for the first time, that you are the one driving the cart. Up until now, Baron had just as soon assumed that he really *was* the talent-less hack he believed himself to be, coasting on his rugged good looks and humor. He'd held in the back of his mind the notion that failure was at any moment imminent. But as he played and sang, maybe a beat faster than he needed to, because of nerves, he noticed in the periphery of his vision a change in his uncle. The old man shifted in his old patched chair, leaning forward, hands underneath his chin. Uncle Fred was listening to him, and it was like Baron was speaking directly to Uncle Fred—singing the lyrics he and Eddie had written together, then easing into the new bridge that he'd written alone.

Oh, the song was a little silly, he knew. Double dutch lyrics about a pretty little bird on her sixteenth birthday, sitting alone in the dance hall, waiting for someone, presumably Baron. But it didn't matter. Uncle Fred had stopped puffing at his pipe. His pupils were miniature pinpricks. When the song was all over and Baron's chords faded, there was a strange gap of silence that was only just long enough for Baron to wonder if he was wrong, and it was all terrible. But then Fred sat back in his chair, shaking his head, his smile breaking out wide and showing where some of his teeth were gone.

"Well, then, Barry," his uncle said then. "Very well then, indeed."

He felt himself blush. Part of him wanted to ask his uncle if he'd liked it, then. Wanted to beg for praise like a little child. But he wasn't a child anymore. He was seventeen fucking years old. So instead he lifted one eyebrow, shrugged.

"It's nothing," he told his uncle, who snorted. They both knew it was a lie.

"This is what you've been doing with that Hammond boy and Dickie Ashby? Your aunt had me convinced that it was a lark, your band. That nothing would come of it."

"Might not yet," Baron grunted, thinking of Eddie and Dickie. The two of them, together and separate, and the problem they posed. "But it might, too."

Uncle Fred was watching Baron, studying him. At last, he rolled his jaw, and offered the following insight: "I know the older Hammond. Drink with him, sometimes. He's a right cunt. You wouldn't know it, how he's all eyelashes and charm. But if his son is anything like him, you want to be careful with him. They're schemers."

Baron frowned. He thought about Eddie's ultimatums. His threat to leave the band. And then he thought about how it felt when they were together writing songs. Like the purest, most beautiful thing in the universe. Baron forced one corner of his mouth to lift, a wry smile.

"Eddie should be careful with *me*," Baron said. "I'm a schemer."

Uncle Fred let out a few loose chuckles. "Yeh," he agreed. "You are."

"What's this?"

Baron and Uncle Fred both turned. There stood Aunt Deedz in the doorway, looking disapproving, as usual, for no particular reason, again.

"Boys' club," said Uncle Fred, winking at Baron, "Mind your business, my treacle tart."

"Well, unless it concerns doing the washing up or helping me chop vegetables, then you can do it in your office, Frederich." Uncle Fred's office was an unfinished portion of the cellar where he played with his radios and whittled and drank. "And Baron, you know better than to litter my furniture with your 'music.'" The emphasis she placed on the word was derisive, sharp. Baron felt his teeth clench and started gathering up the pile of paper. But strangely, Uncle Fred didn't hop to his feet as he usually did when Aunt Deedz spoke.

"Deidre, Baron has something to show you," he said. Baron's eyes snapped up.

"Wot?"

"Oh, don't look so dull, boy. Play your song for your aunt."

His instincts told him that this was a bad idea. But Uncle Fred was staring at him, waiting. Aunt Deedz was staring, too. At this point, it seemed, Baron's hands were tied. If he played, it would probably mean she'd mock him. If he didn't, she'd mock him anyway—tell him that it was proof he wasn't a real musician, that this was all just a laugh, as Baron's schemes were usually a laugh.

But it wasn't a laugh. It was serious. *He* was serious. He needed to show Eddie that, and damn it, he might as well have shown Deedz, too. Because never in this life had he worked so hard at anything. Music didn't come natural to him, not like drawing had. But drawing didn't mean to him what *this* meant to him. Drawing was still something that Deedz wanted for him, and though he'd resisted, drawing those silly little pastiches of Thurber sketches—his own cartoonish rebellion—it had still been a way for him to tie him to her, to tie him down. This—this was something else. His very own escape plan.

And so he locked eyes with Deedz. He would show her that he meant this. Show her how. Her pupils dilated, and then, as he played, gradually came to flood her nut brown eyes. This time he played more slowly, more carefully. He didn't miss a single chord, though he never even glanced down at his hands. He knew this song. It was *his* song. It was the road that would lead him away from here. Away from her.

When the song finished, he sat back on the sofa. Smirked at her.

"Well, then?" he asked.

She pressed her lips together until they formed a flat, displeased line.

"Baron," she said. Laughed dryly, and while Uncle Fred whipped his head around, his eyes a pair of disbelieving daggers, Baron simply watched her and waited for her to twist the knife in, "You can't seriously think that drivel is *good,* can you?"

Baron didn't answer. Uncle Fred answered for him. "Deidre, he worked *hard* on that song!"

"All the more disappointing, then," she scoffed. "It's daft, that he wasted his time on that."

"What's wrong with it, then?" Baron asked, and was surprised to find that his throat felt tight and strange. He'd expected this, really. The rejection. But he hadn't expected it to make him feel anything in particular. And yet here he was, feeling.

Deedz rolled her eyes. "It's the repetition, Baron. Repeating those same lines—it doesn't offer anything *new.* There's no depth to the story, is there?" She phrased it as a question, but it wasn't. "She's lonely, and alone, and then the speaker dances with her. So what? Just another trite rock and roll song. There's a reason only children like this sort of thing. Your rhymes don't help it, neither. They sound like something schoolboys might say, a lark. It's nothing but a lark, Baron, and it only talks to other larks like it. It's not art, that's for certain."

"*I* like it," Uncle Fred said, sticking his pipe in his mouth and letting out a nervous sequence of smoke. Aunt Deedz snorted.

"Exactly."

Baron wasn't sure for a moment what to do. His body, frozen on the sofa behind his still-vibrating guitar. His heart, somewhere on the carpet in a pile of pet hair. And then it hit him, with a sudden violent assurance: he needed to leave the room. He gathered up his guitar, his papers, and got up from the sofa with his head cast down. Aunt Deedz watched him for a long moment.

"Now, Baron, don't be a child about this. Your song is *fine*."

"Yeh, fine," he said, and brushed past her, heading up the stairs. He could hear Deedz and Fred talking about it below him, his Uncle Fred asking why Deedz always had to say such things, and Deedz dismissing her words as nothing but honest criticism, and didn't Baron deserve her honesty? Uncle Fred was telling her how he *liked* the song, honestly, truly, and Deedz let out another snort, wordlessly this time, and then started to talk about the mopping up that needed to be done in the kitchen, how the dining room floor needed a polish, and their conversation moved on as if Baron didn't matter at all.

Because, he knew, he didn't.

When Baron reached his bedroom door, he hurled his papers and guitar onto the floor as though they didn't matter at all to *him*. The guitar clattered with a satisfying *thunk-hum*. The papers flew all around. Baron slammed the door behind him and thrust himself onto his bed. He pulled the pillow over his head and smashed his face into the sheets and for a moment, everything was hot, gray and blank, and he was no one to nobody, and he contemplated smothering himself, wondering if he could do it or if he'd chicken out at the last moment and finally decided he was too much of a self-obsessed coward for suicide, anyway, and pulled the pillow off himself and threw it at the door. Not crying, but panting, feeling the dampness on his own face, he laid there, looking up at the gray of his room.

He hated her. Aunt Deedz. He could feel the list of crimes she'd committed against him stretching back and back. She'd kept him from his mother, who loved him, kept him from having a normal life that looked like the lives of other boys. She'd let him parade around in her dresses when he was young, encouraging his internal perversions, even trotted him out in front of her friends so they could laugh at him, giggling about what a shame it was that he'd been born a boy because he made such a pretty girl. She'd bought him watercolors instead of pencils when he was nine years old and trying to learn cartooning, telling him to go out and paint *en plein air* when all he had wanted to do was draw funny pictures of the teachers who had flogged him to make his fellows laugh. Cartoons weren't respectable, she said. But to be a painter—that was really something. A few months later, she'd left the gate open, let his old dog Jocko out, and when Jocko had been hit by a lorry Deedz had said it was for the best because Jocko had been dirtying the carpets for months, and when he'd cried she said *Really, Baron, it's just a dog*, and left old soft Uncle Fred to be the one to hug him. She hadn't told him how close his mum was living all these years. She hadn't told him anything nice about himself, ever, unless she could frame it as her idea first. She'd thrown out the harmonica Uncle Fred had given him, "on accident," and she'd thrown out all his old cartoons and lied about it, and she'd hit him, often, and it wasn't supposed to hurt because she was an old lady, but it did, it still did, not just physically, but in some raw place deep down below.

She knew how to hurt him. But that wasn't even the worst part. The worst part was that she was always *right*, and he knew it. The song *was* trite. He was capable of better, more, and Eddie was deserving of something better 'n' more, too, but Baron didn't know how to write it yet, and probably never would. Because Baron was a fool. Never any good to nobody. An orphan, but worse, because he had parents—they just didn't want him. Nobody wanted him. Nobody cared.

He was sniffling a little, feeling right sorry for himself, when he pulled himself from the bed and went rummaging through his desk. At last, beneath a yo-yo and several empty pens and two pen knives and a flip book of two ladies fucking that he'd made for Dickie years ago but never remembered to give to him, Baron found a book of matches. He emptied his metal trash can onto the floor, leaving a heap of paper in the corner, and then gathered up the work he'd done that day and chucked it into it. Then he lit a match and tossed it in. It only fizzled out—Baron cursed himself, a failure at even this—so he tossed another in. And another. At last, the paper caught, curled, smoked. Baron watched it, the flame dancing in his eye.

It wasn't long before he heard a pounding at the door.

"Baron! Baron, what's that smell?"

His head felt dull and useless. He didn't move to answer. The door swung open and Aunt Deedz came barreling in, and when she saw the trash can all lit up, she started screaming for help and wailing on him. Smacking him across the face and head. Shaking him. He just sat there, still and limp. It was Uncle Fred who finally came in, gave a yelp, and disappeared for a moment and then returned with a shaving mug of water he spilled over the fire. The flames fizzled out as Deedz gave Baron one cracking blow across the face, the flat of her hand landing square against his left ear. It rang, his ear. He shook his head. When he looked at them—Deedz all red and angry, Uncle Fred, with one hand on his hip in concern, all he could hear was the same weird, empty ringing. He turned his head right, and the words floated in:

"What were you even *doing*, Baron? Didn't you even *think*?"

He didn't know what to say. He just needed to be left alone. "Nothing!" he cried out, hollow at first, then growing more raw. "Nothing! I'm sorry! I'm sorry!" He said and then, when they didn't answer, he crawled back up into his bed, facing the wall with all the pictures of rock stars on there who would all drop dead within a decade or two, and pulled the blankets up over him.

The world kept turning, kept ringing. Deedz kept yelling, but Baron couldn't hear it. For a moment, a slender moment, he was lost to the world.

20 - 1977

The plan all rested on Mikey Alspaugh. Mom was used to Richard Charles doing disappearing acts on weekends, didn't even bother saying anything about it anymore, but she depended on Zachy being around to watch the baby so that she could go out and wait tables or drink at them, it wasn't always clear which. So that Friday, Zach let his mother know that Mikey had invited him for a sleepover on Saturday, and mom had sighed and ruffled Zach's hair and told him she was happy he was going out for once. She said it in such a sweet, gentle, cloying way that he almost didn't resent the implication: that Zach didn't usually go out. That Zach never went out.

Well, this weekend, he was going someplace. He was determined. It had to happen. In the morning in the halls, he wove through the throng of stinky, middle school bodies until he found Mikey, whose hair was golden and feathered now, like a girl, like a pussy angel. Last year, they'd both been small and zitty and dweeby, but now Mikey towered over him and had begun to grow a certain kind of lean musculature from football practice. All that running and weightlifting "Coach" (who was only ever called "Coach") made them do.

"Yo," Zachy said, "Mikey, I need to ask you a favor."

Mikey slammed his locker shut and turned to look at Zach, but his eyes weren't quite touching Zach's, as though the smaller boy was a slippery, near-invisible ghost.

"What do you want," he said, and it wasn't even fully a question. His eyes were scanning the hallway for someone better to talk to.

150

"Me and my brother are sneaking out this weekend. We're going into the city. There are these girls—"

"Girls, huh?" Mikey asked, suddenly interested. He hooked his thumbs into his rear belt loops and finally looked down at Zachy. "Who?"

"These high school chicks," Zachy said, because he knew that Mikey would appreciate that Zachy called them "chicks." "Jennifer and Shay. I don't know their last names, but they—"

Zachy wordlessly held his hands out in front of his chest, indicating a pair of heavy weights. Mikey smirked.

"Sounds hot," Mikey said.

"They *are* hot. I just can't tell my mom about it. You know how she is." Zach rolled his eyes. In a way, he felt at this moment—at many moments—more like a parody of a teenager than an actual teenager. His mother was easy with him, always had been—barely even concealed the fact that he was her favorite. Had Zach said that he wanted to go on a simple date, one that didn't involve a train ride into the city? His mother probably would have bought him a boutonniere and a bottle of aftershave. Mikey narrowed his eyes at Zachy, but didn't say anything.

"Hmm," was his only response.

"C'mon, man," Zach said, and he was careful not to beg for it, careful not to look too desperate. "Do me a solid. For old time's sake?"

Mikey spun the dial on his lock, then turned to lean his muscular shoulders against the peeled-paint locker's surface. He gave the bridge of his nose a scratch as his eyes looked up and down the busy hallway, the only sign—subtle, slight—that he had any trepidation at all about what he was about to say.

"Okay," he said. "But you'll have to do something for me."

"Sure," Zach said, beaming—then he forced the corners of his mouth down. "I mean, of course. You scratch my back—"

"I'll need an eighth, at least," Mikey said flatly. He still wasn't looking at Zach, still looking down the hallway as if he was searching for someone better to talk to. But when Zach didn't answer right away, his blue eyes fixed on him, very briefly.

"What?" Mikey said.

"An eighth of *what?*" Zach demanded. Mikey snorted, rolled his eyes.

"Ask your brother," he said. "He'll know. Bring it over first thing tomorrow. When you ring the bell, tell my mom—I dunno, that I forgot my notebook or something. Here."

Mikey reached into his backpack and pulled out a notebook that was covered in crude drawings of naked women. There were tits everywhere, blown up like carnival balloons. Zach took it and put it in his backpack.

"Okay," Zach said. "So, like, if I get this for you, you'll cover for me? Right, Mikey?"

"Mm-hmm," Mikey said, pushing up off his locker. He started down the hall, Zach following him, until they reached the south stairwell. "Oh, and it's Mike now. Jizz face."

Zach frowned. He was looking up at Mikey, mulling over the thing he'd just called him. Jizz face. Like it was nothing. Almost like it was a term of endearment.

"Yeah," Zach said. "Sure. Mike."

"See ya," Mike said, and then, with a special emphasis on the name, "*Zachy*."

Mike went up the stairwell, leaving Zach standing there, blushing, behind him.

* * *

It wasn't until that night in their bedroom when Richard Charles crawled under their bed and produced a metal change box that Zach understood what *an eighth* was. His brother unlocked the box with one of many rusty keys from his key chain. When he popped it open, Zachary saw that it was stuffed with a good number of Ziploc baggies, and that each one contained an equally good amount of marijuana. His brother rifled through them, picked one seemingly at random, tossed it to Zach, then closed and locked the box.

"You're fucking kidding me," Zach said, staring at the baggie as his brother crawled back under the bed and put the cash box back in its hiding place. Richard Charles arched one eyebrow.

"Where did you think I was getting my money?" he asked. "Selling Girl Scout cookies?"

"I mean . . ." Zach said, holding it up against the light. He'd never smoked a joint before. He'd thought about it, because he knew that by the late '60s Saffron was always fucking stoned. *Templeton ate LSD like it was candy . . . the biography had said*, but somehow despite the warnings sent home about temporary LSD tattoos one might encounter on the schoolyard, Zach never had found someone willing to give away their drugs for free. Now he opened the bag, sniffed it. It smelled like an armpit. Like his brother's dirty clothes. He suddenly understood something that he hadn't before.

"You smoke it?" Zach asked. Richard Charles rolled his eyes.

"Of course I have, you pussy," he said. "And stop sniffing it. I don't want you to get your slobber all over it."

Zach pressed the bag closed with his fingertips.

"Why don't we smoke some now?" he asked. Richard Charles narrowed his eyes.

"I quit," he said. "I don't smoke product. Besides, it makes me lazy."

"When have you ever cared about being lazy?" Zach said. "Isn't that, like, your thing? Being a total waste of flesh?"

Richard Charles kicked him hard in the thigh. Zach let out a yelp.

"Jesus," he said, rubbing his leg.

"I'm not a fucking waste of flesh," Richard Charles sulked. "I just never found anything worth caring about before."

Still rubbing the denim nap of his blue jeans, feeling the tender pain inside, Zach glanced up at his brother. "Jennifer, you mean?" he asked.

"No, you dick," Richard Charles spat back. "I don't give a fuck about Jennifer. She's hot or whatever but she's an idiot. I meant our band."

Zach stared at his brother, furrowing his brow deeply. He hadn't known that the band meant anything in particular to his brother, though, sure, Richard Charles spent most of his time when he was home bent over their radio, plucking out bass lines. But surely, he'd assumed, it didn't mean to

Richard Charles what it meant to *him*. Richard Charles was full of shit. He always was. Never took anything seriously. Not the same way that Zach did.

"What're you looking at?" Richard Charles snapped. Zach blanched, and tucked the Ziploc baggie down into his pocket.

"Nothing," Zach said softly. And then, thinking about it, he lifted his eyes to his brother again.

"Do you really think we're going to find Baron Templeton tomorrow?"

Richard Charles laughed. Dry. Humorless. "No way. But if it gets us a day with Jennifer and Shay, then I guess it's worth *something*. A date, man! Maybe my little brother will finally nab some pussy."

Zach hadn't even thought about nabbing some pussy. He did now, for the first time. Lifted his hips a little. Made room for himself. Found himself smiling. "Yeah," he said. "Yeah."

* * *

Zach made the exchange of illicit substances on Mikey—no, Mike—Alspaugh's front porch before the eight forty train, while his brother straddled his bike from the cracked-up front curb. Zach had awkwardly pressed the baggie between the pages of Mike's notebook, and when he passed it back to his former friend, Mike took it from him with hungry hands.

"Awesome," he said, with a warmth that sounded false and an enthusiasm that didn't, "I swear if your mom calls, I've got your back."

"Thanks, man," Zach said, and trudged on down the stairs, grabbing his bike from where he'd rested it on the railing on the way. By the time he glanced over his shoulder, Mike was gone. He tried to remember what they'd ever had in common as friends, and came up with nothing.

"Mike Alspaugh's a prick," Richard Charles said, as they both got on their bikes and started toward the train station. It was freezing out, like the season had decided to turn to winter all at once. Zach found himself laughing, mostly with relief, his breath fogging the air. Maybe he didn't need friends, didn't need guys like Mike Alspaugh. He had his brother, for once, and the thing that they might grow between them. A band. That had been enough for Baron and Eddie. Maybe it would be enough for Zach and Richard Charles, too.

They tied up their bikes outside the train station, went inside to the dusty space to buy their tickets. Richard Charles paid. Zach was no longer surprised by the thick wad of bills, no longer pondered where they'd come from. He did wonder, in a way, how his brother had come to this. What path had led him to drug dealership, if it was like the after school specials they used to watch back before Mom had pawned their TV. The drug dealers on Dragnet reruns, or the ones they warned you about in notes home at school—they always sounded as sinister as flashers. Zach had imagined greased back hair, sunglasses, long trench coats. His brother was greasy enough—cheeks deeply pocked with acne in several different shades of pink and white—but if anything, he seemed more solid and less slippery than he had before. Richard Charles paid for four tickets, pocketed them, thanked the woman behind the counter with only a little bit of a sneer. Maybe the band, the prospect of the band, had really changed him. Maybe he'd really, truly turned a corner.

"Ah, fuck," Richard Charles said, turning to face the mostly-empty train station. "I think that cunt bailed on me."

Zach peered over his brother's shoulder and saw precisely which cunt Richard Charles meant. Or didn't see her, actually. Because Shay was sitting there, reading a copy of *Rolling Stone*. But she was alone. No sign of Jennifer.

"Hey, homos," Shay said, not looking up. The issue of *Rolling Stone* was three years old. Zachy had looked at it once, in the school library, had thought about stealing it but had pussed out. It had a silhouette on the cover. From the hair, the shape of the nose, you could tell who it was. Baron Templeton. *The stranger in the city*, it read, and Zach had been able to page through the article that day during study hall, skimming the story about how Templeton had vanished and how nobody knew where he was now, how he was lost in the Big Apple, or maybe some place else. But Zach hadn't been able to finish the article before the bell and by the time he came back, next week, the magazine was gone.

"Where's Jennifer?" Richard Charles answered, his frown deep. "I bought her a ticket."

"Sucks to be you," Shay said, closing her magazine and putting it in her knapsack. "Her grandma's sick or something. I dunno. Maybe it's just an excuse. Maybe she hates you."

Richard Charles snorted, but it wasn't a derisive sound. He sounded almost tickled by her humor, actually, and Zach felt a vague flare of annoyance. Shay was supposed to be *his* date.

"Yeah," Richard Charles said. "You're probably right. Hey, that's the train."

His brother broke out into a run. Shay got up, following slowly, and Zachy found himself walking beside her. Their knuckles almost touching. Their hands almost touching. Unbearable. The tightness in his chest. The pain of it.

"He's fast," Shay said, nodding toward Richard Charles as he burst through the double doors and took off for the platform steps. "I didn't expect him to be so fast."

Zach narrowed his eyes, watching Richard Charles run. He remembered something, a flash, a memory, beyond unreal. His father, a long time ago, racing Richard Charles down the road.

"Going to grow up to be a football star," his father had said after, and by football he meant soccer, which he loved. Zachy remembered the slight lilt in his voice betraying his distant origins, the obvious pride in the way he lifted up Richard Charles and threw him into the air. Zachy, a baby then, or practically, toddling behind, slow, as always. Watching and only half understanding, in that baby way, but for the first time feeling that knife's edge of jealousy.

"Yeah," said Zach, holding the door open for her, because it was the right thing to do. Shay just rolled her eyes at him.

"Fast," he said.

21 - 1958

He was lucky, in a way. The worst kind of lucky. Because aside from his guitar, his belongings all fit into three or four wooden milk crates. Sure, it was sad to clean out his old desk, the one marked with all the ancient carvings of boyhood. Horses and swords and tits and drippy cocks and drum head logos for the Bartlebys that had been easier to work on than his drawing homework. But once Aunt Deedz had made up her mind about Baron leaving, he knew it was no use staying around. She hadn't spoke to him since the night of the fire and her silence laid over them like a thick, soupy doom. If the silence was going to break, it was going to break cruelly, and Baron was already convinced of his worthlessness. He didn't need to hear it from her.

Uncle Timo came by that Saturday to help Baron carry out his things. He was a short man, nearly dark as Baron himself, but greasier. He used Crisco to slick back his hair. Easier that way, he said, to use something they had on hand, and he'd winked when he said it, like he expected Baron to do the same. No, thank you, Baron thought. He didn't want to smell like kitchen grease and besides, he'd do anything he could to avoid looking like stout "Uncle" Tim.

It wasn't that Tim was unkind to him. He hefted Baron's boxes in his strong, muscular waiter's arms, only grunting a little at the effort. But he was largely useless, and Baron had never been able to understand what his mum found admirable in him. He had a job, yes, and money enough for a Peugeot and a council home. And sure, he could dance alright when he had a drink in him—Baron's mum and Timmy often spent evenings twirling around the kitchen together—but he wasn't smart and he wasn't interesting and on the rare moments Baron had been able to extract any information about his own father it was clear *that* man had been both.

No. Had to be something simpler here. Sex, probably. baron had walked in once on the two of them going at it, his mum's face down on Timmy's fat prick. Tim had screamed at Baron to get out, which Baron did, gladly. Unlike the incident with his Ma's tit, he hadn't filed that one away for later, but sometimes the revolting image came back to him uninvited, spoiling a wank. But, hell, his mother liked it, enough to keep Timmy around, enough to marry him when she hadn't even married Baron's Dad—enough to swallow down his putrid cum, yeah? It was more than Baron had ever gotten anyone to do to him.

Feeling sorry for himself, Baron tossed his guitar case into Tim's boot. At the curb, Uncle Tim was shaking Uncle Fred's hand, as though one had just sold the other a racehorse or other, more useful animal. Baron leaned against the car, squinting in the pale spring light at them. Unlike Uncle Tim, he liked Fred. No. Loved. But Fred wasn't the type for feelings, and he wasn't the type to push at Deedz if the punishment were going to be too great. He didn't hug his nephew, just gave his hand a quick squeeze.

"Be seein' ye, Barry," he said.

Baron got into the car. It felt too small for his legs, lank and growing lankier, for his elbows, for his arms. But where else was he to go? He was a nobody, without any real prospects or chances. He'd burned his last best chance of breaking out of Liverpool and soon Eddie would fly away without him. Holding a hand over his face, he let his stepfather shift gears and pull the car away from the one and only home he'd ever known. Maybe it was better this way, he told himself. But probably, in all actuality, it wasn't.

* * *

Buddy died. Body smashed to smithereens in a plane crash in a snowstorm in the middle of fucking nowhere. No more "Everyday." No more "Dearest."

No more "Peggy Sue." What could be done about it? Nothing, for no one at all. Baron slogged forward into the new Hollyless future, heart a little heavier and a little more dead.

A new term started and Baron made a half-arsed effort to go to class. Sometimes he'd see Sue Grasso there—she had just started art school herself, wanted to be in fashion, she said, drew these constipated little sketches of women with bodies shaped like Sue's body if you cleaved Sue's body of all its appealing fat. She would take her sketchbook over after class and show them to Baron, her eyes begging for his approval.

"Yeh," he'd say, then look up at her hopeful, wide eyes and full mouth and crooked teeth, "Yeh, they're fine. But they'll take you more seriously in the fashion world if you dye your hair blonde. Like Bridgette Bardot. She's keen."

"Yeh?" Sue would ask, and their eyes would lock and he could almost feel her shivering with excitement but there was no shiver in him to shiver back—he'd killed it, every tremble. "You think I'd look good as a blonde?"

Baron could hear his own voice, dripping sarcasm. It was a game to him—seeing how hard he could push her, seeing how desperate she was, how fundamentally fawning. "Oh *yeeeeah*," he said. "Smashing."

And then he sacked off of class for a week or two. Some days he'd go to the Delph with a bottle in his pocket and get sloshed and listen to Dick and Liam argue about Elvis—whether he was over or not. Some days, he'd sit farting on his mother's sofa, listening to the radio, wanking intermittently while she was gone to the grocer's or the butcher's or wherever it was that women went to escape their children. Sometimes he'd wander the docks alone and then show up at Eddie Hammond's house, pounding at their door in the middle of the day until he came to the conclusion that no one was home. Eddie himself wasn't coming around much anymore. When he showed his face at the Delph, his heavy-lidded eyes were as shaded as a mask and when he laughed, it was a careful laugh, one that never matched Baron's drunken laughter in either depth or length. One day when he was real sloshed and feeling full of something—bravery, or maybe rage—Baron sidled up next to him at the bar and dipped his voice low.

"You quit yet, Ed?" he asked. "You off sucking Dylan Miranda's cock?"

"Cor," Eddie said, with a theatrical roll of his eyes that Baron decided was only fit for a faggot. "Come off it, Baron. You're drunk as a boiled peacock."

"Peacocks don't get drunk," Baron said, his words a slur. He reached out and tugged hard at one of Eddie's blond curls. "They're too pretty for that."

Eddie jerked his whole body away. His face was another kind of mask now, anger matching Baron's anger. But Eddie wasn't a fighter. He had brothers enough to know how to weasel out of a fight. So he let his pale eyes look stern for a moment, fatherly. Then he softened them.

"I'm working on a new song, Barry," he said. "I could use your help, if you let yourself dry out for a minute or two."

Baron sat straighter at that, feeling the words thump into his bloodstream like a missed heartbeat. He knew what was being offered to him. He knew that whatever music it was curling around Eddie's brain was beautiful, and ripe, and most of all, somehow—his. He knew they could do something special together, some magic that wasn't just Baron imposing his will on someone else and someone else acquiescing, or the other way it sometimes worked, with someone beating Baron down with brain and balls and fist. It wasn't like that with him and Ed, had never been like that. They could go somewhere *together*, couldn't they? The two of them? Consenting to it? Mutually?

But Baron didn't have to look behind him to know that Dickie was sitting at the little table there with Liam, boring two bright, beady, hated eyes right into Baron's shoulder blades. Dickie owned him in a way, and he wasn't going to let him go. And Baron knew, deep down, shamefully, that he had *asked* for this. Slipped the collar on himself, handed Dickie the leash. He'd wanted Dickie, wanted this, knowing in his core that he never deserved any better. Eddie was licking his lips, waiting for a response. But Baron knew that ultimately, shamefully, he certainly had never deserved Eddie.

Baron's shoulders slumped. It was too dangerous to hope. So instead he took out his bottle, poured a full slug of Tim's rum into his espresso. Put the cap on the bottle, and the bottle in his pocket. Drank it all, deep.

"No, thank you, son," he said, holding one pinkie out, dainty, like a lady. "I prefer it wet."

Eddie drew a breath in, not even sighing. Holding it. While Baron grinned wide, showing him every single one of his teeth.

* * *

Dinner with the family. Burnt toast and revolting soused herring. Food was one thing Baron sorely missed about living at Aunt Deedz's house—with no job, and her upper class ambitions, she knew how to cook a meal. Baron's mum worked at the movie theater late most days, and all weekend, too. She could hardly be bothered to think about it so it was eggs for most meals and some variation of fish and toast for the rest. Of course the drunkenness that he had bathed in all day didn't help matters, and he stirred the food around his plate with a fork, scowling. His stomach clenched and rolled. Took one soppy bite of herring, felt himself gag, held a wad of paper napkin over his mouth.

"Baron, behave yourself," Uncle Tim said sharply. It had only been a few weeks, but Baron could tell that Tim was growing weary of him already. It was one thing to entertain his wife's son on the occasional weekend. It was another to live with a sad, alcoholic, adolescent waste of flesh.

"But it's disgusting," Baron murmured into his napkin. That's when Tim kicked him square in the shin beneath the table.

"Ow!" Baron yelped, too loud, and Bess jumped as though she'd been hit herself, even though they never hit her, and Mum veiled her face with her hand.

"Christ, are you a ten year old, Baron?" she asked. Baron threw his napkin down on the plate.

"I'm eighteen," he said gruffly. "Nearly eighteen."

"And *that*," said Uncle Tim, "is why he needs a job."

"I'm in school."

"Barely," Tim shot back. "Didn't Freddie get you a job at a barbershop?"

"They never have work for me. Besides, I don't want to work a job in a barbershop," Baron said. "I'm going to be—"

But then he cut himself off. Because for nearly a year now he'd been telling the whole world that he was going to be a musician—that he *was* a musician. But now the future didn't seem so sure.

"Yeh," said Uncle Tim. "Well."

Baron glowered at his greasy little stepfather. He was about to get up and chuck the entirety of his bile-inducing meal in the sink when his mother leaned forward. She was forcing brightness into her voice, as though she thought a quick change of subject would do the whole lot of them some good.

"Oh you know, I've been thinking about your birthday coming up, Baron," she said. "Thought we might have a party for you, here."

"A party?" he asked. Aunt Deedz had never been much for birthday celebrations. Her home, she said, was too fine for too many little boys with their dirty trainers and their trouble. In truth, Baron couldn't remember the last time his birthday was celebrated at all. When they had given him Jocko, maybe? How old had he been then—five or six? Anyway, turning eighteen was nothing special. Was just going to be more of the same bullshit that seventeen was. To Baron, there didn't seem much worth celebrating about it.

"Yes," she said. Baron could see how she was forcing a smile across her painted lips, but the corners of her eyes didn't wink at all. It was a fake smile, just like the color of her lips was fake, just like the color of her hair was fake and the shape of her body poured and molded by the boning of her undergarments. Why he'd once found her charming—even sexy—he wasn't sure. "A *party*. We could have all the boys over, the whole band. Alfie and Dickie and Liam and Eddie—"

Baron scoffed at the mention of Eddie, like his name itself was a joke. He didn't want it to be, but it was. Still, his mum went on.

"And Sue and her friends. Or another girl, if there's another you'd like to invite?" A pregnant pause, probing, expectant. When Baron didn't answer, his mother just kept talking. "Well, I'll call up Sue's mum if you'd like. Saw her on the way to school the other day. Did you see, she dyed her hair blonde?"

Baron hadn't seen. He shrugged.

"Well, she looks lovely," his mum said. "Really suits her, with those dark eyes and all. You should call her up. Maybe get lunch with her one day at the college."

"I would prefer not to," Baron muttered, almost inaudibly. Then at last he picked up his plate and rose from the table. "'m done. Goin' to my room. You." He pointed at Bess. "Stay out for a spell. I need my privacy."

His little sister nodded her dumb, blank head with its dumb, blank face. Baron chucked the plate into the sink without scraping it. But his mother's voice called back to him.

"But Baron," she said. "What about the party?"

"Do whatever you want," Baron replied, not bothering to look back at his mother as he trudged up the narrow set of stairs.

* * *

Once he'd had a bedroom, too small for him, but his own. Now he had a cot in the corner of his little sister's bedroom, a creaky, stained old thing with a holey quilt and thin old Army pillow, one Uncle Tim had gotten in the war. It was clear it didn't belong here, in this room with its smart white furniture and lacy canopy over the bed. His belongings, scant though they were, just fit into their crates, which they had crammed behind the door. His guitar went beneath the cot. Invisible, unseen. He hadn't taken it out once since he'd moved. Now, with the door shut, and his sister's desk chair jammed under the doorknob, he let himself lie down on Bess's bed, smashing his face into her pillow. Thinking about what his Mum said, about Sue Grasso, smiling wickedly to himself.

Because it was wicked, wasn't it? What he'd done to her? She would do anything to win his approval, his heart. He knew it. She'd loved him for years now, mostly in a way that he found grating though occasionally he'd enjoyed her worship, and so he never quite discouraged her from the practice. How big he felt when her dark eyes were full of admiration for him. It didn't matter that he didn't exactly admire her back—in fact, maybe it was better this way. If his heart had been caught up with her heart, then he wouldn't have been as powerful, as safe. Loving someone diminished you. It made you weak. Look at Baron and Dickie.

Look at Baron and Eddie.

Eddie. Unf. Baron breathed his hot breath directly down into the pillow, trying not to remember how Eddie had looked at him at the Delph, remembering anyway. Those ocean eyes stormy, then calm. Wanting to let Baron in. To be with him, writing music *together*. Baron felt his prick throb at the thought and did not chase the thought away at all, for the very first time, like he had countless times before. Lately, all of his wanking had been about Dickie. The alley. The kiss, gruff and stubbly. He'd wanked all over his mum's WC and his cot sheets and the men's room at art college, remembering the slightly stale taste of Dickie's tongue, telling himself he didn't deserve any better. His own uselessness, his own inherent lack of worth, the fact that he was trapped by Dickie, and couldn't get out—all of that had become part of his fantasy. He was bad and so was Dickie Ashby and wasn't it all so *bad*, the delicious and dirty things they'd done together?

But Ed. Ed wasn't bad. Ed was wonderful and lovely, like a girl, only better. Ed, so sweet he believed that his wanking had gotten his own mum sick. Ed, who would undoubtedly be famous someday, who would make more money than Sinatra and Elvis combined, who was better than Baron in almost every way, but it didn't make Baron mad for once, because Eddie deserved every good thing that was coming to him. With his soft hands that were callused at the fingertips, with those pink lips that he had once pressed to the mouthpiece of a trumpet, with those pink lips that Baron could imagine kissing, and it wouldn't be like Dickie's kiss or Sue Grasso's either. There would be no wrestling, no question of who would be on top. Their bodies could answer each other, same way that music worked for the two of them, and everything could be unspoken and everything would be okay. Baron ground his cock into his sister's sheets, and then he turned himself over and thrust a hand down in his pants. He closed his eyes and thought about pale curls. For a moment, instinctive, he told himself that he was thinking about Sue Grasso, who had made herself to look like Bridgette Bardot for him. And hadn't he spent all of fourteen wanking to the idea of Bridgette Bardot? But it was no good anymore. He had let himself think about the worst thing, which was also the best thing, and so he couldn't deny it, not now.

Ed.

Putting it inside Ed, or letting Ed put it inside him. Taking turns. Like a song. Verse chorus verse. Ed, who knew how rhythm worked, whose hips would match Baron's hips. Ed, with whom sex would be a kindness, without a drop of the disdain or hurt that he felt when he thought about Sue Grasso or Dickie Ashby or anyone else. He wanted to touch every cell of flesh that Ed had, wanted to make his body sing. Tuned to a natural E, both of them, and glad for it. And never, ever ashamed again.

Baron's body tensed, then writhed, his orgasm arriving sooner than he thought it would, but not unwelcome. Toes curling, and a little, strangled gasp. After, sweaty and damp on his sister's bed, he laid still, twitching, thinking about it. Imagining Eddie, with his head against Baron's shoulders, the two of them happy, the two of them spent.

22 - 1997

Cymbeline woke in her tiny counselor's bedroom with Sid's head on her shoulder. Their bodies were mutually graced with a thin coat of sweat. When Sid shifted her weight, she left cool, damp patches on Cymbeline's body. The sun through the window was thinly golden. Soon, Cymbeline would have to wake the children, hear their whining, their yawns. It was fascinating to her, how the girls had so quickly come to treat her like a parent or an older sister. When she'd been a child, she had mostly been a solitary creature with only her mother as a friend. She hadn't expected to find any notion of sisterhood here. But it seemed that she had.

She pulled herself out from beneath Sid's weight, watching the other woman tug the synthetic sleeping bag over her bare shoulder. Was this part of Sid's general confidence in the world, her swagger and confidence? Was it because Sid had grown up in a community, while Cymbeline had only a dyad—and a dysfunctional one, at that? As a kid, Cymbeline had never whined and had very rarely complained. She existed, she'd often felt, for her mother's general pleasure and amusement. Her mother loved hearing music, and so Cymbeline taught herself to play her mother's old guitar from a book she'd gotten out of the library. Her mother found it gratifying to have a child who kept a clean house and whose grades were worth bragging about, in a vague way, almost as an afterthought, to the other mothers at the supermarket—so Cymbeline kept a spotless bedroom and did her homework promptly, even when she would rather be watching TV. They never fought because if Cymbeline's mother was mad at her it would have been like rendering herself invisible.

But then Cymbeline's mother had died, and she'd become invisible, anyway. It hadn't been until she'd come to this place with its cool pine groves and green lake slimy with seaweed that any notion of self had begun to return to her. Or maybe it was the first time she was really meeting herself at all. Sid, on the other hand, was in many ways pure ego. She slept heavily now, smacking her lips and snoring now and then. Sometimes, when they shared a teeny bunk, breaking all the rules, Sid farted and then laughed about it when Cymbeline complained. She was a hungry lover, almost greedy, wanting Cymbeline's body on top so she could take every inch of her in. It wasn't that she didn't return the pleasures she felt—Cymbeline had never had as many orgasms with a lover before, had once believed it was a magic she could weave only by herself. Sid had definitely disabused her of that notion. But it was Sid who decided the type of pleasure Cymbeline would feel, and how. If Cymbeline expected Sid to be like nervous, empathetic Pamela, then she was disappointed. Only she wasn't disappointed. She was glad, in fact, that Sid was exactly herself—and that they happened to be tuned to the same fork, naturally.

Cymbeline grabbed her shower caddy and a towel from her cubby and hustled out into the cool morning before Sid or the children could begin, in their expansive way, to intrude on her day. It was August now, but the morning was beginning to have a little bite to it. The door of the cindy slammed behind her, the holey screen doing nothing to keep out the impending autumn. Only three weeks left here at Camp Kaaterskill. And then what? She'd have to return to school. To her ordinary, empty life. She stepped into the shower, shedding her shoes on the tile floor even though they'd been told it was an athlete's foot risk. She didn't fear skin fungus. No, she felt dread only when she thought about the future, and in a way she never had before. Once her future had been so tied up with her mother's. Now?

She knew that Sid had grown up in Poughkeepsie, a strangely named city not much more than an hour's drive south from camp, that she was living with her parents and working in a mechanic's shop even though her mother wanted her to go back to school to get a degree, because she never had finished her own. Cymbeline could tell that Sid was holding herself back for some reason in terms of her ambitions—in terms of her life. Perhaps Sid could see no way forward other than her mother's way, and so, by rejecting that, she was at least carving out a path of her own, even if it was obviously, abundantly clear that it was the wrong path. Cymbeline had let Sid talk about these things, offering no advice. Just listening. It was, after all, what Sid did for her. Holding her hand when Cymbeline spoke of her mother's prolonged, all-encompassing death, but offering no advice. Only empathy.

In this way they had at last begun to trade pasts—though they never spoke about the autumn to come. Cymbeline's college was several hours east by car, but she didn't have a car; a Greyhound had delivered her here. She found it difficult to imagine what their future would look like, whether it would entail letters or mix tapes or train rides or nothing at all. Probably nothing, Cymbeline suspected. The truth was, she wasn't used to asking for anything. From anyone.

She soaped up her hair, letting the pink liquid fall in rivers between her shoulder blades. She was just about to wash it away when suddenly the curtain was yanked unceremoniously open.

"Perky!" A bellowing voice greeted her, and Cymbeline let out a scream. After a moment, when she saw Sid and her wide, waiting grin, the scream gave way to laughter. She hugged the other woman, who was fully clothed, soaking Sid's basketball shorts and wife beater top all the way through.

"Hold on, hold on," Sid said, pulling away. "There's something I have to show you."

Children had begun to file in from Cymbeline's cabin (Spruce must have awakened them; Spruce was twice the counselor she'd ever be) and from others. Cymbeline pulled at the curtain to shield her naked body, but Sid was unperturbed. She pulled a wrinkled sheet of paper out of her pocket, unfolding it, smoothing the edges.

"Here," she said. "I saw this at dinner, but I forgot to show it to you."

"You had your mind on other things," Cymbeline said, grinning, grabbing for Sid's ass even though Sid squirmed away. It was true; Sid had wasted no time after light's out tearing off Cymbeline's clothes. Once Cymbeline would never have flirted, not really. It felt amazing to do it now and dangerous with all the children around, but also somehow safe. Like this flirtatious self, this swaggering and cocksure self, was the shadow of an old life that had been waiting for all these nineteen years to be illuminated.

"Yeah, yeah," Sid admitted—actually *blushing* like some kind of little kid. "I'm serious, Perky."

"I hate when you call me that," Cymbeline said, but she didn't, not really. It was *different* when Sid said it. It was special.

"Bite me," Sid said, and then she held out the paper to Cymbeline. She took it, still clutching the shower curtain around her with one hand.

"Talent show?"

"Yeah, tonight at the library at Berean," Sid said helpfully as if Cymbeline couldn't read herself. "Counselors *and* campers are invited to participate. Compete for the golden trophy. They give it out every year, you know."

"I don't have any talents," Cymbeline found herself saying gruffly. She gave the flier back to Sid and began to turn back toward the shower head to wash the remainder of the shampoo away. Sid snorted once, then twice. When Cymbeline didn't answer, Sid yanked back the shower curtain again—exposing Cymbeline's naked body to the small pack of pre-adolescent girls who had begun to congregate.

"Hey!" Cymbeline cried, grabbing for her. But Sid was just standing there, hands on her hips, brow low and wrinkled and an expression on her face that suggested that there would be no easy escape for Cymbeline—no more invisibility.

"Are you fucking kidding me?" is what Sid said, is all that Sid had ever needed to say.

* * *

The library on the girl's side was different—not much more than a shed tucked behind the playfield with soggy old *Girl's Life* magazines and crumbling horse girl novels packed into a few tiny shelves. Cymbeline had expected more of the same on the boy's side of camp; she'd only passed this building once or twice before, and had then operated under the assumption that it was some sort of boat house because it overlooked the lake on risers and because boys on canoes, indeed, came and went underneath.

But it was not a boat house. At the top of a rickety set of stairs, through a rustic porch and a set of freshly-painted barn doors was the kind of library Cymbeline had always dreamed about in her bookish, introverted childhood. They had every Hardy Boy's novel ever published here; all the old Tom Swiftys; loads of fantasy novels, door-stopper thick and resplendent with images of dragons, knights, and women in various states of undress. Scale models of boats in bottles and outside of them served as occasional book ends, as well as real stone busts of important men: philosophers, founding fathers, and camp directors of years past. In the center there was a stone fireplace. Real stone. A fire simmering behind a screen. Several game boards for chess and checkers and backgammon dotted the room, in between child sized rockers that some boy had probably made for a camp service project, decades and decades before. The sunset was coming in orange and blue and breathtaking through massive picture windows, and boys, and a few girls from Camp Kaaterskill, were beginning to file in. Cymbeline noticed the way the boys walked—different from the girls, like they owned this place, and they did. The girls looked nervous and unkempt here, like they were interlopers. Scuffling and whispering among themselves. Cymbeline wondered if this wasn't part of the *point*.

"This place is amazing," she murmured to Sid, as they stood in the middle of it all, her guitar case in one hand and her anxiety—which she was trying to ignore—in the other. The children were all sitting down in little rows in front of the fireplace, except for those who had decided they would perform, too. A pair of girls in spangly gymnastics suits. A trio of older boys with yo-yos.

Sid glanced at Cymbeline, and it was as though there was something veiled behind her eyes, something she wasn't quite revealing.

"I'm over it," she said a little too loudly. There were times like these when Sid's normally-joyful demeanor would crack and reveal and paunchy annoyance underneath. Now, she fled from Cymbeline's side, leaving her standing there alone so she could go talk to a male counselor who *also* had a guitar slung over his shoulder. It was the boy from the first night campfire, and Cymbeline's mind drifted back, trying to recall his name. Newt? No, it wasn't a camp name. Something normal. Nick? Neil.

Sid was laughing with him, clapping him on the shoulder. Cymbeline knew that Sid was not attracted to boys, though she felt a vein of jealousy, anyway. The truth was, she was too nervous. The truth was, she wouldn't have ever signed up to do this without Sid's encouragement, and she felt like she needed her now, beside her. But Sid was joking with Neil, and they were clearly old friends, and Sid was clearly preoccupied. So Cymbeline busied herself, taking out her own guitar, crouching in a corner to tune it against the voices of the children who were gathered behind her.

It had been years since she'd performed in front of any kind of *real* audience—her serenade of Sid before her cabin that day didn't seem to count, nor had her mortifying karaoke failure at training. The last time had been sixth grade or so, in the gym of her middle school, and she'd known at once that she'd picked the wrong song as soon as she'd opened her mouth. "Crimson and Clover" by Tommy James and the Shondells was a favorite of her mother's, but when it came time to sing that day, she hadn't been able to make her voice *work*, not at all. The song was long, too long, and she had dressed "nicely," at her mother's command, in a long skirt and navy v-neck, her hair parted in the middle, and as she sat there, picking out the notes perfectly, she could sense how this had been the wrong way to gain middle school notoriety. She should have worn something slutty. She should have worn just jeans and a t-shirt, maybe her father's old leather jacket on top. She should have sang something that meant something to *her*. Jonathan Richman, maybe. Or Lou Reed. Bowie. She should have been cool, should have made a mark. Could have, if she'd just been someone *different*. Instead, she had plodded through five minutes of repetitious notes, whispering "crimson and clover, over and over," over and over and over again until finally the song was done and she was released from the prison of their watching eyes.

It had been painful, and in the days that followed, remembering her humiliation, she was struck with her very first migraine, one lasting three whole days. Her mother initially believed that she'd been faking it, that she had merely been embarrassed. She was, but of course, that wasn't the problem. Still, by the time she'd returned to school, the experience had been forgotten by everyone, or nearly everyone. Because Cymbeline hadn't forgotten.

Now Camp Berean's co-director, Lonnie, was asking all the children to be quiet, holding his hand aloft in a symbol the boys called "quiet coyote" (this wasn't used on the girl's side, at all, and now the few girls scattered about looked around in confusion while two of them continued whispering, until a boy elbowed one in the ribs, and she shut up, fast). He seemed too old to work for a camp, a kind of dumpy little guy who really belonged in an office, or wrestling with his own children on some grubby rec room carpet. When he finally had the attention of the campers, he introduced the first talented participant.

He called up Sadie Edelman. But then, when she gave him a look, he corrected himself: Sid.

She'd brought her hacky sacks, and she did what Cymbeline had finally figured was her usual routine—cracking jokes, dropping them once, cracking more jokes, dropping them again. Now the children were really excited. Maybe she couldn't juggle? Maybe it was all a trick? It made it all the more amazing when she finally did it, successfully, and with flourish. Chucking them all high, toward the library rafters, then spinning and catching them all at once. Cymbeline had a sudden vision: Sid as a child, with short hair that was more like the boys here than the girls. Waiting, bored, outside her own cabin for the other girls to finish gossiping or playing *Ouija* board or whatever normal girls might do, while Sid, who was only Sadie then, threw a bruised apple or two in the air over and over again until finally, and without fail, she could catch it.

It was the kind of hobby you only got by being an outsider. The kind that only worked when you needed something to fill your hands. Good for a party, maybe, but also bad for a party—because it meant that you weren't like an ordinary person. You weren't talking. You were doing *tricks*. Drawing attention to yourself, while also diverting attention away.

Cymbeline could understand that impulse well enough. But the simultaneous hunger she saw in Sid—for attention, for worship, for taking up space—was harder to wrap her mind around. She had never really wanted anything more than to be anonymous. So what was she doing *here*, now, shuffled beside a bunch of cross-dressed campers made to look like the Backstreet Boys, waiting for her turn?

Sid finished, catching the hacky sacks in her snap-back cap, finishing with a bow. The campers applauded politely, and Sid, having apparently forgiven Cymbeline, returned to her side.

"How'd I do?" she asked, sweaty and breathless, kissing Cymbeline on the cheek.

"Great," Cymbeline said, and she meant it, but it sounded disingenuous—her attention was mostly inward focused now, on herself, and what was about to happen.

"Hey," said Sid. She took Cymbeline's hand, apparently not caring that there were ten year olds watching. "Hey. Are you freaking out?"

Cymbeline looked at Sid, her eyes wide and wild and almost tearful. And nodded, quickly.

"Hey," Sid said again. "You'll do great. You *are* great. Okay?"

"Okay," Cymbeline said. The gymnasts were performing right now, careful and repetitious handstands. But they were almost done. She didn't feel okay, but Sid wanted her to fake it. So she forced a smile. "Okay!"

Sid gave her hand another squeeze, but Cymbeline's fingers were numb as the assistant director introduced her as Perky. Some boy in the audience whistled, and as Cymbeline stepped up to the little staging area—too small, too rustic for even a microphone—Sid thrust a finger toward the audience and shouted.

"Hey! Watch it!"

Hoots and howls. But in a way, that helped. The attention was off of Cymbeline for a moment and onto Sid. Cymbeline let her eyes scan the small gathered crowd. It was getting darker, the light turning nearly purple in the rustic library, and these were *children*, only children. Why, then, did their presence conjure images of some other sort of beast? Like a biblical angel, with a million arms, legs, more eyes than she could count, and a mouth, made of many mouths, hungry for her. She had seen something like this—felt something like this—before. This expectancy. She put her guitar in front of her, let her fingers touch the strings, and in the back of her head there was a humming and she knew that she would have a headache later, definitely. But she also knew that they were waiting for her—Lonnie and Neil. All these children. And Sid.

She glanced at Sid. Sid was nodding, making encouraging motions with her hands. It was time for Cymbeline to stop dithering. It was time for her to make a noise.

So she did.

* * *

She didn't win the dinky little trophy from Lonnie that night. That honor went to Neil, who, she could reluctantly concede, put on a better show than she did. He'd sung three songs, two by The Ruffians and one of his own, dancing along to them with a certain wild abandon even though his own song was awful, with a chord progression stolen from Canon in D and lyrics that seemed to say the same thing over and over. *My girl doesn't want me. Whoa whoa whoa.*

Cymbeline had sung her own song too. Just the one. A song she'd written for Sid, here and there, while leading her charges down the trail and in the back of her head while fucking. It was a song about a girl who looked like Peter Pan but never made her feel like Wendy, a song for a girl who, she sensed, had been leading her somewhere better all along. *This isn't only Neverland*, the chorus started, and she meant here, camp. Corny, maybe, but the emotion was true enough. Cymbeline did her best with her performance, bobbing up and down a little, belting out the words as loudly as she could stand. It was nothing like her middle school humiliation;

it was passable, cromulent, even, but she could sense how the little boys were bored and the attention of the girls, prepubescent and nervous, was not quite yet enough. Maybe later, with puberty, when everyone's desires boiled over.

She did her best, and it was goodish but not enough to win. As Neil took the trophy, Cymbeline thought about how it seemed easier to be a boy. You were allowed to say ridiculous things, to take up space, to move the way you wanted. She wasn't the sort of pretty that demanded attention, but maybe, if she'd been a boy, she could have been cool and funny the way that Neil was cool and funny—pumping a fist in the air, thanking the academy. She would have liked that. Maybe in another life.

"You did great, baby," Sid said to her after, nuzzling her cheek as they stood on the wide porch outside and watched the moon lift itself over the lake.

Cymbeline snorted. "Not well enough to win."

"You care about that?" Sid asked, pulling back. It was funny. Because she wasn't used to being competitive, to caring about what other people thought. But in a way, it was true, she did. She nodded.

"I've never wanted anything more than I've ever wanted that stupid trophy," she said. Sid snort-laughed.

"Well," she said, "There's always next summer."

Next summer. Cymbeline looked out toward the water, closing her eyes, hearing the tiny waves. This was the first time Sid had mentioned any notion of a future to come. The assumption, then, that Cymbeline would be here—that, undoubtedly, Sid would be here, too.

"Hey! Great song!"

Cymbeline turned, her body still wrapped in the warm hold of Sid's arms. There was Neil, hefting his own guitar case, and Lonnie beside him.

"You, too," Cymbeline lied, just to seem game. Neil shrugged.

"It was fine. I've never written a song before. You have, though?"

Cymbeline bit her lip, nodded. The truth was, she had notebooks full of them. Some with music, some with only words that needed music still, and someday, she knew, she would write them, and the world would be just a little bit more perfect and right.

"There's an open mic next week," Neil said, "At this bar outside Oneonta. They hold it once a month, cash prizes. I think they'd like your stuff. It's a quieter crowd. Older. Not like these assholes."

He jerked a thumb back toward the library, indicating the boys inside and their general raucousness.

"Hm," Cymbeline said carefully. "Cool."

Neil looked at her for a minute, frowning, and added, "You should come. You're really good."

She felt the weight of his compliment, but not the meaning. She couldn't feel anything like *good*, like *pride*. She'd been too carefully trained not to, too deliberately taught that with any triumph came an equal and often worse dose of tragedy. She smiled a little vaguely, and once that would have been everything, but she had Sid beside her, and *that* shifted the weight of the air.

"She'll be there," Sid said, loudly. "We both will. But we'll need a ride."

Neil glanced at Lonnie, and they both lifted their eyebrows as if to suggest something untoward.

"Yeah, sure," Lonnie said. "It's a date."

"No, it's not," snapped Sid, and Cymbeline could see even in the dim porch light how Sid's face had gone ruddy but Neil and Lonnie only laughed and headed for the steps.

"Sure thing, Sadie," Lonnie said. "I mean *Sid*." More laughter, though Cymbeline couldn't see what was funny about it as they walked down the stairs together, leaving the two girls alone under the glittering blanket of night.

"Fucking pricks," Sid said, and she leaned over and grabbed Cymbeline's guitar case for her. "C'mon, Cymbeline. Let's get back to real life."

Cymbeline wasn't exactly sure what she meant, but she trailed after her, down the narrow, rickety steps.

* * *

The darkness that had settled in on the paths between the two camps meant that Cymbeline stepped carefully, heel toe, heel toe, to avoid tripping on a branch or a stone. Sid had no such hesitation. She was all prickly anger tonight, and Cymbeline wasn't sure entirely why, until at last they reached the shoulder of the road that joined the two camps together.

"Finally," Sid said, and exhaled, audibly, "I fucking hate it there."

"Berean?" asked Cymbeline, climbing over the guard rail. "I don't know. It's pretty nice."

Sid didn't answer. Her not answering made a sound louder than any silence, which Cymbeline felt desperate to fill.

"I mean," said Cymbeline. "It seems nicer than Camp Kaaterskill, if you ask me."

Sid snorted.

"What?"

"I mean!" Sid began, those two words an exclamation unto themselves, "Of course it is! Those pricks all network with each other and then get jobs from their rich daddies and come back and pour money into the endowment, but only for Berean, but not Kaaterskill, because they only care if their sons have a good time, not their daughters!"

Cymbeline waited a moment before answering. "But you love Kaaterskill," she said at last.

"Yeah," said Sid. "Yeah, it's *fine*. But . . ."

She stopped on the road, glancing back to where the closest boy's village sat, light in a jagged grove of pine trees.

"Being *there* always felt like a sign I wasn't supposed to be *here*. And, you know, I used to think it was just because it's sexist as hell. Because it is, sexist as hell. And it's bullshit because of that. Because *obviously* the girls should have access to the Magical Hobbit Library, too, and not just the boys. But I also realized that if *they* were in crappy old Camp Kaaterskill, if the *boys* were there, it wouldn't bother me as much that it was crappy because it would be, like, where I fucking belong."

Cymbeline stared at Sid. She narrowed her eyes, taking the other girl's sharp, muscular, tousle-haired silhouette in. And she understood something fully, for the first time.

"Oh, *Sid*," she said, perhaps too gently, because Sid cringed when she said it, hefted the guitar case higher in her hand, and kept walking. Cymbeline trailed after.

"It's fine," Sid said. "It's fine."

"Of course it's fine," Cymbeline agreed. Then she stumbled over the words, not sure if they were right. "If you're a—a transsexual."

Sid snorted again.

"I mean, really, I don't care! You know I like boys, too."

She struggled to keep up with Sid, glimpsing the whites of Sid's eyes as she rolled them expansively. "Sure, it might be okay for you, Perky, but can you imagine what I'm risking? My dad—I mean, he's ancient. He's so checked out he probably won't care. But my brother? And my mom?"

Cymbeline knew almost nothing about Sid's mother except that she was from a wealthy family who had been disappointed when she'd gotten pregnant while still in college. She knew that Sid's mother had forced her into lacy Passover dresses and on mother-daughter spa trips, but she'd thought that had been a more general sort of misunderstanding rather than something deeper.

"Sometimes I envy you, Perky," Sid said, and Cymbeline braced herself, because she knew what was about to come—and she knew it was going to hurt. "Seems to me sometimes that it would be easier to be an orphan."

Don't cry, that's what Cymbeline told herself, standing there in the road, watching Sid walk away. *Don't cry.* So her eyes only went big and watery at the edges, even though her chin trembled. It took a moment for Sid to realize. She stopped in the road, turned. Stared. Then, when she saw Cymbeline, all the tension seemed to dissolve from her body.

"Oh," she said.

"Fuck," she said. And then added, "Cymbeline, I'm *so sorry.*"

It was the sympathy that was the worst, was always the worst. And right now, Cymbeline could do nothing but take it. She dissolved into rough, shaking tears, and Sid came to her and folded her into a hug.

"Fuck," she said. "Sorry. Sorry."

She held Cymbeline while Cymbeline trembled, and cried. And as her tears slowed, she kissed them, and her snot-slick lips, and her hair, moist, now, with tears, too.

"No, no," Cymbeline said, not wanting to be misunderstood, because she knew, in a way, the freedom she had now. Freedom that Sid didn't share. "No, it's okay. It's just . . ."

She reached her hand down and interlaced her fingers with Sid's.

"It's better, not to be alone. Trust me. It's so much better." She laughed a little. Sid laughed, too. Then, Cymbeline added, "You—you don't have to be alone with this. Not anymore."

Sid looked at her, and smiled then. Tight-lipped, but real, her eyes crinkling at the edges.

<h1 style="text-align:center">23 - 1958</h1>

Back at college, ignoring Sue Grasso, who *did* look keen with her hair all pale and her eyes all dark, but not keen enough to want to go talk to her, because he knew she would contain the same small thoughts in her head she always had. Instead, spending all his energy drawing naked ladies, their tits pointed and dangling, with a ground-down charcoal, the dust getting all over his face. Baron wondered what the point was to this all, because this had been Deedz' dream, not his own. He wasn't going to become an art teacher now, was he? Well, then maybe he would become a regular Van Gogh. Cut off his own ear and all of that. See color swirling in every corner in an insane asylum. It was almost like being a rock musician, being an artist, wasn't it? Fame and brilliance and madness all caked up into one. Almost—almost enough that he could pretend—but he knew it wouldn't be the same for him, would never be the same for him. His heart wanted music now, even if music was now out of reach. Fuck. He'd cursed himself, then, for wanting more than this. He tucked the nubby charcoal behind his ear and pulled on his coat, went outside to smoke himself a fag.

He was in the back alleyway beside the art college, a space littered with cigarette butts and broken glass, when he heard footsteps approach. At first, he assumed it must be Dickie, was almost resigned to the idea that it was Dickie, because who else would come find him in this cold, puddly space? Was probably going to rape him, and his heart hitched at the thought of it, the wanting, and the not-wanting. Both.

But when he turned, it wasn't Dickie's dark Irish eyes that greeted him.

It was Eddie. Bundled in a smart pea coat, his school uniform looking crisp beneath. And if the thought of Dickie had made his pulse speed, now it was racing. Baron tightened his scarf around his cheeks, hoping to hide how they burned.

"I found you," said Eddie. "I thought you were dropping out, son."

"You found me," agreed Baron, and said no more than that. He had that fear, which visited him often, since nine or ten or so, that other people could somehow read his thoughts. What if Ed knew what he'd been wanking about? Maybe not mind-reading or telepathy like in the science fiction rags he sometimes read on the khazi but rather because it was plain, somehow, on Baron's face. So he tried to rearrange his features into something resembling normal Baron-ness. A tight-lipped frown, brow low.

"Don't look so happy about it, Barry," Eddie said. Then he reached for Baron's cigarette, plucked it from his fingers like a flower, and took a drag.

His lips, Baron thought helplessly. *His lips touching the paper that my lips have touched. My saliva just inside the pucker of his mouth. And the smoke, which I have tasted, lacing its way inside his body. Tucking itself inside his lungs.*

That strange wave of feeling rushed through his belly, delicious and painful. If he were a girl, this would be called a crush. But Baron was not a girl, and Eddie wasn't a girl either. There was no word for this. He coughed, raking a hand through his dark hair, and looked away.

"Well," Baron said, because it was easier to be cruel. "We're not in a band anymore. We're not really even mates anymore, are we?"

"Cor," Eddie said. "Really? Baron, you're worse than a bird."

"What do you know about birds, son?" Baron pressed, because even at times like these he could not resist teasing. Especially teasing Eddie. "You're as pure as the Virgin Mary." He pressed hands together, looked saintly. He expected Eddie to giggle—had been craving the sound of it. But Eddie looked dire at the pronouncement, finishing up the ciggy and crushing it underfoot.

"Not anymore, *son.*"

This made Baron stand straighter, to examine Eddie with a greater level of scrutiny. And here he'd been worried that Ed could see the changes sin had made in *him*, had never even been looking for signs of sin in Eddie. But could it be true? Ed's face was boyish, rounded, still as it always was. But his jaw was set firmer, making the dimple in his chin more clear. And his gaze had a directness about it that it hadn't always before. Baron found it hard to imagine that this was the same Eddie who had cried once about getting cancer all in his ma's tits.

"Awwww," said Baron, beaming, clapping Eddie on the back once, hard. "That's our kid! That's alright, Ed!"

Eddie laughed a little, a gruff tiny chuckle. "Yeah, Barry," he said, blushing slightly. "Yeah, yeah."

"But who?" asked Baron. Ed's eyes darted back and forth across the empty alley, as though he were searching for prying ears. Then a sly smile curled his lips.

"Not here, Barry," he said. "Come with me back to me house. Then I'll give you all the sordid details."

Baron arched an eyebrow, standing straight. But he could not stop from grinning. "Tease," he said.

Eddie did not deny it.

∗ ∗ ∗

They piled their overcoats and school bags next to the door. Had Eddie's father been home, he never would have abided by it. Ed the senior might not have been one for dusting, was no Aunt Deedz—but the house was tidy enough. Had to be with this many boys in it. Earlier in the year, Baron had begun to grown accustomed to the naval regulations that were often in effect at the Hammond abode. A place for everything. Everything in a place. So he could feel Eddie exhale in a way when it was just the two of them, and his own relief matched it. Him and Eddie. Alone again. Which of course reminded him of his evening fantasies, the throbbers he'd wake with and have to hide from sweet old Bess on his way to the WC.

"I wanted to show you something, Baron," Eddie said, and rushed into the little dining room where the upright piano sat waiting. Baron followed,

182

slowly, carefully, because this felt like an epilogue, somehow, and he was afraid to get too comfortable here, even though his instinct was to treat Eddie's home like the second home it had become.

"A song?" Baron asked, leaning on the door jamb, his arms crossed. Eddie laughed a little again.

"Yeh," he said. "What else?"

He began playing. Heavy hands on keys, working chords out of nothing. It wasn't a rock song, or even the perky dance hall numbers the Hammond boys usually played together. No, instead it was somber, almost tragic—and beautiful. There were no words, just Eddie's fingers working the melody and his voice, occasionally, lifting over the sound of the piano, a sweet, wordless hum.

It went on for awhile. Baron eventually sat down at one of the dining chairs, his arms draped over it, watching. The song was perfect. Complex. More stunning than anything Baron could have ever written, and he felt a small stab of jealousy at that even though he knew it was all wrong, too, for a rock band—whether that band was The Bartlebys or Dylan Miranda's Tempests.

"What's this for, then?" he asked, talking over the chords loudly enough that Eddie stopped playing completely and turned on the piano bench to look at him.

"Wot?"

"I don't see any use of it," Baron said, then added, in his worst fake American accent, "Ain't rock 'n' roll."

Eddie smirked a little bit. "Ain't s'posed to be rock 'n' roll. It's a love song. For Genie."

"What!" Baron sputtered, standing up. Laughed so hard that his stomach ached, or maybe it was another feeling, underneath the ache—but he couldn't admit that to himself. "Eugenia Waller!"

"Yeah," Eddie said, "Eugenia Waller. Who d'ya think I stuck it to?"

Baron, still laughing, barely croaked the words out. "Son, she's twelve!"

"She's fourteen," Eddie said, too seriously. "And she's got bigger tits than your Sue Grasso."

"Yeah," Baron conceded, wiping the tear from her eye. "She does, Hammy. But she's a *baby*. I don't see what you could possibly see in her."

Eddie narrowed his eyes, said again, "She's got bigger tits than your Sue Grasso," as if that were the beginning and end of it. Baron snorted. But now he was sounding harder, less tickled than before. His real feelings, leaking out.

"Dunno why you would want to screw a female version of Liam."

"Oh," said Eddie, one eyebrow raised, "You don't, do you?"

But Baron couldn't act like he understood the implication of that. "Well," he said, "At least you're sticking it to someone. Finally." The last word was pointed, a weapon. Baron knew it was safer, easier, to focus on Hammy's prior, humiliating virginity. Because Eddie had been the last of his mates to screw a bird, or at least to *admit* to being the last of them, too sweet and too good to *pretend* he was screwing birds even if he wasn't, like the rest of them. "Was she good, at least? Did she suck it?"

Eddie stared at Baron for a long moment. Shrugged. Annoyance still clouding his eyes. "Yeah, she sucked it. I finished about half a bar after I put it in her, though. Would almost have a wank, you know? Maybe it'll be better, next time."

"Yeah," Baron said. He sat back down, this time in the chair right next to the piano bench. Their knees almost touching. It was exciting to talk to Eddie about it in a way that was difficult to hide. *Would almost have a wank, yeah?* He reached out and slapped Eddie's thigh with the back of his hand. Not precisely a flirt. But not *not* a flirt. "Plenty a time to practice."

Eddie, blushing again, cheeks all poppy mottled. Whatever Baron had thought about Eddie being newly grown through his loss of virginity had clearly been a mistake. "Yeah, sure. But Baron, the song."

Baron stared at him, then let his gaze flit to the piano. He could have been cruel now, been cutting. But they both would have known it was a lie.

"It's an all-right song, son. Smashing."

"Yeah?"

"Yeah. But you better not let those Tempests hear it. They'll think you're a queer."

Eddie shrugged. "'Snot for them. Told you, it's for Genie."

"Good," said Baron.

"'Cept I can't figure out the words."

"Hmm," said Baron. "Nothing?"

Eddie turned toward the keys again. "Almost nothing," he said. "Nonsense. I thought maybe something like . . ."

He began playing again. The same tender melody. The same angry chords. "Dear love—I'm no fool. I'm thinking of linking my life to you . . ."

Baron cringed. From the corner of his eye, Eddie saw Baron cringe, and the notes faded off.

"I know," Ed said. "It's awful."

"'Sfine," Baron said. But they both knew he was lying.

"You're better at this stuff, Baron. The sappy stuff. I thought you could help me, maybe. You know, write the words for Genie."

Baron sat back in his chair, folding his arms over his chest. His heart felt swollen and painful at the compliment. At the irony. That Eddie wanted him to write a love song. For someone else.

"Dunno. Don't have much time to play anymore. You know. I've got school, and all."

Eddie's eyebrow ticked up. When he answered he sounded serious, which made Baron feel even worse. "That's a shame son."

Baron's cheeks heated. "I'm working on *art*, darling."

"Music is art. Darling," Eddie answered. "You know, I used to think the band mattered to you—"

But Baron couldn't hear the rest of it. He shook his head fiercely, standing up. Shoving his hands in his pocket. Leaving the room.

"Fine," Baron said. "I'll help you with your song for your sweet Eugenia Waller, then."

"Good," said Eddie. He stood, too, following Baron out of the dining room. Standing nearby as Baron pulled on his coat. "And I'll see you at your birthday, then?"

"Birthday," Baron grunted. "Next week, yeah?"

"Yeah, your mum called me up."

Baron snorted once again, an almost automatic response. It was something about the idea of his *mum* calling up *Ed*. The absurdity of it. Ed was his, but he wasn't, really, was he? Not in a way anybody else could have understood. Certainly not his mum, who thought she owned the world, and every man inside it.

"Yeh," Baron said. "Sure."

He would have left Eddie's house and would have left it at that. But Eddie was stepping closer to him over his pile of discarded outerwear and schoolbooks. Until they stood just a little too close to one another, and eye to eye. Eddie was looking at him through his long-lashed eyes, his gaze flickering from point to point around Baron's face. Baron felt his lips open, the breath in his chest gone shallow, and he thought about all the things he'd imagined and everything he'd hoped for and wondered if maybe, finally, it was all about to come true.

But Eddie didn't kiss him. Instead he reached out, his fingertips brushing Baron's rough cheek, and took the piece of charcoal from behind his ear.

"Here," Eddie said softly. "Wouldn't want you to forget about this."

Baron took it. Holding it. Feeling absurd. But the thing that happened next was even absurd-er, for Eddie let his tongue dart out and licked the pad of his thumb, then gently drew his thumb along Baron's cheekbone.

"Had a little there," he said. Baron felt his diaphragm contract, a small breath, of laughter, maybe, or something else.

"Yeh," Baron said. "Thanks. Ta."

And then, before the moment could linger one moment longer, before he could shrivel up and die inside from the yearning and the wanting and the desire, he hoofed it out of Eddie's house, slamming the door behind him.

24 - 2017

Through the peephole Matthew glimpsed Naomi standing on the doorstep to the Edelman abode. The morning was bright, still, and lightly swirled with massive snowflakes. When he looked at her, and the mountain tumbling down behind her, and the lake, all lit up with too-bright sunshine, he saw another ancient flash of childhood: turning a snow globe over, pretending that whatever lived inside was real. Of course, she *was* real. She was here. In the flesh, whatever the providence that that flesh might have been. He hiked his ratty old robe tighter over his belly, which had been getting paunchier than he liked in his descent into middle age, and opened the door.

Naomi had been smiling, a serene, practiced smile—until she saw him, with his robe and his disheveled, thinning hair, and the bags under his eyes, dark, like bruises—and her smile fell. Now she scowled, an adolescent sort of expression crossing a face which *must*, by his calculations and if her story were true, have seen just as many years as his own.

"Christ," she said, "You're drunk. How are we supposed to write if you're drunk already?"

Matthew flattened his mouth into a grim line. "I'm not," he said, even though his stomach clenched a little bit in the moment, and he felt his body sway, betraying him. "I'm hungover."

It was a useless distinction. Her pupils had gone tiny in her dark eyes. "Either way," she said. "You need to sober up."

She locked down at her watch, a slender, plastic-banded Casio, the kind you could find at any drug store. The kind of watch a poor person would wear.

"Ten minutes," she said. "You have ten minutes. Go get dressed and meet me out here. We're going for a walk. The fresh air will do you good."

Matthew felt the simian confusion of his expression, hated it. Hated her. Who was she to tell him what to do? She was a nobody, probably, a great pretender. And he was the son of Edmund Matthew Hammond III, a superstar.

Why, then, did he close the door firmly, turn toward the stairwell, and do exactly as she'd said?

* * *

He couldn't pretend that he looked fresh in yesterday's clothes, his teeth unbrushed and without a single drop of caffeine in him as he followed Naomi down the mountain. But she had been right about one thing: the fresh air felt good in his lungs. He was used to city air, garbagey in patches even in the winter. This was nothing like that. Pines dotted the edges of the long driveway and they loaned a cool, minty quality to the atmosphere, like Christmas distilled. It was sharp and true and almost fake, like the smell of his apartment after the cleaning woman visited. Only it wasn't fake. It was real. Nature. Matthew's stomach felt thick and oceanic; the taste of bile was sharp on the back of his tongue. But these Catskill mountains contained their own sort of magic, and they worked their way inside him, waking him to life, one cell at a time.

Naomi was walking briskly, hardly looking back at his ambling progress. He watched the angular shape of her denim-clad legs. It reminded him of someone, something he'd seen on television or something. And then he realized: it was from Saffron's first movie. Templeton, in black and white, drainpipe trousers and a leather jacket, picking up garbage along the banks of the River Mersey. That had been their artsy period, the early '60s. Heavy French influence, before his old Dad Eddie had wrestled control of the band away from Baron.

He still didn't know what to think. What to believe. Maybe she planned to walk him down the mountain and murder him and sack Edelman's house for its precious music industry memorabilia. Stranger things happened sometimes to the children of celebrities. He thought of Abigail Folger, heiress to the coffee fortune—murdered decades ago with Sharon Tate. There had been a span of time when he'd been obsessed with stories like those, much to Kara's chagrin—staying up all night, reading Wikipedia articles on his phone. *Why do you get yourself all worked up all the time? You have everything in the world you've ever wanted.* Now he heard her voice in his head, and snorted softly to himself at the thought of it. The truth was, right now, any anxiety was manufactured. Despite himself—despite all the paranoia that he rationally knew he should have held as this perfect stranger escorted him away into the middle of nowhere—he held none of it. It felt comfortable here, walking beside her underneath a wide gray stretch of sky.

It felt like he'd known her for years.

"What?" she said, in a curt, snappish voice, whipping her head around. He realized that he'd been staring at her, that she must have felt the insistent pressure of his eyes.

"Nothing," Matthew lied, then added, "I was just wondering what the heir presumptive to the Templeton fortune is doing here in the middle of nowhere."

Naomi seemed to be barely listening. She didn't slow her pace. "It's not an interesting story," she said. "And you know I'm not after his money. Or yours."

"No?"

"No. It's the *music* that matters to me."

"That's nice," Matthew said blandly, not sure if he believed it, though of course he remembered the way she'd pounded at those keys the night before, like her life depended on it. "Interesting or not, tell me the story, anyway."

She looked taken aback, like she wasn't used to being pushed like this. Maybe she wasn't. She had a certain swagger to her that he recognized. It was his own.

"Well," she said, looking in the other direction as she spoke, "My mother was dying. She didn't have insurance for hospice or anything like that. The Edelmans were her friends. They'd been friends for years. Cymbeline told me we could stay in their house. I kind of fell in love with this place. Never wanted to leave. Got a sublet down the mountain, then a lease. You know. The usual bullshit."

She said it so bluntly, though it was a world away from Matthew's life. He'd never rented anything, much less sublet it. Matthew stopped on the road, turning back toward the Edelman house at the top of the mountain for a moment, squinting. "She died there."

"Yup," said Naomi, popping her lips. She hadn't stopped walking, so now Matthew had to scurry to catch up.

"Does it scare you?" Naomi asked. She still wasn't looking at him, "To be staying in the same house where an old woman died?"

"No," Matthew said simply. He wasn't about to tell her about his own mother's death. It was too much for him to talk about at the best of times, and here, with her, wasn't the best—even if he did feel a certain heady sort of comfort with her. Like an old favorite t-shirt forgotten at the back of one's closet, discovered again, years later. He added, "I'm not a child."

It was her turn to stop, frowning, at the center of the path. But he didn't stop to look back at her. This time, Matthew was the one who soldiered on down the mountain.

* * *

There was a town at the bottom, if you could call it that. More of a village, really. A post office, and a hipster cafe that catered to the New Yorkers who had come upstate to laze about in VRBOs, and a divey looking bar that was closed, of course, this early in the day and probably on Sundays, too. Across a two-lane road, in a nest of mountain and scrubby bush, there was a general store. Matthew started to cross, but Naomi put her hand out, holding it against his arm. He looked at it there, feeling the small, steady pressure of her fingers, as a truck whizzed by them. The nails were short and unpainted. The fingers were sturdy, broad. A musician's fingers. He knew the type. But she didn't seem to notice how he was looking at her, or how she was touching him.

"You have to watch out," she said, "These rural drivers aren't used to pedestrians." She crossed briskly, her hand leaving his arm like it had never been there at all.

"I grew up in the country, you know," he said. He didn't know, actually, what she knew about him.

"Oh yeah?" she asked, lifting an eyebrow.

"In Scotland."

"Ex-patriot child?" she asked with a grin as she held the door of the market open for him. He hesitated, not used to this kind of gesture from a woman—not expecting the gentle tease in her voice. It was a reference to one of his father's '70s tunes.

Combat or conquest. Aside from his mother—and even her, when he had been twelve or thirteen or so and briefly decided he hated her—that's what women had always been to him. Naomi was something else though. Congenial. As they stepped inside, she offered: "My mother was born in Trinidad, and lived in London for awhile, but I've never been out of the country."

The market was small, dusty, lit by fluorescent bulbs that both flickered and buzzed. The over packed shelves and strange lighting made it difficult for Matthew to account for what she was saying—the implication of it all, heavier than he liked.

"Trinidad," he echoed. Because he knew that bad things had happened in Trinidad. Unspeakable things. There was an old man behind the counter, wearing a faded red cap and a worn-out flannel shirt, soft with pills. His skin, too, seemed faded, gray and pocked, and when the two of them entered the store and began winding their way up the small aisles, he let out a phlegmy cough at the sight of them, apparently his version of a greeting. Naomi grunted, distracted, looking through the crinkly bags of chips.

"Trinidad," Matthew said again. He squinted. Meanwhile, Naomi cringed.

"Go ahead," she said. "If you have to ask, ask."

But Matthew didn't have a question. He'd already figured it out. "She was part of Peter X.'s crew."

Naomi's mouth went flat. She grabbed a few bags of Flamin' Hot Cheetos, tucking them against the nest of her sweater, and nodded. She wasn't looking him in the eye.

"Yeah," she said. "Sure. But by the time she had me, she was done. Ready to settle down. My dad—"

"We all know what happened to your dad," Matthew said. It had been on every news station in the world, not just in the weeks that followed the murders but every single year after, on the anniversary of Baron Templeton's death. Matthew had been too young to follow the coverage when it happened, and beside—they hadn't had a TV. It wasn't until he was ten or eleven that he'd seen what everyone else had, that he'd learned the full scope of the truth.

The image had burned itself into his mind. It was grainy footage of a grainier photo: Baron face down in the jungle, a burlap sack over his head. He remembered the splatters of dried blood over Baron Templeton's dark arms and the darker dirt that formed his bed. It had been days before the police had found him. By that time—Matthew had been told, on the eve of the fifteenth anniversary, on a rare night when his father had been too drunk to maintain his usual chipper facade—animals had eaten away at most of his face. He'd been cremated in the Port of Spain, and the casket they eventually interred in London had been empty—a hollow pantomime.

Now Matthew cast his eyes to the floor, which was covered in dirty asbestos tiling. Naomi didn't say a word. Instead, she went to the counter and dumped her bounty there. Two bags of Cheetos. One packet of supreme pizza Combos. Two crispety crunchety Butterfinger bars. It was the kind of food that Matthew loved in secret, but rarely ate, especially lately. They were *supposed* to be cleaning up their diets with the baby coming and all.

Anyway, he didn't have much of an appetite.

Naomi looked at him, at his grim expression. "These should fill the hole inside," she offered wryly. Somehow the joke-that-wasn't-quite-a-joke poked a chink in the wall of darkness. Matthew picked up a packet of Hostess cupcakes and squinted at them, considering.

"The famous celebrity father murder-suicide death cult hole?" he asked carefully, uncertainly, glimpsing Naomi out of the corner of his eye. It was the kind of a joke that would have gotten him in trouble with Kara. There were certain things that were serious to her—sacred. Absent fathers were definitely one of them. But Naomi wasn't Kara. She grinned broadly, then let out a cackle. It was the kind of relieved, maniacal laughter that couldn't be faked.

"Will that be all, kids?" the old man behind the counter cut in, laughing a little, too like he thought he was part of the joke. Naomi's own chuckles trailed off to nothing. She took a breath, held it, putting both of her broad, strong hands flat against the counter. Then she sighed.

"I'll take two egg and cheese sandwiches, Lon," she said, and she spoke like she knew this guy well—but didn't particularly like him. "And two coffees. One black. Matthew, how do you take yours?"

Matthew wasn't usually wasn't much of a coffee drinker. Usually went for tea, the last flag of his British heritage. But he shrugged.

"Light and sweet," he said, and the old man behind the counter snorted at this like it was some kind of a joke.

"Sure, beautiful," Lon said, turning away to microwave their sandwiches for them. As he did, Naomi glanced over at Matthew, who in turn stuffed his hands in his coat pockets, waiting. The old guy put their wrapped sandwiches on the counter, then the pair of coffees. As he added them to their order, Naomi got out her wallet, but Matthew rolled his eyes and intercepted her, placing a crisp, bright hundred down on the counter.

"Big spender," said Lon, marking the bill with a counterfeiting pen. His hazy eyes flitted briefly up at Matthew. A line creased the rough, sparsely haired space between his eyebrows. Matthew felt his stomach clench, but wasn't sure if it was the hangover or an emotion he was more accustomed to: dread.

"Do I know you?" he asked. "Former camper, maybe?"

"No," Matthew said quickly, his stomach squeezing. He didn't want this now, here. He let the man, still frowning, count the change into his hand. In the periphery of his vision Matthew saw Naomi watching him. Her lips twisted wryly. "I'm not from here."

The man shrugged. "So many kids passing through. They all run together sometimes."

"He's not a camper," Naomi cut in. She sounded eager, almost excited to spill the beans. "That's Matthew Hammond. You know, Eddie Hammond's son." Matthew cringed. He hadn't wanted her to share that—but he supposed there was no way for *her* to know. She was used to going unrecognized. Maybe this is what *she* had always wanted, to see the sudden, gnawing hunger in the eyes of gross old strangers like this one.

"Shit," said Lon. "Really? Like, Matthew from 'Matthew's Song'?"

"Mm-hmm," Naomi said. She was smirking. Enjoying this, Matthew was sure. Lonnie began to hum, and then, to his horror, both of them began to sing. Together. At once. The old man's garbled tenor, and her lower, smoother voice.

"My bonny boy, precious and true—the path forward has always been with you."

The last note warbled out unsteadily. Matthew felt himself die a million deaths inside. But somehow it wasn't as bad as it normally was. Because Naomi was looking at him with a sort of warm fondness to which he wasn't accustomed, and—worst of all—he was almost, halfway, enjoying it.

"Okay, okay," he said, doing his best to take it in stride. For Naomi's sake, he told himself. No need to make things awkward with the local merchants. The old man laughed, offering him a hand. Matthew hesitated a moment, and then he took it. Shook.

"Alright, then," Lon said. "It's my honor. You know we used to sing that one at camp? The kids loved it. Sobbed like babies on the last night campfire."

Matthew nodded, prying his hand away. He had no idea what the old man was talking about. He'd been to boarding school, but never camp.

He'd definitely never *cried* about saying goodbye to his classmates. He couldn't spare those kinds of feelings, not as a child—and not now, either.

"Lon used to run the camp across the lake," Naomi offered. "The one that Cymbeline went to when she was a kid."

"Nah," Lon said. "She wasn't a kid then. She was almost a grown-up. Brilliant when I met her, already."

Naomi smiled broadly. Matthew wondered, not for the first time, about the exact nature of Naomi's relationship with Edelman and his wife. How had they met, anyway? What had inspired this bald devotion? But he didn't get a chance to ask. Instead, Lon wagged his finger three times at Naomi, changing the subject.

"Speaking of—Naomi, how're the old ladies up the hill?"

Naomi's wide, exuberant smile fell now. It was like a door had slammed inside her. Her eyes narrowed to little slits. "They're fine. Give us our sandwiches, Lonnie."

The old man was laughing as he slid Naomi's snacks and the two sandwiches into a flimsy plastic bag. She took it, hugging it against her chest.

"You tell them I said hello, okay?" Lon said, clueless to the sudden drop in temperature in his little store.

"Yeah," Naomi said, and without another word she turned to leave, the bell on the door jangling behind her. Matthew shrugged, sipping at his coffee.

"Have a nice day, Lonnie," he said. The old man was still laughing, a phlegmy sound that seemed to catch and hitch in his throat.

"Yeah, kid," he said. "You have a bonny day, too."

Matthew smiled grimly. He followed Naomi outside, where she'd squatted on the concrete front steps to eat her sandwich.

"What was that all about?" Matthew asked. Naomi shook her head.

"That guy's a dick," was all she would say.

"Okay," Matthew said, pressing gently. Because, after all, she'd pressed him. "But I thought you hated 'Matthew's Song.'"

She snorted. "Just because I hate it doesn't mean I don't know it. I didn't grow up in a cave, you know."

Her tone was hot, defensive. He sighed and sat down next to her. He reached into the bag between her feet, fishing out his sandwich. The silence between them was heavy now. Strange. He'd fallen into a pattern of easy comfort with her, and more quickly than he had in . . . well, ever. Now he wondered if he'd only imagined it. He picked at the sandwich—the rubbery eggs, the dusty English muffin, the waxy yellow cheese. His stomach felt a conflicted wave of both hunger and nausea at the smell. But beside him, Naomi was eating. It seemed like the only thing left to do was to sip at his coffee and choke down a few bites too.

It had been silly, he thought to himself, to hope. Because there had never been anyone else like him in the universe before—not his sisters, who had been born *boring* despite coming from the same insane family. Not Barry or Charlie's kids. Not Kara. Not Pearl. They hadn't known what it was like to walk through the world with an ache to prove your worth to the universe, but never, not for a moment, knowing if you ever would. When he'd first seen Naomi, he'd hoped for a lover. Somehow, on this strange, queasy morning, that had all changed. He thought about how his Dad sometimes talked about his teenage days when his sister's kids were around—telling them about how they'd skipped school, wandering around Liverpool with a bottle in his pocket and a guitar case in hand, throwing stones with the other boys, being nuisances.

There had been no other boys for Matthew. He'd had followers, but never friends. He was too different, too special, too rich for that. He'd had the music in his head and plenty of girls, but nothing like this. Companionship. It had always been either sex or loneliness for Matthew, all because of Matthew's fucking song. For a moment, he'd thought Naomi could be something different.

Her knee was leaning into his. He thought it might be deliberate. He angled his own leg toward her, just a little. Their legs touching. But then she leaned away.

"Anyway," Naomi said, balling the sandwich wrapper in her hand and chucking it toward a nearby trash can, "Time to head back up there."

She slung the bag of remaining snacks over her shoulder. Matthew stood and felt the weight of his sandwich sink into his stomach like a turd into a toilet bowl. He felt a belch gurgle out of him. By the time he turned toward Naomi, she was already disappearing up the road.

** * **

There was a fact about Edmund Matthew Hammond III that had never made it into any trivia book. Namely, he was horrified about the thought of vomiting—downright phobic about it. So, while the other members of Saffron chewed morning glory seeds and choked down mushrooms—while his youngest, newest wife once dragged him to an ayahuasca ceremony in remote Peru—Eddie abstained. He drank on occasion, though less than the other lads. The others, of course, rarely stayed sober enough to notice. But at the rare moments when he overindulged, his stomach was like a steel drum. Not a leak in it. He'd go to bed queasy, but he never, ever *barfed*.

His son had always figured that it was the loss of control that bothered his father. The sense that your body was *doing something*. Without your consent. Control was very, very important to the elder Eddie, and while he'd softened his stance on trying to reign in the universe in general after Matthew's mum had died, he'd be damned if he let his own body walk away with him. His fear that he might succumb to a dreaded sick, so deep and visceral, had once manifested as anger—and this anger was the one gap in what Matthew would call an otherwise storybook upbringing.

He still remembered it: that night as a child when Matthew had caught a virus from one of the sweet-lipped village girls, when, just a few hours later, he tossed and turned in his freezing bedroom, and his stomach would not be still. The bed was almost like a boat to him, rocking, bucking. He was feverish, delirious—and afraid. When he called out, it was not for his mum. It was for his Dad, as usual. But the man who came to the door looked unfamiliar, white-faced and hesitant.

"Daddy," he'd called, and his ghastly pale father came closer, choking something back that Matthew didn't understand at six or seven or however old he was—too young to understand much of anything. Eddie Hammond had perched himself on the end of the bed, was just reaching out to touch Matthew's brow, when out of nowhere Matthew's body betrayed him—betrayed both of them—and emptied the full volume of that night's dinner on top of his dad.

His father, still for a moment in the sour-smelling room, did something he'd never done before. He raised a hand and smacked it against Matthew's poppy-red cheek.

It was the only time his father ever hit him. His father admitted his error the next day, after Matthew's stomach had been emptied and lightly dusted with soda crackers, and had begged for Matthew's forgiveness. But the anger and the fear were still there, and they both knew it, from the way that Ed Hammond hung back, even then, by the rough-hewn bedroom door. Matthew had only one or two other stomach illnesses in his childhood—less than an ordinary boy. But each time after, his father stayed away.

And so Matthew had, to a lesser extent, inherited the family curse. Emetophobia. He knew that there was no deeper shame than to have a soft stomach, to lose control, to let others see the things that had been churning inside you. Usually he could stave back his belly's impulses even while drunk, just like his old man did. But now, an ancient sense of dread and panic had begun to wash over him as they trekked higher and higher up the mountain.

He didn't speak. Couldn't, because his breath was too shallow, his mouth too full of saliva. He knew that Naomi could *not* see him like this, in a state that even Kara had never seen him. He could not be reduced before her, helpless and exposed. He thought for a moment about trying to duck into the bushes unnoticed. Naomi was already far up the path ahead. Perhaps she wouldn't see him go, wouldn't hear the mortifying noises that were bound to come out of his throat as he was sick over and over again. Because it was becoming increasingly obvious that he was about to be sick over and over again, and any minute now, too.

But it was too late. He'd stopped on the path, wondering if it might help if he caught his breath, leaning his hands on his knees and all of his weight against his hands, doubled over there, swaying. And Naomi noticed.

"Are you okay?" she called, and jogged back down to him. He opened his mouth. He was about to say yes, that she should go on without him, that it was nothing to worry about. But he couldn't manage words. All he could manage was to *not* repeat the mistake he'd made at six and a half. He didn't vomit *on* Naomi, at least. Instead he turned to the edge of the path and emptied the contents of his stomach, rubbery egg sandwich, vodka and all, right onto the base of a scrub pine.

It was humiliating to do this in front of her. To have his insides exposed, not to mention his lack of composure. When he was a child his father's anger had terrified him. Now he understood. It was shameful to have a body, and to lose control of it. And though tears were acceptable for women and children, and for men, at their father's funerals, and their children's births, and at no other time, they were not a means available to Hammond men to express themselves. Matthew vomited, and felt his body fill in the same hollow place with a prickly white hot rage—and that rage only swelled larger as Naomi stepped closer.

"Go awa—" he started to say, but his body overtook him again, and there was another powerful wave of half-digested food. But Naomi didn't go away. She put that broad, strong hand on his shoulder, and said to him in a knowing tone:

"Good. Good. Let it all out. Now that that's out of the way, we can get to work."

She spoke with calm and without a hint of disgust. Angry already, that's when Matthew realized: she had planned this all. She had *wanted* him to gnaw on that disgusting egg sandwich, had headed up the mountain like it was inconsequential, all the while knowing he was hungover, or still half-drunk. He'd been naive to think she was a friend, to allow themselves to settle into a pattern of amicability. They were not amicable. She was not amiable. She was a villain. A manipulator. She wanted to humiliate him in this, the worst, most shameful way—and for what? For music that *she* had decided *he* would write with *her*? Well, she had miscalculated. Underestimating him.

"Fuck *we*," he muttered, after spitting out one last brackish mouthful of bile. "I work alone."

But when he turned back, Naomi had already left him, disappearing up the mountain.

* * *

The gray morning light had faded, giving way to a pale blue afternoon sky. Naomi sat at the piano, back-lit by the sunshine, all shadow and darkness. Her hands were folded between her knees. Matthew sat in the mid-century recliner, his jaw set, looking surly at her. He hadn't gone to get his guitar. He hadn't gone to get anything. It felt like they'd been sitting there for hours in silence, her expectant eyes upon him, waiting for him to act first.

At last he sat forward in his chair. His mouth still tasted sour, like vomit. He knew he probably smelled like it, too. That didn't matter. She might have pushed him toward that mortifying scene on the mountain, but he wasn't going to be ashamed of it. He was the one in power here. The one with wealth. With pedigree. Who was she? A nobody.

"You think you're such an agent of chaos," he said at last, the disdain clear in his voice. She turned toward him, the dimple deep on her left cheek. She was playing coy.

"What?" she said. "Like from *Get Smart?*"

Matthew snorted. It was funny, in a grim way, but he wouldn't let her know it was. Instead, he stood up. But rather then of walking toward her, he went to the bar in the corner and found himself a bottle of expensive bourbon. Opened it. Even without looking at her, he could feel her response. A roll of the eyes, dismissive as he poured.

"You think you can waltz in here," he said, "And upset the apple cart. I have a *career*. I have a life."

"I don't want to upset anybody," Naomi said. He could feel her gaze against him, and hated how warm and calm it was, both. "I told you. I just want to make something worthwhile."

Matthew's hand paused as he put the cork back. She sounded sincere, and his anger almost broke, dissolved. But he couldn't let it. He put the bottle back on the bar, letting the glass hit wood a little harder than it needed to.

"Worth money," he said, turning to face her. He held the tumbler against his stomach, which was empty now—calm, clean. "You're a grifter."

Naomi winced. "I'm not. I told you. I'm friends with Cymbeline. It was her idea that we meet. You can call her if you want. Ask her."

"I don't believe you," Matthew said. "Why would she care?"

Naomi shrugged. "Don't ask me. She said she had a hunch we would get along. Edelman agreed. *He's* probably in it for the cash. But she isn't. She's never cared about money. If she did, don't you think she would put out another album? She cares about diddling around on her piano and talking about art and philosophy over drinks with her husband. *You* know what she's like. *You've* met her. She's not a grifter. And I'm not either."

"Well, she was wrong," Matthew said, ignoring everything that Naomi had told him about Cymbeline, even though he knew deep in his empty, yawning gut that it was true. "We don't get along." Naomi hadn't moved an inch, but she blinked now, as though she hadn't expected his words.

"Clearly," she said.

"Look," she added. "I told you, if you don't want to do this, it's fine. I figured we could make something together. *Music*, you know? Haven't you always wanted to do that? To make something even half as good as what your dad made? Maybe we can even make something that will be judged on its own terms. Separate from him. I thought you'd like that. But if that doesn't work for you, it's no skin off my nose. Here, she's all yours."

She pushed away from the piano and stood, holding one hand out. Offering him the keyboard, which should have been his, he told himself, all along. Matthew didn't hesitate. He walked right over and held out his drink to her. She took it, clutching it now against *her* belly, an almost protective shield. He sat, opening the fallboard. Began to play, lightly at first. Speaking over the notes.

"Sit down next to me," he said. His tone let in no other possibility. Naomi did as she was told. She sat down.

"Do you want this?" she asked, offering him his drink. He hadn't stopped playing, his hands flitting up and down the keys in his studied, skillful way. He had been playing the piano for as long as he could remember. Watching his father work the pedals, then sitting on his father's lap, helping him press the old ivories down, carefully at first, and then with confidence as he got older, stronger. It was a lie, what he'd told her, that he was self-taught. His lessons had been daily, joyful, instinctive. Part of the fabric of the rhythm of his family's daily life, like lunch and dinner and brushing your teeth. Every day that they were home together, until he was tall enough to work the pedals himself, he and his father had played.

"No," he said. "It's for you."

Out of the corner of his eye, he saw her take a sip. Then another. Quickly, she drank the whole thing down, and then she set the glass down by their feet.

Matthew kept playing.

"Here's what I'm thinking," he said. "We could make music together, but we won't. You'll help me take down notation for my next album, just like Edelman told me you would. And then—"

He hesitated only a second. Only his words, not his hands.

"What?" Naomi asked.

"Well," Matthew said, and his chest felt full and light when he said it. "I can see no other end to this. We sleep together. That's the only possibility."

Edmund Matthew Hammond IV kept playing, hands light on the keys. He'd made these declarations before, to other girls, or women he thought of as girls. Kara had been neither the most recent nor the first, but their first night had begun much like this. With Matthew laying out the studied inevitability of their union, and Kara agreeing, quickly—placing her small, pale hand on top of his hand.

Naomi didn't do that. She didn't touch him. Instead, she let the pause stretch out. And then, excruciatingly, she let out a small, hard laugh.

"Matt," she said. "Matthew."

He stopped playing. He looked at her. He saw the gentle look on her face, not incredulous, not judgmental. But certain. He watched her lift up her hands, and put them on the keyboard. They played the exact same notes he'd just been playing.

"It's not going to work like this for us," she said. "For one thing, I mostly sleep with women."

He looked at her, neither of their expressions changing. That had never been a barrier for him before, after all.

She sighed. "For another, think about what it would do to our power dynamics. You *have* a career already. I don't. We fuck, and I become your Meg White. Why do you think she and Jack pretended they were siblings? They *had* to. Once the world knows you've fucked, it's over. It doesn't matter how hard I play, or how influential my sound is. I become some pretty little nobody who you're doing a favor."

"Meg White's a terrible drummer," he said as he watched her hands still roaming over the keys. She looked at him. Gravely. Seriously.

"Okay, she's fine. But—"

Naomi wasn't going to let him finish. She spoke right over him. Maddening. "Anyway, I figure our fathers made a deal, and it worked out well for them. They chose art, not sex. I'm making the same choice."

Matthew felt his hands go numb. His belly flip-flopped, and for a long, terrifying moment he wondered if he was going to be sick again. But then he swallowed hard, forcing it still.

"*What?*" he said, staring at her, at the steady way she played his music, only it wasn't *his* music anymore. It was *theirs.* She shook her head, like it was a sad, sad thing.

"What?" she said. "You didn't *know?*"

Matthew frowned. He didn't know what to ask—how. It felt like an absurd insinuation—what, that their fathers had been *lovers*? Or almost lovers, but not? For the sake of *music*? It was like something out of a gossip magazine. A fan fiction. It *was* absurd, he told himself. But his body was telling himself something else, something equally true. Because every moment of this weekend had been absurd so far. Each and every note. His hands shook slightly as he lifted them up and put them down on the keys. Sober and uncertain for a bar or two, and then with confidence, he began to play. Their song. Together.

Naomi didn't say anything. Their fingers moved in tandem for a long time, until at last the song was over and she got up, and grabbed some scrap paper off the kitchen counter—old take-out menus and to-do lists that the Edelmans had left piled under a cork-board—and began to jot the chords all down.

"Okay," she said to Matthew with certainty, nodding her head as she did it. "Okay, that's the first song. The music, at least." She looked at him, her dark eyes boring into him. "Now what are the words?"

25 - 1958

Eighteen, but Baron didn't care. His mind that morning, instead, was all occupied by thoughts of one thing and one thing only: helping Eddie Hammond write his Christ forsaken song. He'd been here before, with other songs, with this same desperate need for validation. He realized that. But this would prove to Eddie, in a way that no other song would have proved to him, that Baron had *art* inside of him. And so all through the days leading up to his birthday, he spent his time in classes penciling and erasing lyrics, in between the usual fruit bowls and naked tits. But nothing was good. Nothing was right. Not yet. He knew better, now, to ask anyone—be it his uncle or his aunt or his mother—for help. Couldn't have them spoiling the rare, fragile optimism leasing space inside his mind.

He thought that maybe the problem was that he didn't know enough about birds. Once he had, back when he and Sue Grasso had been sharing finger pies, but that had been over a year ago now, and perhaps he'd been too preoccupied with Eddie and Dick to remember what it was all *really* like. And this was meant to be a song for Genie, wasn't it? Who was certainly and most definitely not a lad. So on the morning of his birthday, he rolled his eyes through the cake his mum had made him for breakfast and took off for art college, determined to conduct some new research. For the sake of art.

"Five o'clock, Baron," his mum called out after him as he headed into the spring morning. "Don't be late to your own party."

"Yeh, yeh," he answered sternly.

Sue was waiting outside the school, her legs dangling off one of the damp marble blocks that lined the entrance. Usually, Baron rushed right by her, barely paying her any mind. But not today. Today he stopped just a few feet away from her feet, in their smart little leather boots, and he knew instantly, from the way her smile lit up at the sight of him, that she hadn't only been waiting for class. No, in fact, she had been waiting for *him*. All this time. Weeks and weeks and weeks.

"Susan," Baron said. He stuck his hands in his pockets, wishing he had a cigarette. But he was out.

"Baron, happy birthday," she said. She leaned up on tippy toes and kissed his cheek, and he smelled the cloying, perfumey girl-smell of her; it was chemical, with something else, musky and unfamiliar, underneath. Like old fruit. "How's it feel to be eighteen?"

"Taller," he joked, and she laughed at that a little too hard. Then she searched through her satchel for something, her long, painted eyelashes flickering in his presence.

"Here," she said. "I made you this."

She handed him a card, homemade. Painted up with inks and watercolors. A little cartoon, clearly meant to be the pair of them. Baron playing guitar, his mouth forming a hollow O. And Sue, kneeling beside him, looking adoring. It was cute. Smart. Truly. She was a good artist. Always had been. And he looked at her and sort-of smiled, but only sort of, you see, because there was something perverse to him about it, too. How she was spending her art, her time, telling him something that both of them likely found self-evident. Her bland adoration was so *obvious*. Yawn. He held the card, staring at it and wanting to frown at the lovely cursive text there: "You're my favorite song." He half-wanted to dig into her. Didn't she think about anything else in her stupid little life? But he needed her right now. For research.

"Keen," he said, then looking at her, seeing her uncertainty, made himself smile. "I mean, I do love it, Sue."

"Really?" she asked, then not waiting for an answer, she flung herself at him. Unlike Dickie, unlike Ed, Baron towered over Sue, and so when she wrapped her arms tight around his neck he barely swayed from the weight of her. He was a pillar. And she, a small, inconsequential piece of string, wrapped around it.

He put his hands on the small of her back, felt her general smallness, her heat, and kissed her anyway. It wasn't bad kissing. It never had been. Her soft mouth, and his feeling rougher for it, and his tongue, forceful, the way she liked it, prying her mouth open. Invading.

After, he let himself knot his fingers in hers.

"You'll come to my party tonight?" he asked and she glowed and giggled and didn't really answer and didn't really hafta. They both knew the answer was yes.

They walked up the stairs together, crossing the threshold into the art college. That's when Baron saw a pale Irish face in the darkness. He felt a knot of fear tighten through him, and dread.

"Baron!" Dickie said, stepping out of the shadows, his voice too-big for this dusty space. "Ready for your birthday whacks?"

Baron took a breath, but didn't say anything. Didn't need to. To his surprise, Sue answered for him. "Feck off, Dickie," she said. He tightened his grip on her, glad to have her there for once. Like a shield.

"Ohh, you need Susie to defend you now?" Dickie said. Baron didn't answer him, just rolled his eyes.

"Must be off to class," Baron said, in a small, firm voice. Dickie laughed.

"Yeah, sure, Barry," he said. Then he smacked Baron, hard, once, on the arse. Baron jumped. "You'll get the other seventeen tonight."

Baron didn't answer, just led Sue Grasso up the stairwell toward their class.

"Are you alright?" she asked him, in the hollow silence of the stairs. Baron shrugged.

"Oh yes," he said dryly. "I'm simply peachy."

* * *

Baron's mum lifted Bess up onto a chair so she could string streamers over the curtain rod. There had never been parties at Aunt Deedz' house. Occasionally, to celebrate a good report card, she would take him out for fancy tea, dressing him up in a waistcoat and bow tie, but they never did anything so simple and uncouth as throw a *party*. So it was funny, in a way, to watch his mother get into the swing of it, putting on a Little Richard record and swaying her hips all around. Kind of cute, actually, Baron had to admit to himself. Though this all seemed to him to be a little more for her than for him.

He mulled around the first story of the house, which was not—and never would be—*his* house. By the door, where his uncle would leave his keys and wallet and pocket change when he was done with work, Baron found a package wrapped up in fine paper and tied with dark blue ribbon.

"What's this?" he asked, holding it up in his hand, letting the light catch the ribbon's shine. It was heavy, heavy enough to use to clobber someone. His mother giggled a bit. A high, false laugh.

"Oh, that's from Deidre. She came by when you was at school. Looking for you, Baron. She said she wanted to wish you a happy birthday."

Humm, Baron thought grimly. He remembered in a flash the chaos of that last night, how it had felt when her hand had collided with his ear—the ringing that he still heard, even now, in between everything else.

"She's been waiting, you know," Baron's mum said. He stopped looking down at the book, glancing over at his mum instead. Her dress was especially low cut today—too low for this early spring really.

"Waiting for what?" he asked. Her glossy lips pursed.

"For an apology, Baron! You know we love having you here, but Aunt Deedz' house is your *home*."

Baron gritted teeth. Clenched his hand harder around the book. He wanted to scream out: *an apology! What* for! But maybe he was growing up, because he knew it wouldn't do any good. His mum had let Aunt Deedz take him away, years and years ago, and he'd always suspected there was a dollop of not wanting him, anyway, below the surface of it all. He wasn't like Bess, cow-like and placid. Easy. He'd never been. Probably had been easier for his mum to have him out of her hair. Probably would have been easier, again, if he let himself be carted away once more. To go back to Deedz house, hat in hand, and apologize.

"I won't," was all he said, because he knew it wouldn't do any good to argue about it. He'd lit a *fire*. There was no acceptable answer for such a transgression.

"Stubborn," his mum said, sighing. And then she smiled. "Like me. Well, are you going to open your gift or not?"

He almost didn't want to. Almost wanted to chuck it into the trash. But his mum was looking at him, and she was all made up and beautiful, and it made him feel a painful squeezing in his belly. Couldn't let the old broad be sad. He tore the lovely paper off in one swift movement, balling it in his hand. And frowned.

"What is it?" asked Bess, whom he had almost forgotten was standing there. Baron squinted at the cover and the small, metallic text. Should have been wearing his glasses, but wasn't. Hated them. His mum came over and took the book out from his hand.

"*The Collected Works of William Shakespeare*," she said. She opened it up to the flyleaf, and it seemed to Baron like she'd been waiting for this. Almost as though it had been rehearsed.

"For my dear child, I give you the gift of knowledge on your eighteenth birthday. Love, Deidre."

It seemed to Baron like a shadow had fallen like a curtain behind his mother's eyes.

"*My* dear child," she said wistfully, and he regretted desperately then thinking that his mother had wanted to get rid of him—even as he also suspected simultaneously that it was still true. She took a breath, deep and shivery, like she was doing her best not to cry. "I suppose that's a nice gift."

"It's trash," Baron said, because he wanted to make his mum feel better. But his mum only rolled her eyes.

"It's not trash," she said. "It's *important*. Go put it in your room."

She handed Baron the book, and he took it, feeling the unwanted weight.

"It's *my* room," Bess whined from her chair. As Baron passed her, he took his knuckles and rapped her on the greasy forehead. Clucked his tongue twice. Forced a smile.

"Quiet," he said. "I'm the heir."

Maybe in any other family, he would have been told to be kind to his sister. But this was his mother's house. His mother only looked charmed as he made his way up the stairs.

* * *

That's how, in the moments before Baron's eighteenth birthday party, he found himself alone in his little sister's room, reading Shakespeare.

The pages were thin as an onion skin. The text was minuscule. Baron *had* to take out his glasses now, and he sat on the cot with them low on his nose as he flipped through the pages.

The truth was there had been a time when he would have adored a gift like this. When he was ten or eleven he'd seen a performance of *A Midsummer Night's Dream* at the Royal Court Theater and become briefly obsessed with the whole endeavor. Oh, that Oberon, with his beard and broad chest. That small, waifish Puck. For a time, he stopped drawing pictures of football players, which boys like Dickie had asked him to do because he was good at art, and instead, in secret, drew fairies. Some hidden part of himself had thought that perhaps someday, *he* could enter a tangled wood and become all tangled up. Maybe in the world of fairies, where a man could have a donkey's head, or forget his old true love, he would be permitted to have a woman's body, or at least a woman's lusts. Even then, as a child, he'd known he had them. In small, secret places and in tiny, invisible ways. Knew better than to share that with Dick and the rest of them. But still couldn't help but dream. He'd asked Deedz to take him to the show another three or four times after that, at which point she said she wouldn't be wasting her money anymore on a play she'd already seen. So the last time, it had been him and Uncle Fred—a surprise, a sneak, with Aunt Deedz out at her bridge game.

"Thought one last time wouldn't hurt," Fred had said, and if he'd suspected the queerness of the whole endeavor, well, he didn't let on for a second.

And of course they'd read the great tragedies in school. *Macbeth* and

Julius Caesar, which he hated, and *Hamlet*, whose moody soliloquies Baron admired. He *knew* Shakespeare. Sometimes felt he appreciated Shakespeare in a way nobody else possibly could. But, as he paged through, he also knew that this gift contained another message besides Deedz' general knowledge of him as a human being with likes and dislikes, a childhood full of strange passions. It contained her judgment. He should have been thinking about lofty things, important things, she was saying. He should have grown to be the person she wanted him to be—a scholar, a gentleman. Not a queer, homeless scamp.

Ah, well. He paged through, scouring past the Richards and the Henries. Came to a play he hadn't heard of before. *Cymbeline, King of Britain*. Read the first few lines. Didn't seem to have any real music or charm in it. But his eye lingered on the title. Cymbeline. Cym. Bel. Ine. It almost reminded him of the Chuck Berry—Maybellene. All that hot rod romance and heartbreak, masculine and moody. But it seemed different. Ancient. British. Not like a king's name at all, really. But a queen. He rolled the name over his tongue, played with it. And then, leaving the book splayed out face down on his little cot, he bent over and got out his guitar for the first time in what felt like a lifetime. Tuned it. And started to hum.

He could hear the notes of Eddie's song fading in and out of his head. With his hands, approximating the chords Ed had showed him all those weeks ago as best he could, he began to strum it out. Cym. Bel. Ine. Cymbeline. His strong voice started to pick out a melody, finding places where the name might fit.

My Cymbeline something else of the darkest ocean, will you something a storm for me, my queen, my Cymbeline . . .

It wasn't rock 'n' roll. That was certain. And it sure as hell wasn't about Genie Waller. But it was most definitely some sort of sorcery. He strummed and hummed and wove words in and out, stopping and starting, and for a moment, he saw a flash of something, bright, right between the forehead. A vision of a past life, maybe. Something he'd seen before. Himself, dressed in rich velvet, a lute between his hands. Felt cold stone under his arse. Had he dreamed this? That he'd sat at the foot of a throne, strumming for a woman. A princess or a duchess or maybe even a queen. Her features had been fine and pale and she'd had a knot of red hair that was like a vixen's pelt but those eyes, pale and watery and beautiful—they had been familiar. Eddie's eyes. And he'd sung, and now, in the present, in his little sister's room, he thought of Ed's eyes, the beautiful queenliness of him, his lips and his earnestness and everything they might possibly make together, rolling out into the future. And he sang a tune that was like Ed's song, but different, too:

Cymbeline, I am undressed before. Distressed before you—in your eyes. None comes before you, and so I must implore you, my queen, my Cymbeline . . .

At this point in Baron's life—just minutes into his eighteenth year—he had not yet learned how certain songs would seem almost pre-ordained. Tumbling out of him like something he was certain he'd heard before. In the beginning, he'd sit friends down—sometimes Ed, sometimes Liam, sometimes someone else—and play for them and ask and ask, "Do you *know* this? Where did this come from?" But the answer was always a frown and a shrug. Nobody knew Baron's music. But Baron was sure that he did, that he hadn't written it. That it had just come to him, from the ether.

Like magic.

Baron put his guitar down for a moment, went to Bess's desk and grabbed one of her notebooks and a pencil and tore a page out. In his cockeyed chicken scratch, he began to write down what he'd figured out of the words. Humming something adjacent to that beautiful music that the most beautiful boy had written, all the while knowing that this song—spectacular, true—was not what Eddie had precisely asked him for. But Ed was smart. He knew quality when he saw it. Surely, surely, he would hear Baron's song and he wouldn't be able to deny it, deny him. They could make something spectacular *together*, something more than the Bartlebys, more than Liverpool. This was Gilbert and Sullivan. This was Bach. This was Mozart. This was bigger than Genie Waller, bigger'n either Baron or Eddie individually, too. Forget Elvis. This was beauty, and if Ed didn't care about beauty—well, then, he cared about the pound signs that would follow after beauty. Ed would be a damn fool to deny him. And so, Baron was sure, he would not.

He was still scribbling and erasing when the door suddenly burst open. There was Eddie himself—with Liam and Dickie and Alfie and Bongo Turner, too. They all came tumbling through the door, and before Baron could even finish his sentence, they started grabbing at his arms, his legs, rough-knuckling his hair.

"Ey, son!" Eddie was saying, "It's a happy birthday!"

Baron found himself roughly lifted by the pack of joyful boys. The revels, it seems, had begun.

26 - 1977

When Richard Charles bent forward to watch the castle rotting among the ice floes on the Hudson, his nose left a greasy print on the train car window. He'd insisted on taking the window seat. Had it been up to Zach, he would have let Shay take the window seat. Be a *gentleman*, like their mother had taught them. But it wasn't up to Zach, of course. Richard Charles had shouldered his way in, sat down first, and when Zach stared at him with a frown creasing the corners of his mouth, Richard Charles just shrugged. "What?"

So Zach sat in the middle, wedged between the two of them, uncomfortable, but what had his comfort ever mattered? It hadn't to his brother ever before, and didn't now. The train chugged on and on down the Hudson, and Shay had her nose in a book. *No Exit*. Sartre.

"What's it about?" Zach finally asked. Shay glanced at him, rolling her eyes a little.

"It's a play about how hell is other people," she said flatly, and he had the sudden feeling that her words were aimed at him. He slumped lower in his seat.

"Not everybody. I think some people—"

"Hey, we read that in school." Richard Charles reached across Zachy and grabbed the book right out of Shay's hands. She shouted, "Hey!" and went to take it back, but he squirmed away from her, facing the window.

"It's really gay," he said. "There's an evil lesbian in it. I can see why you would like it."

"Fuck you," Shay said, sitting down in her seat and crossing her arms over her chest. "I'm not gay."

"I don't know. You're sure hung up on the whole 'Baron Templeton is a fag,' theory."

"That's because it's *true*."

"How do you know?" Richard Charles pushed. Shay rolled her eyes.

"How do you know that Elton John is a queer?"

"Because he said so in *Rolling Stone*," Richard Charles sniped back.

"Because you can smell it on him," she hissed, narrowing her eyes at Richard Charles. Her gaze was both pointed and tense, like she was accusing him of something. "Some things are just obvious. This is obvious. Even if it wasn't in a dozen different books, if you ignoramuses would take the time to read."

That rattled Zach. He *had* read about Templeton. Sure, it was the same book, over and over again—but it wasn't his fault if Mom's fines had gotten big enough that the library wouldn't let them take out books anymore, if he didn't have any cash to buy his own books from the bookstore, because he wasn't a fucking drug dealer, like Richard Charles was, if he wasn't going to steal them, because he wasn't a thief, like Richard Charles was, too. *He* knew about Templeton deep down in his heart. Knew that he wasn't a fag. In a way that this stupid girl never would.

But Richard Charles didn't care what Shay had to say.

"I'll tell you what I can smell," Richard Charles said, loud enough that some old woman in the seat across from them looked over disapprovingly. Zach slumped lower and lower in his own seat. When he had imagined their trip into the city, he'd pictured, at worst, his brother making out with Jennifer while he quietly flirted with Shay. This was too much noise for him, too much hostility. "It's the smell of your cu—"

"Will both of you fags shut up?" Zach finally snapped, and snatched Shay's copy of *No Exit* away from his brother before handing it back to her.

"I'm not a fag," Richard Charles huffed. "You're a fag."

Zach didn't say anything, but when he glanced at Shay, she rolled her eyes. Like her point had somehow been proven. Whatever the point. When Zach only shrugged and turned away, she waited a beat, then cracked open her book again and went back to reading.

The train trudged southward, tracing the line of the Hudson.

* * *

The three children spilled out of the train an hour later, along with a bunch of weekend tourists and rumpled day trippers. No one paid them any particular notice as they made their way up the dirty track and into the grubby, echoing lobby of Grand Central. There was trash littering the marble floors, homeless people who had been driven inside by the cold and were scattered around begging. None of that really did anything to detract from the sense of space here—the echo of it. Zach paused, letting his eyes scan the scaffolding that barely seemed to hold up the collapsing walls. He remembered his mother talking about it once, how Jackie Onassis, of all people, had vowed to preserve this space. Someday, it would be beautiful again. Grand. He tried to imagine it, but, with all of the peeled paint, the small of urine, failed. Instead, he had the sense—not for the first time—that he was just one of thousands of souls passing through here, that his tenure on this world would be as limited and fleeting as any who had gone before. He'd read in a book once that there were constellations painted on the ceiling, but he wasn't sure if he believed it, or if it even mattered if he did. His sign—Libra—was buried. Gone.

Shay had noticed he'd stopped and come back to get him. She stood for a moment, watching him watch the ceiling.

"You're going to get yourself mugged," she said, and reaching out, grabbed his hand. Hers was clammy and cool, not at all what he'd imagined a girl's hand would feel like. In the moment, he was so surprised by the damp feeling that he let her drag him. His heart was a fluttering bird trapped beneath the cage of his Adam's apple. A girl. A girl holding his hand.

"Why do you care so much about Baron Templeton?" he finally asked as they rushed through the station, chasing down Richard Charles. "Why do you care about proving this to us?"

She looked back over her shoulder, and he saw in that moment how she was strange and wild and beautiful. Not like a magazine. Like something feral. Vital. Real. Her eyebrows, just a little overgrown. The fuzzy split ends of her hair, forming a soft cloud around her.

"You know," she said. "I play music, just like you do?"

"You do?" Zachary asked in confusion, and his voice squeaked, just a little.

"Well, yeah," she said. "The drums. I've played the drums since I was like six."

"I didn't know," he told her. She'd brought him to the top of the out of order escalator that led down into the bowels of the terminal, where the subway—and Richard Charles—were now waiting. Pausing there, she pried her hand way from Zach's, wiping her palm against the nap of her denim jeans.

"No one ever asks girls that kind of shit," she said. "No one thinks we know anything."

Zach frowned. "Are you any good?" he asked. Shay started down the escalator, turning back just once to shout out toward him.

"Dunno," she said. "Are *you*?"

Zach's frown deepened. He rushed down the stairs, almost tripping, trying not to think about it. Because the truth was, he had no idea if he was good. He and Richard Charles played all the time—every moment they could. They played their only Saffron record, *The Ruffians*, over and over again and stuttered through the chord changes the best they could. Some days it sounded magical, and he was beginning to see the shape of the music in his head in a way he could better feel than articulate. But most days it felt . . . lame. Tinny and wrong. In his heart, he suspected that he was really just as bad at music as he had been at chess.

And he'd been *terrible* at chess.

Richard Charles was standing there at the bottom of the stairs waiting for them. And he couldn't admit in front of Richard Charles that he had doubts about their music. For one thing, Richard Charles *was* good. When he stroked his fingers up the skinny neck of his Teisco, the strings didn't buzz or plod. His music was as smooth as a heartbeat and just as steady.

For another, you could never admit to Richard Charles that you had any fear inside you, any doubt. His brother was the type of boy who would grab a thread like that and leave you totally unraveled. You couldn't be weak in front of Richard Charles. If you did, he would destroy you.

"I'm awesome," Zachy said, and tried to look confident—like his older brother might. But from the look on Shay's face, he could tell it hadn't worked. She let out a snort, and moved her long hair away from her own sticky lip gloss.

"Whatever," she said. "The train is this way, boys."

She led the brothers deeper into the cold, dank bowels of the city.

27 - 1958

The drink of the day was scotch and soda, which Baron's mum said was all the rage in America these days, thick and syrupy because she'd forgotten to make ice. The drink of the day was a slug or six of gin from a bottle Liam Waller had stolen from his dad, which they passed back and forth while sitting on the steps and watching the birds drift in. The drink of the day was sparkling champagne Sue Grasso's mum had bought just for the occasion, served in the Depression-era wine glasses Baron's mum had gotten from a sale in the church basement, whose lips they touched together in a toast, to birthdays, at least 18 more. The drink of the day was whiskey, which Uncle Tim said he was honored to share with Baron on this momentous occasion, but he wasn't looking at Baron but Baron's mum, who locked eyes with him as they toasted, putting the thought of their fucking later right into Baron's booze-addled mind. Baron may not have had 18 drinks and one for luck that day, because what was a drink? Was it a shot, a mouthful, a finger, a chug? Was a drink just enough to get you loose, or silly, or horny? Well, he had that, many times over, and as his mum's house started to crowd with bodies he began to feel all three. Or maybe he was always all three. A clever boy. Cock-sure and hungry. Cock-hungry and sure. By the time his mother's house had filled up with people, Baron had had enough to drink that he couldn't feel his legs. He'd had enough that he couldn't feel *himself*, for once, that small shitty core of shame he'd come to believe was inherent to the life and times of Baron Templeton. In the packed living room, he gave in to wild abandon. He danced with Sue Grasso and didn't care who was looking as she shoved her hips up against his pelvis and wiggled. He danced with Ed and Liam and didn't care who was looking as he found himself angling his body away from Liam and toward Ed, the compass needle inside him turning to its most predictable position. He danced with his Mum and gave her arse a goose and didn't care that Bess was watching and blushing and Timo was watching and fuming because his Mum let out a little squeal. He loved to be dirty. He loved to dance. Letting Little Richard worm through him until he was nothing but a hollowed-out tunnel of music and feeling. As he took a break from all that writhing and groping, went to pour himself another one, the whiskey overflowing his glass, he wondered if this wasn't what fucking felt like. And the clock hands inside him turned again, and he found himself looking over to where Ed and Genie Waller were dancing. It was hot in his mother's living room. The girls looked all greased up. The boys, sweat shining and greasy, too. Both Ed and Genie were covered with a sheen, their hair all sloppy, arm pits circled damp. Genie was looking at Ed with wide open eyes, but when she danced she hardly moved her hips. She had no rhythm. Her hands were balled up into two awkward, clenched fists as she shuffled and Ed grabbed her hand and tried to spin her and she stepped on his shoes. *Christ*, Baron found himself saying to himself, and he wasn't sure if he said it aloud or not, because what was the point of screwing a bird who had no rhythm like that? You could wank better. *He* could wank Ed better. Take him from point A to point B like a song. Instead of the stuttered, awful start-and-stop of Genie's hips and tripped up feet and she was a child and she didn't even understand music but because she had a cunny she got to stand close to him, to throw her hands, small and painted, over his neck and wiggle up against him not so far from the way Sue had wiggled up against Baron, and so he knew how it felt, the soft flatness of a woman against your sharpness—the cavern where there should have been a jetty—and he knew, he guessed, that Eddie wanted to fill her, his water lapping at her shore. But why? Why not his rocks? As far as he could see, there would have been more pleasure in it—

"Liking the floor show?"

Baron wheeled back and nearly spilled his drink, and when he did, Dickie

Ashby laughed an amiable sort of laugh and clapped Baron's shoulder, steadying him. But Baron knew even then that they were not friends. That it was all a pantomime. And for whose benefit?

"Why don't you come outside with me," Dickie said, "For a fag."

For Dickie's benefit, that's whose. But maybe, perhaps, perhaps for Baron's benefit too, because swaying a little on his numb, tingling legs, he found himself putting his drink down on the table and following Dickie through the tiny kitchen, past the clothes press and the refrigerator, and down the steps and outside. It was cold out here still. Bright, but near the edge of winter. After the heat of the house, and dressed only in a button-up shirt, no jumper, Baron found himself shivering. Dickie's hand hadn't left Baron's shoulder and now it moved up to the base of Baron's neck. They were walking through the tiny garden, past the rubble that was always back here, broken tumbled brick that no one had bothered moving after the bombs, after the war. In the corner of the garden was a small building. It had been an outhouse once, but no one used it anymore, not with the WC inside, and Baron knew, in some vague sense, that it would be full of spiders. He hated spiders. His shoulders tensed, and he was still shivering, but now Dickie moved closer to him, *tcht*ing.

"It's alright, mate," Dickie said, even though they weren't mates, not really. Or were they? Well. A different kind of mate. Dickie compelled him forward, and Baron was compelled. Dick's hand was broad and warm and he didn't seem to be cold at all out here. Dick was wearing a jumper, woolen, and it had seemed too thick for inside but seemed just right for now. Baron found in his drunkenness thinking about balling his whole body up inside Dick's jumper, keeping himself warm. Hibernating.

Dick opened the door. Sure enough, the old khazi, spider webs and an earthen smell and the light only coming through one smeared window. As soon as the wooden door slammed shut behind them, Dick was on him, his lips starving pressed to Baron's neck, then throat, then lips, and Dick's prick hard as an ice pick and Baron's hard, too, but Dick wasn't touching it this time. Instead, he was yanking Baron's pants down, his movements almost violent, and yanking his own pants down—his movements almost violent—and his cock was stabbing at Baron already, against Baron's hip, and then he turned Baron around and Baron knew what was coming as he gripped the old split wood around the toilet's hole and looked down into a yawning darkness that was only lit by thin winter light touching down on spider webs. He heard Dick slobber over his own hand, and then the slobbery hand was inside him, and then Dick was inside him, not gently. All roughness. And it hurt more than anything had ever hurt before, and yet his body yielded to it. A yelp first. Then a shudder. Then a moan.

"Shut up," Dick growled. "Shut up." He tangled his wet, spitty hand roughly through Baron's greased hair and pulled on it like it was a rope, forcing Baron's eyes down to the spider webs in the khazi and he thought he saw a brown-legged spider creep silently closer, her legs all fur-spiked and soft but then he felt a wave of pressure inside of him as Dick pounded into him and Baron's eyes shut because he was close, and Dick was close, too . . .

And then. A shaft of yellowy winter light past Dick's humping shadow, falling on Baron's face as Dick turned back and Baron turned back and he saw, for a split second, the pale, beautiful moon of Eddie's face, standing there in the doorway, his mouth slack and open and soft pink inside it and his brow smooth like he was having so much trouble solving the arithmetic of what he was seeing that he didn't know what to feel, what to say, and Dickie Ashby let out a roar of garbled sound then and grabbed the slim creaky rotty wooden door and moved to slam it.

"Get out! Get out!" he bellowed, and Eddie's face was gone while Dickie pumped himself into Baron once more, twice more, three times, then came, and Baron did too. His face down in the ancient toilet, his eyes sliding open only after and as his body throbbed itself out to nothing he wondered where the spider had gone. Where Ed had gone.

"Fuck," said Dickie, pulling himself out of Baron, leaning against the splintered wall of the outhouse, putting himself away. The word was panted, half-laced with laughter. He zipped himself up, laughing more, this time.

"Fuck," he said again, smiling right at Baron, a sweet, friendly sort of smile, and that's when Baron, pulling up his belt, pulling down his shirt, felt himself fill up with rage, white-hot against the cold. Because he realized then how this was a joke to Dickie. Nothing but a joke to him. No real danger. No real risk. Not like it was for Baron.

He hit him then. Not a punch, but more of a shove, both fists into both shoulders, hard.

"You fucking didn't lock the door?" he cried. "You moron! You simpering moron!"

"Oh, come off it, you queer," Dickie said, and though his easy laughter and smile had crumpled into a look of annoyance, when he batted Baron away it was without much force or anger. Like it was nothing. Like he was nothing. The little faggy spider, a tiny creature worth no regard. Dick fished through his pockets for a pack of ciggies, offering one to Baron.

"Did you want that fag or not?" he asked. Baron could see it in his head: how it would look to let his anger loose now, to smash his fists right through Dickie Ashby's cro-magnumically small skull and let his overcooked brains ooze out through his ears and eye sockets. But no. No. Getting sent off to prison would do neither of them any good. So he only let out an anguished cry of frustration and threw open the door, sending himself stomping through the rubbly garden.

He knew that Dick was behind him somewhere, strolling slow and whistling into the cool air. Baron didn't care. He tore open the kitchen door and pressed into the packed kitchen. From somewhere, he heard Bongo Turner's voice call out for him, offering him a drink, but he ignored it. His own brow low, his anger sharp. He pushed through the throngs of bodies, wondering, in passing, but without much concern, if anyone smelled the perfume of sex on him, and at some point he passed a bottle of something—a bottle of cognac, in someone's hand, about to be poured into a glass—and he grabbed it and when they gave a yelp it was only for a moment, because he was the birthday boy, and he took a long swig and carried it upstairs and shut himself away into the bathroom. Tore off his sticky clothes. Sat for a moment on the can, drinking and heaving leaden, wheezed breaths.

Eddie had caught them. Eddie had seen.

He climbed into the claw foot tub, still holding that cognac by the neck. Turned the water on. Hot enough to sear his skin, to slough away any lingering evidence of the things he had done and had been done to him, which he'd enjoyed even if he hadn't precisely asked for them. Below, he could hear his mother's records blaring, all the boisterous voices of teenagers rising up, and he put his face in the burning water and didn't cry and didn't feel anything. Chugging and chugging, then finally letting the bottle drop, still half full, spilling out the burnished liquid against his feet. He groped along the windowsill for the bar of soap, scrubbed himself, then stood there for five or ten or a hundred minutes longer, letting the water rush down, until a knock came sharply at the door.

"Yeh," Baron said. He turned the faucet off, stumbling out of the tub—his big toe catching on the lip of it, and almost crashing to the floor before he caught his own lean body—and he wrapped himself up in one of the ratty cotton towels, which smelled like mildew because his mum was terrible at doing the wash. Grabbed his clothes. Opened the door.

"Go 'head," he croaked out, then saw, through damp eyelashes, Eddie's face looking back at him. His heart throbbed beneath his Adam's apple. He thought he might be sick. Instead, he swallowed the acidy bile down, stood straighter.

"Allo," Baron said. "Need a piss?"

Not waiting for Eddie to answer, Baron stumbled into his sister's room. Didn't bother closing the door. He was aware, sharply, of how Eddie was just standing in the hallway, watching him. He could have—should have—had more shame about the skinny shape of his body, the cleft in the back of it, and the damp, floppy parts in front. The hair, and the small pucker of his belly that seemed to hang a bit no matter how little he ate. But he knew, sharply, that to hide himself now would have been like admitting what he had done. To hide would have been to admit shame. So instead he dropped both towel and old dirty clothes in a heap on his bed and began dressing in new, cleaner clothes, swaying with the effort, but staying upright, while Ed watched at first, then cleared his throat, then dragged his eyes away to some middle distant point that seemed to exist not on his sister's wallpaper but somewhere beyond and past it.

"Um," said Ed, blushing a little. "No. Your mum said to go get you. For the cake."

Baron stood straight, curling one corner of his lip. Like Elvis, but with more disgust. He suddenly felt full of anger at Ed's poppy-bright cheeks, his lovely soft mouth, his beautiful pale lashes. He knew inside that it wasn't Ed's fault. It was his own fault, wasn't it? Or maybe Dick's. Yes, Dick's fault. For putting him in this situation. For making him ashamed of himself, and in front of this beautiful boy who loved him.

"The cake?" Baron said, not a question, really. A sneer.

"Yeh," Eddie said, raking a hand through his blond curls, letting out the start of a breath. Baron stumbled toward the dresser, grabbing his comb, his pomade. Started to try to tame his own curls, which he knew, even in his drunkenness, would be a mess if he let them dry the way they were. Not like Ed's curls. No angel curls. But coarse and unruly. "You know, Baron—"

"We don't have to talk about it," Baron said, putting his comb down. He was speaking maybe too firmly, and he could hear how his words were slurring together, wedunhaffffftotawkabowtit. He swallowed again, putting both hands on the edge of the dresser to steady himself. "I'm going to take care of it. Right?"

In this mirror, his eyes went to Eddie's eyes. Locking. But with a wall of glass between them. Eddie didn't look quite so soft or uncertain anymore.

"Right," he said. "Okay, Baron. Now are you coming downstairs or not?"

"Right," Baron said. He pushed himself off the dresser, somehow managing not to fall over at all. He was still barefoot as he padded down the steps after Eddie. They didn't speak as they walked. Baron couldn't. The effort to walk straight was too much. Instead, as he stepped, he kept thinking to himself, *Going to take care of it have to take care of it take care of it take care of it.*

But as he stepped back into the fray, he had to admit, in his haze, that he had absolutely no idea what he was going to do.

28 - 1997

Over the next week, Sid and Cymbeline's conversations took place in the margins of their campers' lives. At night, after light's out, if they could manage to sneak away to see one another. At the lake, when the girls donned their swim camps and the counselors would have a few minutes off to let the lifeguards worry about whether the girls lived or died. In a way, Cymbeline didn't even mind worrying about the survival and well being of her charges. She often felt as though her own concerns were merely intrusions on the lives of these girls, who already seemed to have bigger, brighter problems than she did. Maybe it was because of their general, albeit temporary, state of parentlessness. A girl would come to her sniffling, because she'd been too shy to ask for a bathroom during the camp's all-day sporting event, and so wet herself, just a little bit, just before she finally made it to the cindy at the closest tent unit, and Cymbeline would magnanimously offer to wash her clothes in the counselor's laundry facilities, which were open seven days a week, unlike the wash and fold service the campers used only on weekends—saving her from the embarrassment of having to tuck her damp shorts into her luggage. Or Cymbeline would walk into the cabin after lunch to find a gang of girls taunting one another, and the smallest among them crying. It felt good to put an arm around her and lead her out of that lion's den, to sit with her in the program shelter, sucking silently on Otter Pops and waiting for the child to spill the dirt. The children needed her. Cymbeline knew what it was like to need someone. Maybe it was because, as Sid had said, that she was an orphan now. But the truth was, she'd always felt an especial affinity for orphans, an obsession with books like *The Little Princess* and *Heidi* and *Pollyanna*. Her mother had once rolled her eyes at her, while simultaneously supplying her with a steady stream of Boxcar Children novels from the local K-mart.

"Is this because of your father?" she'd ask. "Because he's not dead. He lives in Peoria."

Cymbeline had made no retort; her mother hadn't expected one, for one thing, but also she knew there was no good response to make. She had a mother, then. A father, too, though he was mostly distant and unknown. Yet still she felt she knew, intimately and innately, what it was to be parentless. When her mother finally had died (her father, at that point, completely absent from her life for more than a decade) it felt more inevitable than in any way crushing. She was meant to be alone.

And so could speak to these children better than the other counselors, even Sid, who mostly just found them to be nuisances.

"Perky," Sid would say, after hearing a stream of gossip—Tess Swale's bunk-mate had told her to go kill herself because Tess had never tried a cigarette and wasn't interested in trying one— "You realize these little rich bitches will be *fine*, right? They'll figure it out and by the last night's campfire they'll all be sobbing about how heartbroken they are to leave each other."

"But they need me," Cymbeline had objected, and begun to pry Sid's heavy arm off her body, because it hurt her, what Sid had said. She didn't think the girls were bitches, even if they were both little and rich.

"Nnnf," Sid said. "*I* need you." Sid had begun to smother Cymbeline in kisses that were both hungry and possessive, pressing their bodies even closer in the narrow counselor's bed, and Cymbeline, in the dark silence of the night, let her, because she didn't doubt it, not even for a second. Sid did, in fact, also need Cymbeline.

In their snippets of conversation, in between fucking (Sid) and fretting over other people's children (Cymbeline), they talked about the coming performance. If Sid didn't care much about her (his? Sid had given no indication for a preference, and to refer to her summer beau this way would have invited questioning that Cymbeline wasn't sure was yet wanted; still, the word "he" seemed to hang heavy in the air between them now, a constant presence) charges, then Sid certainly *did* care about Cymbeline's impending doom in front of a bar full of people.

"You should wear something with *contrast*," Sid said to her, riffling through Cymbeline's worn out duffle bag, which her mother had bought her before seventh grade, anticipating a sudden increase in sleepover invites which never quite materialized. She finally pulled out a ratty sundress, one speckled with tiny daisies that was so old that the skirt was almost see-through. Cymbeline had loved it once, in high school, and she brought it everywhere with her, to college and camp, though it no longer seemed fit for polite company whenever she contemplated wearing it. "Here. This. This'll look fucking sexy on you. Wear it with your black bra. The lace one. Let the straps show. But you need something edgy that'll go with it. I have an old motorcycle jacket that I think will fit you . . ."

Cymbeline took the dress from Sid, holding the hanger up against her shoulders, draping the fabric over her. She smoothed it with her palm, contemplating the nubby cotton.

"Do you ever think about making music yourself?" Cymbeline asked, angling her chin toward Sid. "Maybe we could start a band. You could play the bass or something . . ."

"Perky," Sid said, and let out a ragged laugh that had little humor in it, "Have you ever heard me sing? I'm functionally tone deaf. My brother is, too. My dad's greatest tragedy. You own a record store, but both of your kids will forever be stuck in the audience, just like you were. He was always to get me to play *something* when I was a kid, but it was a total disaster. You should have heard me tooting away on my recorder."

She pantomimed playing at an imaginary instrument, her cheeks blown up like balloons. Cymbeline laughed at the sight.

"Anyway," Sid said, "I always thought that my real place would have been in, like, management. You know my dad used to have me sort the new releases for him?" Sid had spoken a bit about the days when her father had owned a record store, before CD World had bought it out and he'd retired. It sounded magical—the used sleeves, graffitied with the art of teenagers long-grown, the listening booths where kids would hook up, the education Sid had gotten in music, far deeper than Cymbeline's own. Sid sighed. "They'd come in every Tuesday and it was like Christmas. I'd get to listen to all of them and put the ones that would sell well right up front. *Sadie's Choice*, he called the shelf." She grimaced just a little at the old name. "He used to brag to everyone how I had an 'uncanny ability to sniff out triple platinum records.' Tim"—this was Sid's brother— "Sucked at it, but *I* could always find a winner. You could just hear it. The shine."

"He must have been really proud of you," Cymbeline said. "Your dad, I mean. Not Tim."

Sid snorted. "Yeah, Tim wanted to murder me. As for my dad, of course he was proud, but it's not the kind of skill that's enough to keep a record store going at times like these."

"No," Cymbeline said. "I guess not . . ."

"Anyway, Dad's been depressed ever since the store closed. He sleeps all the time," Sid said, matter-of-factly. "He probably doesn't even remember."

Sid's tone was flippant, easy—but Cymbeline could tell there was loss. Sid wanted her father to remember. Sid wanted her father to understand how she was special. Better than Tim. Better than any boy. More like her father than not. And Sid *was* special, of course. A juggling, hilarious, strange, coarse person who was brighter than anyone Cymbeline had ever met—man or woman.

"Anyway, band life isn't for me," Sid said. "But maybe . . . well, I've always thought I'd be awesome at managing a band. But unless some kind of miracle happens, at my age it would mean going to school for business, I think, and that sounds like a drag."

"Management, really?" Cymbeline said carefully, standing up, peeling off her over-sized pajama pants and the camp shirt stained with tie-dye that had become her night time favorite. Somewhere out there, beyond the thin sheet that provided a hollow semblance of privacy, there were 9 sleeping little girls. But this was not a world of little girls. Sid let her eyes fall on Cymbeline's breasts, possessively, approvingly. "You mean being a mechanic isn't your true calling?"

Sid snorted as Cymbeline pulled on the old dress. It hugged her curves like a pair of familiar, loving hands.

"I tried to get these guys I knew in high school to let me manage them, but they wouldn't take me seriously. No one would. I mean, you know how guys are. Especially musicians."

Cymbeline went to the mirror at the far side of the room. It was hazy and scratched and reflected more darkness than light. The sight of herself there, in her flimsy dress, made her uncomfortable. And yet she could also see how Sid had been correct. With the right sort of leather jacket on top of it, it would be the perfect outfit for a musician. Sloppy, but sexy enough that it just might be intentional. Cymbeline took her tousled hair and piled it high on top of her head, considering.

"I don't care that you didn't go to school for business. I want you to be my manager," she said, suddenly, impulsively. Because she saw in that moment how *good* Sid would be at it. Sid could be charming and suave when she wanted, persuasive. She knew how to move among folks with money in a way that Cymbeline didn't. And she had impeccable taste.

But more importantly, Cymbeline saw how whole it would make Sid feel. How it would be a road out for her, from this box she'd put herself in. Of telling herself she was meant to be a grease monkey, of telling herself that it was enough. Sure, working as a mechanic was *stable*. But there wasn't much of a future in it. Wasn't much of an opportunity to become something more.

Or something *else. Someone* else.

There was a moment of silence and at first, Cymbeline wondered if she had done something—said something—wrong. But Sid came over to her. Standing behind her, she kissed Cymbeline's neck, first, then let her hands drift up to Cymbeline's breasts.

"Okay," Sid said. "But you're going to need to start off with something else. The song you played the other night was too soppy for an opener. You need to warm them up with something. An old cover, maybe something by Buddy Holly or the Temptations. 'My Girl.' Something like that. Something familiar, but it'll sound new when *you* sing it. Give them love songs after you've already won them over."

Cymbeline nodded, a little numbly. She'd never really listened to Buddy Holly *or* the Temptations. But it sounded like a good idea. Hadn't she loved Tiffany when she was young? Especially "I Think We're Alone Now"?

"You're gonna be amazing, baby," Sid said, and kissed her neck again, more deeply this time. *"We're* going to be amazing."

Cymbeline closed her eyes, leaning into the kiss, letting her heart flutter in her chest. Letting Sid's feelings—her pride, her excitement, her horniness—envelop her own. There was no use in feeling what Cymbeline was feeling, that low thrumming dread that said *You have done this before and you know you're going to hate it.*

Sid needed her. So she would do it. Because she needed Sid, too.

* * *

After dinner that night, Sid and Cymbeline stood together in the gravelly parking lot. The sun was just beginning to set beyond the crest of pine trees, casting shots of purple and gold through the sky. Soon it would be dark, and the stars would come out, but it wasn't dark yet, and the air was swarmed with mosquitos, who pricked at Cymbeline's bare legs and collarbones, all that flesh that showed beyond the seams of her well-worn dress.

She kind of hated it, being this bare. When she was a little girl she'd refused to go swimming without a t-shirt over her one-piece. It bogged her down, floating around her like an enormous tent. But she didn't mind. Otherwise, there was too much slippery water, too much air, too many eyes. She often had a feeling of being looked at, even when completely alone. It had made her reluctant to call attention to her physical body, as if the weight of being watched somehow diminished her. Now the whole night seemed to narrow its eyes on her, and she'd asked for it, hadn't she, by dressing this way? Or consenting to dress this way, for Sid. The guitar case was at her feet, waiting. Sid was prattling on about the set list. Cymbeline was only half-listening, if even that, instead focused on one rolling thought: she could not believe she was actually going to do this. To get up in front of people. To sing. Again.

"So?" Sid was asking, eager, prodding, "What do you think?"

"Y-yeah, sounds good," Cymbeline replied quickly. She could see the distant shape of yellow headlights as Neil's rust-eaten Ford Pinto crawled its way into the parking lot. She felt the shimmer of something. Whirling teeth in the left-hand side of her field of vision. Maybe a migraine. She grimaced and tried to will it away. Sid watched her closely.

"I *know* you're nervous," Sid said, misreading the look on Cymbeline's face. Because she was nervous, but it wasn't that, or only that. When had she not lived with anxiety? Her life had been steeped in it. "But all great artists get stage fright. It's part of the process. *Gandhi* hated public speaking."

Cymbeline chewed her lip. The car was approaching on them slowly, the sound of the tires crackling against the stone lot. She wondered if Neil was looking at her. At her silhouette, her tits, sharp and obvious in the cool evening air.

"Does that help?" Sid asked, a fleck of annoyance seeping through. It was obvious that Cymbeline wasn't listening to her advice, though it wasn't like the advice wasn't *good* or she wasn't grateful.

"Yeah. Gandhi," Cymbeline said faintly, as the Pinto pulled up beside them. The figure inside was much too stout to be Neil. As the window rolled down, Cymbeline bent over, glancing in—hating how she knew it made her breasts look in that dress. Hating it even more when she realized who was there, alone, inside.

Lonnie.

"Helllooo ladies," he said slowly.

"Hey," Sid said brusquely back, "Where the hell is Neil?"

Lonnie shrugged. "Sorry, girls," he said, "But Neil is indisposed."

"What the fuck," Sid said. "He was supposed to give us a ride."

"Look, don't shoot the messenger." Lonnie held up his hands. They were sort of gray and grimy, older looking than the rest of him. "His entire cabin has the pukes. But you know Neil—he's a thoughtful guy. He told me to bring this here wagon of folks out to you so you don't miss your 'gig.'"

Air quotes around the word. A condescending smile. Cymbeline hadn't realized how much she hated Lonnie before, but she did now. This was all a joke to him—the two "girls," the music. It seemed like Neil, at least, had taken her *music* seriously, recognizing in her some sort of kindred spirit. But Lonnie was different. To him, she'd never be more than a girl in a dress, no matter how well she played the guitar. She was only a woman. A body. A mark.

"We don't know where we're going," Sid said, glowering. At least Cymbeline wasn't alone in her dislike of the man.

"No worries," Lonnie said. "I took care of it. Or Jeeves did."

He held out a stack of printed directions.

Sid looked over at Cymbeline, who shrugged. This would be an easy juncture, Cymbeline thought, to just give up. Stay here with her girls, who needed her. Go back to college at the end of the summer. Write Sid a letter or two, until they met other people. And then never speak to Sid again. She wasn't sure how, but she knew that if she pressed forward with tonight, it was destined to be a wedding, of sorts. She'd be showing Sid that something could come of her ambitions—their ambitions. She'd be showing both of them that there was something more in this world.

It would have been so much easier to just convince herself that there *wasn't*. Music wasn't magic, after all. It couldn't *take* you anywhere. The only place you could really go was summer camp, maybe. Sure, maybe the right song could be an escape from your crappy apartment with your crappy dying mother, playing your acoustic with a towel stuffed inside so the hum of the strings wouldn't disturb her. But that was an illusion. You were still your same wrong, anxious self, trapped in the same thin flesh, withering under everyone's gaze. For a moment, she told herself that nothing would come of this, even if they *did* go. No fame. No fortune. No union.

But looking into Sid's dark, steady eyes, she wavered. Because she didn't want this, not for herself. But Sid did. And she wanted it for Sid. Sid, who never bothered with college because she figured it couldn't teach her anything she needed. Sid, who had music in her bones, her veins, who had wanted to somehow make her father's forgotten dreams manifest, but hadn't had the rhythm for it, the internal beat. Sid, who said she was a damned good mechanic—reliable, an ace diagnostician—despite the fact that she was paid less than anyone else in the garage just by virtue of her sex, when her sex wasn't even *true*, wasn't right. Sid. Who wasn't an orphan except on the inside, because she'd never been understood, never been seen, much less *matched*. Not until Cymbeline.

Sid, who had just started to hope that life would be more than summers at camp and winters smelling like engine oil, zipping her coveralls over her sports bra, hiding herself. Sid would be her *manager* and they would get out of here, out of the lives they were both trapped in, make money and do something new. What would they do?

Whatever they wanted.

Cymbeline cleared her throat. Shrugged.

"Yeah, sure," she said. "But I can't drive stick."

"Oh, don't worry," Lonnie said, rushing to unbuckle himself. He got out of the driver's seat and opened the passenger's, cranking the seat forward, putting Cymbeline's guitar in the narrow back. Gesturing for them both to climb in. "I can drive you."

Sid looked at Lonnie, her lip curling. Snorted. "No," she said. She reached down and put the front seat back in place, gesturing to the empty passenger seat.

"Perky," she said, with command presence. "Get in."

Cymbeline did as she was told, slamming the door behind her. She watched as Sid planted herself in the driver's seat and started adjusting the mirrors.

"Hey, wait a minute, ladies," Lonnie said. "You can't just leave me here. I'll have to walk all the way back to Berean!"

Cymbeline tried not to smile as Sid shifted, stepped on the gas, and peeled it out of the parking lot, leaving Lonnie in the faint cloud of evening dust, behind them.

* * *

The car rattling down a highway, a stream of light in darkness. Sid talking too much, then getting annoyed at Neil's poor taste in cassettes, throwing them pell-mell into the backseat, and the headache blooming to life over Cymbeline's left eye, like the peonies her mother used to cut and leave in cups in the spring, how they would explode, and wilt and their fragrance would touch everything, the food they ate and the medicine her mother took and even Cymbeline's own saliva, it seemed. Cymbeline could almost smell them now, and a wave of nausea washed through her.

"I'm going to close my eyes for a few minutes," she said, not wanting to tell Sid what was happening. She wasn't sure that Sid would even believe her. Sid might think it was an excuse like she had last time. Sid might think that Cymbeline was preparing to let her down.

She wouldn't. Couldn't. Maybe if she just went to sleep . . .

"Go for it," Sid said. She flicked her fingernail against the flock in the dash. "We'll be there in about an hour."

Cymbeline put the seat back. Shed her flip-flops, put her bare feet up on cracked hard vinyl. The window was open and she could smell those peonies as she let the darkness close its arms around her. The wind on her face, nauseating. She heard the oceanic sound of the cars on the highway, their own, noisy, puttering, and the trucks around them, and how the rust bucket Pinto swayed and Cymbeline felt it, her stomach a knot, her head a knot, her anxiety not even mounting because it could not get any higher.

She closed her eyes. And still, in the darkness, through her slitted eyelids saw the lights on the side of the highway, and through her slitted eyelids she saw headlights glide through the black. There were those open mouths, those teeth. Soon she would get up on stage and even if there were not many eyes facing her or mouths smiling or unsmiling they would be hungry mouths. They would want to devour her. They would be starving. Hands reaching out for her. Ready for her mistakes, her victories, her flesh, her songs, eating them up, hungry hungry hungry, biblical angels many-eyed and wing innumerable and wanting and she would know that she volunteered for this, she asked for it. Once. Twice. Again. Fame.

The wind was on her face, which was slick now with a sheen of sweat and something else, clammy, oily and she heard a baby crying, somewhere, here and not here—in the car and somewhere else, and she heard a knock on the door and she felt herself pass through a space, a hallway, a kitchen, saw a guitar in pieces on the table, and there was a baby crying and there was music playing somewhere, not hers, but a song she'd once loved long ago, and she was humming even though she was silent, and there was a knocking, *thunk thunk thunk*, and her head was full of teeth and her mouth filled with smoke and she shed ash down into the ash tray on the table before reaching out through the cigarette haze toward the doorknob.

That's when Sid smacked the dash once, hard, waking her up.

"That's not good," Sid said.

"What?" Cymbeline asked. It wasn't a conversational *what*. Cymbeline had felt momentarily untethered from reality, unsure of where she was. Her stomach lurched as Sid pulled into a parking lot.

"The noise. Doesn't sound good. I think it's fucking rod knock . . ."

That was meaningless to Cymbeline except for the grim tone in Sid's voice.

"Shit," Cymbeline said, "Do you think we'll make it to the open mic?"

"Well," Sid said, she gestured out the window, to where a seedy-looking bar sat on the edge of a black, endless-looking lake, flanked by sparse trees on either side. There was a sign on the roof: *The Lighthouse*. And then, below, in black letters against white, *Live Music Every Friday and Saturday 10 - 1.* "We already did. But getting home might be another matter."

Sid killed the engine. The knocking, incessant, urgent, hummed to a stop. Funny, though, how Cymbeline could still almost hear it, echoing out in her head. *Thunk thunk. Thunk thunk.*

29 - 1958

oing to have to take care of it, Baron thought, staggering down the stairs after Eddie, his shoulder hitting the yellowed wallpaper as he went. Eddie's small, square shoulders in front of him, his arse (round, more like a girl's arse, really) in front of him, his blond fucking curls in front of him, beautiful and shining. And Baron knowing in his heart that he had ruined everything. That he had fucked it all up. The party had quieted somehow, the music off now—but a loud kind of quiet. Folks trying to keep their voices hushed, like it was a fucking surprise party, which it wasn't. Everything was wretched to him now, especially this—everyone he knew, or almost everyone, since Deedz and Fred weren't there—all packed into a corner in the living room. Raising their arms up at the sight of him.

"Oi, there's the birthday boy!" and "Surprise, Barry!" and all of that, but they were all almost invisible to him except for Eddie, who went to the corner and found his guitar and slung the strap over his shoulder. And except for Dickie, who was still there of course, perched on the edge of his mum's sofa, thimbles on his fingers, washboard in his hands.

"Is he here?" came his mum's chirpy voice. "Is he ready?" And some bird—Sue, probably—chirped back a *yeh, he's ready* and that's when the crowd parted for his mum, looking young and beautiful, her pointed boobs almost being lit on fire by too many candles in a pink fucking frosted cake.

Eddie counted them all out. Eddie started strumming. They started singing *Happy birthday to you*, the whole lot of them, playing and strumming, and for a moment, with his mum's tits over his very own birthday cake, his name glowing out in red icing script on top, he was happy, the little sad boy in him was happy. A birthday party! And a cake! And a boy like Eddie singing to him. Made the cockles swell. But then, before the song was over, he heard it. Something off and very wrong, and his eyes went to Dickie, who was scraping the washboard off tune as the last *happy birthday to yoooooooooou* warbled and faded. *Fuck,* thought Baron, because Dickie was ruining it and *he* had already ruined it, and his arsehole hurt and he couldn't forget it, what Eddie had seen, what he had done, how he had failed. *Going to have to take care of it*, he reminded himself, as his mother said, in a sweet sexy voice, "Blow out the candles, Barry, and make a wish."

He leaned over, getting a good look at that soft, pink rack, took in a deep breath, and blew. What was he wishing for? An answer, that's what. And just as the candles flickered out, and he stood straight, and everyone cheered, he looked over at Dickie and realized that he knew what he needed to do.

People were clapping their hands. Someone—was it Ed?—gave a whistle between the teeth. Someone else asked him to give a speech. He didn't, couldn't. But he walked straighter now, and less drunken. In that brief, narrow moment, restored to sobriety, restored to himself.

He towered over Dickie in that brief, narrow moment. Dickie was sitting on the sofa, looking up at him, eyes mocking and expectant.

"What'dja wish for?" Dick asked. Baron held out one hand, gesturing.

"Give us the washboard," he said.

Dick hesitated. He looked around him, like it was a joke, all at Baron's expense. Looking for Liam or someone else who would confirm that he did not need to give Baron the washboard. But it was Baron's fucking birthday. He was the *fucking* birthday boy. His mother only laughed from where she still held that pink cake in trembling hands, said, "Oh, give it to him." So after just one more moment, Dickie did.

Baron held the washboard in his hands, examined it. Dickie's fat Irish mother's ancient fucking washboard. Paint-peeled, but sturdy. "Looks good," Baron said thoughtfully, and he didn't wait even one more minute, not one more *second*, before he lifted it up and let it come down crashing right over Dickie's stupid little greasy head. It hurt, it must have hurt, for how hard Baron did it and the thickness of the wood. But it didn't matter. Or maybe it *did*, because Baron had wanted to hurt him.

Everyone was quiet, except someone laughing a little, then stopping. Liam, maybe. The wood frame had splintered around Dickie, and now it hung useless like some sort of ruffled Victorian collar around his neck.

"My wish," Baron said, not sourly, but easily, and with a smile, "was for you to be out of me fuckin' band."

Dickie blinked. Dickie shook his head like his ears were ringing. Looked around him, blinked again. Maybe he could have cried, could have made a joke at Baron's expense, could have let Baron be the villain. But how would that have made Dickie look? Only small and weak. So he forced a laugh then, and a few folks, uncomfortable, laughed with him.

"Far be it from me to spoil someone's birthday," he said, his voice a little raw, but kind enough. Pretending to be kind enough. All around him, Baron could feel people exhale. Laugh a little more, comfortably now. There would be no more fight than this, not from Dickie.

Baron had won.

"Alright, then," Baron's mum said brightly, "Who wants cake?"

* * *

There were strawberries inside the cake, and they tasted like summer. There were cherries in the bottom of Baron's glass, the drink someone had given him, whatever it was. He held them between his back teeth as he drank. Dick went home with a sulk in the middle of it all, casting a dark look to Baron, but Baron didn't care. He'd won. He'd *won*. He had fucking won. Now if Dickie tried to tell anyone what had happened, if he tried to use Baron's *weaknesses* against him, it'd look like sour grapes.

Baron danced. Baron drank. Baron swung, full of life. He had *fucking* won.

Hours later, moon high in the sky, he stumbled out the front steps to smoke a fag, last one of two in his coat pocket. That's when he saw Eddie standing in the yellow porch light before his mother's house. Not smoking. Just standing there, beautiful, his hands in his pockets. Baron swayed, still pickled drunk, of course, as he lit that fag up.

"Want one?" he asked Ed. Ed looked at him, face a soft mask. Shook his head.

"Suit yerself," said Baron, inhaling deep. It felt good to smoke. Good to be alive. Though he coughed a bit on exhalation. And laughed a little, too.

"What a fuckin' birthday, eh?" he said to Eddie. Silence stretched out. Ed didn't answer. So Baron gave him a tender punch on the arm.

"Well?" he prodded. "Got rid of Dickie for yeh."

Eddie didn't look at him. He laughed now, too, but it was a dry laugh, without any warmth.

"Yeah," Eddie agreed. "You got rid of Dickie."

Ed started down the steps as if to leave. Baron felt like his heart was walking down the steps with him.

"What's all this?" Baron called out. Sloppy voiced, stupid, and when Ed didn't answer he added: "You leavin' then? What? Is it because of what you saw? Is it because I'm a *queer*?"

He'd reached the front walk, but now Eddie whipped around, his eyes narrowed, his voice low. "Baron!" he snapped. "Do you think *I* fuckin' *care* if you're *queer*?"

Baron didn't know what to say to that. He stood there, the ash turning into a tower at the end of his fag, the cold biting his numb drunk hands.

"It's not—it's not because you're *queer*," Eddie said, his voice full of anger and grief and yet still dropping low when he said it, like he couldn't stand anyone in this dark silent night to hear. "It's because you're a *foocking mess*. Can't you see where this is all going to lead you, Barry? Because I can."

Baron's pride, usually a prize fighter inside him, swelled large now with anger and muscle. "I sacked him," Baron said, "For *you*. So we can be fucking famous. And that's where it'll lead. Piles of money, isn't that what you care about, Hammy? The piles of fucking money waiting for us?"

"No," Eddie said, with a fierce shake of his head, so angry that he didn't care what Baron called him, or if Baron called him anything at all. "I was wrong. Dickie or no Dickie, you're a fucking drunk. Gonna be old and fat and toothless in a bar someday, bitchin' about everyone who ever wronged you. How Dick ruined your chance and I ruined your chance and how your sweet old mum ruined your chance. Or else—or else—"

"Or else what?" Baron said, taking a drag, trying his best to look like he didn't care about what Eddie was saying to him. Trying to look like it wasn't slashing him into a million pieces.

"Or else you'll be dead in a ditch. You're fucking sloppy, Baron Templeton. I'd be a fool to hitch my star to you."

Eddie tugged his coat tight around him, turned around, started off again in a huff. Baron felt his lip curl, let it. It was better than than the alternative, to cry like a fucking baby on his mother's front steps. He took one sharp, dangerous step down the slate steps, determined, maybe, to prove Eddie right.

"Yeah," said Baron, "You fucking *go*. Run off to your Dylan Miranda. Suck his bollocks for all I care. I'm not the queer. Everyone has to just take one look at *you* to know it."

The only indication that Eddie gave that he even heard what Baron was saying was to shake his head a little, to laugh a little, his breath making clouds on the winter air. He didn't stop, not for a second, as he took off into the night.

That was the end of it. Baron let him go.

* * *

There was one more event of import on that night, the night that Baron turned eighteen.

Somehow, as the party dwindled away to nothing, as the girls and the boys drifted away, as his brain started to sober up and pass into the dry, painful, throbbing domain of drunk's aftermath, he found himself on the sofa next to Sue Grasso. Her head on his shoulder at first. His hand on her thigh, then her breast. Then she stood and walked him upstairs to his sister's room, and Bess wasn't anywhere to be found as, giggling, Sue closed the door behind her. Baron was sure his mother had had something to do with this, with orchestrating this entire encounter. Both of their mothers together, probably, conspiring with Sue to solve some sort of problem, together.

The problem of queer little Baron Templeton.

They tumbled down on Bess's bed together, giggling, both, and for a moment, as she kissed his neck, he wondered if he were too drunk and his life too grim for him to get a throbber—but that had never been a problem for him. Before he knew it, he was pressing into the billows of her dress, pressing hard into her softness, lifting up the cotton, feeling the scratchy nylon cage that birds like her kept themselves in, and they were still giggling, unhooking latches together like they were breaking into some sort of hallowed ground. Her skin, at last, warm and free, and his hands, hard with callouses and narrow, feeling it, and him hard against her.

"You'll pull out," she commanded, wriggling out of her knickers. He was still in his trousers, his cock hard as a glass bottleneck, nodding dutifully, undone, like a little boy.

Oh, how it felt to be undone at that moment, not thinking, not miserable, and it was different than wanking with Dickie. She was all softness and velvet save for her sharp nails, which scratched a bit, accidental, as they took out his cock, but then there was more softness and wet and he shuddered into her, too close, too soon. Gave a yelp, shook his head, laughed. Flipped her over in one smooth movement, laughing more, and Sue laughing with him, Baron feeling glad to be bigger than her, stronger, in that moment, a different beast than the one who had spilled seed with Dickie in an alleyway, in the old outhouse. It was different for him, for there to be soft sweetness and light.

He moved in her. A poem. A song.

This is how I would fuck Eddie, he thought, then hated himself for it, for reminding himself of his misery and pain and so he buried herself deeper into her, on top now, in control, smiling, laughing, cunning, brave, and Sue's eyes were open and she saw him, and what she saw was not the whole truth but neither was it a lie.

Soon, anyway, both their eyes were closed, and they were crying out, both of them, not caring if Baron's sister or stepfather or mum heard, or maybe that was the point, crying out together, a chorus, until he was close again, and she stopped him and obediently he pulled out, spilling seed all over her soft fat belly.

"Good boy," she said, stroking his cheek, and he would have hated her for speaking to him that way, except he didn't. In the moment, he loved it, to be *good*. His body throbbing, trembling, still. But not done.

"I want to see how you do it," he told her, and Sue didn't say anything, only frowned for a moment, like she didn't know what he meant, so he bent low and began licking her soft belly clean, and then moved his head downward. It was *her* turn to yelp, as he moved his mouth over her already-damp thatch of hair, finding easy the bundle of nerves that, in their way, matched his own softening bundle. Inhaling the walnut and wood smoke musk of her. Undulating that tongue. Letting her thighs tighten over his ears, her hips bucking, her fanny throbbing. *There*, he thought, as she let out a small, strangled sound, her cunt and arsehole ticking against his face. *Not so different. Not such a mystery, then.*

After, thinly asleep and then awake in the gray dawn, his head pounding. A question answered, but not the whole question—perhaps not answered in the way his mum had wanted. He had enjoyed Sue, yes. His body had certainly enjoyed it. His mind had enjoyed it. Going inside of her, setting off sparks, turning off the world for a moment for the simple pleasure of it, for the magic of what their bodies could do.

And yet it didn't change what he'd felt for Dick, what he'd felt for Eddie, what he'd felt for young Puck in his green sheer tights, for Elvis, shaking his hips on TV, for poor dead Buddy, shaking his hips on TV, a soft voice worming into his ear, a soft music making his cock twitch. Had he still wanked to those thoughts, would he still wank again? Yes, yes, and to Bridgette Bardot and Jayne Mansfield and his mum and Sue, once twice or a thousand times. It wasn't that he liked one thing, and not the other. It was not one thing or the other to Baron. No, he didn't love Sue, not like he loved Eddie. And he wasn't starved for her, either, like he'd been for

Dick, but that didn't matter. The *point* was that it wasn't a whole new song, fucking Sue. It was a leitmotif, really. Ed had taught him that word once. A repeating theme. Happening once, twice, again and again in the same song or maybe a different song, a different form. The same melody. And he knew, lying there, as the day dawned over his mum's house, the gray winter light waking over Sue's bare skin, that he'd fuck her again, soon, maybe in just a few minutes, and he'd be doing it so that he wouldn't have to *think* about how Eddie Hammond had broke his heart.

But not because Eddie Hammond hadn't broke his heart at all.

30 - 2017

Hours and hours of writing and noodling, pages scattered around like autumn leaves, the ink dragged over the heel of Naomi's left hand and up her forearm. At nearly sundown, Matthew finally stood, stretching his body, letting his spine, which felt stuck in its curve after hours stooped, unfurl to its full length, and he was spent enough that he almost didn't notice how Naomi's eyes went to him, watching where his shirt lifted up over his belly. Or if he did notice, he told himself he imagined it. Naomi had been clear. This was not about sex for her.

Besides, who needed sex? He had suggested that the song be about love at first. A love song. You know, that sort of simple hit that Edelman had told them he needed this summer? Something just a little nostalgic, a little world-weary, to appeal to guys his age. But a love song, none-the-less. Naomi had scoffed, and secretly, he'd been relieved by her dismissal.

"C'mon, what does *love* even mean to you, anyway? Greeting card sentiment. *Who* do you love? *How* do you love? What do you risk when you love someone, Edmund Matthew Hammond Junior?"

"I'm not a junior," he said, and Naomi made that scoffing sound again, phlegmy, in her throat. "I'm the fourth."

"Alright," she said, "Number Four, tell me about love. Use a few *details*. I don't have the pedigree to coast by on sentiment. So neither can you."

There it was again, that crass discussion of class, money. Matthew, still stooped over the piano then, had closed his eyes. Thought *love love*. Felt nothing, not for Kara, not for the baby to come. *Love.* He'd put his hands down, blindly playing the chords that Naomi had helped him wright. *Love.*

And the first image was his father's foot, pressing the pedals. He knew, then, what the song would be about.

"My very first memory. I couldn't have been much older than two, three. A pair of wellies," he said, "Covered in mud, because my dad had been mucking about on the farm all morning. I'd wanted him to play with me, but he said he had to go feed the sheep. So I waited and waited, and then he comes in for lunch, but he doesn't go to the butties my mum had made him. He goes over to the piano instead. That thing was so big it took up our whole dining room. He was humming already, and he sits down, and he just starts playin'. Matthew's Song. Like it was fully formed. And I realized as I watched him that he'd been goin' around for days humming that. Carrying me in his head, while he was doing chores and making oatmeal and helpin' my sisters with their maths. He might have been *busy*, but he hadn't forgotten me."

Naomi had watched him, wide eyed, from her chair. Her pen paused, before the writing began.

"That's what I know about love," Matthew said. Naomi blinked, began furiously writing.

"Okay then," was what she said, and she'd sighed at first, like she had almost hoped he'd failed. But then he hadn't, had he? And that's how they whittled the day away. Trading phrases. Him remembering, her pushing. About Dad and his wellies and the sheep and being a little boy, pressing his face to the floor and listening.

But at last, the evening had come, and he hadn't eaten since he'd voided his gut that morning.

"Man cannot live on music alone," he declared, marching to the kitchen, finding those takeout menus. He bowed a little to Naomi, "Or woman."

Naomi rolled her eyes. But she didn't look unhappy about it.

He'd been hoping to find something decent, Thai, or maybe Vietnamese. But all there was to choose between here was a place called Village Pizza and two Chinese joints—China House II and China Palace.

"Stick with the original," Naomi said. She was still curled in her chair, jotting down words. "China Palace."

"You've got class," Matthew said, and winked, as he called to put in his order for egg foo young and for Naomi's for four seasons lo mein, whatever that was, Matthew wasn't sure. When he got off the phone, he told her it was his treat. More snorting.

"Yeah," she said. "Of course."

He bristled, but tried not to show it as he sat back down on the floor and examined their work so far. He didn't like her poverty, of being reminded of it. It made him feel guilty about everything he had, which, in turn, made his stomach knot up. There had been so many birds who had wanted something from him before Kara. And *she* never seemed to mind the many fringe benefits of being tethered to a Hammond, even if she had celebrity and money of her own right. He coughed, frowned, tried to make himself focus on her sloppy handwriting, the words she'd transcribed:

Heavy boots made light again/he'll write you a song again/while he's working in the ~~garden~~ farmyard???/he'll keep you in mind.

"Farmyard feels very pastoral," Matthew said. "Very agrarian. It's not right. Maybe garden is better."

"Only if we mean it in the American sense," she said. "But with your accent, it sounds like you're talking about palace grounds."

"I've lived in the states for decades. I don't have an accent," Matthew groused. Naomi didn't answer for a moment, so Matthew looked up over the top of the paper.

"What?"

"*Wot?*" she snapped back, like a teenage girl, then snickered at him. Matthew felt himself flush, but he could see she meant nothing by it. He could play at this, too, he decided. He crumpled the page into the ball and threw it at her. It hit her on the shoulder, bounced off.

"Watch it, Matthew," she said. "I've got a lawyer."

"Have you?" he asked. The doorbell had rung. Food. He got up.

"Sure. Well, Edelman does. He tells me that his star client has pretty deep coffers."

"Sure, sure," said Matthew, as he opened the door and paid, and tipped well, and thanked the delivery girl. Trying to ignore it again. The money talk. *She's only joking*, he reminded himself. *She says it because she doesn't know that she's not supposed to say it.*

"Wouldn't want a lawsuit," she added. "For reckless endangerment."

He put the bag of food down on the counter. His stomach gurgled. Still sour, a bit, from earlier. But mostly just starved.

"Are you going to come eat or not?" he asked.

"Sure," she said with a sigh, "Just a minute."

She got up and crossed the room, going to Edelman's hi-fi. He kept his eyes on her back, her slender form. She picked a record. Arthur Alexander. *You Better Move On.* Violins and vaguely Caribbean vibes filled up the room.

"Now that's what I'm talking about," she said, and started dancing. And. Well. She might have been slender, smooth skinned, lovely. But lord. She crossed the room, shuffling her arms, her hips swinging, remarkably off-rhythm for someone who had such a stunning sense of *music*. She was a *terrible* dancer.

Matthew laughed, then stopped himself as he carefully scooped his food onto a plate. Didn't want to offend her.

"What?" she said. "People who don't dance aren't allowed to laugh at people who do. That's my rule."

Matthew frowned. "I dance," he said, then immediately regretted it, because he knew what was coming next. She gestured to the space between the piano and the kitchen. The white carpet, waiting. It was a dance floor, of sorts.

Matthew sighed. He really *was* hungry. Really *didn't* want to make her feel bad. The record coasted to the next track. Slower. Groovier. Tinkling and a little wild. He offered her a hand, and she took it, and he tried to pretend that he wasn't thrilled somehow, like a teenage boy at a school dance, which he'd once been, but back then he hadn't figured it out, that all it takes is to move like you're really feeling it. Back then he'd been awkward in his skin, utterly unfucked.

He wasn't now.

She tried to lead at first. He stopped her. Laughed. Shook his head. Started over. And they danced together, slowly at first, their eyes locked together, something trembling between them, pregnant. Until the song faded. Changed again. Grew upbeat. That Arthur Alexander. Bringing him just what he needed so that he wouldn't lose his head. He spun her. Let her go. Snapped his fingers, mashed potato a little, felt it. She laughed at him, stumbled.

"No," he said gently. Not cruelly. "Watch what I'm doing. Follow me."

She hesitated, for only a second. And then she did.

And. Christ. Christ. Arthur Alexander was singing, the words filling up that room overlooking that winter mountain, that lake: "Hey baby," Arthur was asking—no *they* were asking—Arthur Alexander and Edmund Matthew Hammond IV, both, at once, as she mirrored his motions perfectly, "I want to know, will you be my girl?"

* * *

Forty minutes later, sweat-slick from dancing, a bottle of Edelman's Pinot Noir drained into his vintage juice cups and those juice cups drained into their bodies. Their meals eaten, or mostly, and for the first time that day, Matthew feeling settled, too, even if his heart was going wild inside of him. It had been Naomi's idea, after the Arthur Alexander album, to put on Saffron. Matthew had campaigned for *The Ruffians* but Naomi said she liked the later stuff better. She pulled out an album, ancient looking, well loved, from the band's psychedelic period that immediately preceded the breakup. There was a name in the corner in permanent marker: *Sadie.* Was he mistaken, or had Naomi's hand lingered for just a moment over Baron Templeton's dark face, over the image of his now-dead body, clad, as it had been, in a bright red suit. The rest of them had been wearing white, pure white, except for a red carnation in his father's lapel. There had been theories for a few years that Baron had received a premonition of his death, that this was why he was set apart visually, that Eddie had worn a carnation to show the bond between them which would transcend even the veil between the world of the living and the dead.

Fan-fictions. Stories traded between teenage girls.

"Don't be daft," Matthew had heard Eddie say to a reporter on tour once. "He dressed in red because it looked better with his coloring. I wore a flower because I'm fond of flowers. Used to do it all the time when we was young, at shows. The birds dug it. Sometimes, dearest Abby," he said, addressing the squirming reporter, "a cigar is just a cigar."

Everyone had laughed. It struck Matthew then and stayed with him for years after that his father's humor was underrated. This Baron Templeton, a man he'd never met, was said to be the funny one. But *his* Dad was funny too.

Now, the two of them sitting on the Edelman's white carpet, and perhaps not caring as much as they should have about the noodles they dropped here and there. On the hi-fi, his dad was doing his solo, now, the big one, in the quiet dark of the studio, all alone. "Cymbeline."

"I always liked this one," Naomi admitted, almost reluctantly, like it hurt her to give Eddie Hammond praise, on a song that had gone quadruple platinum, on a song that could have sent him to boarding school forty times over on cover rights alone.

"Yeah," Matthew said. "It's okay."

They both laughed. But as their laughter faded, he looked at her, reading the strange sort of quiet in her face. He was going to ask what was wrong, but then she spoke before he did.

"I'm jealous, you know," she said. "You have all these memories. The boots, but not just that. I bet you were a dick to him when you were a teenager. He's probably a pain in the ass at holidays now. I don't have any of it. A few memories, but I might have invented them for all I know. He wasn't even with my mom for four years, you know that? Before he insisted on following Peter X. down to Trinidad. She tried to convince him to stay. She always said they loved each other. But how much could he have loved her if she couldn't convince him to stay?"

Matthew stirred his fork around his takeout container like he thought me might be able to find an answer there. "Hmm," he grunted. "It was practically a cult, wasn't it? I think it's stranger that your mom broke free than that Templeton didn't. Charismatic leader and all that."

"Charismatic," Naomi said. Snorted. "Isn't that how the press used to talk about my dad? *The charismatic leader of Saffron since the beginning.*"

Matthew grimaced. If you spoke to his dad, he told a different story. That they were a pair, the two of them, and also a group. A family of sorts, not so easily understood by outsiders.

"Just think," Matthew said finally, "What would have happened if your Dad hadn't of blown it all up. Hadn't gotten wrapped up in all those *causes*, hadn't forced my Dad's hand in breaking up the band. Hadn't have followed Peter X. to America."

"Is that why he broke them up?" Naomi asked sharply, then shook her head. "Well, thank him for me. If he hadn't done it, I wouldn't be here."

Will you weather this storm for me, my queen, my Cymbeline? Eddie Hammond asked them from the speakers wired to the ceiling.

I'm glad you're here, is what Matthew wanted to say, but couldn't. This wasn't about sex, right? And there was Kara and the baby to think about. As much as he wanted to fuck her, as she sat there, looking moody and tragic and so, so lovely, it would have been wrong—what with the thought of little Naomi and her poor Black immigrant mum burning so brightly in his mind. Begging Baron Templeton not to go. Begging him to stay. To be a father. To survive.

"Still," Matthew said, listening to the music fade. The next track, more typical for Saffron. Hard rock back beat shot through with veins of lysergic acid, jostling the soft, mellow sounds of the album opener out of place. "Can't help but feel sad for the loss of the music."

Their dads sang together. Sweet silly nonsense. Matthew could almost imagine it—or maybe it was footage he'd seen somewhere. The two men, so young, if you thought about it, grinning at each other from across the studio.

"So," he said, narrowing his eyes on her, harder now, because he felt he had to be. "You think they were queer?"

"That wouldn't have been what they would have called it then," she said. "At least, not like we mean it now."

Not like she means it about herself, Matthew thought. He poured himself another glass of wine, topped off Naomi, too. No, he supposed his father wouldn't have used those words then, unless he'd meant it as a deadly insult. He had heard his father speak politely about *the gays*, or even joke regressively about *queens*, but to be *queer*, to actually name it, that would have been something else entirely.

"They loved each other," she said. "More than anyone else in the world. My mother—she was jealous. Not because she had to share my father with Peter X., or the groupies that sometimes found their way to him. Male and female. Both. But because of Eddie. Because Eddie was his first love, and no one could ever top him."

A glint in her eye. A wicked dimple. "So to speak," she said.

Matthew took a mouthful of wine, swallowed hard. "Platonic," he said. "It was platonic. They loved each other. Like brothers. That's what my dad always says."

Not that his dad spoke often of Baron. Not that Matthew had ever really asked. Naomi lifted her cup close to her mouth, but didn't drink for a moment. She didn't speak, either. Considering.

"He left everything with mom when he went to Trinidad," she said. "We have . . . his guitars. His records. She sold some of those when money was tight. His MBE. And . . . . journals. We have his journals."

"Journals?"

"Not, like, diaries. But notebooks. Papers. Stacks of them. Going back to—what do you call high school, in the UK?"

"Secondary school," Matthew said. He drank a little more, stared at her. "And you've read these?"

Naomi's eyes were owl eyes. She didn't answer, but she nodded, and finally drank a little, too. Verifiable—it was all verifiable, what she was saying. Whatever she was saying. It could kill his dad with the press. If it was a lie? Some kind of forgery, or a joke on Baron Templeton's part? It could kill his dad. *Kill* him. His sweet old soppy dad.

"If what you're saying is true," he said, "Then those journals could be worth millions. Why didn't she sell them, if she was so poor? Why didn't you?"

Naomi cringed. "I told you. It's not like that. It's not about money. And—at first, my mom didn't want to. She could have been implicated, you know? In all that shit that Peter X. was doing. Funding the Panthers, that kind of thing. You know the CIA followed them for years? She wasn't here legally. She didn't want the press. Not for her *or* me. We laid low. And now—I mean, it's one thing, to tell *you,* now. But it seems to me like it isn't really anyone's business."

"I'm not sure that it's *your* business," Matthew said, sounding angrier than he intended. Naomi opened her mouth. Closed it. Laughed just a little bit.

"You're right," she said. "You're right. When I was a kid—a teenager—I used to pore over them. They were all I had of him. And that it was so different from what everyone else knew about him, the biographies and all of that, it felt—it felt like a secret. The one thing that I had with my dad, just for the two of us, alone. But if anyone deserves those journals, it's probably your father. The way Baron *wrote* about him, Matt. The poetry of it! Sonnets about his music, his eyes, the way his armpits stank." She laughed at the memory. "All the way up through the '70s. Your dad carried songs about *you* with him. Mine was busy writing pages and pages about your dad's *toes.* Among other things."

Her gaze flickered toward him, checking to see if he was shocked. Matthew wasn't.

"Plenty of people have written sonnets about my father's *other things,*" he said, and couldn't help but cringe to say it, because it was his Dad, and because his father was embarrassing, and it was embarrassing to acknowledge that your embarrassing old man was a sex symbol or had been, once. But still. Not shocking. "That doesn't mean it was in any way mutual—"

"There were letters too," she said softly, in a rush. "From your father. Other people, too, his Auntie in England, his sister. But mostly from your dad. They were—they weren't like the stuff my dad wrote. But they were very, very affectionate."

"He's an affectionate guy. If you'd ever met him—"

"*Matthew*, he talked about lying in bed with him. As teenagers. Deciding—I can't explain it to you. I don't have to. I can bring them to you tomorrow if you want. I should. You can give them back to him. They don't—they're not mine. They're his. All of them. I think they should be with him."

"Fine," Matthew said, a little too sharply. He wanted to shout at her. To accuse her. This was just jealousy. It had to be. She wanted to hurt him. Because she was covetousness for the life he'd had, with his sex, his skin color, his wealth.

His family.

The record had hissed to a stop. Other than "Cymbeline," his father's masterpiece, the first song he'd ever written alone, supposedly—claiming it came to him in a dream, a story which he'd heard so many times that Matthew had hardly paid attention to a single word—Matthew had barely listened. He'd heard them all before. On commercials. Piped into airports. Those songs were the fabric of everyone's lives, not just his own.

He rose to his feet. Put the album back in its sleeve. Touching *his dad's* face with his thumb. The full lips. The clear, bright eyes. He was the opposite of strange, smoldering Baron. In the photo, that fleck of pink was the only thing that connected them. But it was more, wasn't it? Different than what the other boys in the band had shared. Matthew touched his father, felt him. Before sliding them all back onto the shelf, tucking them away for eternity.

Then he looked at her. "I have an idea," he said. "For the album. A leitmotif."

Naomi frowned, like she couldn't quite keep up with the change in subject. He hadn't meant to confuse her. Only to move on from this—and onto to more pressing matters.

"Yeah?"

"Musically *and* lyrically," he said. "I think if we do this part, repeat it in, what, five or six of the songs? Space it out. You forget about it, then it comes back again . . . "

He went to the piano and sat down. Played a few bars. It had been a part that Naomi had conjured, a part which Naomi had added to his melody. Not an important part on the surface of it. But it had stuck in his brain. Wedged itself in there. And he could see how it could spin out, complementing *other* songs. Hers. His.

"Okay," she said carefully. "And what about the lyrics?"

"I'm not sure," he said to her. "But I have an image. A *specific* image," he added, and the corner of his mouth ticked up a little, because he knew the song they'd already written was better for how she'd pushed him.

"What's that?"

"Feet. Maybe yours. Mine."

She cracked a bright grin, and started to joke, "Kinky—" but Matthew shook his head, cutting her off.

"No. I'm serious. Because I think we start with my father's feet, and we end with yours."

Her smile fell. Was it a bad idea, wrong? But he knew it wasn't. When she didn't answer him, he sat straighter. Wanting to prove himself to her.

"We can talk about him walking in the Port of Spain. The history of it. Mudflats and mangroves. And *his* history, the one he carried with him. His history with my father, and his own father. And his history with you."

The silence trembled now between them. She was frowning, shaking her head, only slightly. Not quite saying no, but not saying yes, either.

"I've never been there," she said softly. Matthew shrugged.

"It doesn't matter," he said. "I have. I can tell you what it's like."

She hesitated only a moment longer, watching him. Then she rose from the floor and went to sit beside him on the piano bench.

* * *

When he next took out his phone, it was dead. So he glanced over where Naomi was curled in the chair again, jotting lyrics, and then above and past her, to the mid-century metal clock on the mantel.

1:45 in the morning.

"Jesus," he said, and when she glanced up, he gestured behind her, to the clock. She blinked for a moment like she couldn't believe it either. Then laughed.

"Jesus," she agreed.

They had written four songs since dinner. Five songs for the day, if you counted the opener. "Eddie's Song," Matthew was calling it in his head. Or maybe "Answer Song," because it was an answer to "Matthew's Song," written forty years before. They'd written half an album or thereabouts. In a day. He laughed again, rubbing the heels of his hands in his eyes. It had never been like this for him, this easy. He couldn't have said for certain who had written what—the music or the words, the melody or counter melody. He heard his dad's voice in his tired brain. *We both wrote both,* he'd told a reporter once. *Except Cymbeline. That was all mine.*

Back then, Matthew had taken that to be a statement of the song—and his father's—superiority. Art was supposed *to be made in isolation,* coming through the haze like a dream. If you were a real artist, you could catch it easily all on your own. Now, he wondered how he had ever thought that. Wasn't this better? The push and pull of it, the muddling up. Both of their brains, their talents, working better in concert. The building rhythm, and how it made it better to . . . build.

"Christ, I'm tired," he admitted, and he looked around at the messy living room, at the take-out containers still lying about the carpet, at the paper strewn everywhere, and shook his head. Naomi was yawning, stretching out. When she yawned, she reminded him of a particularly adorable sleepy cat.

"You could stay—" Matthew said, at the exact same time she said, through a yawn, "I should go." She looked at him, her brow wrinkling skeptically.

"I thought I made myself clear that—"

"I'll be a gentleman!" he protested, holding up his hands. He hadn't meant it like that. He didn't think. Maybe. "There's a den, isn't there? Down here? I just thought, it's pretty late to drive, and we could get up to work earlier—"

"I sleep better in my own bed," she said decisively, rising from the chair. Suddenly, she wasn't catlike at all, but brisk, efficient in her movements.

More like a skittish colt. She started to pick up the takeout containers. Matthew rose and made a *shoo*ing gesture.

"Stop," he said. "I'll take care of those."

He took them from her. She was looking at him strangely as if this, of all things, was the last thing she expected from him. Then she shrugged.

"Suit yourself," she said, heading toward the door. As she shoved her feet down into her boots, she added, in a low voice.

"Besides, I need to get a few things for tomorrow. Those journals, for your dad. And my guitar."

"You play guitar?" he said, still standing there on the white carpet, clutching the takeout containers to his chest. He realized then that there was so little they knew about each other. She hadn't touched his guitar at all, only the piano. He'd assumed she didn't play.

"Of course," she said strangely.

He was still frozen in place. He knew that the strangeness was his fault. That he was being strange. It felt *wrong* that she was leaving. Severing whatever steel-wound string connected them. He wanted—he wanted to go to her, to kiss her forehead, to kiss her feet, to give her some sort of more fitting goodbye for what had transpired that day. But he knew he couldn't. It would have been even stranger if he did. She didn't want him *like that*. And he wanted her to know that he respected that, for once. Respected her.

"I'll be here at nine," she said. "If that's okay with you."

He could feel it, how he was smiling like a dumb ass. "It's . . . early," he admitted, still smiling. "But it's fine. Nine it is."

"See you," she said, still strangely.

"Goodbye!" he chirped back, and they both cringed at the sound of his voice. As if to escape the awkwardness that had descended upon them, Naomi rushed out the door. And was gone.

"Fuck," Matthew whispered. He sighed, moving slowly toward the kitchen garbage, where he chucked the cardboard containers inside. Sighed again. He looked around at the general chaos of the living room. So much paper strewn about. Lyrics dashed off and revised, in both of their hands.

Their words lying over each other. Like—like *bodies.*

"Fuck," he murmured again.

Lust was nothing new to him. But this was. Feeling so . . . . giddy, so smitten. So tender. But, well, he'd never experienced anything like this before, had he? That is to say *creatively.* It reminded him of high school. Sixteen. His first hand job, from a girl named Michelle. He'd rushed home from the theater to call his mate Harry from school, to tell him all about it. For those two weeks when he was sixteen—before Michelle consented to more complex pleasures—a hand job was the epitome of sexual bliss. Because, after all, before sixteen the only person who had been giving him hand jobs had been himself.

He told himself that it was simply this: the new, procreative magic of collaboration. He knew he was fooling himself, of course, but it felt better than the likely truth, that he had a stupid, childish, hopeless crush.

He went over to the hi-fi, found that Saffron album again. Took it out. Stared at it. Baron Templeton in that oxblood suit. His head angled, just slightly, toward Eddie Hammond.

He slid the record out of the sleeve, put it on the spindle. But this time, when he set the needle down, he skipped the first track. What new blood could be squeezed out of the stone that was "Cymbeline"? It was in Zales commercials, played at the emotional climax of romcoms, the heroine's eyes wet and trembling. He knew every beat of the recording, every breath his father drew. Once he'd been captivated by that. But that wasn't what he needed to understand, now.

He skipped to the second track. Heard the paired voices light up the darkness. Dragging his feet a bit on that white carpet, he pulled himself over to the chair and tucked himself in, to listen to the tapestry both men had woven—together.

31 - 1958

It was a bright, clear Saturday, the last Saturday in March. Saturday mornings were quieter than most in Eddie Hammond's house. None of the usual work and school day runabout for the Hammond men, except for Tom, who worked down on the docks on weekends and was gone before dawn. Now, just after seven, all was the soft, muffled silence of boys, sleeping the deep sleep of the dead. His brother James was snoring up above him, and the mattress shifted and creaked when Eddie's alarm went off, but that was the only other sign of life in the room. In the bed across from him, the youngest, our kid Billy, was only visible by the few feathers of blond hair that peeked out between his blanket and the pillow.

Eddie rose alone then, in that thick, cottony quiet. He imagined sometimes what it would be like to live alone, or nearly. In a family with a normal number of kids, or even one, like Baron's maybe, when Baron was at his auntie's and not his mum's. He smiled grimly at the thought of that. At the thought of Barry. It had been nearly six weeks since Baron's eighteenth, since the party. Since the . . . row, if you could call it that. The end of things. He hadn't seen Baron, and he'd refused to entertain conversations about him with Liam or his Dad or anyone else. Told them, in no uncertain terms, that the band was over and it weren't worth talking about. But that didn't mean he didn't think about it. Him. Often. All the bloody time. If something wasn't reminding him of Baron, it was reminding him of how it was nothing like Baron.

Like now, how he went and got the clothing that hung in his closet. The cheap hand-me-down suit. The skinny tie. And went and drew himself a bath while he still could, while the other boys were still asleep. He never took a *bath* before rehearsals for the Bartlebys. And he certainly never wore a *suit*. A *tie*. Baron would have laughed at him. *Smart noose, Hammy,* or something like that.

He dropped himself down into the bath water, soaped up. Well, no choice now, was there? Dylan Miranda demanded that the members of *his* band look *professional*, and so for three Saturdays now, Eddie had gotten up early and washed the week's *junk* off of himself, freshly coiffed his hair, and put on Tom's old suit, which he'd recently outgrown. Would have rather worn his sports coat, the white one, which Baron had complimented once—*Fab, Hammy, like something Elvis might wear*—if he had to look sharp at all, but Dylan did not want the other band members upstaging him in comportment, if not in looks. He hadn't *said* so, but Ed was good at reading people, so Ed knew it was true. Tom's old suit would look better, for now. The right uniform for the right job, as his Dad would say.

He scrubbed his armpits, his ball sack, his hair. He hummed a little, hearing his voice echo. It was the melody for "Shake, Rattle & Roll" by the Comets, which Dylan had them learning. A bit passe, if you asked Eddie. A bit 1957. But Dylan at the ripe old age of twenty-two couldn't have been expected to be as up on the next thing as Eddie, a teenager.

Though honestly, if Ed had his way, they'd be doing originals. Dylan had a wailer of a voice, and it seemed a shame to waste it on only the exact same songs every band on this side of the Mersey was playing. But Dylan didn't write songs, couldn't even play guitar. To be fair, even Hank Wren, the Tempest's rhythm guitarist, was clumsy on an ax. Slow and soggy. They'd asked Eddie to come in on lead, but he had a thought in his head: maybe he should be rhythm, maybe he could bring in young Liam Waller for lead instead. Liam would need a suit and a better guitar, but the sound would work so much better. For "Shake, Rattle & Roll" and whatever else they wanted to do. Then, with Dylan's voice, and Charlie Peck—who was fab, just fab—on drums, they'd be a real, *proper* band.

Only he wasn't going to risk any of it by *telling* Dylan any of that. It had been a stretch, them letting not-yet-seventeen-year-old Eddie in. No way they were going to let Liam in, since the boy was, admittedly, at fifteen, a soddin' *baby.*

He dipped himself down into the water, flooding his ears. Looking up at the cracks in the ceiling. Thinkin' about it. No, he wasn't going to be able to ask Liam into the band, not anytime soon. Which was a shame, because they'd been best mates forever, really. Forever and a day. But if he brought Liam around to a practice then they'd think he was a kid, a hanger-on. They wouldn't take *Ed* seriously. And Ed needed them to take him seriously.

And he wouldn't bring Dylan his songs. Didn't matter how many were piling up in his notebooks, or how good they were—good bit better than anything decrepit old Bill Haley was writing these days. It wasn't *Eddie* Miranda and the Tempests. It wasn't a group like the Bartlebys were a group—where he and Liam and Baron all knew that the glue was the music, before any of their individual selves. No. He'd keep his head down for the time being. A year, maybe two. Make himself obedient, but indispensable. Bite his tongue, chew it to pieces. Be good. Sock away a few quid, and then, someday, when the time was right and Dylan was certain of his own superiority, Eddie would bring him a song, act blushing and young and embarrassed about it, almost like a bird. Treat it like an accident. Ask Dylan for advice. *I don't know how it happened, Dyl, but what do you think? Do you think the band could use it? I know it's not very good—the middle eight isn't done yet—but they say that if you write your own songs then you get more back from the record labels, in royalties.*

Yes, that would be the ticket, indeed. Money. Dylan Miranda knew—appreciated—money. It was business for him, really. Well, birds, too. But also business. They were alike in that way, and if he just made it out like he didn't realize he was a *little* bit more talented and a *great deal* more handsome, then Dylan would continue to tuck him under his wing.

A knock on the door—Billy, needing a shit. Eddie pulled the plug on the bath, told his brother to come in. Toweled himself off in the vague miasma of his brother's shit smells, put on his pants, his kecks, his dress shirt, draped his tie over his shoulder, greased the sides of his hair down and the top part up. Looked at himself in the mirror. He looked good. Cool. Older, he thought, which was just what he'd wanted. Needed a bit of a shave, maybe, but that would have to wait. He had places to be. Or one place, at least.

"Tara, Billy," he said, "Don't forget to flush."

He went downstairs where his Dad was having a fag and a paper and a cuppa, poured himself a bit of tea himself.

"Ey, Eddie love," his Dad said to him, "How's the band?"

"Why?" he asked, taking a sip, "Did you want to join?"

His father barked a laugh at that. He stubbed out his ciggy, leaving his paper and his teacup on the table. And then went to Eddie and did his tie for him, making the knot square, as he always did.

"I think I could show those lads a thing or two on the piano if they wanted," his father said, smirking. Eddie smiled back, his mouth closed and tight. His Dad was right—he probably could. Hadn't it been his Dad who had taught him the piano, when they couldn't afford lessons anymore? Hadn't he been the one who taught him "Oh When the Saints Go Marching," on the trumpet, and how to tune up his guitar, too?

"Now you say they'll be paying you soon enough, Eddie?" his Dad asked him, not carefully, not caring if he was careful. Eddie was a child, after all. His child. Eddie's money was his Dad's money. Shared. Ed ignored the whiskey on his Dad's breath, what must have been in that teacup.

"Soon enough," Eddie said. "£5 a week, as soon as we start playing the Star."

"Good boy," Eddie's dad said, giving his son's cheek a tender slap. "The Star Theater? Used to take your mum out dancing there. Fox trot."

"Lovely," Eddie said, as his Dad began crooning out Hoagy Carmichael's "Georgia on My Mind," spinning himself through the tiny kitchen. He stopped only briefly to tuck his paper under his arm. Then kept on singing, spinning, out of the kitchen, down the hallway, singing himself into his cap, and out the front door. *Of course,* Eddie thought sourly, *the pub would be open soon.*

But he paused for a moment on the threshold.

"Oi, Ed," he called back. "Your mate is here. Tara, boys."

Mate? Eddie thought, and for one, absurd moment he wondered if it might be Baron. It had been so long since he'd seen him, hadn't it? So miserable and long. Maybe Baron had finally come crawling back to him. With an apology, or at least—at least a song. Eddie put down his tea and grabbed his coat.

But when he got to the door, he saw that it wasn't Baron slouching up the front walk as Eddie's Dad walked briskly down them. No, the narrow-shouldered boy in his jumper was paler, more pinch-faced than Baron. Liam. Looking—well, miserable.

"What is it, Waller?" Eddie asked, cringing at the pitiful sight of his old friend. Perhaps it was time, them, for the two of them to hash out all the old marital strife. How Eddie had promised Liam could be in his band, and then left them all behind. Eddie closed the door—didn't want his brothers hearing the whole sad story or else he'd never hear the end of it. But then he put his hands in his pockets, angled up his jaw. "I have band practice to get to. Well? What do you *want?*"

Liam looked up at him, those beady hazel eyes pale and insufficient. Gave a snuffle. Wiped his nose on the wrist of his jumper. That's when he realized that Liam had been *crying*.

"Hammy," Liam brayed, sealish, awful, "Hammy, it's Baron. Well, 'snot Baron. His Mum, Hammy."

Hands out of his pockets now. Jaw softening. "What happened to Baron's Mum, Liam?"

"She got hit by a lorry. Off duty copper. He was drunk, didn't see her on her bicycle—Hammy, she *died*."

Ed sometimes thought he had a secret heart, one he kept locked up in his throat, with its own beat, its own rhythm. Now that heart was swelling, painful. He thought of Baron's Mum at the party. Bent over that pink cake, her alabaster skin all goose pimply. *Me mum's got a pair, too*, Baron had told him once, and what a thing to remember now. He had *danced* with her, at the party, half drunk, half thinking about dancing with Baron, an absurdity, knowing he couldn't, not really, not the way he wanted, knowing that dancing with his mum would be the next best thing instead. She wasn't like other mums, was she? Certainly not like Eddie's had been. His mum had been soft pretty lullabies and secret Catholic prayers, despite her conversion to CoE, back before she'd married his Dad. But Baron's mum—she'd been rock 'n' roll, son. Twisting pretty narrow ankles and hipbones and all the boys, every one, wanting to dance with her, wanting her for *their* mothers, especially a boy like Eddie, motherless.

And now gone? Those pretty little ankles—cold and broken somewhere? Like his own mother's ankles, and all of the rest of her?

"When?" Ed asked Liam. Liam snottily sniffled again.

"Yesterday mornin'," he said. "I went round to their house last night. They carted off Baron's sister somewhere to an auntie's house. I don't think they even told her what happened. And Ed, they're sending Baron back to his Aunt Deedz'. His step-dad doesn't want him, the cunt. He's—he's not doing good, Hammy. He's not—he's a mess. Worse off than you were, last year—"

Liam didn't want to say what had happened last year. Liam didn't need to. Eddie could remember the things the mothers all said from up and down the street. How the father had gone to shite at the bottom of the bottle, but how young Ed—not the littlest one, the second to littlest—had somehow seemed to be keeping them all together. Cleaning up the house and doing the wash, keeping the littlest one fed and in school. Would make a good husband someday, a good father. Not like his old toss pot of a dad.

Ed had kept it together, mostly. Ed had only ever let himself cry at night when the others were asleep. Had to be strong for Billy. For Jamie and Paulie and Tommy boy, too. Had to be strong for Dad. Had to be strong for Mum, especially, who would have wanted him to be strong. Especially.

Who did Baron have to be strong for? Who would be strong for him? He had nothing. Nobody.

"You said he's at Deidre's house?" Eddie asked. He went over to the gate, where his bike was there waiting for him. Waiting to take him to Dylan Miranda's flat. To practice.

"They said they were taking him there last night. He was hardly talkin', Hammy. Like King Tut or something." Liam paused, watching Eddie get on his bike. "I thought you should know. I thought you could help. Because of your mum—"

"*Yes*, Liam," Eddie said sharply. Not wanting Liam to say it. The scar that he and Baron now shared. But then, when he saw Liam's face shining with tears under the morning's pale March sunlight, he added, "Thanks, love."

"Cheers, mate," Liam said to him, as Eddie started down the road.

He should have been heading off to Dylan's flat. Shouldn't have missed rehearsal. If Dylan had said there was one thing he hated, it was lads who skived off. Said there would be no loafers in *his* band, and the threat had been there, implicit. *Well, skiv this*, Eddie thought, standing on the pedals to coast, the wind against his face. There were some things that mattered more than a shitty rock 'n' roll band and £10 a week.

Even to Eddie Hammond.

32 - 1977

222 West 23rd Street. Even in the bite of the winter air, you could practically smell it before you could see it. The piss and grit and dirt of it. The prostitutes in their fishnets, the white squares of their flash shining through dark threads, the goose pimples showing in between. Zach tried to be respectful, because he'd been taught to look away, because Shay was right there. His brother, it seemed, had been raised in a different household, had different standards entirely. He gawked openly as the three teenagers positioned themselves against the cold red brick face, just down the street from the front door and the doorman and everything that barred them from their shared, triplet hero.

"I wonder if we'll see Warhol here," Shay said.

"I wonder if we'll see some hot open beavers," Richard Charles responded, his lascivious gaze still on the pair of prostitutes who stood not far from them on the street's edge. That's when Zach elbowed him in the ribs, hard.

"Shut up," he hissed. "There's a *lady* here."

"Oh, don't be such a pussy," Shay told him. "It's not like *I've* never seen one."

Richard Charles glanced over at her, a smug smirk dawning over his mouth underneath his sketchy mustache. "See?" he said to Zach, "Told you she's a dyke."

Now it was Shay's turn to hit him. Her fist fisted hard, pounding the shoulder of his shearling coat. Richard Charles didn't even wince.

"Fuck you, man," she said. "I meant my own."

They were all jangly, bright with nerves that they'd never admit to each other. Because the truth was, they were young in the city, within striking distance of *prostitutes*, the smell of pot mixed up with garbage and urine on the air. The sidewalk was the type of cold that went right up through your sneakers and into your leg bones. The wind whipped between the avenues. Trucks were rattling down the street; cabs drove erratically. Their parents didn't know where they were, but they were alive, teenagers. Immortal. And somewhere inside that building, maybe, was Baron Templeton. The *real* Baron Templeton, not just a figure in books. Waiting for them.

"So what's our plan?" Zach asked nervously. He watched as Shay fished a piece of folded paper from her pocket.

"This is where he's supposed to live," she said. It had *Chelsea Hotel # 909* scrawled on it in jagged handwriting. It didn't have any of the bubbles that a girl's handwriting usually held.

"Where'd you get that, anyway?" Richard Charles asked. Shay curled her lip.

"Fuck you, I know people," she said, and then, seeing Zach's face, she sighed. "I have a friend who works at Edelman's. Her name is Cassie? I guess she's really a friend of my brother's. They're in college together. Anyway she got it for me, from some of Edelman's industry buddies."

Richard Charles' brow lowered at the mention of his nemesis, his true love, the record store girl. "Dykes," he muttered, stamping his feet on the ground as though to shake the cold from them. Shay ignored him.

"Anyway, we have this, so it's just a matter of waiting until the doorman is distracted and going in. Right?" She sounded, suddenly, nervous too, and Zach remembered that she was also fifteen, just like his brother. A girl, really, not some kind of ethereal, knowledgeable, impossibly cool adult. He'd always figured that girls *knew* things that boys didn't. Isn't that what they said? That girls matured faster? But they were all just a couple of stupid kids, weren't they? He had an enormous sense of it just then, how stupid their plan was, how they were merely a bunch of children. Apparently Richard Charles agreed.

"Retard plan," he said with a snort. "It'll never work."

"Okay, *genius*," she said. "Let's hear *your* plan, then."

Richard Charles didn't look her in the eye. He was staring at the hookers, hazy and distracted. "I'm working on it," he muttered. And then, to Zach's horror, he pushed his foot off against the concrete building and crossed the sidewalk, greeting the prostitutes with one raised hand.

"Oh, God," Zachary said, turning toward the wall, burying his face in his hands. Shay looked between them for a moment. Snorted.

"You know," she said, "I don't know why you'd put up with a guy like that in your band. He's a mess. Can you imagine what he would do if he ever had access to *money?*"

Zach half wanted to defend Richard Charles. It was his brother, after all. They'd shared a womb. A bed. He had *never* known a world where he wasn't standing in his brother's jagged, dangerous, fire-shot shadow. Anyway, he didn't have to imagine what Richard Charles would do with money. He had money now, and apparently, that meant soliciting prostitutes.

"He's a good musician," Zach offered bleakly, the best—only—defense he could conjure. It was true, at least. Richard Charles was an amazing musician. Rhythm was inside him in a way it just didn't live inside Zach. It pulsed. It throbbed. And sometimes it heaved up out of his fingertips and mouth. And then Zach would get to sit next to him, awkwardly strumming the chords his brother had written in his math notebook, whose only arithmetic was the music of the spheres. Zach didn't have the same skill, nor that magic. But he didn't need to. Not with Richard Charles right there beside him, willing, for the first time in their lives, to share with his baby brother.

"I'm a good musician," Shay said. Zach glanced over his shoulder to where his brother was still chatting up the two women. How old were they anyway? They had to be at least forty years old. Maybe older. Grandmothers, practically.

"Oh yeah?" Zach asked, distracted by his brother's conversation, which he couldn't hear over the rush and mumble of the street.

"*Yeah,*" she said. "*Really* good. You should let me in your band. In the Ruffians."

"The Dervishes . . ."

"No," she said. She was looking at him strangely, intently. And . . .. kind of squirming, a little. "You were right. The Ruffians is a way better name. The band should be the Ruffians, and you should let me be your drummer."

"It's not up to me," he said, blushing to say it, because it was embarrassing, sort of, to be younger, to have to ask his older brother for permission for *anything* really.

"Well, it shouldn't be up to *that* asshole," she said. Squirming even more, kind of cross and uncrossing her legs. Zach snorted in her general direction.

"Do you have to shit or something?" he asked.

Shay turned bright pink. "Fuck, I—I've had to pee since we got off the train."

"So go piss in an alley or something," Zach said, his nostrils flaring in disbelief. A little fucking kid, indeed, if Shay couldn't even hold it in.

She blushed even pinker. "I can't, you dip shit. I don't have the right anatomy."

"So go into a bodega or something," he said. "I think we passed one down the block."

Shay glanced toward the doorman, who was still standing there, immobile as a gargoyle. Collecting pigeon shit, practically.

"You won't go in without me?" she asked. Zach, who had never been a Boy Scout, held up three fingers. Saluted her with them.

"Scout's honor," he said.

Shay sighed an audible sigh of relief like she'd been holding *that*, too, all the way since Poughkeepsie. Without another word, she raced off down the road, not looking back once . Zach watched her go, then noticed Richard Charles coming over to him.

"Where'd the dyke go?" he asked.

"Had to take a wazzer," he said. Shrugged. Richard Charles' teeth glinted at that.

"Good," he said. "It'll be cheaper if it's just the two of us."

"What?" Zach asked, blinking back shock at what was being implied. Richard Charles elbowed him.

"Sshh," he hissed, bits of spit flying everywhere. "We're not going to *fuck* them. We're just going to let them *think* we're going to fuck them. They live there. With their pimp or whatever. So we can use them to get into the building. Then we'll take off."

In a louder voice he added, "Ready to lose your v-card, bro?"

At the curb, the prostitutes giggled.

Zach's cheeks heated. Squinting against the wind, he looked up the road, searching for Shay. He didn't see her there. But if he had, would it have changed anything?

"Come on," Richard Charles said, *sotto voce*, "The ship is sailing."

"Okay," Zach said with a sigh. He tried to think of what Richard Charles would do in that moment, to make it less awkward. A joke, maybe. He spun on his heels and offered one of them—the older one, with honey-toned skin and long black hair that kind of, sort of, if he used his imagination, reminded him of Shay. "Ladies?"

The woman rolled her eyes, but took the offered arm anyway. So it was Zach leading the way, up the steps of the Chelsea hotel, past the smiling doorman.

And Richard Charles, for once, trailing behind.

* * *

The lobby was bigger than Zach expected. Grander. Shinier. With fancy-looking artwork on the walls, even though there was garbage here and there, too. An odd sort of dis-junction. Junk, and high culture, right there, all mixed up together. Richard Charles led his charge to the elevator. He stabbed his finger into the door hold button.

"After you, girls," he said, and there was more general eye rolling and giggling at the boys. Who probably really did look foolish to these two old women, gritty and beautiful and experienced in wise of the ways of men—real men—and the world. This, Zach thought, as he let Richard Charles snatch him back to keep him from walking inside the elevator, was probably the closest he'd come to screwing in the next decade. Especially

270

now that they'd screwed over Shay.

"Oops," Richard Charles said breezily, as he dragged his finger down to *door close*.

Just as the faces of the two women disappeared behind the door, Richard Charles grabbed at Zach's shirt.

"*Run*," his brother whispered, and they took off, then, toward the stairs, the two of them, both of them, racing, even though no one was chasing them and no one was paying attention to them, either. Zach thought about what he'd read about the fans—the Saffron fans. How the four lads from Liverpool had to wear disguises on the street, how eventually they couldn't even perform, because the *birds*, as they called them, would flood the stage in hunger for them, how Templeton's anxiety eventually got too much, and they had to quit performing, because he, he told the rest of them, he was worried they'd eat him alive. Or shoot him. Or something. Zach wondered if he'd ever be so lucky to be chased and afraid and wanted. He wondered if anyone would ever want to eat *him*.

Meanwhile, his brother, screaming his head off like a maniac as they ran higher and higher up the spiraling staircase, lit like a ghoul by the yellow flickering lights, his shadow sharp against the wall, against Zach, who almost—but couldn't quite—keep up. By the time they hit the fourth floor landing, he felt like there were knives in his side. He felt like he was gonna vomit. He was covered in sweat in his leather coat, practically wheezing. But it didn't matter to Richard Charles. Richard Charles was an animal. Richard Charles could not be stopped.

"All the way to the top, Zachy!" he screeched, as he made it to the ninth floor. Zach, trailing behind him by almost two stories, had started to slow, coughing, his feet feeling heavier on every step. To his surprise, as he reached the ninth story landing, Richard Charles went to him and outstretched a hand. Pulling him up that last step, so they could walk into that long, dark hallway together.

They didn't have Shay's shitty little piece of paper. But he remembered what it had said. Before he knew it, they were standing there, outside #909. He looked at the numbers, golden against white wood. Thought about the *person* who was supposed to be beyond that door. His hero. A living God. Baron fucking Clement fucking Templeton.

He wanted to race back down the stairs, through the lobby, outside into the frigid light of day. What could *he* possibly have to say to Baron Templeton? He wanted to find Shay, to run back home to Poughkeepsie. On foot, if they needed to. There was no way he could possibly knock on Baron Templeton's door.

But he didn't need to. Because Richard Charles was there, and before Zach could stop him, his brother put heavy knuckles on the door and started pounding.

Silence. Except for Richard Charles' incessant knocking.

"Maybe he's not home—" Zach started to say. Just as the door swung inward. And they saw him.

It was too much to take in all at once. From beyond the door, a thick cloud of smoke and sound wafted in. There was music, something raucous and sweet all at once—maybe something from the '50s. And the sound of a baby crying. And the smell of weed and cigarettes and—and he was *there*. Both skinnier and shorter than Zach expected—not much taller than either of *them*. Five seven, maybe, max. But also more compact, more muscular. In pair of impossibly worn out, impossibly tight, faded blue jeans, torn over the knees. And an old t-shirt, orange, tight fitting too. Mazatlan, it said. And a button shirt, open, on top—or was it a blouse? Floral and synthetic. diaphanous. His face was just like it was in photos and album covers, except older and—and different than he expected, his hair longer now, coarser, and certain things were suddenly shockingly more apparent.

"Holy shit," Richard Charles blurted, "You're *Black*?"

Baron Templeton cracked a smile, a slight one, put his hip on the door jam and took a drag of his cigarette.

"Who is that?" a voice called from somewhere inside, over the music, over the sound of the baby's ragged crying.

"Fans," Baron Templeton said. In his voice. Which sounded just like it always had, on the records, in interviews, in Zach's imagination, for months and months now. "I think."

Zach didn't know what to do, what to think, what to say. They'd come here with a question, but now it escaped Zach entirely. And beyond his racial faux pas, it seemed that words had suddenly failed Richard Charles too, for once.

Baron stood there smoking for another moment. Then stubbed out his cigarette on the jamb. Zach thought he heard the wood sizzle, or maybe he imagined it.

"Right, boys," Baron said, and was he doing what Zach *thought* he was doing? Holding the door open, gesturing to the room inside. "Why don't we come in, have a cuppa?"

Baron fucking Clement fucking Templeton was standing there, waiting for an answer. For once, Richard Charles didn't have one. It was Zach who answered, saintly, polite, for both of them.

"Uh, okay," he said softly, "Sir."

Baron let out a small snicker as he turned and walked inside. Richard Charles elbowed Zach then in the ribs.

"He's a *rock star*, you idiot," Richard Charles hissed, "You don't call rock stars *sir*."

Only Zach had. And now he stepped inside, into Baron Fucking Templeton's suite at the Chelsea Fucking Hotel.

33 - 1958

Eddie almost coasted right past the floral shop on Woolton Road. He'd been preoccupied, his mind nearly cleansed of everything else, of thoughts about Storm and the Tempests and his sodding drunk father and everything else, all except one word: *Baron*. But then a flash of red and yellow caught his eye, and he slowed, hopping off his bike to walk it round back the other way.

Was early, still, he figured. Couldn't be wrong to stop and bring something. There had been a death, after all. Was only right.

Didn't have much in his pocket. Dylan hadn't paid him yet, since he hadn't yet played a show. But he knew how, at times like these, any token could have meaning. He looked through the buckets on the sidewalk, the roses and irises and early spring daffodils, with their thick green stalks and spiky beards. They were lovely. Wild. Enough like Baron that maybe . . . but no. He just didn't have enough. At last, he found a bucket of carnations. Reds and pinks. Meager, in a way, but lovely, and their smell was strong enough that maybe they'd be a comfort. A reminder that *Baron* still lived, yeah? Lived and breathed and pissed and whatever else. And he knew that Baron needed to remember that, if he were going to pull through. That he hadn't gone up the river Styx with his poor dead mother.

Not the pinks, though. That had been *her* color, in Eddie's mind. That stupid bloody birthday cake, with the frosting and her tits. No, the red was more like Baron, his own dark, swarthy tones and his broiling brightness. He gathered up a dozen of them and brought them inside to be wrapped and to pay.

Better then, a few minutes later, to be back on the road *with* the flowers. An offering of sorts. Rushing to Baron's Auntie's house, which he couldn't think of as Baron's house, because did Baron really have a home of his own? Ed supposed that was another thing that wedded them. Ed's home was never *his* because there were too many people there. Baron didn't have any place that belonged truly to him, neither.

Funny how empty the house looked so soon after a death. When his mum had died his own aunts and uncles had kept their house packed for days, not wanting his Dad to be alone. There were lights on inside, past the curtain, but no extra cars outside, no sense of *community*.

He left his bike by the gate, staring for a moment at the mangled bike frame that already stood beside it. A woman's bike, the wheel all bent. Eddie took the bouquet of flowers in one hand, touched the crooked handlebar with the other.

"Fuckin' hell," he said softly. Then he carried the flowers up the front walk and rang the bell.

It took only a moment for Baron's Auntie to appear at the door. Ed hadn't liked Deidre before, though he was polite with her, like he was with all parents, as a rule. She seemed too stern, too impatient. When she looked at Baron, it was only ever with contempt—either thinly veiled or all-too apparent. Not that Baron wasn't occasionally worthy of contempt, but . . .

"Deedz," he said, and, bending forward, kissed her face, feeling the cool, thin skin of her cheek. She looked paler now, her eyes shadowed and under-slept, though it wasn't clear if she'd cried at all yet over the loss of her younger sister.

"Oh," she said in dull-voiced surprise. "You're Baron's mate, then, yes? Was it 'Bongo'?"

Eddie frowned. He'd met her a half dozen times at least. But then, he told himself, grief could be muddling.

"Eddie," he said. "Eddie Hammond, from the band." Well, lately from the band. But not from the band lately. Did she know they'd broken up? No use worrying her about it now, he reckoned.

"Oh, yes, Eddie," she said, politely but without much enthusiasm. Until, looking down, she noticed the flowers.

"Oh, for me? Thank you so much, darling. Flowers are a comfort at times like these."

Before he could object, she whisked them off inside, leaving him in the doorway. He took an uncertain step inside before she called out from the kitchen.

"Do close the door! You'll let the cats out."

"Oh yes," said Eddie softly. "The cats."

The cats were nowhere to be seen.

"Come in, Eddie," she said. "I do need to be off to the funeral home soon, but I suppose we have time for a cuppa. Milk?"

Eddie followed her slowly into the kitchen. *Where's Baron?* He wondered. Was he even there? There was no sign of him in the clean, staid place. There had been little sign of him there before, when he'd previously lived there, but you would occasionally see *a* sign. A sketchbook etched with dirty drawings. A copy of *The New Music Express*. His specs left somewhere, discarded and forgotten. Now it was like it had been scrubbed clean of Baron.

"Please," Eddie said. He stood in the doorway watching as she made them two cups of tea, then set them on the table to steep. She didn't sit, though. Only kept buzzing about like a manic mosquito. Cutting the ends of the carnations under running water, bustling about for a vase.

"Please," she said. "Sit."

Eddie sat. Eddie sipped his tea.

"I'm sorry about your sister," he said, as Deidre at last set the vase between them and finally sat down. Her eyes flitted off in another direction, and he saw then a flash of tears caught up in her mascara.

"Yes, well," said Deidre, her hands casting about the tablecloth until she found a pack of ciggies. She didn't light it, only held it out, until Eddie realized that *he* was supposed to light it. He had no lighter but saw one sitting not far from him on the windowsill. Grabbed for it. Lit her fag for her. Put it back. "We always did know that Evelyn would leave us first. She had the type of personality that you just knew wasn't long for this world, from a young age."

"Evelyn," Eddie said. He hadn't known her name before. He took a sip of tea. "Awful, though. An accident like that. I saw her bicycle, out front. Must have been a shock."

"Yes," Deidre said. She was smoking furiously. "I suppose there are worse ways to go, aren't there? At the very least it was fast. Clean. Could have been beaten to death by one of her horrid adolescent beaus. Oh, did she give our father palpitations. Always some tragic romance with Evie. Or she could have wasted away in a drug den somewhere. Seemed to be on that track for a while, before Timothy. Or she could have even got cancer."

She said it in such a pointed way that Ed glanced up, wondering if she knew.

"That's how our mother went," Deidre added, seeing Eddie's surprised face. "Cancer of the uterus. They didn't tell us that when we were girls, of course. Didn't want to scare us. But we were scared anyway. I was ten. She was eight. Took months, her wasting away to nothing. Miserable pain. If it's that or a lorry, well." Deidre cast about for an ashtray. Eddie pulled the one on the table closer to her.

"Mine died of cancer, too," Eddie said gruffly, as she flicked away her ashes. "Breast cancer."

Usually he avoided saying it in mixed company. *Breast.* But it didn't seem to bother Aunt Deidre.

"I'm sorry to hear," she said. "You're very young to lose a mother."

"Yeah," Eddie said, laughing wryly, despite himself, because he could have cried if he didn't. "You were, too. And Baron—"

"Baron," Deidre said, letting out a thin stream of smoke. She didn't *precisely* roll her eyes upon speaking Baron's name, but she sat forward in her seat. "Well, she was never a *proper* mother to him, was she?"

"Wasn't she?" Eddie asked. He wasn't drinking his tea now, only holding his cup close to him.

"No, she was rubbish," said Deidre. "And not much better with young Elizabeth, either. She loses interest when they're no longer babies. That's what I learned about her. You know, she didn't see him once between ages seven and fourteen. Only came back when he was grown and *handsome.* But she's always been weak for a beautiful boy."

"It's terrible she didn't see him," Eddie said, because it was, that she'd left Baron like that. He knew Baron loved her. He did. Had *thought* the feeling was mutual. "And now, to lose her again—"

Now the wretched woman *did* roll her eyes. "He's probably better off, really," she said. "To be in a proper home where he belongs. With me. I'll have him back in school soon enough. Not lost at the bottom of a bottle somewhere, running off with his skiffle band."

Eddie put his teacup on the table.

"Pardon?" he said, but at the same time Deidre interrupted him, as though she'd been chewing over something for a good while now.

"What did you say your name was, child?"

"Hammond, ma'am," he said. "Eddie Hammond."

She sat back in her seat, satisfied. "Yes! That's it. Eddie. One of Matthew Hammond's brood. Was a shame about your mother. I didn't know her well. But I knew *of* her. A kind woman. Uncomplicated."

"Yes," he said stiffly, looking down at the table. "Thank you, ma'am."

"You're not like your father, are you?" she asked, cutting right to the heart of the matter. "No, I can see you're not. I must say, I appreciated those days when you were coming around. Didn't see much of the worst lot of Baron's mates after he added you on. That dreadful *Dick.*" She made a sour face, like she couldn't stand the taste of his name. Eddie let out a laugh at that. He couldn't disagree that Dick was, indeed, dreadful. He drained his tea, put down the teacup.

"Another?" she asked. He shook his head.

"No, thank you."

"I guess it's always been Baron's way, to follow a stronger boy. I'd rather that boy be you than Richard Ashby. That's the father's doing, I think. Leaving Baron and Evie like he did. Left a hole in Baron, I've always believed. I'd hoped my Fred would be enough, but he's soft. Not stern, which is what his kind needs."

"His kind?" Eddie squinted at her. Thought of what he'd seen in that bog, which he'd tried to forget in the six weeks since. She couldn't have possibly meant that Baron was a *queer* kind, could she? She couldn't have possibly known?

"Well, yes," she said crisply. Lowered her voice, as though someone might hear. "Did Baron not tell you that his father was a negroid?"

Eddie laughed without thinking, believing it to be a joke. But Deidre didn't laugh.

"It's not a joke, love," she said. "I know Baron's *pale*, but his father is Black. The mother was from one of those Afro-Caribbean nations. Tobago or Jamaica, I can't remember. *His* father was a dock worker of course. Dead after a bar fight is what I heard. But I've always thought that it explains *so much* about Baron. I tried to raise him proper, with *culture*. But you can't fight nature."

Eddie, not laughing now. Staring.

"Does Baron *know*?" he asked, because surely, Baron would have mentioned *this*. They'd traded their histories early on. Eddie's tragic history with his mum. Baron's roaming pirate dad. The things Baron had occluded—Dick, especially, what he was up to with Dick—he'd learned soon enough anyway. But Baron had never said his Dad was *Black*. He would have told Eddie, Ed was sure. Because why hide *that*? From your best mate?

Now it was Deidre's turn to laugh, as though the question were absurd—but she broke off after a breath or two, and her face fell.

"I'm sure Evie must have told him. He *must* know."

Eddie, still, stared.

"Oh, look at the time," Deidre said suddenly, stubbing out her cigarette, rising to her feet in a rush. "Freddie is waiting for me down at the funeral parlor. We need to pick a coffin, and I know if I let him, he'll waste a month's wages on something we'll be sinking into the mud."

"Don't let me keep you," Eddie said. He got up and began tidying—putting the teacups in the side, all that—in the hopes that it would get Baron's aunt out of there sooner. But she stopped and looked at him.

"Aren't you coming, then?"

Eddie ticked up an eyebrow as he washed the cups with a wash towel. "No," he said, his annoyance seeping through. "I'm here to see *Baron*. I was hoping to, at least."

"Oh. God," said Deidre, as she went to put her coat on. "Good luck to you. He's been in his room sobbing all night. It'll be a miracle if he's slept at all. I'd be careful. He can be a beast when he hasn't slept. But perhaps you know that."

Something about the way she *looked* at him when she said that, the insinuation buried there, made Eddie want to sock her. But she'd just lost a sister. And Eddie didn't hit women, as a general rule.

"Thanks," he said, nodding. Added, when she still hovered there, "Tra."

Baron's aunt looked like she wanted to say something else, but at last she shut her gob, grabbed a clutch purse, and was out the front door. Gone.

Ed, alone in Baron's aunt's kitchen, the washing all done. Leaning against the counter, observing the patterned tablecloth, the clean tile, not a crumb in sight. Sighing.

He turned and headed up the stairs.

34 - 1997

The Lighthouse was, ironically enough, a space of very little light. The dark wood, low rafters and the smoke which fogged the air beneath the ancient Tiffany lamps didn't help much, giving the place a subterranean appearance—like a place one might find a den of voles. Cymbeline suspected no one had cleaned—or even cracked open one of the shadowed windows at the edge of the room—in ages. She hefted her guitar case, casting her gaze all around in search of the stage, which she did not find, trying to ignore the way her boots seemed to stick to the floor, crackling, as she walked. They passed the bar, darkly glittered with bottles, and the old man behind who ignored them as they walked by.

"Where's the open mic?" asked Sid, putting her hands in her pocket. Cymbeline noticed how she stood a little taller when she spoke to the man, commanding more space than she would have if addressing a camper or female counselor or even Cymbeline. She wondered if Sid was used to this, doing the work that she did, being the *way* that she was. Subtly shifting her body and its language to take on new modes.

The bartender grunted, angling a thumb toward a closed door at the end of the room. They passed a trio of stooped, silent men at the bar as they headed to the back.

Better. Slightly. Through the swinging door, a larger room, more recently swept, with small round tables dotting a dance floor here and there, a votive candle burning in red glass in each one. There were maybe thirty people in attendance, all sitting, silently watching. Many of them had guitar cases of their own. At the front of the room was a low stage—what passed for one, anyway. There was a man, standing, playing guitar at the stage's center. Dressed in a flannel, shaggy hair leaving his face half-veiled. It was difficult to tell how old he was. He could have been a twenty-five year old who had led an exceptionally hard life, or a sixty-year-old who had led an exceptionally good one. There was a bottle by the toes of his dirty work boots. The beat he stamped out, the soundtrack, a familiar one.

Know that I'm here, he rasped into the mic. A lovely voice, though worn. But not a bad worn. More like an old pair of jeans. *That I'm waiting for you, where the sea rolls green and the grass is tumbled blue.*

"It's our song," Sid said, looking back at her, giving Cymbeline a jagged grin. "The Ruffians."

Cymbeline smiled vaguely as she found an empty table at the side of the room and settled in to watch. Sid was hardly paying attention to the music, to Cymbeline as she sat. She was more focused on the procedure of the thing, finding a woman at a table in front with a clipboard, jotting down Cymbeline's name at the end. But Cymbeline was listening, cocking her head to one side, considering. Maybe it was the pounding in her brain, subtly thundering. But this version of the song seemed different from the other ones she had heard. A minor chord turned minor and seventh here, a lyric different, by a slant rhyme, there. She sat forward, listening more closely as Sid pulled out a chair and settled in beside her. This man *had* something, sang the song in a way that elevated it beyond what Neil had done and Cymbeline had done and even—even what the Ruffians themselves had done. Like he was *feeling* the song, more deeply than anyone had ever felt it before.

By now, by the time the last verse began to fade, Sid was sitting forward and listening, too. She glanced at Cymbeline. Their eyes locked. Cymbeline nodded. Acknowledging that they were *witnessing* something which they hadn't expected to witness here.

The song faded. A smattering of applause rippled through the room—less, though, than Cymbeline expected. And after a moment, she understood why.

"The fucking radio," the guy said, bending over to grab his beer, taking a long swig, wiping his mouth on his sleeve, putting his boozy mouth back on the mic, "Will tell you that that song is by a band called the fucking Ruffians. But it's my song."

"Here we go," an elderly gent at a nearby table whispered.

The man took another swig. "*I* wrote that, when I was fourteen fucking years old, for the fucking love of my life. And he fucking *stole* it. Stole her."

There were a few snickers from the audio. Cymbeline shifted, uncomfortable, as they began to egg him on. The man at the next table cupped his hands around his mouth, shouted, "Who fucking stole it, Dick?"

"Who said that?" the man—Dick, apparently—shouted, squinting, pointing blindly into the stage light. When no one answered, he went on. "My dweeby kid brother fucking stole it. I never asked for his *millions*. A 'thank you' when he got the Grammy would have been nice, though. Maybe a phone call, Zachy, if that's not too much to ask?" Dick mimed making a phone call on his beer bottle. There were more snickers—heartier laughs now. This was getting uncomfortable. Cymbeline sank lower in her seat. At last, the woman at the front of the room, the one with the sign-up sheet, lifted up her hands.

"Okay, guys, okay," she said. Weak. The kind of tone that would have campers plowing right over you. But enough. "Richard, do you have another song for us tonight?"

Dick looked back out at the audience. Nodded, once. Put down the bottle. And played another song. A different one, this time, something new, something Cymbeline had never heard before. It was about the passage of time, about how he had felt it slip through his fingers. About how he'd go back, if he could, to set all things right. Simple enough. Romantic regret. But there was a story in it, and more, the way his fingers glided over the fretboard was light. Tender. Beautiful. Part of it was the disjunction, Cymbeline thought, between this man's grizzled appearance and the sweet tones of his music. But part of it—another part of it—was pure talent. Spark. He had it, whatever *it* was. Cymbeline, also in knowing possession of *it*, saw it, felt it, knew it, too.

Her anxiety flared briefly in her belly. She saw teeth in the corner of her vision. He would be a hard act to beat.

At the end of the song, Dick bowed. There was more scattered applause. Cymbeline watched as he staggered down the stage, settling in at a table not far from theirs. Empty bottles were scattered all around him. He cradled his guitar in his lap like it was a precious baby.

The woman walked to the stage, announced the next performer. There was a barbershop quartet who sounded like every other barbershop quartet. There were two boys who played an off-key cover of "Cymbeline" that made *our* Cymbeline want to stab herself in the temple with a fork. There was a woman who did a spoken word performance which ended with her full undressing. There were no other real threats.

Dick, apparently, felt it, too. Through each performance, he muttered and mumbled and drank and occasionally shouted. Clapping too flat and too loud at the end of it, managing to make a whistle at the performer sound pickled in sarcasm.

"Come on," he said loudly at one point, swinging to look at Sid and Cymbeline just behind him—as if they'd been already engaged in conversation. "I mean, do you hear this crap?"

"Watch it, bud," Sid mumbled. Cymbeline tensed in her seat, dreading conflict. Dreading—well, everything, really. As the woman climbed the stairs at the stage's edge one more time, leaned into the microphone, and announced that there was one last performer for the evening.

And then, with a smile, maybe, at the irony of it, she called out Cymbeline's name.

* * *

It's not that Cymbeline *wasn't* nervous that night. She was incredibly, unspeakably nervous. In fact, "nervous" wasn't even half an adequate way to describe the bile that rose in her throat as she felt the stage light over her, the pressure of all of those eyes. She saw, as she always did, at moments like these, eyes. And hands. Hands and eyes. And teeth. And at first, she felt the pressure, simultaneous, of two possible futures tugging at her: how they might laugh her off the stage, but also, how they might consume her, if she gave them what they wanted. She felt their hunger for her music, for her. They wanted to imbibe the magic she had, intrinsic, in her hands and voice and mind. They wanted it for themselves. They didn't care about her as a *person*, because she wasn't a person. More of a medium, channeling a spirit, and once they had that spirit they would spit her out, leave her physical form to be eaten by wild animals.

For a moment, almost a split second too long, she might have fallen into her fear and never climbed out. There was shuffling, and that booze-hound Dick was cracking some kind of joke, but she couldn't hear it over the crackling rush in her ears, like some echo of something she'd known well, once, but had since forgotten.

And then, somehow, through the light—the light and the hands and the eyes and the teeth—she saw Sid. Sitting there, tousle-haired, waiting for her. Her broad, boyish face. Saw, in her posture, Sid's own warring impulses. Her comfort in herself. Her inherent discomfort. And Cymbeline's heart squeezed, and somehow that squeezing was enough. Because she knew that she could resolve these impulses for Sid. All Sid needed was money, support, and then she could be the person she was meant to be—the person she already was. If Cymbeline had been a painter, she would have covered a thousand canvases in oil paint, thick and gloopy. If she'd been a bank robber, she would have driven her car through the window of a bank. But Cymbeline wasn't a painter, and she wasn't a thief. No matter what anxiety gripped her, she was a musician. She *knew* music. It lived in her. And so she would play, and play her heart out.

All for Sid.

Somehow, against every impulse in her body, she pushed down her fear. Ignored the buzz saw grinding in her skull. She went beside herself. Outside herself. Flashed a grin, and a dimple she hadn't known she had, at the audience, said something funny into the microphone—she couldn't even tell you what—and somehow, against all rationality, the audience responded. Warming. Laughing. She cracked another joke, this one about tuning her guitar. As she tuned her guitar. And they laughed again, and they waited for her. And then she started strumming. She started singing. And in that moment, even drunk old Dick shut up. Taking a long draw from his bottle. Swallowing. Listening.

Listening to the magic she made.

* * *

"Three hundred *fucking* dollars," Sid said, after, counting out the thick stack of bills Cymbeline had been given. "Three hundred dollars, Cymbeline! Have you ever seen anything so beautiful in your life?"

Sitting at the table there, nursing a beer one of the other performers had bought her, Cymbeline watched Sid kiss the stack of bills. Both of their eyes were shining. It was a beautiful moment, pure triumph. And still, Cymbeline knew, it was only a start. They were at the bottom of the steps now. There would have to be more gigs, better gigs. Finding a band, finding an interested label. So many steps before they—her, too, but really Sid—would be able to become the person they were meant to be.

Now, though, Sid glowed, giddy from Cymbeline's victory. She finished counting, went to hand the stack of bills to Cymbeline. But Cymbeline only shrugged.

"You hold onto it," she said. "It's both of ours, anyway."

Sid fluttered her eyelashes. She leaned over, kissed Cymbeline on the cheek.

"I'm going to go get the car started for us, okay, Perky?" she said. "You enjoy your beer."

Cymbeline nodded, glowing, too, as Sid took the guitar case and carried it off through the swinging door.

Maybe they should have been more guarded, because he didn't waste much time at all. The door had barely closed behind Sid when there was a great scraping of chair legs, and Dick dragged his chair over to her table. Inviting himself.

Cymbeline braced herself. She knew enough of the world to know that there were many possibilities here, and few were good.

But despite the beer smell on his breath, Dick just looked at her, big-eyed, gawking. Full, not of lust. But honest admiration.

"You have *pipes* on you," he said. Cymbeline felt it, how slyly she smiled.

"I know," she said.

"And that song," he went on. "Not the cover. Who was that, anyway? Arthur Alexander?"

Cymbeline nodded just a little, impressed. She'd believed that to be a deep dive, obscure enough for this crowd. Apparently not.

"I love that song," he said. "But I *really* loved the second one. It's original, isn't it? Man, you sang your heart out. Something fucking *real*. At last."

"Is he bothering you?" the woman who had run the open mic asked from the next table. She was cleaning up, putting chairs up on top of tables. Cymbeline looked at the man, considering. He was younger than she thought. Probably no older than forty. And there was no malice that she detected there, no danger.

"Oh, leave us alone," he said, but she saw that the way he rolled his eyes was more like a sad teenager than a grown man. Cymbeline shook her head.

"No," she said. "I'm fine. I'm Cymbeline."

She held out her hand to him. He gave her a firm handshake, like she was a man. An equal. So she shook firmly, too.

"Like the Saffron song," he said. "I fucking loved Saffron when I was a kid."

"Everyone loves Saffron," Cymbeline said, and it was true. The band had outsold everyone. Frank Sinatra, Elvis, *Mozart*. None of them had anything on Saffron.

"Yeah, but it was different for me," he said, his lips cracking, showing chipped, yellow teeth. "I loved them more than anyone. When Templeton died I went on a bender like you wouldn't *believe*."

"Somehow I believe it," Cymbeline said, her eyes flashing. Dick brayed with laughter.

"Fair's fair," he said. Then he added, "You know I met the guy once, in the '70s."

Twice, Cymbeline thought, and felt her head throb, like a knife, a dull and ragged knife.

"Oh yeah?" asked Cymbeline.

"Yeah, he was nothing like you would expect. A fucking fairy, for one thing. You could just tell. And about four feet tall. *I* was taller than him, and I had to be, what, fourteen? But, man, just brilliant. You could see it in the way he lit a cigarette, the way he dialed the fucking *phone*. Tragedy, what happened with him with those Black power freaks. Didn't seem like the kind of guy who would off himself."

"He was murdered," Cymbeline said. Hesitated, added, "That's how it seemed when I looked it up online. For a school report. A few years ago. That he was murdered. I think he must have gotten in over his head with those radicals. Not that he didn't *believe* in Black liberation. But I think he thought he was using them, to a certain extent, and maybe it was the other way around."

"Could be," Dick said. Looking at her oddly. Shrugging. "Waste, though. Of talent. All those songs he and that douche bag Hammond could have written had they only gotten their shit together."

"Hammond's still writing music, isn't he?" Cymbeline asked. Dick snorted, finished off his bottle.

"I wouldn't call it *music*. Would *you*?"

Cymbeline's eyes shone, but she didn't answer. She didn't need to, anyway, because that's when Sid returned.

"Hey," she said, and Cymbeline saw how her brow was furrowed, how she clutched Neil's keys in her hands, oddly worrying them. But then she noticed Dick sitting there.

"What're you doing talking to this asshole?" Sid asked testily. Cymbeline laughed. She wasn't used to anyone acting possessive toward her. Not even her mother had cared when she spent time with strangers, even older men. Wandering through the guitar store down the street at thirteen. Barely speaking to them, but feeling like she belonged there.

"We're just talking about music," she said. She glanced at Neil's keys again, jangling in Sid's hands. "What's up?"

Sid turned a chair around backwards, sat down in it. "There's no way the pony is getting us back to camp tonight. It's the engine rod. Fucking pain in the ass. I bet it's been knocking for months and Neil just ignored it."

"Can you fix it?" Cymbeline asked. Sid shrugged.

"Of course I can. But I'll need *parts*. Tools. A garage. And that's not what this is supposed to be about anyway, tonight. It's not supposed to be about me stuck under Neil's fucking Pinto."

Stuck, thought Cymbeline. She realized that that was what Sid had been, up until tonight. Stuck. Same old job, no matter how good she was at it. Same old body. Same old life.

Sid grabbed the beer from Cymbeline, finished it off. "Tonight was supposed to be about *you*."

Cymbeline wasn't sure what to say, so for a moment, she didn't say anything. Dick did, though. Looking back and forth between them.

"Oh," He said. "*I* get it. You're *dykes*."

Cymbeline tensed, looking at Sid. But Sid was mostly elsewhere.

"Not exactly," she grumbled at him. Dick was not deterred by the roll of Sid's eyes, or the look of consternation on her brow.

"Fine," he said. "*Lesbians*. You know what I would do if I were you?"

"Kill myself?" Sid muttered. But Dick only laughed.

"You're alright," he said. He was reaching hands, glove-like and worn, into the pocket of his flannel shirt. He pulled out a stack of business cards, held together by a dingy rubber band, yanked one free and passed it to Cymbeline.

"You hitch a ride with Sheila over there," he jerked his thumb at the woman who had run the open mic, who was now sweeping the flowers clean. "Have her drop you down the road at Motel 88. Then in the morning, I sober up, pick you ladies up. And you—" He pointed a grimy finger at Cymbeline. "—Will come record at my studio."

Cymbeline examined the card, lifting her eyebrows. Then she handed it over to Sid, who read it, too.

"You own a studio?" Cymbeline asked, trying her best not to put the emphasis on *you*.

"Yeah," he said. "Bought it with my inheritance. Zachy might have gotten the millions, but at the eldest son, I at least got that."

Sid looked up from the card, carefully setting her gaze on Cymbeline. She could see that Sid was interested—they could record a demo! Something *useful* to both of their ambitions—but it was clear she didn't want to give herself away yet, either.

"What's in it for you?" Sid asked, offering the card back. But Dick waved his hand.

"Keep it. All I ask is $100 an hour for the rental and to pay my guy. He'll engineer it. In an afternoon, you could have a demo. I know a couple of schmucks in the business. They'd be interested in that one."

At *that one* he pointed at Cymbeline. She shifted in her seat, trying not to look uncomfortable. Trying not to feel like a piece of meat. But still, she said nothing. This was what Sid wanted. To manage her. So she would let her answer. She glanced at Sid, waiting for her to answer. She glanced at Sid, wondering what the answer would be.

"Seventy-five an hour," Sid said, leveling her gaze at him. "And *you'll* pay for the motel."

Dick didn't answer for a moment, looking Sid square in the eye. Waiting for something. Something, apparently, he did not get.

"Fuck," he said, sitting back, fishing for his wallet. He took out a handful of wrinkled bills and offered them to Sid.

She took the stack of money, counted it, nodded. "That should be enough. Now go talk to Sheila for us about that ride."

Dick looked at her. He brayed out a breath of laughter. "Cymbeline, your girlfriend here is a shark. You should make her your manager."

Cymbeline smirked. "I already have," she said.

* * *

When they got to their motel room at nearly three in the morning, they discovered that the air conditioning had been left off. The air had that soggy, muggy, chlorinated quality that one only seems to find in late August, in shared spaces that have been disinfected one too many times. As Cymbeline latched the door behind them, and put her guitar case on one of the double beds, she gazed at Sid. The other girl peeled off her shirt, leaving it where it fell, on the damp carpet, put her wallet down on the nightstand, then went to turn on the air conditioner.

"What are we going to do with Neil's car?" Cymbeline asked, sitting on the bed, feeling it sag under her weight.

"We'll call him first thing," Sid said. "See if he wants to tow it somewhere. It's not really our problem."

"Do you think the campers will miss us in the morning?" Cymbeline asked. Sid laughed at that. She jumped onto the bed beside Cymbeline, landing on her knees, making the mattress shake.

"Perky, who the fuck *cares* about the campers? Tomorrow we are going to record your demo. You were transcendent tonight. Tonight isn't about those brats, Cymbeline. It's about *you.*"

Perky cared about those brats. But now, in this moment, with Sid leaning her curved, naked shoulder into hers, it was easy to forget that she cared. They kissed, both of their breaths beery and hot. And something seemed to lift and swell in Cymbeline's belly. She put her hands on Sid's narrow waist, flipped her over onto the bed. Usually she let Sid be on top. Sexually dominant. The "boy," if there was one. The aggressor. Not tonight.

She pressed her lips, the edges of her teeth, against Sid's neck. And that was enough to unravel her. Sid moaned. Her hands, at first clutching at the thin fabric of Cymbeline's dress, fell back against the scratchy motel duvet. Cymbeline traced a line downwards, half kissing, half biting, her hands drifting down, too. Only gracing Sid's breasts through the thick fabric of her sports bra, because she knew how and where Sid liked and did not like to be touched. With an almost violent force of motion, she tugged down Sid's zipper, cast off her shorts, Sid's y-fronts all tangled up in them. She was kneeling on the floor then, her knees against the hard, scratchy carpet, a supplicant before the altar of Sid's body, and in the still-musty heat the smell of Sid was pungent and rich, less musky than her own, somehow more earthen, and she drew close, inhaled, then plunged her tongue in.

Sid's moans were guttural. Her body convulsed. Her hands ineffectually tore at Cymbeline's hair, and it wasn't clear if she was trying to pull her away or not, until—Cymbeline's tongue deep inside her, because she could feel the resolution of this bridge already, stunningly close—her legs clamped tight around Cymbeline's ears and she croaked out.

"Oh God, I'm—"

And then a full body convulsion, back arching up, muscles taut, even her toes arching, trembling, and Cymbeline felt Sid's body twitch against hers, but she didn't stop, her tongue still circling, and Sid pulling with fisted hands at her hair. She let the almost-painful pleasure roll on and on. For Sid's benefit, but also for hers.

* * *

Later, or maybe earlier, Sid was sprawled out on top of the blankets, wearing only her socks and her sports bra, the air conditioning prickling her skin. Cymbeline couldn't sleep. Her headache throbbed, worse than before. She leaned over to the nightstand, opened Sid's wallet. She saw there, beside the stack of neat bills, their day's earnings, Dick's business card. Her ears rang. Biting down on her lip, she let her eyes, half-clouded with wings, settle on the black-on-white text.

Richard Charles Ashby Studios
Recording. Mixing. Engineering.
"It's all about the experience."
www.notthatRCA.com
comboRCAshby62@aol.com

Well, she thought wryly, through the pain, At least that weird old cunt has a website.

Her stomach squeezed, as if in response to that thought. Cymbeline grimaced. She shouldn't have had that beer, she thought. Dark beer always wrecked her. She got up, padding over toward the bathroom, scratching herself. It was amazing that she was able to stand. Usually when it got this bad, she couldn't. She'd learned to leave class when she saw the teeth, had learned to tuck herself in bed until it stopped. Sometimes it would take three, four days. Now, somehow, through some kind of magic, she found herself able to walk through it. To be alive *through* it. She got herself a paper cup of water from the tap, drank it, tasted something gritty there, like fresh clean soil. She drank another cup. A third. The pain was still there. She looked at herself in the mirror, found her reflection surprising to her for the thousandth time.

She understood, instinctively, deeply, this *thing* that Sid felt. This *incorrectness*. It didn't plague her like it did Sid. She knew on some level that this had been a choice she made, and not an incorrect choice. But still, there were days when she saw herself and was surprised by her own pale, freckly skin, her breasts and the heavy weight of them, the narrow span of her shoulders, her stung lips. Now, the strap of her dress was falling down. Her ponytail had half come undone, trailing into feathers down her neck. She knew she looked *pretty*. But in some ways, hadn't the prettiness always been with her? In other lives, in other forms. This body's prettiness didn't matter, the same way that it didn't matter that Dick looked like a drunken waste of flesh at not-yet-forty. Because there was something else there. A certain soul's inherent magic.

She drank one last cup of water, crushed the cup, tossed it into the trash. Then she turned out the light and stepped back into the bedroom. That's when she found herself in the wrong bedroom, the wrong place, the wrong life. The light here was not the gray light of dawn outside Oneonta, New York. It was brighter, sharper, coming in the wrong way through the window. The walls. Too narrow. Not a motel room at all. White plaster she'd once memorized. A crack over the small window at the end. Album covers, stolen, glued to the walls. She'd caught hell for that. Hadn't cared. Drawings pinned up, and postcards from exotic locales. And beneath them, a single narrow bed, and two bodies shivering in it. Animal sounds, instinctual, shared. A chorus. There would be other choruses, she knew. But now, in this feral, everlasting moment, she watched the shapes move. A pale head and a dark one. She watched and she felt herself split then, outside herself, like she would on stage for the next half-decade or so, as long as she would tolerate being on stage again, for Sid's sake. She felt the heat under the blankets, and the stale, air conditioned air outside it, felt hands, flesh, a certain explosion of stars, a certain wetness of faces, a certain stickiness. Felt her knees weaken, reached for the dresser and tried to steady herself, as one of the shapes lifted down the corner of the blanket, and looked at her with her own coal-black eyes.

Sorry, but not in this fucking lifetime, those eyes were saying. *Not him.*

She felt herself fall, *thump,* on the carpet, saw Sid sit straight up in bed.

"Cymbeline?" she called, rushing over. Just as the image was fading. The voice, ringing out still in her mind, but softer now.

In this lifetime, the voice was saying, *him.*

Cymbeline took Sid's hand and stumbled to her feet.

"Sorry," she said, taking staggered steps toward the bed. "Sorry."

"Why are you *apologizing*?" Sid asked. Cymbeline squeezed her eyes shut, reminding herself of where she was. Who she was.

"God," she said, sinking into the covers, "My head is *killing* me."

She squeezed her eyes shut, willing away everything in the world but the body beside her, the hand that still squeezed tight her hand.

35 - 1958

As Eddie made his way up the narrow stairwell, he realized he'd never seen the second story of Baron's aunt's house before. On past visits, they'd always been restricted to the first floor—the sun room, mostly. She hadn't even wanted the boys to use her downstairs bog, though she'd relented eventually, after Baron had screeched at her that she couldn't very well want them all to piss in her bushes.

Now, as he made his way up the stairs, he was surprised by how small it all was. Brighter, yes, and more smartly decorated than most of the houses he knew. Bongo's or Liam's or even his own. He glimpsed through an open doorway at the top of the stairs, at a wallpapered room with a bed nearly made with a flowered coverlet. Deidre's room. It looked as fussy as she was—though a long-haired cat saw him and slinked down from his spot in the center of the bed to lace himself around Eddie's ankles. Eddie found himself softening despite himself. Usually he prided himself on remembering the names of pets and younger siblings, but nothing came this time.

"Hallo, Puss," he finally said, and, bending over, stroked the creature's fine, soft fur. Puss mewed, leaving auburn hair all over his pants legs. Eddie laughed a little, brushing it off.

That's when he heard it, coming from the end of the hallway. A small sound, like a mouse. Like a baby's cry. Hiccuping, off and on. Starting, stopping. It didn't sound *human*. It definitely didn't sound like *Baron*. But Eddie knew that it was who it must be.

He left Puss sitting at the top of the stairs licking his paw, and went to the small door at the end of the hallway. Rapped his knuckles on it, softly, twice.

"Barry?" he called. No answer. Only more mewling sounds. "Baron, can I come in?"

When there was no answer for another moment, two, Eddie opened the door. The room was like a closet. You could practically stand in the middle and touch either of the white plaster walls with your fingertips. At the far end, a desk. A window over it, with a crack snaking its way down from above. A guitar case, Baron's familiar guitar case, sat cradled in the chair, and there was a milk crate on the floor in front of him, piled with books and papers and clothes, nearly blocking his entrance. He turned, looking left. To the wall, covered in Baron's dirty drawings, tits and cocks and pirates brandishing bloody knives. Edges of postcards, pinned to the wall. And album covers, the ones they'd nicked together, and at least one that Baron had borrowed from Eddie himself, swearing he'd return it, glued down with mucilage to the plaster. *Deidre must have had his head for that,* Eddie thought, and then he looked down into the narrow bed beneath it and saw that head, with its black hair, tightly curled, peeking out from beneath the covers.

He didn't seem to notice that Eddie was there. His shoulders were a hunched up shape beneath the pillows like a craggy mountain, and his face was smushed into the pillowcase, eyes squeezed tight, blocking out the world. Eddie closed the door behind him, reached down, touched Baron's shoulder.

"Baron," he said, the word coming out now like a whisper. He felt how tight Baron's muscles were, how tensed up he'd been, probably all night, probably for hours and hours. He heard Baron take a painful gasp of breath—and then say nothing at first, and for a long moment Eddie wondered if Baron was going to say nothing at all.

But then, that ragged voice. Raspy, raw as blood. "She's gone, Ed. She's fucking gone. That fucking copper—"

And then all unraveled again, shredded away to nothing but tears.

For a moment, Eddie said nothing. He took a slow breath, then stepped over the milk crate, gently moving the guitar case from its seat at the desk. He sat down, and began untying his shoes, slowly, listening to Baron wheeze and cry. Set them on the floor at the edge of the bed, one right next to the other, right next to Baron's trainers, too. Like they both belonged there, in a row. Like they lived there together.

He took off his coat, draping it on the chair. And then, moving slowly, like he feared he might break something if he moved too fast, he peeled back the covers. Exposing the sight of Baron's muscular back, clad only in a white undershirt, the brown backs of his muscular arms, the nape of Baron's neck. The older boy tensed for a moment, exposed. He was facing the wall, not looking at Eddie, drawing in a breath, his eyes half-shut.

"It's alright, love," Eddie said, and though for a moment he wondered if the tiny bed would fit them both, he climbed in beside and behind Baron, putting his arms around Baron, drawing him close. "It's alright. I know. I know."

Tense, for just a moment longer, and then the grief overtook Baron again. Baron cupped his hands over his face, crying into them, as Eddie held him and gently rocked him, kissing his shoulder, his cheek, finding his own face wet with tears. Remembering his own Mum. And the space, hollow, painful, that she had left behind—that would always be there. The first scar. The worst scar.

"She's gone, Hammy," he sobbed. "Gone. How could she—? I'm—" A gasp. A terrified whisper. "I'm all alone."

"Tch tch," Eddie said, pursing his lips, making a noise like one might make to a cat. "You're not, love. I'm here. I'm here."

Their bodies pressed tightly together, they cried together, Eddie holding Baron in his childhood bed. Grieving together. And that's all it was.

At least at first.

<h1 style="text-align:center">36 - 2017</h1>

Matthew woke early in that Eames chair, unable to remember having gone to sleep. The light over the mountains was pale and feeble. His neck ached, his spine, even his ankles. Once he'd been able to sleep anywhere—that had been the family joke. He'd fall asleep backstage in a pile of stinking old curtains. He'd fall asleep under the old willow tree after chasing his Dad's sheepdogs all afternoon. Into his twenties, even, he'd fall asleep standing up on the New York City subway after one of the early gigs, those days when his rise had seemed meteoric and he'd been sure that age would never, ever catch up to him.

Well. His body had showed him, hadn't it? Aching, he rose, stretching, scratching. The mantel clock said it was just past seven. Earlier than he would have expected. But it wasn't entirely unwanted. His body needed a piss, for one thing, like a sodding old man. He headed upstairs, drained the dragon, went into the shower. Showered off. Thought only for a moment about beating it, about, well, *her*. But pushed the thought away. She had made herself clear last night. It was her body—*hers*—not his to co-opt for his lecherous fantasies. And besides, he told himself, giving himself just one little squeeze, he would see her in the flesh soon enough. And they'd make music. It had worked for their dads, hadn't it? Well, it would have to work for him.

He got out and dressed. Old blue jeans and a tour t-shirt, one of his dad's from the late '70s that he'd filched on the last holiday visit to London. He'd had the same one when he was a little boy, and it had been his favorite, had worn it until it was practically tie-dyed with stains and cried when his mum insisted he throw it out. There was a picture somewhere of the elder Ed Hammond in this one, of Ed Matthew Hammond the younger in his, their arms around each other and kind of preening, like a coupla peacocks. He wondered if his Dad had noticed the missing shirt, if he'd cared. Thought about texting his father a selfie of himself in the foggy bathroom mirror: *Missing something, old man?* His father always texted him, pictures of the cats and of himself in stores with sunglasses he was thinking of buying and bits and bobs in the newspaper that made him think of Matthew. Normally, Matthew answered about a third, and curtly: *lol.*

But when he went to find his phone downstairs, it was dead as a brick. He sighed, plugged it in on one of the kitchen sockets, then looked around the scene before him. Creation, it seemed, was messy business. Papers everywhere, pens. A few lingering cardboard remnants of their dinner feast, and half-drunk bottles and the records they'd left strewn about, and his guitar left out on the floor, ready to be tripped on. *Well, this won't do*, he heard his Dad say in his head, and began tidying. Cleaned up the old noodles, put the records back in their proper place—alphabetical, it seemed. Edelman's wife was a fastidious sort even if Edelman was a bit of a slob. He put the bottles back on the bar, brought the glasses to the sink, and started to pile up the papers. Sorting them so that the same songs were all together, then started to put them in order too. In his head, he could hear the larger body of work that was forming, going from start to finish. But there were still gaps. They'd need seven or eight more, at least. But, he thought, putting the stack on the coffee table, he was closer to an *album* than he'd been in a very long time. He set a pencil on top of it, and then went and found some note pads by the phone. Brought two over. Set them out. Better, he thought, than writing on whatever scraps were sitting around. Would be easier when they went to record.

He glanced at the clock. Not yet eight, still. And still not right, the whole scene. So he went to the hall behind the stairs—where the day before he'd glimpsed that small den, with an ancient VCR and a pull out sofa, and opened doors until he found a stick vacuum. And started properly cleaning up.

Forty minutes later, he sat at the kitchen counter, eating an egg he'd found to fry in the fridge, and some crusty gluten-free toast. The sun was up now, shining yellow at a slant through the picture windows, almost too bright, and the sky was clear, the kind of blue that seems almost supernatural. He couldn't remember the last time he had a morning like this. He and Kara were late risers who never cooked. And they rarely cleaned up after themselves. They ate take-out and paid well—above market wages—to have other people do the cleaning. Funny, because they'd never hired help when he had been a kid. His Mum and Dad did it all, his Dad helping more than most, at least until Mum got sick and he was preoccupied taking care of her. But Kara's schedule was all over the place, and somehow, it seemed, Matthew's always was, too. There was always a radio program calling him up over some Saffron anniversary or another, or that breast cancer foundation his Dad had formed asking him for a new recording of one of his old songs. There was the school in Brooklyn where he'd been the visiting musician and helped a bunch of little kiddies learn to play the ukulele. He'd enjoyed that one, but it had taken more time than he thought it would. Kara, annoyed, always, by his distraction.

"You don't understand," he'd told her, barely glancing up from his laptop, "They need my help. This one, his name is Ramon, he'd be amazing if I could just figure out how to teach him to read music. He's dyslexic. I need to research this, Kara—"

"Learning how to read music isn't going to save him, Mattie," she'd said in annoyance. Well, easy for Kara to say. She'd been in voice lessons by the time she was four. *What did Kara know about saving anyone?* he thought bitterly, *she's never been in any* danger.

Not that life had been dangerous for Matthew either. But still, he thought, it was the fundamental difference between them. Yes, he had a pony growing up. But he'd mucked her stalls himself, brushed her, slept outside with her when she'd gotten sick once, woke up to the sight of the sunrise coming through the slats of her stall and the rhythm of her still-beating heart beneath him.

He put his fork down, thinking. Wondering if Naomi had once been like Ramon, so eager to be filled up with music, so hungry for it. That year that he'd taught at PS 51 had been one of his better ones. Waking up every morning to take the subway there in his natty suit, stopping home on the way for dinner, gossiping about students with Kara as they ate, a glass of wine before bed, then doing the same thing all over again the next morning. The entire rhythm of it. He'd even started Googling—secret search histories, late at night—teaching programs nearby. Remembering how his Dad had said his grandmother had been a teacher. But Kara hated it. It had been only their second year living together, and they almost lost each other because of the gig.

That had been the Christmas they'd had that rocker of a row in Kingcausie. The problem, he thought then, and now, was how fundamentally *different* they were. They weren't like his Mum and Dad, teenage lovers from the same neighborhood, having grown up together and gone through fame together and all of that. And they weren't like his Dad and the new woman, either, a pair of staid old souls who wore slippers all weekend and were friendly and open with the press and generous with charities. But then, had he *ever* met *anyone* with his sonar? Not a bird, anyway. And Kara was pretty, and a kitten between the sheets, and ambitious, in her own way, and supportive of his music, so long as that music did, for Kara, what it needed to do.

He remembered the aftermath of that fight, the Kingcausie fight. Kara upstairs, crying to his Dad's wife about it. And him downstairs, having a whiskey with his father before the hired car came to get them. His father pouring in another finger, lowering his voice, asking Matthew about it.

"Now you know I like her. I do, Matt. But son, are you sure she's the one for you?"

Matthew, drinking, not wanting to hear it. His father was warm and generous with his girlfriends—but Matthew had known, secretly, truly, that his father liked none of them.

"Yeah," he said. "She is, Dad."

When he said it, he said it like an American, like Kara might. A flat, nasally syllable, a crisp D at the end. For a moment, Eddie didn't say anything.

"Alright," he said at last, lifting his glass. "Cheers, then." Clinking the edges of their glasses. Drinking. But then Eddie added, with a wince, "But be careful, right? You know we Hammonds have a tendency to mate for life."

Matthew had hated him for saying that. But it did seem to be true. In six years, now, there had been no talk of marriage—Kara said she was philosophically opposed to it—and of course there had been other girls. He wasn't *happy*—had never really been *happy*—but he figured happiness was for other blokes. And Kara had chosen him, and let him sow his oats so he could still feel young and relevant, and now there was going to be the baby, and, well, hard to go back now, wasn't it?

And if you had asked him a week ago if he wanted to be with her, anyway, he would have told you that you must have been smoking something. Kara was a *catch*. And she was *still* a catch, and that hadn't changed. But still . . .

He was washing his plate when the doorbell rang, and he came to the door with a dish towel still on his shoulder.

"Morning!" he cried brightly, because it *was* bright. Only it didn't look that way, for Naomi. Her hair was frizzy, and she was still wearing the same clothes from the night before, and there were bags under her eyes. She looked much older. In her arms there was a file box, and another on the ground there, and a guitar case, covered in stickers for bands he hadn't heard of.

"Can you help me with this?" she asked testily. Matthew let her dump the box into his arms.

"Sure," he said, only after she'd grabbed her guitar case and brought it in. "Where do you want it?"

"Wherever," she said, then added, "You can put both of them wherever you want. Those are the journals and the letters, for your dad. I kept the ones from the Templeton family. Figured it's all I'm going to get from them. But he can have the rest."

Matthew carried both boxes over to the coffee table and put them down beside the sofa. He closed the door behind her, turned. She was looking around.

"You cleaned up," she said in confusion. "Didn't think a guy like you was capable of that."

"A guy like me?" he asked, snorted a little. "Yeah, well, I went to some of the best schools in England. Parents didn't pay all those thousands to have a son who can't use a vacuum."

She turned, looked at him. The corner of her mouth was cocked up.

"Should we look at them?" he asked, gesturing from where he still stood by the front door to those file boxes. Waiting for him. "Settle this argument about our fathers?"

"It's not an argument," she said. She rubbed the heels of her hands over her eyes. "It's—God, I don't care. I'm starving. I should go get some McDonald's or something. I didn't have time to eat. Was up all night going through those for you."

He felt his belly twist a little, an unfamiliar feeling. Guilt. She'd lost sleep over this. Over something that was only half-serious to him, mostly. A joke to him, mostly.

"No, no," he said. "I'll make you something. A pot of coffee, too."

Naomi stood there in her coat, watching him, frowning, as he went to the kitchen and got out another egg.

* * *

If he expected thanks from Naomi, he would have been disappointed. She inhaled the eggs in a breath, scraped the plate clean, dumped it in the sink without much acknowledgment at all. Another difference between her and Kara, then, because the few times he'd cooked Kara breakfast, she *oohed* and *aahed* over his efforts, then posted emoji and hashtag-filled snaps of her breakfast to her Instagram account. #lover #blessed. To Naomi, it seemed, his efforts were expected, ordinary. She took her coffee over to the sofa, sat down.

"Are you ready for work?" she said.

He laughed a little. An easy laugh.

"Yeah," he said. "Soon, but—I'd really like to take a *look* at these." He came

303

and sat on the opposite end of the sofa, touching one of the file boxes with the flat of his hand. She grimaced.

"Are you *sure?*" she asked. "Why?"

"I mean," he began. "They're *historic*. Baron Templeton's lost journals. His private thoughts! We can find out what *really* happened with Peter X. His actual state of mind. How he felt when he was up there with my dad, playing in front of thousands of people. How it felt to know the whole world loved him."

"Ah, I get it," Naomi said. "You're a *fan*." Her eyes fell on his t-shirt, the one that read, in square letters *Hammond III: Live at the Nippon Budokan*. Something about her expression suggested she was trying to make a point, in looking.

"And you're not?"

"It's complicated," she said. "Anyway, I've read them. I can tell you, in a nutshell: Peter X. convinced Templeton that his long-lost father was waiting for him at his brand-new commune outside the Port of Spain, and bled him dry of his money while he strung him along. He was naive and trusting. An idiot, basically. As for performing, he hated playing those stadium shows at the end. He used to have panic attacks. He'd get the runs before concerts or puke his brains out. He was afraid someone was going to come up with a gun and murder him. He said he never wanted to go back to that. And as far as knowing that the whole world loved him, well—" She took another sip. Shook her head.

"What?" asked Matthew.

"I don't think he did. He knew that the music was something special. Even he could see that. But he doubted *everyone*. His aunt. My mother. He was incredibly jealous and incredibly insecure. Called himself a fat pig when he weighed all of a hundred and thirty-five pounds. Said he was wretched, disgusting, a coward. He hated the sound of his own voice; did you know that? Talked about giving his songs away so he wouldn't have to hear himself sing them. He barely seemed *aware* of the world, never mind its love for him. Said there was only one person he could trust in it."

"Who?" Matthew asked, and realized as he said it that it was a stupid question. Because he knew. "Oh. Dad."

Naomi just sighed, sitting back on the sofa. "But go ahead and read them," she said. "It's your funeral."

She was watching him, waiting. So he went and lifted the lid of the first box up. It was packed full of old notebooks, papers, letters, photographs. He pulled out a steno pad that was on top. *December '74 - ,* it said, and there was no end date. Maybe Templeton had never finished it. He opened to a random page. There was a drawing on the side, a cartoon of a man, balloonish, naked, clutching his own cock, semen spurting out of it. Like something a teenager might draw. Templeton's handwriting was jagged and wild, odd peaks and valleys. Hard to read.

February 16

Call from Liam this morning. Ostensibly about his album but all he wanted to do was gossip about the in-laws. That old sibling rivalry. Genie's knocked up again. You think the two would have been enough for the Hammonds, but that Ed's always wanted a flock. Must be those old Catholic genes. Liam thinks I should ring up Hammy, offer to pay him a visit. Would sooner hang myself than to see all that domestic bliss. I don't think he thinks he's rubbing my nose in it. He never does, Waller. Thinks he's making me feel included. Convincing me of something, their way of life. Doesn't understand that it was never going to be away in a manger and a sweet sainted Mary for me. Have made my own happiness, besides. Alana. Lovely Alana, legs that go all the way. Alana, Alana let's talk about the coming rise of the Left, the lack of radicalization of Blacks in the colonies, read me the words of Frantz Fanon, whisper your secrets in my ear. She doesn't understand music at all but she knows what its like to walk around a shadow and when we fuck I float all the way up the mountain to Shangri-La. She wants me to meet her guru, this Peter Charles. I told her I never trust a man with two first names and she shouldn't either. She says he has plans to change it. What other plans have they shared? I know she's fucking him, too, and I don't want to see her drooling over him but she insists he's going to blow my mind. He's getting a crew together, planning to head out to New York next year, connect with the Panthers. I suspect we'll be among them. But I'm not ready to be blown yet.

The chat with Liam was of no help. Never is. Can't talk about Ed without thinking of other lives, universes other than this one, better ones. And the deal I made with the devil in 1958. And yes, I consented. Put my name on the line. But I would have done anything that Hammy asked me. Still would. It's why I can't go to Kingcausie. Gotta keep my head screwed on. Gotta keep moving. He has his family. I'll have mine. Alana and Peter Charles and whatever else might come after.

Still, thinking about that day in me little bed, after my Mummy died, of Hammy's cock pressing into me and how I never wanted that moment to end. Sometimes I think maybe it hasn't. A moment that rips through the universe, through every universe, a signal post, a pin in the map. How I reached down and felt the broiled hot skin of Edmund Hammond III's uncut seven inches, that old magnificent Hammond organ—

"Ew," Matthew said, and threw the book away from him, onto the coffee table, like it had bitten him. Naomi laughed.

"I told you," she said, only a little meanly. Matthew laughed now, too.

"You did."

"So you ready now?" she asked. "To get to work?"

"Yeah," he said, still laughing, wiping the tears from his eyes. Christ. "Let's go."

* * *

If he had any doubts before that this was Templeton's daughter, he no longer did. For one thing, the guitar that came out of its case that day was Templeton's. A cheap little plywood thing, an Antoria according to the swooping script on the head stock, Templeton's first guitar, the one he'd had as a teenager, predating the pilfering of their amplified gear. Matthew recognized it from old photos, had filed it away into his memory without even realizing. Now, sixty years after the instrument's purchase, the finish was worn, of course, only Naomi had strung it up backwards, because she was left-handed, so that it was not only worn across the pick guard, but under it, too. Because of the way she played. Hard and fast. Like she was dying. Like she was her father. The two shallow spots in the finish, reflections of each other.

Easier this way, he thought, as the two of them sat on the sofa with their guitars. This way, they were perfectly mirrored, and it made it faster, easier, to play with her than he'd found it to play with anyone . . . ever. They strummed together, bumbling through their burgeoning music. He watched her fingers and avoided looking too deeply into her eyes. Every time he did, he found himself unmoored again, tangled up. It felt like fucking. And she didn't want to fuck, and that was embarrassing, a bit, and the day had already been embarrassing enough. Revolting thoughts of his father's member kept flashing in his head.

Anyway, the song was a good distraction. Naomi on her guitar. Singing. Playing. She was good, too. Strong voice, and you could feel it, and you could tell that *she* could feel it. He'd been around enough musicians to know that there were some who had that, and some who didn't. The technical players—sometimes even studio musicians—who could do a complex arpeggio and back. Steve Vai. And then there were the raw ones, for whom music existed as a simple means to transmit feeling. Cursed Robert Johnson and that lot.

His Dad, actually, he'd always thought, a unique case—something in between. An incredibly proficient musician, could pick up almost anything with strings, plus piano, plus drums, plus the trumpet, plus a brief, odd love affair he'd had with the saxophone in the late 1980s. His father had all the musical ability of a studio professional, of a conductor, which he was, in a way. Could read sheet music at a glance, though he lied to the press about it, for some reason that was forever beyond Matthew, and Matthew perpetuated that lie for him without even thinking, as he did other pieces of family lore. Maybe because it was important, this myth of his father as a working class bloke, a self-made man. He and Templeton, both teaching each other the names of chords. Templeton had been more like Johnson, clearly, and not just due to his race. An intuitive musician. And Hammond Sr. could certainly be intuitive, feeling his way through songs, the possibilities of them, melodic and emotional. But then if you asked him about it, he could tell you the theory of it, too. Why the music needed to work the way it did, and, if he was breaking rules, why. Matthew had a bit of that, from growing up in it. But Naomi, he sensed, didn't. When he asked if something she was playing was in 6/8, she looked blankly at him, said, "Is it?" and then bent back down over her guitar and just kept on playing.

And yet the way that the music wormed its way out of her—it was remarkable. Her fingers were long and nimble and could pick out a counter melody without a problem. She could find little variations in chords that woke him up a bit, made him sit straighter. If she sang along with it, it was even better. Her clear, untrained voice, immediate and real, and the flash of her fingers on the acoustic strings beneath it. Around noon, as she was working out the middle eight to a song without any lyrics yet save for a line about some ocean come to shore, he got up to make them both sandwiches, but his eyes remained fixed on her. Magnetically attracted.

He set a pair of ham sandwiches on plates, set plates in front of them on the coffee table. Then he sat down across from her, but didn't pick up his guitar this time, even though he halfway *itched* for it. Finally, the notes faded off. She looked up at him. Grinned, jaggedly, looking more like her father than he'd ever noticed her to look.

"What?" she asked.

He'd tucked his hand in under his chin to watch her, and now he pulled it out, flashing it through the air. Something he tried not to do, normally. Talking with his hands was known to be one of his Dad's tics. If Matthew were ever caught doing that in public, in an interview or whatever, all the teenage girls who, improbably, obsessed over a seventy-five year old man on Tumblr would be posting animated gifs everywhere, squealing about their similarities. But Naomi was not a teenage girl. He was safe, here, to be his real self, genetic quirks and all.

"You're an amazing performer, is all," he said. "I don't understand why you wouldn't want to play these songs, too. On an album, or on stage. We could do it together. Be a proper *band*. I mean, why be Bernie Taupin when you could be—"

"When I could be Baron Templeton?" The grimace that pulled Naomi's mouth down was slow-developing, but clear. She leaned her guitar up against the end table and started stuffing food in her face. She ate like a pig, again. Like she'd never seen food before, like she didn't much care about it except to get it in there and done with.

"What?" it was his turn to ask.

"I have performed on stage exactly once in my life and Matt? That'll be the only time." She shuddered, as though she could feel it still.

"Why?"

She shrugged. "Choked. Was supposed to get me into conservatory. Well, forget *that* plan. Took one look at those stage lights and all those eyes on top of me—you know, the professors who were there to *rate* us?—and I could barely see the keys. Couldn't even *feel* them. Played about two bars, and one was a different song entirely, and then just sat there shaking. They told me to go, so I went. And never went back."

"You said Templeton had stage fright," he said. "Genetic, maybe. Could take a Xanax. Kara does that sometimes before shows. I think it makes her dull, takes her edge off and she needs the edge to be halfway decent. But it gets her through it."

Naomi frowned. "Who's Kara?"

Matthew drew in a sharp breath. He hadn't realized that she didn't know about Kara. "Oh, my—my partner." Kara hated being called "partner," actually. Preferred "lover." But it seemed crass to say that now. "Girlfriend."

"Oh," Naomi said. She put down her sandwich. Was he imagining it, or did she look a little green?

"Sorry," he said, uncertain, even as he said it, as to why he was apologizing, then remembering, with clarity, how he'd propositioned her. "We have an open—"

"No, it's fine," she said. "It's none of my business." She rubbed her palms against her thighs. Anxious, now, he saw. Generally anxious. Genuinely anxious.

"Anyway," he said, because he wanted to go back to what mattered—how amazing she was. "You could be fantastic on stage. I know you would. You should consider it. Both of us together could do our songs better justice than one of us alone."

"No," she said, shaking her head, hard, "you'll be the one to play them. *You'll* be fantastic. You grew up on stage, right?"

"Yeah," he said, shrugging. "On and off. It helps how much my Dad loves it. When I'm up there, I have to go outside myself, sort of, pretend I'm an actor in a play. Ask myself: *what would a decent performer look like, what would they do?* And then do that. Works, though."

"And your dad?"

Matthew shrugged. He picked up his sandwich, tugging away at the crust before taking a bite. "It's just him. He loves it. I think he was born to be on stage."

"Must be nice," Naomi said. Matthew looked at her.

"Yeah," he said.

Naomi got up then. She dumped her plate in the sink, once more without clearing it or washing it.

"Anyway," she said. She crossed her arms over herself. A shield. "I'm a forty-year-old dyke. I'm nobody. No one wants to see me perform. You've got a history in the industry, at least."

It wasn't funny, but Matthew found himself laughing. Dry laughter. Hard, painful laughter. "A history composed largely of false starts and failure."

"But you're Eddie Hammond's *son*."

"And you," Matthew said, "Are Baron Templeton's daughter."

Naomi's turn to laugh. "Well, they don't know that."

Matthew leaned forward. He picked up one of their notebooks, the chord names she'd written down, the words he'd added. She'd crossed out his corny ones. Made them better. He hadn't minded.

"They will," he told her.

37 - 1958

Ed Hammond had never undertaken a serious contemplation of homosexuality.

The other boys had, for him. Because one cannot be a boy as pretty as Ed without attention of varying sorts—whether lust or jealousy or admiration or some queer combination of the three. He had those eyelashes, you see. That bee-stung mouth, just a little crooked. Those eyes, heavy-lidded and, in the right light, such a clear, bright blue it was nearly turquoise, it was nearly sea glass, it was nearly Caribbean waters at midday, it was nearly impossible not to fall in. And the curls, soft, loose over his forehead, and the way he dressed, well-considered for every occasion, and the way he held himself, and the movement of his hands. He was a lovely animal, and so of course the other boys had called him a queer and a pouf and a queen and made jokes about sticking it in his arsehole or whatnot but he'd never listened to it because he figured their words had nothing to do with him. He liked birds. He'd always liked birds. It was unquestionable, that he liked them, since back when he was a little baby boy in primary school, getting all excited by little Margaux Taylor showing him her knickers behind the back fence during recess. *I'll show you mine*, and all of that, and he had and had even let her touch it, and it was good, felt good. Who even needed to think about *boys*?

He hadn't needed to, until Barry.

Had heard rumors, of course, before the two of them ever met. That day at the parade, when he'd stopped with his mate Teddy, who was trying to make everyone call him *Bongo*, of all absurdities, to listen to the band play, and saw the bloke in the pink checkered shirt, the dark one, with inky eyes smoldering like Elvis, heard him singing all of the lyrics wrong, leaned his shoulder in against Teddy's shoulder.

"'Ey, Ted, you know him?"

Bongo smirked, as though in asking, Eddie had confirmed something about himself Bongo had long suspected.

"Baron Templeton," he said. He held his wrist limp. "Goes to the art college. Bit of a fruiter, that one."

Eddie's cheeks heated then, wondering if the boys said the same thing about him, suspecting they did, from what little he knew.

"Yes, but, cor, listen to him *play*," he said. Bongo listened then, and grinned.

"Yeah," said Bongo, "He's alright. The two of you, mate, I think you could get along. Don't you write songs or something?"

Poems, actually, or one poem, about his dead mum, which the school paper had printed last year and about which he never heard the end from his brothers. But. Close enough.

"Yeah," he told Bongo, lying easily, the plan fermenting in his brain.

There had been some days, in their friendship's short tenure, that he'd felt sure that what he'd been told about Baron wasn't true. Couldn't be true. Because if it was true, wouldn't it be more like being around a bird, to be around Baron? He never felt west when he was around him, never got those first date jitters. Christ, when it came to girls half the time he couldn't get any words out at all, instead preoccupied by when the game would start. Y'know, *I'll show you mine, etc.* But it wasn't like that with Baron. It was comfortable. Like being with any other mate, like being with a brother. Sure, Baron talked about *wanking* a lot. Drawing those dirty pictures around the edges of the music he'd written, talking about his throbbers, being crass. But so did his brother Tom, and Tom was no homosexual.

And yet. And yet. He'd seen what he had seen in that bog, that disgusting worm Dick Ashby plowing into him. *Into* him. He heard, but hadn't known, that fairies did it like *that*. In the bottom. Did it hurt, Ed had wondered?

Seemed like it might. But seemed like Baron hadn't minded it. Eyes half closed. Moaning. And strange, how in recalling it, Ed's own parts would start to tingle. Well, he told himself, shouldn't have surprised him. Fucking was fucking. He'd once gotten a throbber watching two cats pin each other down in an alleyway. Was normal to respond like that to another person's private pleasure.

Private, he thought. He'd never understood all that snickering about queerness, anyway. What two people did was private. And none of his business, except Baron was always making such a mess of things. The band. The drinking. The fights. How many songs had Ed given him to finish, how many chances to sack Dick, how many days wasted strumming away together? And they shouldn't have been wasted, because they were beautiful—the *best* days, his *favorite* days. What they made in those moments, transcendent. Better than anything he could have made by himself. Before Baron had been in his life, he hadn't even known what he was missing. For six weeks now, Baron's absence was an ache in him. It was the music, he told himself, all that music they'd never write. But nothing could be done about it.

As for the issue of Baron's proclivities, he reckoned they had nothing to do with him at all. He only thought of it so often because he was a bored, randy boy. Like any other boy. Not a queer like Baron. No. Of course not.

* * *

Perhaps it happened because they were young, sixteen and eighteen respectively, full of hormones and trouble. Perhaps it happened because their pre-frontal cortexes, which regulated impulse control, had not yet fully formed.

Perhaps it happened because they were bodies. Strong bodies. Muscular bodies. Smelling of sweat and unwashed hair and a faint bottom note of semen even on the days they didn't wank, which wasn't often. Because of the hair in their armpits and legs and groins, because of the whiskers, growing from their chinny chin chins. Perhaps that was why.

Or perhaps it was because they were so *different*. In some ways, perfect mirrors. Because Ed was melody where Baron was harmony. Because Baron was rock 'n' roll where Ed was dance hall. Because Ed was cool alabaster where Baron was warm mahogany. Because Ed had so many brothers where Baron had none. Because Ed had a stupid drunk father where Baron's had walked off.

Or because they weren't different, really, at all. Because they had both lost their mothers. Because they both had converted to the church of the holy trinity: Elvis Presley, Buddy Holly, and Little Richard. Because music *did* something to them. Because they could do something to *it*. Because it was musical, to touch body to body, Ed's arms under Baron's torso, Ed's stockinged feet touching Baron's bare feet, touching Baron's bare legs, and he held Baron and let him cry and quiver, and at some point he realized Baron *wasn't* quivering from crying. That there had developed a rhythm between them, Baron rocking against him, and he had realized that Baron wore only a t-shirt and a pair of Y-fronts, was almost undressed in the bed next to him, rubbing against Ed—because, Ed realized, he'd gone hard against Baron, was rocking *himself* against Baron, that this was happening mutually, as though they both wanted it, and in that moment, in Baron's bed, with Baron's body beside him, beautiful, Ed very much did.

And perhaps because he *hadn't* ever seriously contemplated homosexuality, because he simply viewed the things that people, in their bedroom lives, did behind their closed bedroom doors, as private, Ed did not in that moment think to be ashamed. He drew Baron Templeton tighter against him, pressing kisses to his neck, his jaw, his cheek, until finally Baron turned his head back to face him and they kissed for the first time, a strange kiss, a rough kiss, too much stubble on both of them, their teeth knocking percussively together, and Baron drew back for a moment, wincing, laughing, but Ed was undeterred, because he *wanted* to kiss Baron, so he pressed closer to him, until his body was half on top of Baron's body, and kissed him again. No teeth this time. Better this time. Perfect this time. Their tongues touching and their hearts touching and their cocks touching and their legs all tangled up.

(Here, the author almost wishes to demur; here, at this moment close to climax, the union of at least one and perhaps two intensely private men, who would later give so much of themselves to so many. Here, it is tempting to turn away because for them, this moment was sacred, a marriage of sorts, a contract, a vow, but also a secret, tightly kept between the two of them, against the world. And yet this moment, when they vibrated together, their very different bodies singing the very same song—they were not merely a pair of keys, struck, in an empty room. There would be not only the fingers—theirs, groping for each other—to press the keys but also the ears to hear it, ours, though we could not possibly know what we had heard. There would be oscillations, because of what happened in that room. There would be *repercussions*.)

For Ed, this was different than what had come before, with Genie. Their fucking had been hesitant, studied. The rubbers he'd bought off a friend, only three, and Genie lying prone and scared and waiting while he stuffed himself into her, wondering if maybe it might feel better without a rubber at all but the last thing they needed was a *baby*. Tight and dry the first time, then less so the second, the third. But still, a certain division between their bodies, as though she owned herself and he owned himself and never would either of them truly trespass upon the other.

Now, because there was no fear of a baby, yes, but also because he and Baron *loved* each other, Ed trespassed. Rubbing his cock, hard in his trousers, up against Baron's cock, his head cast aside, grunting, moaning. Kissing. Rubbing. And Ed could have been content with that, the magnet at the center of him drawn toward the magnet at the center of Baron as they kissed and rubbed and were writhing, unthinking creatures.

And perhaps it was that it was easy not to think, to just allow their bodies to clash together as impulse and instinct demanded. Their eyes closed. Their mouths making wordless sounds.

But Baron was more experienced—with girls, with boys, or at least Dick Ashby—and it seemed he wanted more from Ed than just grunting, just instinct. Now, with deliberation and a low, throaty groan, he stopped the bucking motion of his hips. Eddie opened his eyes, watching as

Baron—beneath him now, with Ed's legs straddling his hips, reached down between them and unbuttoned Ed's trousers, and in one clean motion, tugged down the offending layers of clothes. Ed found himself *helping*, kicking his pants down. Their legs touching. Heat on heat.

Baron's black eyes had not broke contact with Ed's eyes. But his hands. His hands went all over, over Ed's tie, his shirt, and down, to hips, and lower, until Ed felt the first beads of wetness against the palms of Baron's hands. Baron's mouth moved up, kissing him, kissing the corner of Ed's mouth, his neck, the base of his throat, and Ed felt his toes curl, felt himself hitch himself up higher in the bed, moving to meet Baron's mouth, Baron's hands, down below, pressing him up higher still, touching belly, thighs, arse, until only one conclusion was left foregone, and Baron's mouth met Ed's body. *There.*

Momentarily, Ed was surprised. He'd told Baron that Genie had done this, *sucked it*, but it had been a lie, a boast. Genie was a *good girl*. But Baron was neither good nor a girl. *Had Baron done this before?* he wondered, but there wasn't much time for wondering, as Baron's hands and mouth enveloped him, so tight and warm that Ed felt the pressure build already. Baron's wet, sweet mouth was all around him, and yet Baron still let out a groan of pleasure himself. Ed found himself casting his head back, looking, saw a flash of something brown in Baron's hand. It was Baron wanking down below him, as he pushed his lips all along Ed's length, swallowing him. Both of them gurgling, letting out sounds of pleasure. Close. Close. He saw and he found himself tensing, the pressure building, but it was Baron's body that bucked first, his orgasm spilling out across his own body, across the sheets, his lips going even tighter around Eddie, who throbbed once, inside Baron's mouth, and then came too. Baron did not turn away from him. Just held fast to his thighs as Eddie cried out and Baron swallowed him all down.

Ed stayed there frozen for a long moment, the only movement that of his throbber, throbbing itself out. His body softened. He was still, his eyes closed. At last, as he reached out and touched the wall in front of him to steady himself, and then gently drew himself away from Baron's mouth, his hands, and Ed laughed to himself a little bit. Softly. Gently. Looking down, he saw a certain look of fear behind Baron's eyes at even *that* laughter, and wondered, though he did not want to wonder, how it had been with Dick, after. What sort of cruelty Dick had ravaged upon Baron? Or maybe Baron had ravaged some kind of cruelty upon himself, hating himself for being fucked, hating himself for letting Dick fuck him? But Ed had no intention to be cruel to Baron now, not in this moment at least, and not for this—as he tugged up his trousers again and stuffed his softening, wet prick back inside his pants.

What had happened between them had come—*heh*—as naturally as breathing to him. As singing. And what shame in there was *singing*? It was just something your mouth wanted and your lungs made manifest. No, nothing like shame here, not now. He bent down and kissed the corner of Baron's mouth, and Baron was stiff at first, then softened into it, as Eddie put his head on Baron's shoulder, draped his body over Baron's body, suddenly sleepy. Baron, still sticky, still surprised, some, put an arm over Ed's back and held him, and their eyes both began to close. Until Baron's eyes opened wide again. He looked at the door, which made Ed's eyes go winder, sitting up, just a little bit.

"What is it, Barry?" he asked, worrying for a moment that Baron's auntie was home. Baron frowned.

"Just me ghost," he said. "Did you know I have my own ghostie? A poltergeist, they might say. Been following me around since I was a baby."

"Cor, Baron," Eddie said, and settled back in. "You're a nutter."

Baron didn't argue with Eddie. Instead, he just barked out to the closed doorway: "Go 'ome, ghostie. Yer not wanted here. 'Sprivate matter!"

Then Baron turned back to Eddie, apparently satisfied by his ghost's retreat.

"She's gone now," he said to Eddie. Kissed him on the lips, full and warm, one more time. Eddie let him.

"Good," he said, and nuzzled Baron. Closing his eyes, too.

38 - 1977

Baron Templeton sauntered into his hotel room, and Zach followed, feeling like a strange duckling following an even stranger mother duck. His eyes were firmly welded to Baron's back, to the floral pattern there. Definitely a blouse, he thought—but then, Templeton was a reclusive rock star. Even a teenage boy like Zachy, so infirm in his own masculinity, could forgive him his stylistic excesses. Zach barely took in the sight of the hotel suite around them, only registered brief impressions. A contrast: heavy regency furniture, painted up in white and gold, moved to the edges of the room to create space for things like a mini fridge, a hot plate, a tea kettle, a folding table draped with a plastic dime store tablecloth. Everything one needed to live, but, strangely, nothing immediately apparent which implied wealth, beyond the fact that it was the *Chelsea* and he was *Templeton*. As they passed through the makeshift kitchen, Richard Charles elbowed Zach. He glanced, and noticed in fleeting surprise the guitar, half strung and the pickups in pieces on the kitchen table, like Baron had just been fiddling with the wiring. Green paint flaking away, showing pink. That guitar. Baron's guitar. *Eddie*. They were *here*. They were truly here.

And yet, still, how bizarre a place. The ceiling and the wainscoting were carved, but cracked if you looked long enough. There was ornate damask wallpaper, but it was dingy from cigarette smoke, wrinkling at the seams. The bed at the back of the room was a king, but unmade. Et cetera. There was a general sense of mess. Books everywhere—by Engels and Gibran and Baraka—and records scattered about, abused, left outside of their sleeves.

The room was absurdly hot; the curtained windows cracked open, and a mildewy smell lingered in the air around them. And there was something else, too. A familiar odor, from Marigold. Cloth diapers in a pail in the corner, which seemed to be in desperate need of taking out. Not a bad smell, exactly, but milky and alive.

Not something Zach had expected to find *here*. With *him*. He'd expected, maybe, the records. The three or four guitars scattered about, and the amplifier with a towel shoved in it. He'd even expected the books. But not anything so pedestrian as a *baby*. He could hear crying somewhere beyond a door that was closed in the corner, kittenish mewls that rose over the tinny of the speaker portable record player that sat on the floor next to the bed, playing some old rock record. Something that seemed familiar, but Zach had never heard before.

Baron perched on the end of the bed. He gestured to a pair of overstuffed armchairs—one whose arms looked like they'd been torn to pieces by cats—that formed a seating area around a black and white TV in the corner. The television was on to *Rocky & Bullwinkle*, but the sound was off.

"Sit, children," he said dryly, puffing away at his cigarette. Zach hesitated. And then sat down.

The two children regarded their hero. Baron leaned his weight leaned to one side, his thin neck extended as he smoked. Looking regal and almost feline. That's when Zach remembered that they had come here to settle an argument, to ask Templeton something. But it seemed inconsequential now. Gossip. Besides, how could he ask the man something so *personal*? It would make them look—sound—like a bunch of dumb teenagers. Which they were. But. Still.

"Well?" Templeton asked. He reached for an ashtray in the nest of sheets, stubbing out his cigarette. "Have you come for an autograph, or just to pay tribute? Or perhaps you'd like to interview me for your school paper?"

Templeton's amused, weary tone told Zach that he had been here before, with other boys. And in a way, that stung. Knowing that he was not special, even in this pilgrimage.

"Nah," Richard Charles said. "Nothing like that. We came here to settle an argument between us and a friend of ours—"

Oh God, thought Zach. *Don't—*

But Templeton slyly smiled and said, "What's that, then?"

"We don't need—" Zach began, but Richard Charles spoke too firmly and loudly, and drowned out his brother's protests.

"Are you a fag?" Richard Charles asked.

At that, Templeton stared for a moment. And then snickered, a wicked snicker, like a sound a little boy might make when he's placed a whoopee cushion on the teacher's chair. Not that Zach had ever done that, but he never stopped it when it had *happened*, either, giggling just as much as the rest of them, waiting for the hilarity to start.

"You mean you came all the way here from, what, Paramus, New Jersey, or Wallington, Connecticut, or wherever it is you lot are from, to ask me *that?*"

Neither boy knew what to say to that. Templeton drew his feet up onto the bed and sat cross-legged upon it. He was barefoot, Zach realized, and had really large, ugly feet for a man his height. Brown feet. Dirty soles. Templeton cast his head back, and called out toward the doorway in the corner.

"Alana?" He pronounced it like "Alaner," said it twice.

A long pause, more crying. At last, a Black woman appeared in the doorway. She was dressed in a simple dress, slinky blue. No bra underneath it. She had curves like you couldn't imagine, or Zach couldn't, at least. On her fat hip was an equally fat baby, dressed only in a fresh diaper with no cover, who she jiggled with what looked like increasing agitation.

"*What* is it, Barry?" she asked, looking exasperated at the man. Baron just smiled, gestured for her to come closer. With almost palpable annoyance, she did.

"Boys, I'd like you to meet me wife. This is Alana. And my Naomi." He reached out to take the baby, cooing at her. She was almost instantly quieted, gurgling in his arms. Feeling the topography of his face with fat fingers. For a second, a split second, it felt like everyone else in the room was an afterthought except father and daughter.

"Yeah," Richard Charles said, rolling his eyes, untouched by the tender familial scene, "But just because you knocked *her* up doesn't mean you're not a fag."

"Christ," Alana said. She looked relieved to be free of the crying child, and headed toward the kitchen area, where she shoved the guitar to the side and began to fix herself a drink. Nothing fancy, just a scotch and coke, no ice. "Not this, Baron. Again. Peter's supposed to be coming over in two hours. You were supposed to clean up. Unless you were planning on canceling, like I asked. Well?" No answer. Alana sighed, took a gulp of her drink. "Do you think we even have time for your bloody sexual history again? Because I don't."

When Zach glanced back at Baron, he was lying on the bed now, dangling the baby above him. Making airplane noises at her. She was giggling, stuffing a fat fist in her mouth. A thin stream of drool was dangling down from her mouth, about to fall on him, but he didn't seem to care. Alana returned to them, sitting on the edge of the bed, looking at Zach and Richard Charles directly.

"What business of it is yours," she asked, "Who *this* one sleeps with? Why are boys like you so afraid of it, anyway? Do you worry it makes you a little bit of a queer yourself, if you love the music of a man who loves a man?"

Zach started frowning, deeply. Didn't answer. Couldn't. What she said cut too close. But Richard Charles, as always, was unperturbed.

"Neither of you have answered the question," he said. Alana glanced at Baron, one eyebrow ticked up. He grinned, too.

"Sharp one, you are," he said. Those four words seared themselves into the bottom of Zach's belly. He could have burned down that hotel—no, all of *Manhattan*—for the jealousy he felt. Baron Templeton, calling his asshole older brother *sharp*. While he just sat there in dull, brain-dead silence.

"Now," Baron said, "The wifey's right. We have guests coming, really should be cleaning up. D'you blokes have anything else you'd like to ask me?"

Richard Charles was opening his mouth again, taking a breath again. But

Zach knew he couldn't let him speak for them again—what other idiocy would pop out of his brother's brain if he did? So instead, Zach cleared his throat, just loudly enough that his brother turned his head.

"Um, well," he said, blushing. Because he wanted to know. Because he hadn't figured it out yet. Because he wasn't used to not having something *figured out*. "I wanted to ask, sir. You see, my brother and I have started a band and—I think we could be pretty good, but . . . I mean, I want to know how you and Hammond *did* it. The two of you. How you made such *amazing* songs without getting in each other's way?"

Zach's voice rose and even squeaked at the end just a little bit. Mortifying. But maybe not so bad. Baron sat up now, setting baby Naomi on his lap. He looked *interested*, which was gratifying, too.

"Now *that*, son," he said. "That is a *great* question."

Zach sat a little straighter, feeling vindicated, a bit. Baron was looking at both of them, gesturing to some middle distance between them. The little baby kept her eyes on her daddy's long, callused finger.

"We made a decision, early on, me and Hammy. It'd be the music for us. Always the music. That's what we would exist for. We could have been alright as music makers, either of us alone. And you know, Hammy's done alright by himself since. I got bored with the 'industry'"—implied air quotes around the word, a grimace— "but he's not half bad at it. Has it written on his soul or something. But we all know what we made together was better. I know it, when I'm noodling around here, keeping Alaner awake. He knows it, in his mushy parts, too. When we were lads, we realized that whatever we made together would be better for us being together than apart. So we decided we were going to set ourselves aside—all that angst and pain—and do it for the music. Now, I'm not a man who has transcended mortal weakness. Heard his song on the last album, what's that one?" He started singing vague strains of music, snapping his fingers.

"'Matthew's Song,'" Richard Charles said to Zach's surprise. He thought that Richard Charles *hated* Ed Hammond's music. Hammond was corny as fuck, wasn't that what they had decided? But Richard Charles was clutching his hands into fists, looking at the crumbling ceiling as if it were the heavens. "I *love* that one. That fucking *hook*."

"Yes!" Baron exclaimed, slapping his leg. Both the baby and Alana jumped, but Templeton didn't seem to notice. "I about wanted to off meself when I heard it. So bloody good. But that's now. Was never jealous of him then. When we were together, we decided it would never be like that. What I wrote was his. What he wrote was mine. Because we knew the *world* would be better for it. Now boys, I know it can seem like the hardest thing in the world. But if you're going to be a band, an actual, real, band, then you'll need to do that. If you can't work for something greater than your own glory, then you might as well go write yourself some solo albums or something. I don't know."

He said it like it was a simple solution. Of course, for Baron Templeton, it probably was. *Write yourself some solo albums*, like music would come to either of them just as easily as it did to him. A certifiable genius.

"Of course," Baron said, "The two of you have a leg up. Brothers, right?"

Zach nodded, though it felt, as it always did, almost embarrassing to admit it. That they had come from the same womb, the same variety of seed.

"Never knew what that was like," said Baron, letting the baby chew one of his fingers, "To have a real, proper family. Me mom and me dad couldn't hack it. He ran off for warmer climes while she went cold in the ground. S'pose it's almost like a band. A *family*. You have to choose it, eh? That's why I'm going to make sure this little one has everything she needs."

"Really?!" Alana cut in, turning to Templeton like she had been holding this in for hours—mostly unsuccessfully. "Is that why you're still letting Peter come around, after I told you—"

"Hush, woman," Baron said, though more in a joking than a serious tone. He shifted the baby in his arms, letting her rest her face on his shoulder. Pacing around the bed a little bit, jiggling her. "These children don't need to hear our dirty laundry. In fact, boys, 'sprobably time for you to be off."

Zach began to pull himself to his feet, but Alana let out an exasperated noise and gestured for them to stay in their chairs.

"Barry, they're *children*. Runaways, probably. You can't just let them off into the streets of New York City. We should call their parents."

"If they're runaways, why would they want us to call their bleeding parents?"

But it was like Alana couldn't hear them. She leaned forward, whispered to the two of them—like her questions were an intimacy. "D'you have someone to pick you up, boys? A mother, perhaps?"

Zach tightened his grip on the arms of the chair. No way he wanted Baron Templeton's ball and chain to call his fucking *mother* right now.

But luckily, somehow, for once, Richard Charles saved him. "You can call our dad," he said. "We don't see him much, but he lives in the city. I don't know his number, though."

"Oh?" said Templeton, rising. He carried the baby over to an ornate, ancient desk, where there was a phone and phone book waiting under a pile of singles and take-out containers. He brushed them aside with his free hand, cracked the thick phone book open. "What's his name then?"

"Dick," said Richard Charles. "Dick Ashby. Or maybe it's under Richard. A-S-H—"

Baron stopped flipping through the pages and turned to look at the boys. His eyes flickering rapidly back and forth between the two, from Zach to Richard Charles and back again. Zach had the feeling that Templeton was looking at them—truly looking at them— for the very first time.

"What?" said Richard Charles.

"Your father is Dickie fuckin' Ashby?"

Richard Charles glanced at Zach. The two frowned at each other. Richard Charles shrugged. "Yeah, that's our dad. Why? Do you know him?"

"Yeah," said Baron. He picked up the telephone receiver and, without even glancing again at the book, he started to dial. Like he knew their father's number. Like he had it *memorized*. "I fuckin' know him."

Zach's eyes got wide. Surprisingly, so did Richard Charles'.

"Allo, Dick?" Baron was saying. "Yeah—yeah it's me, Barry. I have a coupla visitors here, you'd be interested to know." Baron looked up at them again, his coal-black eyes impenetrable.

"It's your kids, Dick. Payin' me a visit. Your fucking sons."

39 - 1958

In Baron's little bedroom the day ticked on. Even their tryst, their lustful eruption, could not quite shake off the gloom. Of course it couldn't. Baron's Mum was still dead. Their band was still over. The loneliness, inherent in being two bodies, separated, two people living two individuated lives, still present with them. Maybe an hour later, Ed found himself holding his left hand up against Baron's right palm. Obvious, now, he thought, how much darker Baron was. The *reason*. Did Baron see it? Did he understand? Ed wondered if he should say anything, tell Baron what his auntie had said. But the moment seemed too terrible for it, and after *that* moment, Baron drew away, turning his back to Ed again so that he was facing the wall.

"I'm an orphan now, Ed."

Ed looked up to the wall over Baron. All those loosely drawn tits. And the postcards beneath them.

"That can't be true, right? Your daddy is out there somewhere, love. Roving. Sailing the oceans."

Baron snorted. "Haven't gotten a letter from him since I was six. What good is a pirate father when you're stuck on this bloody island, anyway?"

Ed sighed. He knew there was no use in arguing with this sort of thick grief, this sort of sullen self-pity. He'd seen it before, in his Dad. The way his Dad would cry over the bottle at night. *Oh Sheila why'd you leave me.* There had been no comforting his old man, either. Just rushing young Billy out to leave his Dad to his pitiful, snotty-faced grief.

"Well," Ed said, "Maybe it's a boon. All the best heroes are foundlings and orphans."

Baron glanced back at him. A smile, very small, very sly, curled his lips. "What?" Ed said.

"Corny," said Baron.

They laughed a little together, roughly and for no particular reason except that it felt good to laugh. But then the door opened. Ed tensed for a moment, wondering if he hadn't heard Baron's Auntie and Uncle come in. But instead, that fine feline, the one with the long marmalade coat walked in the door. "Oi," he said. "It's an interloper. Allo, Puss."

Ed climbed out of bed and went to greet the creature. Puss arched his back into Ed's palm, luxuriating with his touch.

"What's this one called?" Ed asked, glancing back at Baron. Baron had sat up in bed and was now busy peeling off his black t-shirt and wiping down his still-sticky belly with it. He tossed it easily into the basket in the corner, then yawned, pausing for a moment with his arms outstretched.

"That's Doot," Baron said, putting his chin down on the heel of his hand. Watching Eddie in a way that made him feel more undressed than he *really* was. "Old Deuteronomy, Aunt Deedz says, after Eliot, but I think the name's too big for him. He's a stinker, that one. Old Stinky Doot."

Eddie laughed a little, though it creaked out self-conscious. "Brilliant," he said, trying to ignore the shakiness he felt from the weight of Baron's gaze. "I've always wanted a cat. I think someday when I'm a grown-up I'll have a whole flock of them."

"A herd?" Baron grinned.

"Maybe a cavern. A cavern of cats."

"Maybe you could borrow a case of ours sometime," Baron said. He slid down off the bed then. Went to where Ed was sitting and sat himself behind him. His arms reaching past Ed's arms, touching Doot's fur, too. Putting his chin on Ed's shoulder. Comfortable and only a little bit sexy. The weight of him pressing against Ed's back. The heat. Baron kissed Ed's cheek. Ed turned back to see Baron and kissed him full on the mouth—a kiss without tongue, but not a quick kiss, neither. Nothing you'd give your Gran.

But then, pulling away, Ed glanced at the half-open door.

"When's your aunt and uncle coming back?" Ed asked. Baron grunted. He got up, leaving Ed's body feeling lonely in his absence. Old Doot meowed quizzically.

"Too soon, I reckon," Baron said. He closed the door again, reaching into his pants, giving his half-hard prick a bit of a shake. Then went into his milk crate and started to pull out clothes. He added dryly, "The cunts."

"Too bad," Ed admitted, then blushed after saying it. Felt dangerous to be this open with Baron. Who knew when he might use it against you. But Baron only smiled as he pulled a fresh t-shirt over his head, and tugged on a pair of trousers which were in dire need of a hot iron. Then he sat down again, right beside Ed. Letting his knee touch Eddie's.

"Don't worry, Hammy," he said. He put his hand in Eddie's hand. Squeezed it. "I'll love you even when me Auntie and Uncle are around." Then he brought Eddie's hand to his lips and kissed his knuckles. Ed, momentarily dumb-founded, frozen, could only watch.

"I love you, too, Baron," he said, very softly, words he had never said to any girl or boy, not even a grown-up, not since his Mum died. Stupid, naked, wonderful words.

If what they did that afternoon could be called *making love*, then they did not make love again that day. In fact, it proved to be a rare occurrence. In the next decade of their friendship, they would tumble together perhaps a dozen times. When very stoned, or very drunk, or very lonely, on the road together, surrounded by sycophants and birds. Once in a van rumbling down a road in a storm in Scotland, sure they were going to die, while Liam Waller, on the cold metal floor beside them, either slept or pretended to sleep so he could pretend that he could not hear. Once in Hamburg. High off their gourds on uppers, that day that they stole Baron's first electric guitar, and then for hours after when the rest of them were away somewhere, at a strip club or who knows where. Finally realizing what they could do in the boggy silence of their filthy room. Twice in America—once, in a celebratory mood on the night of their first US television appearance, again, five years later, when someone threw a firecracker on stage and for a moment, in the confusion, Baron was sure he'd been shot. He'd needed comfort that night. They both had. A handful of times in London, when they could manage, through the haze of marijuana and acid. Playing on Baron's baby grand together, and then their bodies melting together, and their fingers, and their minds. Twice on the night of Eddie's wedding, when he'd tried to break it off with Baron, after, and broken his heart. What was meant to be a goodbye fuck. Tender. Sad.

And that might have been the last time, for all the fighting that followed. For the drunken brick that drunken Baron would throw through Ed's window two days after the wedding while Ed was on his honeymoon, and the way the tabloids spun it. For the press conference Ed realized he *had* to give, alone, breaking up the band without telling the rest of them—before the baby came and Baron was a real danger to his *real* family. That wedding night, that divorce night, could have, *should* have been the end. But it *wasn't* the last time. Because that last time would be 1975. Scotland again. Eddie's farm. When a pissed-out-of-his-mind Baron showed up after the girls had all gone to bed. Told Ed that he was going to America with that radical woman, that he was going to make brown, beautiful babies with her and Ed knew he had to let him and felt it all finally slip away, in his ratty bathrobe, on his doorstep, but he took Baron in and took him down into his wine-cellar-turned recording studio where no one would hear them, and they tried to make time stop for one last time. In the morning, Ed would tell Genie that Baron had showed up pissed as he tried to hide his own tiredness, but when he went down to check on him and bring him some toast and jam, Baron was already gone.

No, fucking would never be the cornerstone of their relationship. And of course, all along, the two of them—fucking other girls and boys, too. Fans and wives and press secretaries and artists. Photographers and radicals and strangers. But *touching*—that would be different. That was *theirs*. It was noticed in the press, by teenage girls who sneaked into their dressing rooms, by teenage girls on LiveJournal or Tumblr decades later, how often and easily the two of them touched. Clasping hands and dancing on stage, throwing their arms around each other during interviews. Making strange, spidery motions with their hands during press conferences, secretly signaling their spidery secrets to one another. Stroking one another's hair, or pulling on it, teasing. It was noticed by their record producers and engineers, how they would sometimes snog each other first thing in the morning during those early morning sessions, Baron moving in on Ed, and Ed pulling away after, scowling, *God, your breath, Barry*. But never really saying *no*.

Their bodies, somehow communally owned, and communally owned without *shame*. No, they never were ashamed of *that*. Nor their love for each other. They spoke of it simply. Openly. Barry even admitting he'd named his pilfered Rickenbacker after Eddie, though Eddie kept the name of his first electric bass—a shiny black Supro Pocket bought on credit and which he dutifully paid off with the proceeds from their first single, which he called in secret corners of his mind *Baron*—his, and his alone. Still, *the two, close as brothers,* the press would write, and they weren't correct but they weren't wrong, neither. Even after the break-up, in 1972 Baron told *Rolling Stone* that his favorite songwriter was Edmund Matthew Hammond III. He sounded like a teenager when he said it, so full of giddy, girlish love. And then in 1996, Ed told Howard Stern that after Baron died, he'd hardly been able to get out of bed for a week. Howard said, "Baron Templeton was said to be a difficult man. Combative. Temperamental. You knew him better than anybody. What was he *really* like?" and Ed shrugged, saying only three words: "He was beautiful."

40 - 1997

Cymbeline woke with a clear mind, the headache gone, returned to her physical self again, without any other presence, without the shadow of what she sometimes referred to as *her ghost*. It was always remarkable, to wake up empty and ordinary after a day or two or three spent clouded and with so much pain. Sid had been up for awhile by the time she rose, and she sat on the bed in her dirty clothes, arguing with Neil over the hotel phone about how they wouldn't be paying for the car repairs *or* the tow, thankyouverymuch.

"I don't care that you spent the last 24 hours puking your brains out," she said testily, "You know just as well as I do that that Pinto has been making that noise for months and you've ignored it. It has nothing to do with my *driving*, you dweeb. Now I'm happy to find you a place to tow it back but you're going to have to wire us money first. Or else we're happy to dump it here for you. Your choice."

Cymbeline smiled wryly, rose, and went to shower off.

She only had that one ratty dress, of course, which had seemed so right for that gig in the smoky old bar but now stank of cigarettes and beer and sex—hers, Sid's. Seemed wrong to wear it for something so momentous, her first time in a recording studio. Even if it was only a crappy recording studio in Oneonta. She felt like she should have had something better for it. A suit, maybe, though she'd never worn a suit. But she could imagine how it would feel, the clean, heavy crispness. A freshly pressed shirt. A skinny tie, knotted squarely. Like a coat of armor, bolstering her. But the dress would have to do. She toweled off her hair, ran her fingers through it, headed down to the lobby for their complimentary coffee and scrambled eggs. In a few minutes, she and Sid were sitting outside of their hotel room with Cymbeline's guitar on the road in front of her, waiting for that asshole Dick to come pick them up.

"This is fantastic," Sid said, eating with sloppy relish. "I'm starving."

Cymbeline looked at her, a wry smile twisting her lips. "I'll bet you are. Wonder why."

Sid barked out laughter at that. "*You* know, Perky. I mean, Cymbeline. Guess I need to stop calling you that, if this thing is gonna be real."

"Thing?" Cymbeline asked carefully. Funny, to have Sid raise the question first, the one that had been on Cymbeline's mind for weeks. Though it didn't really seem to be a question to Sid. It seemed to be an answer already, instead.

"You know," Sid said. "That I'm going to manage you. Can't call you *Perky* around record execs, can I?"

"Oh." Cymbeline looked out into the parking lot. There was a car pulling in, some kind of shiny red sports car. Sid would have known what it was, but it wasn't important enough to ask right now. They didn't have much time. "I thought you meant us. Me and you. *Romantically.*"

Sid frowned. She put down her plastic fork, reached out, put her hand in Cymbeline's. "Hey," she said. "*Hey*, look at me."

Cymbeline looked at her.

"We've been real since the first moment we met," Sid said. "By that campfire. I was *so worried* you were going to be one of those stupid little girls who flocks to a guy like Neil. You know, any asshole with a guitar."

"Little did you know that *I'm* any asshole with a guitar," Cymbeline said. She rested her head on her own knees, looking up at Sid. Grinning.

"Not just any asshole," Sid said. "*My* asshole."

Cymbeline wrinkled her nose at that. But she didn't fight it. She was, indeed, Sid's. The car was pulling up closer now. Behind the tinted glass, the driver—Dick Ashby, presumably—leaned on the horn. Sid started to stand. But Cymbeline hesitated.

"So I guess my question is," she said, "If we're in this, really in it, then what's next?"

"Well," Sid said, picking up Cymbeline's guitar for her. A real gentleman. "There's only one answer, isn't there? I quit my job. You drop out. We move to the city, and we make it."

"Make it?" Cymbeline asked, standing. Sid opened the door for Cymbeline, putting the seat forward, putting her guitar in back. Climbing in, so that Cymbeline could take the passenger's seat, because *she* was the one who mattered now.

Sid rubbed her fingertips together. "Yeah, make it," she said. "Hand over fist."

Cymbeline grinned at her. "Okay," she said, as Sid pulled the seat back again so Cymbeline could sit down. Buckled herself in. "Sounds good to me."

Dick Ashby turned to her. He looked younger, brighter in the light of morning. "Ready, ladies?" he asked. Sid snorted.

"Shut up and drive, Dick," she said.

* * *

Ashby's engineer didn't end up showing for their session. "Fucking cunt," he grumbled, as he went around turning on the lights. "I keep saying I'm going to fire him but somehow can't bear to do it."

"Just do it, man," Sid said sharply. "Why hesitate? You're not doing either of you any favors, if you're going to end up doing the work anyway." Ashby looked at her for a long time, considered—like it was the first time he was really considering it.

"Yeah, maybe I will."

Not that it was their problem. Not that there was a problem at all. For someone who had been so soggy the night before, Dick Ashby had dried up nicely. Had combed his long hair back in a small ponytail, and his face, when revealed by the light of day, made him look younger than Cymbeline had previously assumed. She began to get out her guitar, to find a seat in the booth. He looked at her and laughed.

"No," he said. "*You* go out there."

She glanced through the glass at the seat waiting there, looked doubtfully at Sid. Who grinned, laughed, nodded.

"Your moment to shine," she agreed.

Cymbeline carried her guitar into the studio, feeling strange, as though she was living halfway outside her body. It was nerves, but it wasn't only that. A simultaneous feeling like she knew exactly what to do—and had *no idea* what to do. She sat on a stool in the middle there, started tuning up. Through the glass she could see Dick saying something, first to Sid, then to Cymbeline. But she couldn't hear anything. Sid gestured, hands around her ears. That's when Cymbeline found the headphones dangling from a mic stand and put them on.

"Go ahead," Dick was saying. "Do a warm-up, then we'll get started on your set from last night."

She squinted into the light. No sign of a headache, now, but she couldn't say that the moment wasn't overwhelming even without it.

"Uh . . ." she started. "What should I play?"

"Something you know," he said, with surprising gentleness. Like he had some empathy for her, for all his roughness. Like he wanted her to be *good*. "Hey, your name's Cymbeline. What about that one? Beautiful song from a beautiful girl on a beautiful morning."

She started to grimace. She knew that Sid hated that song, had a litany of complaints against it: it was dated, the emotion was false, it sounded like old person music, Ed Hammond was out of key for the first bar of the recording and no one seemed to notice and everyone in every cover did the same damned thing, like it had been *intentional*. Sid's hatred of the song had just about wiped away any sentiment Cymbeline had once had for it, though in some ways, that was a relief. It wasn't as though it was without baggage for her, too. Her eyes went to Dick, through the glass. Cymbeline saw Sid flick the switch that powered the mic on just for Cymbeline's benefit. So Cymbeline could hear the argument, too.

"I can't stand that Hammond crap," Sid said. "Templeton's solo stuff was better."

Dick laughed. "How *avant-garde* of you. Anyway, you honestly think it's a *Hammond* song?"

"Well, yeah," Sid said. "Everyone knows it was. What was the intro, on the record? Templeton said it himself. *A real Hammond original.*"

"Don't believe everything you're told," Dick said with a snort. "Listen to the lyrics. Hammond would have made a soppy mess of that. It's a Templeton song."

Sid snorted back. "You have no idea what you're talking about."

Dick glanced at her. Then at Cymbeline.

"Sweetie," he said to her, speaking into the mic. "Settle an argument for me and your old lady, okay?"

Cymbeline chewed her lip. "Yeah?"

"I take it that with your name that you're well-versed in Saffron's oeuvre, right?"

Cymbeline nodded. How could she *not* be familiar with it? It wasn't just that they were everywhere—the most successful band of *all* time. It went beyond that. It was personal. Her mother had been a massive Hammond fan. She'd had first pressings of all the Saffron releases, even the 45s, and everything Hammond ever did, and some of what the others had done—Peck's '80s kid's tunes and one or two of Templeton's protest records and even Hammond's weird jazz albums in the 90s after his first wife died. The collection had been worth a pretty penny, though, and that penny had been worth more to them after her mom got sick than any sentiment—Hanukkah gifts for a year, and a new winter coat for Cymbeline, and a used fridge when theirs died. When Cymbeline had helped her mom cart in all those milk crates to the record store, the clerk's eyes lit up like a pair of illuminated dollar signs. Money came first. Eating came first. But she never doubted for a second that her mother loved Ed Hammond.

He's just so beautiful, her mom said once when Hammond came on a late night talk show, on the television above the hospital bed. She was wasting away by then, but she still sat up straighter for *Hammond.* Cymbeline had watched him, had seen it, had agreed. Yes, he was beautiful, even though his babyish face had started to get puffier with age, even though he had obvious, terrible hair plugs.

Just get old like a normal person, Ed, Cymbeline found herself thinking, in a voice that wasn't quite her own, *There's no shame in it. It's better than the alternative, innit?*

"Sure," Cymbeline said now to Dick, carefully, very carefully.

"Then do me a favor," he said, smirking over at Sid, "Sing us 'Cymbeline' in the style of Templeton, will you?"

"Um," Cymbeline said. But Dick had already turned to Sid.

"If you agree with me, then you give me twenty dollars. But if you still say I'm wrong when she's done, then I'll give *you* fifty bucks."

"You should give fifty bucks to me anyway," said Sid. "We're burning our booking time with this bullshit . . ."

"I'll do it," Cymbeline said. Not quite sure why she *wanted* to do it. She told herself that it was just to prove Dick wrong, told herself it was just because Dick had called her *sweetie* and referred to Sid as her *old lady*. The condescending ass. But that couldn't have been the whole story. The truth was, she *wanted* to play the song. Properly, not the Hammond send-ups she used to play for her mom. First line off key and all of that. She'd been waiting for this for a lifetime, it seemed. As though it was automatic, she began to drop her sixth string to D, to put it in its proper key. And then, without any more preamble, she launched into the song.

It was easy. Deliciously easy. To bend the strings hard, like Templeton might've on his protest albums much later, in spite of the tenderness of the song. Hammy always played it too soft, fey, made it into one of his old lady tunes. It wasn't meant for that. And Hammond's voice had been so pretty when he sang it, but there were other ways to approach it, with more urgency, with the feeling of it naked and a little under-cooked. She let her voice feel raw and undressed. She couldn't quite hit the notes exactly like she knew he might have—not in this body, with its smaller vocal chords, with all its limitations. But she played hard and fevered and she sang the words like a boy might have in Liverpool in 1958—and not like a different boy might have nearly ten years later, on an album, or at dozens of solo concerts after that, repeating always in his introduction the myth that he dreamed this song, that it was *his*, and his alone—the first solo effort. The one that had spurred him past fame, to the money and security he'd always wanted.

Everyone had heard *that* song, played *that* way. Dozens of artists had covered it. But it had been a long time since the song had been played like *this*. And there was a rightness to it, a going back to the source of things, and as she closed her eyes and played, she thought of poor old Ed Hammond, alone now, with his grand-babies and basement studio and the new wife, as simple as the first one, with his hair plugs and sheep and his secrets—and no one to tell them to, no one who might understand his depths, his loss, his pain.

"And in another life I might find you again," she sang, "But in this life, Cymbeline, I'm only a man. Let me love you until our dying days. Let me squander this world. Let me give it away—for you. Will this do? It'll have to do . . . "

Her voice hitched a little on the last note. She cleared her throat, the ghost gone as soon as it had touched her. Then she looked up at the glass. Both Dick Ashby and Sid were staring.

She saw Sid curse, once, softly, in the recording booth. She watched Sid get out her wallet and hand a twenty over to Dick, who pocketed it, laughing. They spoke to each other for a minute, leaving Cymbeline tetherless in the circle of light. Finally, Sid leaned forward to speak into her mic.

"That was amazing," she said. "I want you to do it again. Dick's going to lay this take down, okay? Watch the vocals. Don't go flat on the last verse. You've got this, Cymbeline."

Cymbeline sniffled once, sat straighter in her seat, nodded. Heard Dick's voice in her ear, telling her to go ahead.

It was the only time she ever saw Sid lose a bet.

41 - 1958

The sucking was all done. The sucking and the sticky snuggling, too. The sucking and the sticky snuggling and the talking about Old Doot, because they couldn't very well talk about what had *happened*, and then Baron breaking the reverie and getting up to dress because, for one thing, Ed was right, Baron's aunt and uncle *would* be home soon, and if they caught the boys *in flagranto whatevero* then he'd really be up shit creek and paddleless. But also because Baron couldn't very well let himself sit around and be *happy*, not on this day. Not twenty-four hours after his mum had—well. Gone fucking splat.

Fucking world this was, he thought. When the spirits or absent gods or whoever was floating around in the ether around him would take away his mum and give Hammy to him, all at the same time. He got a fag out of his desk drawer. It was months old, one of the French ones he'd stolen from Deedz. She didn't like him smoking up here but it was his mummy's death day, wasn't it? Fuck Deedz. Fuck all of them. He was here with Hammy, in the room where he'd grown up but which had never been his. He was going to smoke a fucking fag.

"Smoke?" he asked Hammy. Hammy shook his head.

"Been trying to quit," he said, the apology that was there telling Baron that Ed really *wanted* it. "Me voice."

"Yeah," said Baron, gravelly, "Gotta protect them pipes. For Dylan and the boys."

He didn't mean to say it mean. But it came out that way.

For a moment, Ed stared bleakly ahead. Finally nodded. "Yeh," he said, and scrambled to his feet. Went and grabbed his shoes, and as he passed Baron on the way to his desk chair, their shoulders brushed. Not angrily. Felt, actually, like Ed was inviting the contact. Wanting it as much as Baron did.

Christ, thought Baron, *we really are a coupla fruits for each other.*

Baron sat down on the bed, watching as Ed began to lace up his shoes. Ed's pretty pale eyelashes trembling like he were afraid to look up at Barry.

"It's alright, pet," Baron said finally, gently. "It's only me."

Ed tied off his left shoe tightly. Only then did he permit himself to look up. He was so *controlled* all the time, that pretty Ed Hammond. Methodical. Even now, Baron sensed how any relief Ed felt in looking into Baron's eyes was relief that was only there by nature of asking himself permission to be able to even look. Still. Brown eyes touched blue. They exhaled, both of them.

"I know, Barry," Ed said, rubbing hands over eyes, hands through hair, worrying his entire face with his expressive, fruity hands, "But I sacked off on a practice with Dylan to come see you. If I don't show up at all, that'll be it for me. There're dozens of guitarists just waiting to take my space. Older ones. Better ones. And you—you know how I need it."

Baron took a long drag, let the smoke settle into his lungs. Held it for a moment. He did know, actually. Music had never been a whim for Ed like it had for the other blokes. It was a path. A door. A means to fucking *escape.*

Baron knew because it was all those things for him, too. Still.

Baron exhaled. Ed was frozen, watching him. Mouth softly open, lips full. Lusty. Lusty looking at *him.* It felt absurd to see it, realize it, be able to name it now, just as soon as he could name Sue Grasso's lust or even the ugly, possessive lust of Dickie Ashby. Baron *knew* he was handsome, but he wasn't handsome like Ed—and Ed wasn't a queer. Not a queer like he was. And yet.

For a moment, he just luxuriated in the weight of Ed's trembly, gooey gaze. Taking another suck of his fag. Letting Ed think about the *other* sucking that had just *happened,* the raw, animal truth of it. He could see how he could hold this over Ed, how he could tug at him. Become a beast not unlike Dick. How maybe in the weeks ahead they could sack off from school and wank each other in the bushes at Seaman's orphanage like Baron and Dick once had. And maybe do more than that, if he wanted. If he asked. He could see that Ed would do any of it now, for sad, tragic Baron. And of course Baron wanted Ed to do *everything*.

He considered it: letting Ed's sweet, pale body lie against his, letting their lust be a light in this shitty world that otherwise held only a feeble, dying spark of flame. He'd drop out of school, probably, finally. He'd get Sue knocked up. He'd go to work on the docks, and drink all day, and show up at Ed's house pissed after work, and get into a fight with one of Ed's brothers or maybe his Dad. Someone would sock him, and he'd start to wander home bleeding and pitiful, and slump down in an alley somewhere, and that's when Ed would find him, and when he kissed his broken mouth it would hurt, but not too much. Maybe they'd wank, and maybe it would be the fortieth or fiftieth time in a coupla months, but it would be the last time. The end of it. Baron could *see* it, just as soon as he could see the past that had already happened, how no matter how much they grinded their throbbers together, that with Ed off, distracted, in Dylan's band, it wouldn't matter. Because music would come first. Money would come first. Not being a *foocking mess,* as Ed had so eloquently put it, would always come first. And no matter how much they *liked* it, what their bodies could do together, he would only ever keep being a *foocking mess* if he let Ed go. Today. Or any day. To Dylan Miranda and the Tempests.

"You don't need Dylan," Baron said, setting his jaw, letting his cigarette dangle. Ed laughed at him. Really, fully *laughed.*

"Cor," Ed said. He started to get up. "Not this again."

But Baron stood, first. He put a hand on Ed's shoulder. Half wanting to shove him, but he needed to show he was in control here. Needed to show he was on top. Otherwise he knew what Ed would do. Ed would leave. If he let himself be at all pitiful, weak, temperamental, messy, he'd lose Ed, truly.

"I'm serious, Ed," he said, in a soft, serious voice. "Sit down. I need to show you something."

Ed looked at him—and then sank slowly into his chair.

"I'm sitting, Baron," he said.

Baron crouched down in front of the milk crate on the floor. Began riffling through it. He wished he'd been better prepared for this moment, but how could he have been? He found it buried at the bottom, beneath a tangle of dirty underpants, the pages all bent under one of his heavy figure drawing textbooks. His music notebook. Full of snippets of songs he'd written, alone and in tandem with Ed here. All the words. All the chords. He paged through, taking his time, taking one more drag of his fag.

"No," he said, "No. Ah. There it is."

He found the scrap of paper he'd torn from his sister's notebook. His own messy writing was on top. *Cymbeline*. He passed the book over to Ed, sitting cross legged on the floor then, waiting. Trying to make it look like he wasn't waiting. Putting his fag out against the door jamb where it joined a dozen other cigarette burns, where it could hide from his aunt behind an open door. He was trying to look like his heart wasn't in his throat. Trying to look like he didn't want to vomit as Ed eyed his writing, one eyebrow arched, and considered.

"What's this?" Ed asked.

"Words," Baron said dryly. Ed laughed.

"Well, yeh, they're *words*. But to what?"

"To that piano place you played for me. The one you'd told me had needed words." He paused, added, in a wheedly tone, "For *Genie*."

"I thought you'd forgotten," Ed said, ignoring the acid-tone in Baron's voice. Baron snorted. Wished he'd had another fag.

"I never forget. Not about *music*. There's more in there, too. Words to the other ones you wanted me to finish, chords, all of that. But that's the best one."

"Why didn't you say anything *sooner*?" Ed said, pain in his voice. But Baron couldn't share his reason, not with Ed, not now. Because Baron'd been drunk. Because he'd been a *foockin' mess*. Because he'd been too lost in his bullshit, no fault of his own, but not *not* his fault either. Because he hadn't been brave enough. Because there hadn't yet been enough on the line.

"It wasn't ready," Baron said.

Ed looked back down at Baron's writing. Pulled a foot up onto the chair, bit his fingernails. Read. Smiled, briefly, and Baron's heart *did* something, but then the smile fell just as fast, and Baron's heart did something *else*.

"I don't know," Ed said. "I can't *hear* it, anyway. Not like this . . ."

Baron sighed. He held out his hand.

"Give it here, Hammy. And me ax."

"But it's a piano song."

Baron just sat there. His hands out. Waiting. Ed sighed. Gave Baron back his book, and his guitar.

He tuned. This, he thought, was the problem with Ed. He was talented, but he was *limited*. His mind only saw the music in one form, one mode. And then got stuck there.

He'd have to show Hammy another way. With music. With their path forward. With—with the two of them, yeah? Because it didn't have to go one way. It could go another way. Choosing something different, besides simple artistry or industry. Besides fucking and—well, not. A third path. Their path. Together.

He started to strum, and then, after a moment, began to sing.

There were some days that were too much for Naomi Templeton. Some weeks, in fact, because often those days came in sticky succession, five or six or fourteen in a row, when a black mood would descend upon her, often—but not always—for reasons she could not divine, when suddenly she'd barely be able to get up out of bed, and when she did she'd barely be able to get dressed, or make herself food, so she'd slump around in sweats for days, eating ramen soup, if she ate at all. Those days would snowball, tumbling into each other—sleeping most of the day, or else dully watching television, and then up all night, frenetic. Playing guitar or piano like a creature who was practically possessed, even if she hadn't played a note in months before that. Then, the next day, sleeping all day again. It hadn't happened often or consistently. Every four years, maybe, or five. But she always knew when those days were coming, and no therapist had been able to help her CBT or EMDR her way out of it, no pill had cured those dark spells. Those were her seasons, her winters, grim and heavy, and there wasn't much she could do to solve or fight them.

She'd lost her last girlfriend to one of those spells. Her mother, when she'd been alive, had hated it, too. Her mother, always so driven, even though her own whims shifted sometimes on a dime. But whether her mother was focused on her own activism or going back to school to get her nursing certificate or getting their apartment in order or organizing a new union or whatever it was she wanted at the moment, her mother was always *focused*. Sharp. Whereas Naomi, it seemed, had inherited her father's jittery and inconstant nature, which sometimes trembled out into a whole lot of nothing. That was it, supposedly, for her mother. That she was like her *father*. Sometimes useless. Sometimes depressed. And no amount of "up, up, and out of bed!" ever seemed to work.

She only had herself to blame this time. Up too late, which always did it, and trying not to think about everything she'd felt the day before—it was the type of avoidance that often did it, too. And then, lost, in sorting her dad's letters. Searching through them like she was looking for something. And then, somehow, she'd found it.

Not a letter from Hammond, soppy and loving. Not a stern talking-down from Templeton's Aunt Deidre about how he was being too political on the telly again. No. A letter for *her*. For Naomi. Only one. She'd read it before at age seven or eight, avoided reading it since or even thinking about it most of the time because it made her cry, made her *really* lose herself. All those hopes the man had held for a tiny, newly born baby. All those promises—that he wasn't going to be in Trinidad long. Just long enough to bring his own father back to the states, and then they'd have a grand family reunion, all three Templetons. Together. Of course it would never happen. Her granddad had been dead almost twenty years by then, though her dad couldn't have known. A fool's quest, for fool's gold. With a fool's death at the end of it.

She'd read it before, when she wanted to hurt herself. She was careful now. Didn't let her eyes even grace the paragraphs. But she saw, as though seeing for the first time, that first line of address: *To my Angel Naomi—*

Now, the folded letter felt like it was burning a hole in the pocket of her jeans as she somehow, despite the soggy weight of her body and brain, sat and wrote songs with Matt Hammond. The music was easy, just like it had been the day before. Easy in a way nothing her life had ever been. She told himself it was just because of his general privilege. His *maleness*, his *straightness*, his *whiteness*, his *money*. She was borrowing that for the first time. Letting herself think that she was somehow entitled to the world as he was. And that was definitely a *part* of what was happening here. Who else talked like this, like an album, a record contract, a show, or a tour, were all forgone conclusions? But she sensed, on that day and in the days before, that it couldn't have been *all* of it. She would catch him looking deep into her eyes as she played, as though transfixed, and she would find herself transfixed back, and the music—the music would just spill out and over everywhere. Lust? Maybe that was some of it. He'd made it clear he wanted her. But also clear now that he would not press, because of what was happening, really happening, between them.

Still, though, that note in her pocket, and the frantic, confused way her mind was racing. And then Matt *said* it. That soon, the world would know who she was. Her notes broke off. Her stomach squeezed. She stood and started packing her father's guitar into its case.

"I—I think I have to get out of here," she said. He stood too, his pale brow gathering in confusion.

"I'm sorry," he said. Really, truly confused. "What did I say?"

Her hands were shaking. She shook her head. What she said then was only halfway a lie. "I'm sorry. It's not you. I'm—I'm a mess. I'm sorry."

She headed for the door, and for a moment, she thought he would let her go. But then she heard him sigh.

"Wait, Naomi," he said softly. She could have gone, but she was weak. She turned back to look at him. "I only have one more night here. This is it. And I don't want to leave it like this. So—unfinished. Do you?"

The strength of the afternoon sunlight through the big picture windows made him look younger. More like his Dad. She thought about the note in her pocket. She thought about the letters she'd read, the diary entries. She thought about the photos she'd seen in the television documentaries as a teenager—grainy, distant. Hammond and Templeton, back in 1958, at their first shows, before they were at all false or polished or professional. Her mother watched her watch those documentaries in the doorway of their Brooklyn living room and shook her head, clucked her tongue. *Don't know why you watch those things,* she said, practical, as her mother always was. *It's not going to bring him back.*

Her mother was right. It hadn't brought him back. But it had told her something. Those photos of the two boys, holding guitars together, looking nothing alike but somehow twinned. She was nothing like Matt, either.

That much was clear. She wasn't even sure how much she *liked* him. Rich, entitled ass. And yet. And yet. She'd felt it. Whatever *it* was. Looking at him, she felt it now.

She put down her guitar case.

"What do you propose, Matt?" she asked. When he spoke, he spoke with his hands. Little bits of his father, spilling through.

"I have a joint in my luggage," he said. "Let's get some fresh air, take a walk. Smoke it."

She squinted, grinning a little despite herself. Bits of her father, spilling through, too. "Best idea I've heard all day," she said.

* * *

There was a path back through the scrubby trees behind the house which then turned into a narrow path over moss-slick rocks. The pair of them followed it, Naomi leading the way, since she'd been there before. They hadn't smoked yet. She still felt queasy, unsettled. *Off.* But Matt was right. The fresh air was helping. It tasted sharp and false, like the thing that pine cleaner was trying to emulate but headier. It was part of the reason she'd moved up here. The heaviness came to her less regularly when she could be outside, in empty, beautiful nature. In the city, it was harder for her to escape.

She couldn't call what she felt lightness. But she was certainly lighter. It made her want to talk a little. To share something of herself. Not all of it. But . . .

"Do you know how I met Edelman and his wife?" she asked, parting the branches with her hand.

"No," Matthew said, and she could hear his curiosity bubbling up and almost spilling over. She'd shared so little of herself with him. That had been deliberate, of course. And it wasn't like he'd shared much of himself either. (A girlfriend? A fucking *girlfriend*?) Still, she wasn't the type to usually keep herself so well guarded. Normally, she was an open book. And she felt guilty for having closed herself to him, just a little.

"My mother was having her first biopsy. This was—God, more than ten years ago now. Maybe fifteen. I was in my twenties. She had a bad reaction to the anesthesia, and they wanted to keep her overnight for observation. I walked into the room, turned to my mom to hand her some flowers, and this deranged woman with her head all bandaged sat up in the other bed and said 'Hello, Angel!' Like she'd been waiting all day for me. That was Cymbeline."

"What was she in the hospital for?" he asked. Naomi tripped over some rocks, steadied herself. Felt Matt's hand on her arm, helping to steady her. Didn't pull herself away.

"Oh, I thought the Edelmans might have told you," she said. Matthew's turn to pull away from her. She shrugged, but could see it rattled him a little, to be on the outside of this story, looking in.

"We don't have that kind of relationship," he said. Naomi sighed.

"Well, don't go tweeting about this," she told him. He snorted softly, not meanly. "But she was in there for brain surgery. She had a tumor pressing on some nerve. Had been having migraines. Seeing things. They thought it was cancer, but it was just a — growth. Benign. But that's why she gave up her music career. The surgery fucked with her vision, her ability to write. Her melodies would go all over the place. Like some kind of experimental . . . well, no more headaches, at least, though, after they took it out. No more hallucinations. Sid said the music's been coming back lately, and I know he hopes she'll do something with it, but I'm not so sure."

"Shit," Matthew said in a low tone. Definitely annoyed to be out of the loop, Naomi thought. But also just a little stunned, as though he'd never considered this. "I had no idea."

"Most don't," Naomi said. By then, they'd reached the final leg of their walk where the path curved upwards. They were quiet for a moment, Matthew's breath heavy and distinctly middle-aged behind her, even though they were just about the same age. He seemed so much older. But they were still kids in a way, weren't they? Both of them always would be, by virtue of who their fathers had been. Most people got out of those shadows by their late teens, their twenties. Matt and Naomi probably never would.

Up the iceberg-cleaved rock and over. The path ended, the trees cleared and scattered, and the ground was only rock coated with damp moss, sloping down into the glassy lake.

"Wow," Matt murmured, and Naomi's chest squeezed because she could hear how he *meant* it, this small, childish note of amazement at the sight of the water. It made her feel the same way, actually, every time. But who else did she know who would *say* it? No one. She watched as he sat down at the base of a tree, got out his joint. Gestured for her to sit beside him. She did.

"Matt," she said at last, "Do you ever get the feeling that the universe is fucking with you?"

He lit the joint, took a deep draw, passed it to her. Exhaled, coughing, laughing a little.

"Most people don't call me Matt," he said. "Except my dad."

"Oh," she said, contemplating the joint. Taking a small draw, tiny puffs. "Sorry, I can stop—"

"No," he said. "'Sfine. And yes, I do frequently feel like the universe is fucking with me, but absent of context, I cannot ascertain whether I know precisely what you mean."

She looked at him for a long time. He finally cracked a smile, and she let out a cackle. Handing him back the joint.

"Okay," she said, "Well, after the hospital my old lady and Cymbeline became best friends. We're talking, up all night painting each others' nails and gossiping together, and then in the same book club, and then the Edelmans over for dinner twice a week. And like, it was great—they're great. They've never been anything but great. This year I went over there for Christmas, because I *always* go over there for Christmas, because Cymbeline says that we orphans have to stick together. And Edelman said you were coming up here to write, and I made a crack about how we should get together and write something, be Templeton and Hammond, volume 2. It was a joke. I didn't mean it. Sid, I think—I mean, you know him. He just saw the dollar signs. But Cymbeline took me into the kitchen, and while we were drying dishes, she looked at me and said, *You know, you really should. I think the two of you could have something special together."*

Matthew looked out onto the lake, his gaze hazy and distant. "Like she was setting us up."

"Yeah," Naomi said. "And, like, you know, I'm about the same age as them. But it's always seemed like they were so much *older*. My life's a mess. I've never held down a job for more than a year."

"I've never held down a job at all," he admitted. When she narrowed her eyes at him, he winced. "Not the point. I realize. Sorry. Go on."

"You've been a musician since you were, what, nineteen?" she asked, reluctant to admit that she'd followed his career closely for as long as she could remember. The other Saffron kids, too. Barry Waller with his shitty band of C-listers. Matthew's older sisters. The boring old Pecks. But there was something different about *him*, she always thought. His music was halfway decent, for one thing, even if it had the same tendency to go saccharine and simple that his father's did. It seemed real*ish*, unlike his sisters' charitable causes, their forays into ceramics and travel photography. It had potential.

"Yeah, I guess," he said, "But I can't claim that I haven't had doors opened for me."

"Maybe, but you tried, at least. And I've always wanted to *do* something with myself, too. Something that was even half of what my dad did with the world. How could I not go for it, when they told me to come up here and help you? They even said they'd pay me and lord knows I can use the cash. But when I think about the way she was *looking* at me, it wasn't just like it was a set-up or a gig. It's like she *knew* somehow what would happen when we hung out. Like she was telling me how to pick the right college or something. Like she was my mother or whatever, and she could tell I was wasting my life, and she wanted me to make something of myself, finally—"

Naomi knew she wasn't making any sense. She put the heels of her hands over her tired eyes, rubbed hard.

"So we've made some beautiful music together," Matt said in a low voice, gravelly and thick. She winced. His words were too cheesy for her. Fuck, this wasn't what she wanted. Not like this. "No harm in that."

"No," she said, determined to stay on topic despite the way the weed had started to unravel her, "But, I keep thinking about that first moment I met her. In that hospital room. *Allo, Angel,*" Naomi quoted brightly, in a voice that sounded neither like her own nor Cymbeline's. "And I keep thinking, why didn't she have a private room? They definitely could have afforded it, the two of them. But she was there. In my mom's room. *Waiting* for me, Matt."

He didn't respond. She pulled the letter out of her pocket, handed it to him. He opened it up.

"Look," she said, "At what he called me. Baron. My dad."

He sucked on the joint. Read. Winced.

"I am *incredibly* stoned," he admitted, handing the letter back. Naomi stuffed it back down into her pocket. Took the joint from him. Sucked it until it was done, then stubbed it out on the rock. The lake began to glitter as though someone had filled it up with stars.

"Me, too," she admitted, though it wasn't entirely true. Wasn't the whole truth, at least.

"Whether or not the universe is plotting against you," he said, and that's when she realized that his eyes, with their flooded pupils, were fixed firmly on her. She felt unmoored by the weight of his gaze, like she was a balloon cut from a string. "I'm glad I had this time with you. I know it's—it's only about writing music, the two of us. I know I can't convince you to get up on that stage and sing with me, or to fuck me, or anything else. I know I can't convince you of anything. That's not how it works. But I'm glad to be here with you right now."

When was the last time she'd been spoken to like this? Not by her high school girlfriends. Or the few men she'd dated in college, the usual experiment in reverse. Not by her girlfriends after, who found her therapists and argued with her about finding better work. They'd treated her like a sloppy child. She'd long thought that they were right. All because she had no father. She hadn't learned how to grow up into a proper person, a person who understood herself and her own impulses. Of course, neither had Baron Templeton. It was the shitty scar they'd both inherited. Past lovers had thought her *damaged*, and they hadn't been wrong. But Matt—somehow Matt saw her as more than a floundering foundling. If he thought she was a mess, he didn't say it, and he didn't seem to care, either.

She looked at Matt. Really looked at him. Yes, his pale hair was thinning on top. Yes, he was thick around the belly a bit. But he had broad shoulders beneath his coat and worn-out concert t-shirt, and deep set, thoughtful eyes. Teeth just a little bit crooked, like his British parents hadn't bothered with orthodontia despite their massive wealth. A little dimple in the left side of his face. She could see, looking at him, that he was more than just his body, his skin, his inheritance—especially now that he'd given up his entitled pretense, now that he'd relaxed beside her. In their music, and the silences between them, she sensed a certain sort of hunger. He wanted to *do* something with his life. *Make* something. And she knew enough of life to know how rare that was. Her last girlfriend had only ever wanted to binge Netflix shows and gossip about her co-workers. The one before that hadn't read a book in ten years. They'd both liked music, but they didn't understand it at all. Nor did they understand why she wanted to make it, when she couldn't even post videos of herself playing guitar to YouTube without dying inside.

When she looked at him, it was like a call coming from inside of her had finally been answered. She knew it. She saw it. She felt it, too.

She looked out toward the lake, resting her head on her knees. "Yeah," she said simply. "Me, too."

* * *

The weed did its work. A half hour later, they were stumbling back toward the house, giggling like children over nothing in particular. Singing together. Saffron songs, of all things. Old favorites, which had been with them since the beginning of awareness, the beginning of thought. Matthew admitted a reluctant love for "Lima Bean Sunset," which was Templeton's most impenetrable work of psychedelia. Naomi shot back that she'd always loved "Empty Knapsack." Cringing at herself.

"Well," Matt said, "It's hard to argue with my dad's major key children's songs. They were, like, written in the universe. Before the universe even began."

And then he snickered to himself. "Christ, I'm stoned," he said, as Naomi, beside him, launched into the quirky little bridge of "Empty Knapsack,": *A feller a feller says Cinderella can't keep up with sister Stella she keeps that glass shoe somewhere new, in her mummy's—*

"Eeeempty knapsack," he crooned along with her, and their voices matched in a way even though they sounded nothing like their fathers.

"How was it empty, anyway?" Matt asked, as he stumbled up the front steps of the house, "If it had a shoe inside. Never did understand that one."

"I think the contradiction is the *point,*" Naomi said. "I always figure that line came from my dad. You just didn't get that kind of turn of phrase with either of them working alone. Your dad was all sunshine and roses, mine was sour milk and dandelions. But when they collaborated, man, it's like there was tension all over the place. I think that's what made their music different."

She waited as Matt entered the door code, blowing warm air into her numb hands. They were full of pinpricks and lightning. *Cold,* she realized, shaking them. Feeling, in the moment, only the sensation, and her own exhilaration at the culmination of their climb—her heart pounding hard, her cheeks flushed. Matt opened the door for her.

"I thought they were different because they were in love?" he asked, arching his eyebrow to show that he was still just a little bit dubious about her claim. She wasn't surprised. She'd grown up knowing that there was something more between the men; her mother had never hidden it from her, nor her father's trysts with Peter X., nor his frequent patronage of the gay bars on the Lower East Side. Matt, on the other hand, had grown up under a veil of secrecy—maybe even shame.

"Well," Naomi said, suddenly feeling sober as she said it, because she knew she wasn't, couldn't be, "What's a lifelong, secret love if it's not tension?"

Matt didn't say anything, only watched her as she walked past him and stepped back into the Edelman's home. Her shoulder brushed his chest as she did. In a way, she didn't mean to do it. But she didn't *not* mean to do it, either.

"Anyway," she said, glad for her dark skin tone, and how it obscured the ruddying of her cheeks. "Time to get back to work, isn't it? We're wasting daylight here."

* * *

They decided to write something different next. A children's song, or something like one—a send-up of the kind of thing Hammond had written in the early '70s, but bringing in the leitmotif on the bridge, puncturing the sweetness with a rusted blade. Naomi had been carrying around the melody for years. During her manic phases, she often tried to set words to it, but they had always come out either obnoxiously cloying or so removed as to sound sarcastic.

"No," Matt said, "That won't do. We need to simplify."

"There are only three chords," she said irritably. They were sitting on the floor beside each other, their knees touching. Matt laughed.

"I meant the lyrics. It's too cynical. It feels like it's written by an adult who can't remember what it was like to be a kid."

She gave him a pointed look. He shot back a glance that was appropriately chastened.

"Sorry," he said. She rubbed her eyes.

"No, you're right," she told him. "I just hate that you're right. *You* try."

He looked down at the jotted sheet of chords and hazy lyrics. Then he crumpled up the paper and began to play.

Naomi laid back on the carpet to watch him, her arms sprawled out over her. Matt was singing about his own wellie boots now, about floating autumn leaves down a muddy stream. She closed her eyes. Thought about her own childhood—how the laces of her second-hand sneakers had looked in the rain, how on the days when it poured, they had kept them inside during recess, how the gym had sounded like a submarine. She hadn't wanted to play dodge ball with the others. She'd sat off on the side, her back up against a sweaty gym mat, gotten her CD player out of her backpack and put on her headphones. Listened to her Daddy sing. Imagined Trinidad. Water that stretched out as far as the eye could see. How his hand would feel at her back.

"I have something," she said, rolling halfway over. She propped herself up on her elbows, began jotting it down. "A bridge."

He was leaning over her, close, quite close. Reading over her shoulder. She could feel the heat of his body, smell the scent of him.

"It's good," he said softly, "But it's a song for two voices, innit? Wouldn't make sense to sing it all myself."

She felt her shoulders stiffen, suddenly hyper aware of her back facing him, her shoulder blades.

"Artistic license," she said softly. But she sat up anyway and grabbed her guitar.

"Start from the top," she said.

He did. She'd noticed already how he made corny faces when he played, the corners of his lips twitching, his shoulders grooving up and down. She had the thought that he wouldn't look like that if he'd been able to stop it—he was sophisticated, unlike his sweet, simple dad. But he couldn't. The rhythm moving through him. His eyes searing into hers. Singing about his brown wellie boots, hand-me-downs from a sister. About how he hoped that the leaf could drift off somewhere, into another life.

This time, she didn't look away. She strummed along with him, humming a half-formed harmony. And then, as the last note of the verse faded, started singing the middle eight. It was more a litany than a bridge, really. A list of images: second-hand shoes, rain on the drum of the roof of the gymnasium, that silver CD skipping and taking her somewhere else. She saw Matt bite down on his tongue, his body bobbing a little as he counted the beat. And then she was back in Scotland, chasing sheepdogs through the freezing rain.

And somewhere beyond both their lyrics, simple though they were, there was something else. Someplace else. A warm, wild kingdom. A boat on the bluest ocean, coasting toward the setting sun. She launched in at the chorus, adding a relative minor, taking that song into it. The places she didn't dare to go, normally. An imaginary kingdom of long-dashed hope.

She didn't realize what was happening until he broke off playing, watching her, his pale brow furrowed.

"Naomi," he said. He reached out, put his hands over her hands, which had been vamping through the chord sequence by then, over and over again. "Naomi, stop."

She stopped. And the tears gurgled out in a humiliating stream. Growing up, there hadn't been room for tears about *this*. She hadn't even known her father, not really. If there was grief, anger, any feeling at all—that had belonged to her mother. She hadn't cried to her girlfriends about it, or boyfriends, or friends. Not even Cymbeline, her courage-teacher. Not even Sid. If it happened, it happened privately, in her little bedroom, and only when she was very young. Turning the music up so that her mother wouldn't hear. But now, sitting there, her knees touching Matt's knees, she sobbed. Big, blubbery, snotty tears. Audible, undeniable tears.

He put down his guitar, and came closer to her. Before she could put up her walls, create that distance, he was holding her with only the body of her father's guitar between them, her wet face against the smooth, warm slope of his neck. He rocked her. She cried and cried.

At last, she pulled her sticky face away.

"So embarrassing," she said, dabbing at her eyes with the sleeve of her sweater. "Forty years old and a fucking mess about my dead Daddy. Still."

"I don't think there's any shame in it," he said softly, letting his broad hand rest on the side of her neck, just below her ear. His fingers, callused from years of playing, gently stroked her skin. She found herself leaning into it despite herself. Despite her most calculated and best intentions. "If the music doesn't move *us*, then what's the point in writing it?"

"Did your dad teach you that?" she asked, snuffling. It was a reflex, the snarky edge to her voice, the knife twist. And for some reason, she felt compelled to just twist it in further: "Because it always seemed to me like he was in it for the cash."

But Matt didn't seem to care right now if she insulted his father. He laughed softly, but kept his hand right there, on the side of her neck.

"No," he said simply. "You did."

"Fuck," she said, looking back at him. Matt frowned, only for a moment, as she took his face in both her hands, and kissed him fully on the lips, her father's guitar pressed between their bodies.

43 - 1958

On that afternoon, Baron played like his life depended on it. As, of course, it *did*. The chords were tricky, a bit, on guitar, the way that Ed had written them—and he wasn't that good at bar chords, not yet. But though he'd struggled with this one before, musically, you wouldn't have been able to tell that day, as he bent his strings and went through it. Eyes on Ed, even, not on his fingers or his ax, because it was a song for Ed. Ed's song. About how much he loved that fucking boy, who sat listening, hand under his chin, controlled. Considering.

Baron promised to love Ed until his dying day. In this life. In any other. He *felt* it, as he looked at Ed, felt the depths of what had just transpired between them, too. The importance. Ed wasn't a boy who would just wank with any boy. He was too careful for that. It meant something, that Ed had let himself be unguarded with Baron. But now, the guard was back. The *care* back. His gaze gave Baron no license, no room. Once, Ed had auditioned for Baron. Now the tables were turned, as he sang Ed "Cymbeline," the song that he'd already begun thinking of, secretly, in his head, as "Ed's Song."

Even as the last chord faded, Ed's bright gaze had not softened. He was silent for a moment, watching Baron, his hand still tucked. Under such scrutiny, Baron felt his cheeks heat. He wanted to look away, but knew he couldn't. To be shy now, receding, would be to lose him.

"It's lovely," Ed said, in that simple, bald way that Ed spoke sometimes, without artifice or hesitation.

"Lovely with an asterisk?" Baron asked, leaning forward, because he could *hear* it, the "but" coming on.

"Well," Ed said, finally dropping his hand, "I'm just not sure what I can *do* with it. I can't give it to Genie, like I wanted. It's too lofty. It sounds—it'd sound queer, Barry."

Baron winced. Ed was right, of course, but it hurt in a way, that Ed had even thought he might be offering his spectacular fucking song to Ed for Genie Fucking Waller.

"'snot a song for Genie," he protested. "It's a song for *you.*"

Now Ed untucked his hand, letting it drop down by his knees. A soft, pained look dawned over his eyes, and he leaned forward, worrying his face with his hands, sighing.

"Christ, Baron," he said.

There it was. The knife twist into a tender bruise. Baron sat back straighter, feeling his throat tighten a knot, feeling his chin tremble. No, no, he told himself, he wouldn't cry.

"'sbeautiful song," Baron said, and it was like he couldn't *stop* talking, even as he sensed himself talking himself right off a cliff, "And you know it. Beautiful song for a beautiful boy."

Ed winced, his hands still over his face.

"It *is* a beautiful song, Baron," he agreed. Ed's tone suggested he believed it, was telling the truth. Couldn't deny the song's beauty, or his own. But. But but but. There was a *but* there.

"But?" Baron said sourly. Ed sighed. Dropped his hands down on his knees, the sound slightly percussive.

"But what are we gonna *do* with it?" he said. "It's not a song for the *Bartlebys.* It's not a skiffle song, or a rock and roll song. Isn't even a proper ballad."

Ed, looking to him, waiting for an answer. Baron could have burst into schizophrenic laughter then, or ragged tears. Or maybe stood and smashed up his guitar against the wall over Ed's head. But he couldn't do any of those things now, could he? So he only sat there. Sitting frozen.

When he didn't say anything, Ed went on:

"I love you, Barry. You know I love you," and in truth, from the heartbreaking sound of it, Baron *did* know. "But we can't play that song on stage together. Everyone'll know—I mean, they'll think we're a bunch of queers. They'll know you're sweet on me. And I can't—it's illegal. Innit? For two men? They arrest us, or beat us bloody, or cart us off to the loony bin for some electroshock therapy, to cure us of it. And that's it. The band'll be over. But it can't be *over*. This music thing—it's real for me. I need it. I want to be a *Dad*, Baron. I want a wife and a *proper* home and a whole litter of children. And I want them to have better'n what I had. I don't want them to have to fight for it, like me and my brothers have had to. I want life to be easy for them. Not a drunk fucking father and a shared bedroom where they hear their brothers wank all night. Not—not hand-me-downs and veg without meat because Daddy hasn't been paid yet. As far as I can see it, music's the only way I can do that for them. I want them to have it *good*."

Baron heard what Ed was saying. Baron listened. In truth, he didn't know what it was like to covet a life like that. For Baron, who had never learned how to dream of something better, something more, his days were usually limited by their feeble beginnings—the sun rising hazily over Liverpool—and their equally unambitious ends. The sun sinking into the ocean. Had he wanted to be famous, to get out, to get money and birds? Oh yes, yes, of course. But he hadn't let himself *see* it, not like Ed had. Dreaming was too dangerous, too intoxicating, too guaranteed to end poorly. Usually.

But then Baron sat straighter, made still his chin. "Y'never told me yer father is a drunk."

Ed let out a sigh. "Cor, Baron. You never asked."

The look on his face! Bruised and pretty and indignant. Baron couldn't stand it anymore. He gazed down at his guitar, at the strings, at his own lap.

"Baron," Ed said again, his voice gentle and just a little pained. "It's a beautiful song. Better than I could have imagined. Certainly better'n what I could have written. *Thank you* for writing it for me."

God. God, Baron was *not* going to cry. Already the humiliation in bed with the two of them, not the sucking but all those tears and Ed holding him, like he was weaker, lesser, a *baby*. Even if Ed knew what it was like to lose a Mum, to feel so raw and open and empty. Even if what had come after had made it better, somewhat, he was *not* going to cry now, to let Ed think that he was still small and trembling and undone.

Baron swallowed hard, clenched his back teeth, forced back the wave of emotion. Looked up at Ed, seeing the kind and slightly patronizing way that Ed regarded him.

"It's your song," Baron said gruffly, his voice low because of everything he was trying to hold in. "Consider it my promise to you, Eddie. My gift."

Ed frowned. When he did, he looked older, less lovely than usual. His gears turning over what Baron had said.

"What d'you mean?"

"Take it," Baron said. And did it hurt to say it? Oh yes, of course it did. The best thing he'd ever written—the best thing he'd ever made. Would ever make. But it was Ed's anyway, wasn't it? Not just the melody, which Ed had written, mostly, more or less, but the words, too. The magic wouldn't have been pulled out of him if it weren't for knowing Ed. His music and his lips and his sweet, stupid voice. "Band or no band. It's your song. Wait a decade, 'til you're already famous a bit, 'til they're all hungry for you the way I'm hungry for you. Wait 'til no one cares if it sounds queer or not. Tell them you wrote it. All by yourself. You'll get rich off it someday. You know you will. And I'll keep my big gob shut on this one. I won't tell a soul."

Ed's frown even deeper. As he chewed over this proposition, leaning forward in his seat.

"You can't be *serious*, Barry," he said, his blue eyes growing wider like a pair of lakes after a heavy season of rain. "You *wrote* those words. They're yours!"

Baron shook his head. His body still felt taut with emotion, with all that terrible feeling. But carefully, he set his guitar on the floor, and rose. His steps toward Ed were small and stiff. He knelt on the floor in front of the younger boy and gazed up into his eyes.

"It's *your* song, Eddie. Take it and make loads of money and keep your fat bonny babies fed," he said hoarsely. Then reached up, putting his hand next to Ed's cheek along the side of his neck. Ed didn't lean away from his touch. No, no, he leaned into it.

"As for the band," Baron said, "As for *us*, it'll be the music for us, won't it? You don't have to worry. I'll—I'll tidy m'self up for you, if that's what you need. I'll be straight as a whistle."

"As an arrow," Ed said, correcting Baron and smiling a little. Baron felt himself grin back.

"As an arrow, Ed," he agreed, thinking to himself *and all for you*. Their eyes locked. It was done then, the devil's deed signed, and then Ed leaned down, to seal it. Not with Baron's blood, but with Baron's kiss. Their lips meeting, their bodies sinking into each other.

Which is right when the door

44 - 1977

Fuck, it must have been three years by seventy seven since Richard Charles Ashby Junior had last seen his father. And the last fucking place he expected to see the cunt was in the doorway of some fucking fag musician's semi-permanent shack-up space. But there he was, the asshole, getting even balder, the bags under his eyes flabby and gray like two pieces of over boiled lunch meat. He'd always been a weird looking guy and now he was even older and even weirder looking. Richard Charles was freaking thrilled, for the millionth time, that he looked more like his hot fucking mom, who had bagged enough boyfriends in her life to have kids by three different ones and had her fun on her nights off, still. Aside from judging his dad for getting old—because who gets old, really? Pussies too scared to die, that's who— Richard Charles *tried* to tell himself he didn't feel a fucking thing when that queer Baron Templeton threw open the door and saw Dick Sr. there and—th'*fuck?*—threw his arms around old senior like they were old fucking friends.

Richard Charles looked over at his weenie little brother, who was sitting there with mouth hanging open like a fucking idiot, and Richard Charles rolled his eyes and let out a snort. "How come you didn't fucking *tell* us that you knew Baron Fucking Templeton, dad?"

His father pulled away from the teeny weeny rock star, wiping wussy-ass *tears* from his eyes, and laughed.

"Hi, too, Richie," he said, in that weird fucking lilt he had that was halfway between British and American, on account of living here so long—Richard Charles' entire fucking life plus nine months, when (he'd once claimed) he came here for business but ended up knocking up their mom instead. What month would that have been? Richard Charles did quick math in his head. March '61, or maybe April. Of course. Saffron's first US visit, backing The Shirelles, before they broke out big, themselves. Dad was always such a fucking tag along. "Nice to see you. Long time no see."

Because you didn't want to see us, you asshole, Richard Charles thought, clenching his back teeth so hard that he thought the second molar, the one with the bad cavity that he hadn't wanted to tell his mom about because he knew it would cost too much to fix, might crack in two. He could have fucking leaped out of his chair and *wailed* on his old man, just beaten him to a pulp. He was probably taller than him now, right? Finally fucking taller than him. But they were in Baron Templeton's fucking *house*—well, more or less—and he didn't want to screw things up for poor widdle Zachy. Meeting his faggy-ass hero and everything.

"Well?" Richard Charles demanded, harder even, "Why didn't you tell us you knew a fucking rock star?"

"I didn't think you cared, squirt," his dad said, keeping one arm around Templeton, almost like he *owned* Templeton. Like he was laying a claim. "I used to play Saffron for you all the time when you were little. Never seemed to give a fuck then."

"I was fucking *six* when you left," Richard Charles howled, and that's when the two men shared a look at each other and started snickering. Like it was a real fucking hilarious joke.

"He *is* a squirt of you, innit he?" Templeton asked Senior and thumped him on the back, real congenial, the sort of gesture that is by nature a slamming of a door in one's fucking face if one is not on the inside of it.

"My fucking clone," Dick Senior said.

"I'll have you *know*, boys," went Templeton, stepping closer to them, away from their faded failure of a father as he did, "That Dick Ashby is one of me oldest mates. How old were we when we met, Dick?"

"Christ," said Dick Ashby, "Four or five? Remember how you pissed yourself on the first day of school?"

Baron laughed a little, but Richard Charles could see that this guy—this fucking *rock star* was *actually fucking embarrassed* at his Dad bringing it up. And yet his Dad just kept on fucking going, because that was the kind of asshole that Dick Senior *was*.

"You were a total bloody baby back then. The future celebrity! No one would have known."

Baron, leaning his weight against one of his folding make-shift kitchen chairs, was actually fucking—blushing? Or sort of getting redder at least. It made Richard Charles want to wail on his dad. A-fucking-*gain*. Because Baron might have been some midget fag but he'd been pretty fucking nice to them, so far, all things considered and it wasn't that often that someone was nice to Richard Charles, much less a *famous* person.

"If you'd have asked me," Dick was saying, "I was the one who seemed like a rock star. Birds always did go for me, didn't they?"

Baron, dark unshaved cheeks going even darker, shaking his head. "Yeh," he agreed, "they always went for you, Dick."

A silence, but a short one, one that was punctuated, by (of all fucking things) this little shaky voice. A voice that cracked at the end, still barely fucking pubescent. Little Zachy, looking at their dad with this intensity in his eyes like the cherries at the end of two cigarettes.

"But Dad," Zachy was saying, "You can't carry a fucking tune."

It was times like these, when the little brother finally grew a fucking spine, that Richard Charles was full of fucking love for him, his baby brother, the best and worst thing that had ever happened to him.

"Cor," Baron was saying, guffawing, "That one's a squirt of you, too, ey Dickie?"

"Yeah yeah yeah," his father said, shrugging because it was true, his father had like four different guitars, or used to, at least, last time they went to his place, years ago but he couldn't play a chord on *any* of them. Chuffed, Richard Charles gazed at his baby brother, who was sitting there staring his father down with bullet eyes and he knew they'd always be together in this, above all: their shared hatred for their sorry excuse for a dad.

"Well, boys," Alana, who had been standing in the bathroom doorway with her tits fat and heavy and leaking milk right through her dress, with her cooing baby and her womanly fucking tension, said, "We really *don't* have time for a visit today."

"Oh, stuff it, you old bag," Dick Senior said sharply, glowering at her right through Baron's laughter and Richard Charles had the feeling this was an old conflict, and while Alana's nostrils flared at the name, not liking it, she didn't even *look* at Dick Senior. She looked at Baron. Instead.

"Unless you want to cancel our dinner plans tonight," she said to him, her eyes saying *I want to fucking cancel our dinner plans tonight*, "Then we have to get the place ready."

"Christ," Baron said, wiping tears away, "But Alaner's right, Dickie. Company's coming. Must tidy up. Put the wee bairn to bed."

Dick Senior looked from Alana to Baron, and Richard Charles had the sense that under normal, different circumstances, maybe his old man would have pushed his way into getting whatever he wanted. Installed himself right there at their kitchen table, company coming or not. But then his dad glanced at his kids, and Baron's baby, and sighed, because to Dick Ashby, kids were always a burden.

"Fine," he said. "C'mon, kiddos. Party's over."

Out of the corner of his eye, Richard Charles saw Zach rubbing his palms on the arms of the chair. Real nervous-like, like he didn't want to do it, didn't want to leave. And Richard Charles couldn't blame him. The last thing he wanted to do was to walk out of this fucking rock star's home and leave with his *dad*. But them's the brakes, Richard Charles told himself. Sometimes you get a fucking minute with greatness, and that's it—but it's better than not having that minute at all. Right?

"Let's go, Zach," Richard Charles said, and got up, but while *he* was trying to gather up his little brother, he heard his Dad go over to Baron and start talking in a low voice.

"The supermarket's fucking failing," he was saying, "Those employees are threatening to fucking *unionize*. Can you believe it? I'm gonna need some cash, Baron."

What a fucking scene. His father begging Baron Templeton for money, and doing it like he'd done it before. His Dad owned a Grand Union out in Queens, and Richard Charles had never thought much of it, except it was a fucking fancy gig for someone so desperate and weaselly and generally useless. But now he found himself wondering where he'd gotten the money to open the place up in the first place. Probably here. From sucking Templeton's cock and begging him for cash.

"I dunno, Dick," Baron was saying, "Funds are tight." Behind him, Zach had slipped out the door and into the hallway. Too embarrassing, maybe, to watch this transaction. But Richard Charles lingered, watching. Richard Charles wanted, for some fucking reason, to understand.

"What?" Dick Senior replied and Richard Charles could hear him warming up to it. The insult that was about to come. He'd heard it enough with his old man and his mom, over child support payments. *You cunt, I'll ruin you. Running off with those assholes with* my *money. You're not getting another red cent.* "You too busy blowing it all on that fucking Black Panther like the papers say? You're naïve, Baron. A chump."

"Dick," Baron said, "It's not like that. You know he's found me old man? We're going to go out to Trinidad to get him. Me and Alaner and the baby. For a real family reunion. He just wants us to help build up the commune in return. Fair's fair. A family for a home. A home for a family."

Dick Senior snorted. "Sounds like a scam to me. Don't forget where you came from, Baron. It wasn't fucking Trinidad."

A silence, sparking, electric. Dick Senior had pushed it a foot too far. And it hurt, in a way, to hear his Dad so piddling and pitiful and petty, to hear him *begging* so Richard Charles, standing there, said in a voice that sounded soggy and girly and weak, "Let's go, Pops. Let's get out of here."

No answer at first, only tension. Between Baron and Alana. Between Baron and Dick. Between Richard Charles and Dick, too. That's when Baron looked at him. At Richard Charles. His beady black faggy little eyes looking at him and—fuck, making him feel like they weren't so different, somehow.

"Not gonna embarrass you in front of your kid, Dickie," Baron said. He got out his wallet and took out a wrinkled-up check. Grabbed a pen off the table. Richard Charles tried not to watch, because it felt fucking humiliating, watching his dad take Baron Templeton's charity, but he couldn't help it. Baron Templeton started writing a number with a lot of zeroes. Too many zeroes. His own eyes turning into fat fucking zeroes, watching.

"'slast time, though," Baron said, in a grim voice. His Dad grabbed for the check. Stuffed it down into his pocket like he was fucking starving and the piece of paper would fill him up.

"Sure, Barry," he told the man, and clapped him on the shoulder. Too hard. Purposefully too hard. Sending Baron off his balance. Proving something. "No hard feelings. Enjoy your date with the Black Panther party. Give my regards to your old man. Ta-ra, Alana."

"Leave, Dick," Alana said, her voice full of fury even halfway across the room and even the baby felt it—started crying then, too. Dick shoved Richard Charles out the door and closed it tight behind him.

"God," their father said, taking out a cigarette and lighting it right there in the hallway. "I hate that cunt. C'mon, kids. Let's get you home."

Richard Charles glanced at his brother, who gazed silently back. And they headed down toward the elevator, the three Ashby men, together.

* * *

Their Dad had double parked his Oldsmobile at the curb outside the Chelsea hotel and when he got down there, there was a ticket waiting, tucked under the windshield wiper. Richard Charles felt something tense up tight inside him, as he braced himself for his dad's fucking rage, which he'd seen before, felt before. Zach, beside him, didn't know he should brace himself. He'd been too young when Dickie Senior had left to remember ever being hit. But Richard Charles remembered. The way he'd gotten backhanded for spilling juice on the carpet, for touching his dad's records or guitars, for standing in front of the television. Usually just a slap, but a hard slap. Across his cheeks, his other cheeks, his ear, and his ears still rang from it sometimes when he was drunk or stoned. The fucking asshole. But for some frigging reason, this time, his father's anger didn't come. His dad just sighed.

"Fucking pigs," he said mildly, and grabbed the ticket and tossed it into the gutter. Unlocked the door to his pristine Olds, and let the boys inside. Richard Charles climbed into the back. Let baby Zachy sit up front. Because he didn't get as much time with their dad, anyway. Hadn't. Over the course of his whole life. Because he knew that Zachy was always fucking hungry for it. For *Daddy*.

"With the dough that Templeton just gave you, you could pay that ticket," Richard Charles muttered. His dad looked at him for a minute, proddy and pointed, in the rear view mirror.

"Don't be a little bitch," his Dad said. "That's your fucking inheritance, you know."

"Oh joy," Richard Charles said, waving his finger in a circle.

"What dough?" Zachy asked, as their Dad started down the road. Neither Dicks answered him for a minute. Richard Charles wondered if his dad was going to tell him. About the check. So much fucking money. But he didn't. Finally, Richard Charles said, "Don't worry your pretty little head about it."

"Fuck you," Zachy muttered under his breath. Christ. Always so fucking sensitive. Couldn't understand that there were some things you were better off not knowing, anyway.

Zach turned then to his Dad, and Richard Charles could see how his eyes were big and gooey and full of fucking admiration, even now. Missing how miserable a moment this was. Missing it completely. "I can't believe you're *friends* with Baron Templeton. He's, like, my hero."

Richard Charles winced. No good could come of admitting something like that, not to *him*.

"Oh yeah?" his dad was saying. Then his dad snorted. Like a flabby freaking pig. "He might be a so-called 'genius' but don't be too impressed by him. That guy's always been a mess."

"Oh yeah?" Zach asked, eager for more tender morsels about Templeton.

"Yeah. Fucking daddy issues. You kids are lucky your old man is around to keep you on the right track. But Baron—the guy bailed on him. Vanished.

It really fucked him up."

Dick Senior gazed out the window, looked like he was chewing over it for a minute. The tender fucking memory or whatever. "I've got a bad feeling about this Peter asshole. You know Templeton bailed him out of jail once already back in England? He *sold his Afro* to do it. Like cut his hair off and *sold* it like something out of a Charles Dickens novel. The cunt had beaten some guy nearly to death, over a chick, supposedly. I hope Barry doesn't get himself fucking murdered."

Both boys were silent then. What was there to say? Richard Charles didn't know anything about this guy Peter—or Baron Templeton, for that matter. Not really.

"Maybe you should say something to him," Zach said. Dick took a drag of his cigarette, stubbed it out in the gum-filled ashtray. Slammed on his horn as a taxi braked in front of them.

"He'd never listen to me. Maybe if that pansy Ed did . . ."

"You know Ed Hammond too?" Zach asked, his eyes big. Dick laughed wryly.

"Yeah I know all of those assholes."

But it seemed like Dad wasn't going to share the wealth with his youngest son, whatever that wealth was. He said nothing, just stared out the window. Finally, Dick Senior glanced at Zach.

"Did your mom know you came down here, anyway?"

Zach's cheeks turned bright bloody pink. He didn't answer. Dick Senior sighed.

"What am I saying? Of course she doesn't. You kids are teenagers now. I fucking forget."

It shouldn't have hurt to hear that, but it did. How little his dad thought about them. He probably went years without them crossing his mind. Richard Charles glanced out the window, wanting to be anywhere else then that smoky Oldsmobile, with the ceiling coming down in billowy patches and cigarette burns on the plastic upholstery.

"Why'd you want to meet him, anyway?" his dad finally asked. Richard Charles glanced at Zach, trying to will him with his psychic mind beams not to tell the truth. It was all too ridiculous, too babyish, too fucking *gay*.

But Zach. Stupid little Zach. Kind of laughed, half-laughed, sheepish.

"It was a bet with this girl we know," he said. "She said that Templeton's—get this, she said that Templeton's a fucking *queer*."

There was a silence in the Oldsmobile. Thicker than the cigarette smoke.

"Ridiculous, right?" Zach chirped up, too fucking eager to fill every beat.

Dick snorted again, hard. But his voice was low as parking lot gravel when he answered.

"Fucking ridiculous," he muttered. Agreeing enough to satisfy sweet little Zach. But he glanced at Richard Charles, and Richard Charles knew what was being said there.

Shut up, his dad was saying with his eyes, *Keep this a fucking secret. From him. From everybody.*

Well, whatever. Richard Charles slumped low in his seat. Who was he going to fucking tell, anyway?

If Little Zachy had hoped for even a second that they'd go back to his dad's apartment in Queens and have an actual freaking Day with Daddy, he was sadly mistaken. Instead, Dick Senior dropped them off outside of Grand Central, ignoring the cars that leaned on their horns behind him.

"I don't have any cash for your tickets," his dad said. Of course he didn't. Just that wrinkly check, and his own greasy paws weren't gonna let it go. "Can you kids cover it?"

"Yeah," Richard Charles said dully. "'sfine."

"Good," said Dick. "Now, don't tell your mom you saw me. I don't need her hounding after me for child support a-fucking-gain."

Zach was looking at Richard Charles, hurt in his eyes, but Richard Charles didn't look back at him. No use looking like a weak-ass little girl in front of the old man.

"Yeah," Richard Charles said.

"See ya, kids," Dick Senior said. Richard Charles started toward the building before his dad even drove off. Zach cried out to him—*Hey!*

Wait!—in a whiny little voice but Richard Charles just kept walking, long strides that made him feel like a man. Like he didn't care. Fine fine fine it was fine. He went inside, past piss-scented homeless assholes and terrible fucking buskers and bought them a pair of return tickets with the money he himself had earned, and headed for the train. Inside, Zach sat down next to him. Looking at him, like he was waiting for comfort, or some kind of fucking story.

Richard Charles closed his eyes. Pretended to go to sleep. Until he actually freaking did.

* * *

Woke up in a better mood, just as they were passing the decrepit castle on the polluted old Hudson. His brother was sitting there, arms crossed over his chest, looking sad and dopey. And Richard Charles felt bad about it, okay? He knew what it was like to see the old man and be let down a-freakin-*gain*. Okay so maybe Richard Charles had learned to be a little hard about it, outwardly, but it didn't mean it didn't hurt.

"Hey," he said, elbowing Zachy. When Zachy didn't answer right away he said it sharper, elbowed him harder. *"Hey."*

"Ow!" Zach said. "What?"

Richard Charles, grinning, pulled something out of the rotting lining of his shearling coat. A notepad. He carried it everywhere lately. Jotting shit down whenever he could. During class or whatever.

"I wanna show you something I've been working on."

He paged through until he found it. Passed it to his little bro. Little bro, dutifully, looked.

"Poetry?" he asked, arching an eyebrow. Richard Charles snorted. Heard his father in the slobbery sound. Hated it. Hated himself.

"It's a fucking *song*."

"What for?" Zach asked, frowning.

"For the *band*, man," Richard Charles said. "The Dervishes." Zach wasn't saying anything. Was staring at the jotted lyrics, the chord changes Richard

Charles had dashed off without really thinking anything of it.

"Well," Richard Charles added, and felt himself fucking heat up. A teeny tiny bit. To admit it. "For Shay, too."

Zach glanced at him, sharply, like a sharp-edged knife. "What?"

"Shay. What? You didn't know I'm fucking in love with her?"

More staring. Stupid little Zach. "I thought you were in love with Jennifer."

"Jennifer's an idiot," Richard Charles said, putting his notebook away. "I only got with her because she's Shay's friend and she puts out. I figure she could be, you know, a stepping stone. A ladder. Whatever you wanna call it."

"To Shay?" Zach asked. God, the fucking *idiot*.

"Yeah," Richard Charles said. "To *Shay*." Zach, still staring at him.

"*What?*" Richard Charles said.

"She doesn't like you," Zach said, shaking his head. Oh fuck, a jealous little bitch. Well, that wasn't his problem. Once Shay heard Richard Charles' song—which was good, which was really freaking *good*—she'd fall for him for sure.

It's not like *Zach* knew how to write a fucking song. He could barely even play guitar.

"Whatever," Richard Charles said, smirking out the window. "You'll fucking see."

Zach didn't say anything. The train *chugga chugga*'d it's way all the frigging way upstate.

45 – 1958

flew

46 – 1997

Outside the recording studio in Oneonta, New York, Sid Edelman gave Richard Charles Ashby Junior a hearty handshake. Sid had been perfecting his since he was six years old, when he'd gone with his dad to sell their old car, their mom trailing in hers behind. They'd met this greasy little man at the Park & Ride on the side of the Thruway. Sid, supposedly a little girl then, though everyone always correctly thought he was a boy in his hand-me-down jeans and hair shoved up under a cap, leaned his weight against their old Mercury Bobcat, his kitten, to which he was unfortunately preternaturally attached. He watched the men circle each other, negotiating—and then finally shake on it. His dad's wrist was lax. He barely squeezed. Not the other guy.

"Easy, bud," his dad had joshed, shaking the pins and needles out of his fingers, "You're gonna take off a finger or two."

But it hadn't really been a complaint, because his dad had accepted the man's offer—five hundred off the listing price and the cost of the new registration, to boot. In the car ride home—Mom driving her boring old station wagon, Sid in the way back, pretending not to listen—his dad said how it had been a fine price. Even though it was two hundred lower than he'd told Sid he wanted to take on the ride over. He'd accepted it. And seemed almost *happy* about it.

That's when Sid figured out the value of a firm handshake.

He softened his, actually, when he shook Dick Ashby's hand, because there seemed to be something more fragile about the guy than he'd initially detected. Sure, he was rough around the edges. But Sid knew what it was like to build armor for yourself. And, *fuck*, the man was an *artist*. It's not everyone who could coax that kind of music out of a performer, especially one as high strung and nervous as Cymbeline. He couldn't help but feel like he'd learned something, actually, from watching him.

"Thanks, man," Sid was saying—and that's when Dick pulled him in for a *hug*. Sid felt a flare of panic, wondering if this was meant to be a come-on, feeling himself shrink, as he often did, from the possible contact between their two chests.

But he needn't have worried, because Dick just thumped him across the back. As—as a brother might, maybe. He'd *seen* those kinds of hugs, between his father and his brother, between guys at the other side of camp, but never experienced one.

"Yeah, no problem, man," Dick said, and as he slid away from the embrace, he slid the burned CD into Sid's hand. *Cymbeline – Demo*, it said on it, in green sharpie pen, in Dick's messy handwriting. "Shoot me an email when it's all done, let me know what happens with that. She's a special lady."

Sid glanced over to where Cymbeline sat in the waiting taxi, her knees pushed together, her unruly hair tucked behind her ear. She noticed the two men looking at her, and self-consciously glanced up, giving them an uncertain smile through the open door.

"I know she is," Sid said.

***

They got back to camp just after dinnertime, almost twenty-four hours after they left. Were it any other summer, Sid would have worried. To miss an entire day's activities would have meant almost definitely that they would be sacked. He'd seen it before, with a counselor when he was ten. A favorite counselor, actually. A counselor with shaggy hair and a killer sense of humor, a counselor whose camp name had been Dan. Later, Sid had wondered what had happened to her and if—maybe—Dan had been a creature out of step like *he* was out of step. But it wasn't like anyone was going to give him Dan's phone number or anything, wasn't like there was any way to find her, way back then when Sid was nine. Dan had just vanished into the ether like something out of a dream, leaving Sid lonely and aching in his absence. It hadn't been love, not then. Only a kind of kinship. Later, when it came time for Sid to pick his own camp name, he'd picked a boy's name. In honor of Dan, he told himself—friends absent but hopefully not dead.

Though in truth, he knew, sort of knew, that he just liked the name Sid. It thrilled him when he'd heard it in the record shop even though he didn't even like the Sex Pistols. Now, when someone said it, the sound made him stand straighter, feel more *himself* than he normally did.

The two of them walked through the parking lot, heading out toward the distant pavilion in front of the dining hall, swarmed at this hour with mosquitoes, where some of the girls were playing an enormous game of freeze tag.

"Should we go straight to Lonnie?" Cymbeline asked, "And face the music?"

"Fuck Lonnie," Sid said sharply, then he looked over to Cymbeline, his smile ragged. "Let him come find us. I'm going to enjoy these last few hours."

"But wait," Cymbeline said, tugging on Sid's hand. Sid stopped in the parking lot. Looked at her. Waited.

She was traced in the light of the golden sunset, her unwashed hair a mane, her freckles looking faded against her tanned skin. She was beautiful. Of course she was. Her tits, ripe, beneath her dress. The dimples on her knees. Sid had seen that right away, how he *wanted* her, to plow into her, to make her cry out in endless pleasure. But.

What he hadn't known, hadn't expected, was how brilliant she was beneath that outer layer of lovely, nervous skin. At first, she'd seemed like a pretty bauble, something to possess. He hadn't realized how she was a locked door, and that, once he managed to pick her, another kingdom would lie waiting on the other side.

She was looking at him, wrinkling her nose.

"Cymbeline," he said, taking her hands. "What is it, baby?"

She laughed a little. "I just—are we *really* doing this? I don't have money for an apartment in the city."

"Don't worry," he said. "My dad'll loan it to us. I'll play your music for him. He'll love you. You don't have to worry, Cymbeline. We're in this together."

Her nose wrinkled even more. "And then what?"

Sid stopped. He looked around, to the mountains all full of greeny gold light, to the children, playing in the distance. To the girl. His girl. Standing there before him.

"Well," he said. "I always thought that one day, if I were rich, I'd buy a place here. One of those fancy mid-century places. Up in the mountains, looking down on all the silly little kids and their dumb little games. A place that was just mine, where no one could tell me I didn't belong. But . . ."

He hesitated, but there was no real hesitation there. It was mostly a tease.

"But what?" Cymbeline asked, looking so sweet that he could have kissed her, right there and then.

"But I think it would be better if I could share that place with you," he said. She grinned. Smitten, utterly smitten. By little ol' him. He tugged at her hand again.

"C'mon, Cymbeline," he said, leading her through the parking lot. "It's our last night on earth."

He took off then toward the pavilion, great boyish strides, full of mischief and wonder. Cymbeline trailed after him, lugging her heavy guitar case, laughing. He could feel her watch as he dove into the children's game, leaping out of their grasp, sticking his tongue out, taunting them. He could feel her watching as he played for the last time, leaving his former self behind him, in the tawny light of dying August.

O^{pen.}

48 – 2017

Matthew felt like he existed somewhere outside his body as Naomi set her guitar aside and climbed on top of him. Her hands—long, lithe, callused (he saw now, though he hadn't noticed it before) touched his face, his neck. Hungry, searching. Her mouth met his again, and that's when he remembered that he, too, existed. Put his hands on the small of her back, slipping them inside her sweater, feeling the heat of her skin, her smoothness. She wasn't wearing a bra. Her tits were small, the nipples erect against his palms, and she kissed him and she kissed him, and he felt her, and let his body melt into hers, sharp meeting soft, angles meeting curves.

Matthew had fucked and been fucked plenty by plenty of girls, but this felt different, in the growing afternoon stillness in the quiet house in the middle of nowhere, as though the whole world were holding its breath. Of course he *wanted* it. He'd felt determined to have her from the moment he'd seen her. But now, it felt as if there were no having. Only touching, mutual, shared, and the universe sharing in that touching, wrapping its thick hands around both of them, pressing them together. As if it were beautiful. As if it were right.

She peeled off her sweater. Sat looking at him for a moment, a certain hardness in her eyes still, as if she were waiting for him to say something, to lob some insult or criticism. There was none to be lobbed. He leaned forward, tasting her throat, her breasts, her belly. He could feel how she was hesitant, distracted, too—outside herself. He pulled away. Looked at her, letting the corner of his mouth lift, just a little.

"It's only me," he said. She rolled her eyes at him. But kissed him, anyway, and lifted off his t-shirt, so that they could touch, body to body, heart to heart.

She was angular and dusky brown. He was soft and freckled, the hair over his chest ruddy and spare. And yet, when he kissed her, and he closed his eyes, he couldn't tell where she began and he ended. His pleasure was mounting, pressing at her through the soft fabric of her leggings, and her body was warm and open to her, and they were shoving themselves up against each other right through their clothes like a couple of teenagers, and he could feel how she was returned to her body then by the pleasure of it, casting her head to the side, moaning low, like a song, a song, and one he couldn't improve on at all if he tried.

Then, suddenly, cold hit him. She peeled herself away from him. And his mouth opened, just a little, in silent disappointment and lust, painfully aching. But then she smirked, and offered him her hand.

"It's only me, Matt," she said. He laughed a little, gruffly. Then he took her hand, and followed her up the stairs.

* * *

Sitting in the nest of that unwashed down, he watched her undress. He watched her take those long, nimble fingers, and unbutton his jeans, and peel them off him, slowly, carefully, like he was some kind of ripe fruit. She kissed a line down his chest. He leaned back, letting her, feeling her mouth wet his belly, his hips, and his back arched as he anticipated the place where her mouth would fall. Wanting it. Aching for it, like a teenage boy, and momentarily afraid—wondering if she would tease him.

But that wasn't Naomi. Before he knew it, her mouth enveloped him, settling deep around him, and he let his hands fall against the nape of her neck. For a moment, she was still, and he was still, and he could feel how quickly it would end if they continued this way—if either one made a single movement. And so, fighting nearly every one of his body's impulses, he touched her ears, the back of her neck, gently, and drew her away from him.

379

In the dim light of the room—curtains drawn, shadows in every corner—he saw how she frowned. Worried, maybe, that something was wrong. That she'd offended him.

So he bent down and kissed her. A long, deathless kiss. Touching the backs of her arms, the tops of her thighs. Not to grip her, to hold her, to keep her. But with the backs of his fingers. Just feeling. Simply wanting to touch.

"You, first," he said gently. She looked at him, squinting, the top of her nose wrinkled. And she could have rolled her eyes, but she didn't. Instead she just let out a sigh, as if resigned, and let her body fall back onto the pillow. Still for a moment, her arms over her face, like she was embarrassed, as he began to kiss her. Her throat. Her collarbones. A line down the center of her chest, between her breasts, his lips on her naval, and lower. Meanwhile, her fingers wrapped around his cock and stroked gently, slowly, as he moved lower, and buried his face in her warm, slick bush.

It worked how music worked for them, he thought, him reading her, where she needed him, needed *more*, and him pressing deeper there, and when he drew away her hips rose to meet his mouth again, so he waited a beat, a long beat, and then plunged in deeper. The sound she let out was strangled, gasped. He could have paused then, but he didn't. Her body began to shudder. She pulled at his cock, more instinct than intent, and, with her other hand, almost painfully at his hair. He took her right to the edge, then paused to kiss her sweet, musky thighs. Her breath was hitched. Jagged. Waiting.

It occurred to him for the first time how much sex—how much music—how much all of life was like this. A series of patterns. But not flat, repetitious. He realized how he and Naomi were doing the same thing now, together—waiting for the build and then the dispersal. His favorite moment in sex was always this moment. When it was inevitable. The same way an A minor was inevitable in the key of G. You could disrupt that pattern, of course. Unsettle someone. Make them queasy. Unravel them. Create little tender wounds, so that the conclusion, the return to the G, would be that much more earned. But right now he had no impulse to art, to wounding. He would be simple, kind. Build a simple song. It would be a comfort. Like coming home.

She stroked his soft belly—usually he hated to be touched there, like that. But it didn't matter to him now. He was right at the edge of her, both of them moist and trembling. She said, in a soft voice, "I'm not on anything. You won't—"

He leaned down and kissed her. "Promise," he said, his voice low and warm and as they kissed he felt her open to him, felt himself inside her, so slick that it happened almost without *thinking*, without knowing, her fingers down there, moving in circles, and him moving in circles inside her, and he cast his head to the side as his movement became more frenetic, more animistic. Her body was tightening around him, and she began to twitch, and he was close, too, so he drew out and let himself spill over her belly, as she came, too, her body trembling just below. Both of their eyes closed. Going somewhere else, together.

After a moment, still, the pleasure still a crescendo inside of him, he leaned down and kissed her, and was kissed back. And then kissed a line lower, kissed her clean. She wove her fingers in his hair, less ferociously now, and he let his head rest on her skinny belly, heard her heart beating inside, heard his own heart, inside her ears. The two of them beating out together. Another kind of chord.

* * *

He could have slept. Normally would have, at his age, after fucking. Wanted to, in a way, with Naomi's body cradled against his, the two of them not speaking and not needing to speak—only holding each other.

But it wasn't long before she started moving against him again. Wasn't long before his arms, feeling strong against her skinniness, clutched her tighter to him, and he was hard again, and she was open to him again—trembling, wanting, and him hard and wanting, too.

The second time, she got on top. Less urgency, desperation. But no less wanting. Taking it slow. Enjoying each other. If there even was an "each" or an "other." So much of his life had been solitude. Individuation. He wondered if she had felt this way too. And then he didn't have long to wonder, really, because looking at her, he saw, for the first time, how her guard was down. She was present in the moment with him. The same way it worked when they made music together, their eyes locked. But if the chords rang out and they were still looking, she would look away, embarrassed. Now, though, there was no self-consciousness. Only the two of them. Truly wed.

The first time, he was on top. The second time, she was. The third, they only touched one another. He didn't come that time; she came two or three times. It didn't matter. He loved watching her. The two of them, naked in every way, with all the scars and stretchmarks and stray hairs of approaching middle age, and none of it mattering. Him enjoying her. Her enjoying him.

* * *

Eventually, thin sleep, and then waking. An hour or two later, or maybe more, or maybe less, waking with her smell around him, her arms around him.

"You're awake," she said softly, and kissed him. He kissed her back. Then grinned a jagged grin. Couldn't help but to gloat.

"I thought you mostly sleep with women," he said. She pinched him a little, in his tender ribs, with her long, sharp nails.

"Matt," she said wearily, "Bisexuals exist."

Sticky, sleepy kisses, punctuated by sticky, sleepy laughter. He felt his belly tighten again, his cock stir between them. He wasn't as young as he used to be. Twice in the span of an afternoon was rare these days, much less four times, five. But for her . . . there was a word in his mind, one he couldn't yet touch. What was it? He felt like he'd forgotten, though he knew it was there. He kissed her more deeply. But then she drew away.

"I have something that I think might work after we do the kiddie's song," she said. He rolled his eyes toward the dark ceiling, laughing wryly.

"Can't you set aside work for a minute?" he asked, though he *wanted* to hear her suggestion, of course. The music was almost as good as the fucking. Or maybe they were one and the same.

But when she answered, it was in a voice that was smaller and more timid than he expected. "But you're leaving tomorrow, right? We don't have much time. We have to finish the album. Unless you want to stay. I'm sure the Edelmans won't mind . . ."

She trailed off. He could feel the wave in his belly still, at the way her body was pressed up close to his. He could feel that word rattling round the back of his brain. He could feel—well, a fantasy. Coming up to see her on weekends. Seeing her apartment, which was probably a shithole, inviting her to the city, dinners with the Edelmans, pitching the album, recording with her, performing with her. Sleeping with her. Making her breakfast, which she'd eat in ungracious abandon, and somehow he'd never mind. A whole future rolling out in front of them. It felt sweet inside him, everything he could imagine. More days with Naomi. More nights. More years.

And if she were nobody, just another fuck buddy, then maybe he would have promised her all of that without thinking of the repercussions, about the world outside these walls. About Kara. About the baby. But she was waiting for an answer, and he didn't want to lie to her. Couldn't.

"I need to go home this weekend," he said, "I'll need to—it's. It's complicated."

"Oh," she said, her voice flattening. "The wife."

Matthew winced. "No, no, we're not married. Kara—it's not Kara. She's not the problem. For this, I can dump her in a heartbeat." Under the covers, his hands found hers, and their fingers interlaced, and she squeezed his hand back. He could hear, as he was saying it, as he was *meaning* it, what a tired cliché it was. You know, *oh, of course I'll leave my girlfriend for you.* That old tired verse. Even if he *meant* it.

"But?" Naomi said sharply. Their hands still clutched, palm-to-palm.

"But," he said slowly, carefully, "She's pregnant. We're pregnant. We're due in May. We—"

"Oh," she said. She drew her fingers away from his. Her heard the door slamming shut, inside her.

"Naomi," he said. "This doesn't mean—" She turned away from him in the heavy covers, her back to his face.

"Of course it doesn't, Matthew," she said. She suddenly sounded very, very tired. He suddenly felt it, too. "It's fine. Congratulations."

"Thank you?" he said, his voice rising weakly at the end of it. She didn't answer that, only wadded up a pillow and stuffed it between the crook of her arm and her head. She didn't leave, he told himself. She was still *here*.

"I'm beat," she told him. "Let's get some sleep."

"Okay," he agreed. Turning away from her. They were, still, irrevocably, perhaps, like one creature then, joined in the center, even as they turned away from each other. Ignoring—willfully, painfully—how they should have been true, and truly joined.

He closed his eyes, willing himself to ignore the way his heart twisted. And it was only as he finally, impossibly drifted off toward sleep that he remembered the word that he was trying to recall.

It was love, of course, he said to himself, as his consciousness turned to nothing. Of course it was love. Matthew, you old idiot.

49 – 1958

In a flash, Baron fell away from Ed, the only lingering sign of their kiss a ruddiness around the other boy's pink, wet lips. As Baron scrambled back against the bed, his heart beat wildly. With the fear of animal—desperate, trapped, caught caught fuckin' caught—he looked at the open doorway.

And then sighed when he saw it was just old Uncle Fred standing in it.

The man, in his wrinkled suit, rumpled hat in hand, blushing. Was clear he'd seen it, what the boys were doing. But looked more embarrassed by it than anything else. Had it been Aunt Deedz, would have all been over. Baron would have been murdered. Dead. But no. *Not dead yet*, as Ed's pissed old father would have said. Uncle Fred, he could handle. Out of the corner of his eye, he saw Ed's fear at being caught, at being seen. Time to stamp out that fire, then. Baron stood.

"Oi, Freddie," Baron said, "Knock knock first, willya?"

He clapped his hand against Fred's arm like it was nothing that he'd seen two boys snogging. That he'd seen Baron snogging. Baron snogging Ed. *Treat it like it's nothing*, Baron thought, *An' it* will *be nothing*.

"Sorry, Barry," Uncle Fred squeaked out, and his eyes went to Ed, and there was more squeaking. "'Allo, 'ammy."

"'llo," Ed said, in a very low voice indeed, which made something in Baron's belly stir but he couldn't touch that feeling now. That feeling was beside the point.

"Baron," said Uncle Fred, "We're headin' over to yer Auntie Alberta's soon. The sisters have decided it's time to tell Elizabeth." He paused, drawing in a breath. "Ah, they want you to tell her. Since her Dad won't. I think it's only right, that you—"

"Yeah," Baron said flatly. "Fine."

Uncle Fred stared at him, trying to tell if Baron was pulling his leg. Baron gave no indication either way back. Wouldn't let any light in, not right now. His own position was too precarious. Time to be hard. A stone. Like Aunt Deedz might when challenged. Refuse to be soft. That's what he had learned from her.

It wasn't a bad lesson.

"Right," Uncle Fred said. "Well, I'll leave you boys to . . . get ready. We'll be leaving in ten, Barry. Ta-ra, Ed."

"Ta-ra," Ed said lowly, as Uncle Fred turned from the room, and closed the door behind him.

Both boys frozen, for a moment, listening for Fred's footsteps making their retreat on the stairwell.

When he was gone, Ed rose from his chair, put his hand into a fist, and slammed it, hard enough, into Baron's upper arm.

"Ow!" Baron howled. "What's that for?"

"*No one will know,* eh? *Straight as an arrow,* yeh?" Baron saw, then, the wild, panicked look in Ed's eyes. Saw what it meant to him, then. The depths of his promise. "He *saw* us, Baron. He saw!"

Baron lifted a hand, wrapped it around Ed's hand before he could swing and punch again. Said "Shhh" through his teeth, the way he said "shhh" when Deedz had him wrap old Doot in a towel to get his claws trimmed.

"Ed," he said. "Fred won't tell anyone. He knows about me. He's always known. He doesn't care. Promise. He won't tell. I won't tell, neither."

Ed, breathing hard, vibrating with anger. But the anger pulsing slowly, painfully back.

And then, absurd, irrational, bizarre. Ed launched himself forward, fixed his mouth, angrily, hard, against Baron's mouth. And pulled away just enough that his words fell right on Baron's lips. A second kiss—a second kind of kiss.

"They can't know. Ever."

"Ever," Baron agreed. He couldn't look into Ed's bright, angry eyes. Could only look down at the ground. It hurt too much, to look.

"Edmund," he said softly, "I need to go tell our kid about me bleeding dead mum, now. If you'll excuse me."

The look in Ed's eyes trembling, cracking. Melting away to nothing. Baron sensed how Ed could have held him then again, could have comforted him. But not right now. Now was not the time.

"Right, Barry," Ed said. He took a step back. Grabbed his sports coat. Draped it over his shoulders. Baron found his shoes, and stepped inside them.

"I think I'll skip practice today," Ed said, at last, like he'd been mulling over it for awhile. "But I've been thinking. The drummer. In the Tempests. A bloke named Charlie Peck. He's older, at least twenty, but—Christ, Baron. He's a stunner. You should hear him on the toms. Left handed, but he plays a right handed kit. It's like nothing you've ever heard."

At the door, Baron paused, looking up at Ed. Trying to read him. Mostly failing.

"We'll ring him," he said plainly. "See if he wants to be in a *real* band, one that's going places."

Their eyes met. Ed firmed his jaw. Nodded.

"Great minds," he said to Baron. Baron nodded back, then headed off, down the hall.

50 – 1977

By the time the train pulled into the Poughkeepsie Station, Zach knew what he had to do. It had been all laid out for him, after all, by Templeton—the God himself.

If you can't work for something greater than your own glory, then you might as well go write yourself some solo albums or something.

Templeton had made a choice once, Zach thought, as he followed his brother through the train station. It was nearly dusk; the shadows were growing longer. Their bicycles, when they reached them, had taken on sinister shapes. Templeton had made a choice to work *with* Hammond. And look how that had worked out for them. Living in a hotel room now, a dirty flipping hotel room, with stinky diapers and a nobody wife. While Hammond—alone now, right?—toured the world. Neither ever as famous as they'd been together, and while Zach couldn't help but think what they'd made together had been—well, fucking *awesome*—he knew they would never get out of the shadow of it, either.

The boys rode their bikes through the shadows, through the deepening winter night. Richard Charles seemed demonic, off his head. He was screaming Saffron lyrics as he rode. Swerving through traffic, ignoring the bus that nearly hit him, leaning on its horn. To Zach, the day had been a rousing success. A brush with greatness, a brush with fucking Daddy—and a song tucked into his pocket. His own song, and *good*, for Shay, like Shay was his to own, like Zach was nobody.

Well, they would see about that, soon enough, Zach thought. He stopped for a moment, watching Richard Charles duck and weave through the rush hour traffic. And then, with a sigh, he followed. Like he always had.

But not for much longer, he thought.

***

It took longer than he'd hoped. Once, they'd barely moved their lives in the same spheres *at all.* But now it felt like Richard Charles was some kind of shitty, zitty barnacle, hanging off of him—hanging around outside the middle school, pressuring Zach to skip. Dragging him back to the apartment to play music together, like playing music together even *mattered* to Zach. Which it didn't. Not anymore.

Shay had called him two, three times. Asking when they could practice together. Complaining about Richard Charles following her around at school. Richie hadn't played the song for her yet. Said he needed to practice more. Every time they got together, he made Zach strum while he crooned. And, fuck, the song was good. The song was getting better. It wouldn't be long now, and worse, the notebook was filling up with other music. Zach knew, with a sinking sensation, that it was just a matter of time. Shay didn't seem interested in either of them sexually. Not yet. She said she just wanted to play drums with Zach. Not a screw. She wasn't like that. But for some reason, he didn't trust that she'd stay so strong when she heard Richard Charles' music. Because when Zach played with him, and Richard Charles sang, so sweetly, so softly, Zach found himself softening too. Did he really have to do *it*—to throw his brother to the wolves? When he found himself doubting himself, late at night, he'd look at the pictures they'd pasted to the wall. Baron Templeton in his leather pants and cowboy boots in the early '60s. And he'd hear that Scouse accent ring out in his head, and it sounded almost like his father's voice, grumbling at him: *For Chrissake, Zachy, grow a pair.*

Finally the opportunity presented itself. Richard Charles skipped one too many classes, earned himself in-school suspension—and a week of after school detention, too. Their mom, more exhausted by this news than anything, asked Zachy if he could pick Marigold up from daycare that week, take her home, and take care of things until either she or Tim came home from work. The first two days, Zach was too scared to do anything. But on the third, with Marigold down for her nap, he finally went into their shared room, climbed under the bed, and took out Richard Charles' stash.

He sat with it at the kitchen table waiting. He had everything he needed now. The music and Shay, all lined up. Soon, they'd be his. And a bed to himself, and then no one would be able to stop him. The minutes passed slowly. Finally, at quarter after four, the door opened. Mom stepped inside.

"Zachy?" she called.

"In here, mom," he said, feeling his hands sweating against the kitchen table. She came into the kitchen, not noticing at first at the bags set out in front of him. Came over to him, kissed his head. And then looked up.

"What's this?" she asked.

"I think—" Zach began, making his voice sound sad and small, like a little boy's voice, like he was afraid, and truly, at what he'd found, "I think Richard Charles might be dealing *drugs*, mom. I think—I think he might be some kind of drug addict."

For a moment there was no answer. In the silence, he heard the door open again, and heavy, galumphing steps come through the apartment. Both he and his mother turned to see Richard Charles standing in the doorway to the kitchen, smirking, like he always did—not realizing that this time, *he* was the butt of the joke.

"Hey homos," he said, and his smile had not collapsed yet, though it would, soon, "What's up?"

* * *

Three weeks later, Richard Charles was shipped off to military school, and freedom, blessed freedom, stretched out in front of Zach.

It was a Tuesday when he first went to Shay's house. She lived on the outskirts of Poughkeepsie, far enough that it was a pain in the ass for him to bike over there with his guitar case slung over his back. It was a nice house. A *normal* house. White picket fence and fucking everything. There was a dusting of snow over everything, the first snowstorm of the season. December, now, but if winter were here, spring couldn't be far behind.

When he knocked on the door, she appeared, her hair still damp from a shower, dressed in a pair of low-slung jeans and a worn t-shirt. Looking soft, if a little fat for his tastes, and so fucking huggable. But he didn't hug her, not yet. It wasn't time. Yet.

She took him inside, making apologies for the mess of their living room, which was one of the cleanest rooms Zach had ever set a foot in, and they went down into her basement den, which had wood paneling, but had been soundproofed. Her drum kit was all laid out there, and she sat down, and looked at him, ready to play.

"So what do you have?" she asked him, leaning forward expectantly. He hadn't written the lyrics down in a notebook. He didn't need to. He'd practiced enough—first with Richard Charles, and then, in the weeks that followed, alone in the room that was now his, and his alone.

He played. Sang. And something shifted as he played, and she saw how she leaned in intently, the pupils of her eyes flooding them black. Her lips falling open. Stunned.

"I'm still working on it," he lied. "It's a little rough." He forced his lips up, sheepishly. That sheepishness was a lie, too.

"Okay," she said. "What's it called?"

"Oh," he said, and pretended to blush. "Shay's Song."

That was the beginning of it all.

51 – 1958

Sitting in Aunt Bert's sitting room, which was even fussier than Aunt Deedz's, Baron thought about how he would have very much then liked to peel off his own skin and collapse into a puddle, then and there, thank you. Fuck the floral pattern on the sofa. Fuck the oriental carpet, the ashtray. It was the bloody *keening* that was doing it—Bess holding both hands over her face and wailing on and on. Behind her, Aunt Bert tightened both hands around Bess's shoulders, not crying herself, probably squeezing too tight to *keep* from crying, herself, or maybe she was trying to will Bess to cut it out, but it wasn't working, because she just cried harder, louder. Baron looked at Aunt Bert, with his eyes, imploring, *Stop her. Make her stop.* Bert cleared her throat. In the doorway, Aunt Deedz watched, frozen, judging.

"Bess . . ." Bert began, and Bess turned to Rose and buried her face in the woman's black dress. Baron exhaled. At least the sound, now, was blotted out.

Terrible, he thought, to have to be clung to by a child like that. All sticky and snotty and freely feeling. No wonder the sisters had contemplated not telling her at all—no wonder Timo refused, too. Even Baron didn't want her clinging to him, wouldn't have known what to do with his hands, his arms.

(His Mum, he thought grimly. His Mum would have known what to do. His Mum would have been free and easy with her love, and maybe if she'd raised him, he would have felt free and easy too, would have let Bess crawl right into his lap and—fucking *kissed her tears* or something soppy like that.

But Baron's heart was hard. It was one thing, to snog Ed or to snog Sue or to tell Ed he loved him, even. That was—that was lust. You were *supposed* to love people you *screwed.* But this. This, he didn't know how to wrap his brain around. So he just watched. Frozen. As Deedz watched. Frozen. As even Bert, delicately patting Bess's hair, was apparently frozen inside, too. Saying nothing.)

Bess hiccuped. Brayed. In the corner of his eye, Baron saw Aunt Deedz flinch.

"Baron," she said sharply, and he was on his feet in a flash.

"Right," he said. "'scuse."

And then he *bowed*, he fucking *bowed*, to his fat fucking bawling little sister who was all tangled up in his aunt's pleats. Just because he didn't know what fucking else to do. His cheeks burning, he followed Aunt Deedz from the sitting room into the kitchen.

Uncle Fred was there at the table, playing solitaire, acting like he didn't exist. Aunt Deedz sighed, shaking two French fags out of a pack she kept in her coat packet. Handed one to Baron, then stood there, waiting for him to light it. He felt around for a lighter in his pocket, found it. Lit the ciggies for them both.

"Dreadful scene, Fred," she said aloud, though her eyes were more on Baron than they were on her husband. "That child. A mess. Didn't you think, Baron?"

Baron held the smoke in his lungs. Let it out slowly, across the kitchen, over his Uncle's head. His eyes were boring into Deedz's eyes. "A *foockin'* mess," he said. She winced.

"Language, Baron."

He ashed into the ashtray.

"Sorry," he lied. Felt full of anger and grief and something else, something he could not name. A dangerous emotion. Drunk. He felt drunk. Even though he'd had not a drop to drink that day. "I'll tell you one thing. I'm never fucking spawning. You'll never see me leaving some fat bonny baby a fucking orphan."

Deedz didn't scold him for his language this time. But she did roll her eyes. Her gaze, for a moment, went to Uncle Fred. She glanced at his cards, gestured to the matched suits he missed. Her hand touching Fred's shoulder carefully—pointedly. Like she meant to make a fucking point with it.

"No," she said thinly. "We wouldn't expect *you* to be a father, Baron. Fatherhood wouldn't *suit* you. It's just not in your nature, is it?"

Baron's eyes went big and wide. He took a hot drag of his ciggie, nostrils flaring, glaring at her. Did she *know*? Had Fred *told* her? And did Baron even fucking care?

"Wot you mean by that?" he asked, angry, but still not sure. Whether she knew. Whether he cared.

"Deidre . . ." Fred said softly, in a voice that was almost inaudible. She laughed. High. Giddy. Fake.

"Oh, it's just a *joke*, child. Though I can't imagine what sort of father you would make. Why, you don't know the first thing about fatherhood. Not as if you ever had a father yourself."

Baron clenched his jaw, shook his head, slowly, slowly. His cigarette was still half-unsmoked. But he stamped it out.

"Ta-ra," he said gruffly. Deidre clucked her tongue.

"Baron, really . . ." she said, as he went out Aunt Bert's kitchen door and into the garden. As it slammed behind him, he heard Uncle Fred saying something.

"Deidre, you didn't have to—"

But before he could hear how his rejoinder ended, Baron hopped the garden fence, and was gone.

52 – 2000

The dark was never truly dark in New York City. In their little apartment in Hell's Kitchen, the restaurant lights from the watering hole below always gave their bedroom a blue cast even on the deepest, most moonless nights. Neither of them could complain of course. It had been a triumph when they'd found this place, and found they could afford to buy it—they'd basked in that sudden glow of adulthood, which they were feeling more and more now, since the album had come out and all the success with it.

There had been a price. Of course there had—and not just mortgage payments. No, it had been mostly Cymbeline's price. Mostly paid with her anxiety. The pills she had to take to get up there on stage to sing or perform or accept an award. But once she swallowed them down, she'd almost forget that edge she felt, instead letting an easy good humor slide into its place. The animal tamed, she could joke or dance or stop to pose on the red carpet, giving her wild hair a shake.

It was the girls she liked best. The ones who approached her in the street, thirteen and fourteen years old, asking for an autograph on a copy of *Bust* or *Jane*, asking for an autograph on their own arm, an autograph on a train ticket they'd found in their pockets. At those moments, Sid would step back, would let her take over, lapping up their praise of her. They told her how they'd picked up a guitar just because of her.

"You're an inspiration," Sid would point out after. "A triumph." She glowed beside him, feeling it. Loving it. In that moment, at least.

During concerts, she tried to remember. She told herself that it was *different* now then it once was, that these girls didn't want her in exactly the same way the girls had a lifetime ago, that she was a promise to them, an *inspiration*. But still, if she let herself look too long, she'd see their mouths, their shining teeth, and if the pills wore low by the end of the opening act the fear would start creeping back. Her hands would shake. Her keyboardist would give Sid, backstage, a secret signal, and a glass of whiskey and another pill would appear from nowhere to quiet the terror that was always there, growing inside.

She felt it now, waking in the middle of a bright, noisy night to an empty king bed and a screeching headache. The fear. They were going to get her. To murder her. Here, in her lonely apartment. Or else—or else—someone was coming. She closed her eyes, saw a glint of moonlight on a blade's edge, willed the thought away. No, no, it was all wrong. There was no moon tonight. But there was something she was supposed to be doing. Here, now, in the city. She had come back for this and—and she was failing. She pulled herself out of bed, her feet making contact with the wood floors, sticky in the August heat. The window units never seemed to do anything at all. Hot. It was too hot. She opened the bedroom door and stood there, staring down the hallway, which seemed to expand and contract like a tesseract, unfolding and then collapsing in on itself. A tunnel from here to there.

She was so *thirsty* as she walked down the hallway. It was like she'd never ever had a drop to drink before. She walked down the hall to the kitchen, ran the tap until the water was cold, filled up one of the Crate & Barrel glasses she and Sid had gotten as a wedding gift from some cousin of his. Drank and drank and drank.

She heard something outside. Out past the open window, on the fire escape. Swallowing, wiping her mouth, she put the glass down in the sink and looked. There was a boy standing there, his shirtless body looking like blue marble in the moonless night. His hair was disheveled, tousled by the wind. And Cymbeline thought, as if it were the world's most rational thought: *Ed! I must tell Ed what's gone wrong.*

She leaned her head out the window, tasting the sticky August air, the garbage in the dumpsters below.

"Oh, you're up," the boy was saying, but her words poured out before the boy could even register his surprise at the sight of her. There was too much to tell him. She had too much to say.

"Ed," she said, "Ed, it's the *baby*. I've forgotten all about the *baby*. She's been waitin' for me, Ed, all this time, and I—I just fucked it all up, Ed. Went and got myself murdered and—and you've got to help me fix it. Please!"

She reached out and tugged at the hem of the boy's blue jeans and that's when he turned, fully, his face twisted, and for a moment she saw two faces, two boys. One sweet and pale—the other sweet and decidedly less pale. One, his chest scarred and skinny. The other, a little plump, who had never worn any scars at all. Both schemers, naturally. She'd always loved a schemer, hadn't she? But then she blinked through tears, and the one was gone, and it was only Sid, her Sid. Her manager. Her husband. Crouching low on the fire escape, putting out the clove cigarette he wasn't allowed to smoke in the apartment, then clutching her face in both his hands.

"Hey, hey, Cymbeline," he was saying, kissing her lips, her tears. "Hey, baby, what are you *talking* about?"

She was shaking. The world seemed to sway above and below her. Her ears rang out, playing that sharp dial-tone that it always seemed to play at times like these. When her headache was killing her. When she was trying to live in two different worlds at once.

"I—don't know. I don't know. I think something's wrong, Sid. I think something is really wrong."

He kissed her one last time. Warm and deep and full. "Okay," he said calmly. "It's okay. We'll go to the emergency room, okay?"

She nodded, relieved a little to have him here. To solve the problem. To make it all go away.

To not have to carry it alone anymore, the way she had been for all these years.

"Okay, Ed," she said, and tried to tell her hands to stop shaking as Sid climbed back into their apartment, and went to get his coat and keys.

53 – 1958

Finally, finally, bright, true spring. Baron sat on his front steps, coat on the stone beside him, tuning up his guitar. The whole world smelled like an explosion of pollen and dirt and sex and though it had been a typical week of Liddypool rain and clouds, the sky had cracked open for a moment, and he'd be damned if he wasn't gonna take advantage. Under the sunlight, he strummed out the chords to the Crickets' "Dearest." Had been planning, for awhile, to get it down perfect and then to play it for Ed. It was almost there. Not quite, yet. But closer than he'd ever been. Funny, how a few months ago he wouldn't have been able to really tell the difference between an A and a D. But here they were: the differences, and he could see them, feel them, *taste* them.

"You're a quick study," Ed had said at the last practice, the corner of his mouth snaking up and Baron had been glad that his blushes were invisible since Liam was there, and he had socked Ed in the arm and said something stupid and nonsensical back to cover up for it—his sheepishness.

Yeh, well I'll study you, or someaught like that.

He was learning though, and quick, to be sure. Not only guitar, but how to hide it. Now he could tuck his feelings into other feelings, creating plausible deniability, always. Soon, he would play Ed a song. Singing "I love you," right there, in front of Liam, even. And no one would be any the wiser. Even if *they* knew, the two of them, what it really meant.

"I love you," he sang now on the front steps, low, hesitant, "I love you."

"Do you now?"

Baron's head snapped up at the hard, familiar voice. Dick Ashby, standing at the gate like he'd been waiting there for ages. Baron narrowed his eyes.

"Richard," he said, seething. Dick let out a snort.

"*Baron*," he shot back. "Still wasting your time with that queer guitar, I see."

"Did your mum make you buy her a new washboard?" Baron asked, glowering. Once it would have been banter, a tease. Not anymore. He looked at Dick, trying to understand what had ever appealed to him about the other boy. How he had ever found him funny, or clever, or sharp. Now, it was abundantly apparent that he was none of those things. A schemer, maybe, but not even a very good one.

Certainly, he was no *Ed*.

"She did," Dick said, squaring shoulders. "You owe me two quid for that."

"Sod off," Baron said, rolling his eyes. Looking down at his fingers on the strings. A D E. It wasn't hard, but he wanted to play the chords barred, and his fingers still didn't feel nimble enough for it. He wished, not for the first time, that the fretboard was just a little *smaller*.

"I won't," said Dick. "You'll owe me a lot more than that, too, Templeton, when this is all over."

"When *what's* all over, Dickard?" Baron said, not even looking at him now. A. D. E. Simple. The simplest song, really, once you let yourself feel it.

"Oh, you know," said Dick. "The 'band.' The Bartlebys."

"We're the Saffron Dervishes now," Baron said. "Found out the Bartlebys is a band out in Toxteth."

"The Saffron *Dervishes*?" Dick practically squealed. "That's a queer name, innit?"

Baron shrugged. "Queer enough," he said. It had been Ed's idea, and he hadn't really given it a second thought. Ed's ideas, he'd found, were usually good ones.

"Well," Ashby went on, "I think you Fairy Dervishes are going to be making hand over fist soon, and I'll expect you to give me some of it."

"Sod off," Baron said a second time, but more weakly this time. His chords faded. He looked up to Dick, who was standing there, eyes narrowed, staring.

"You know you owe me, Barry," Dick said. "Wouldn't be anybody without me. Wouldn't even be funny."

Baron stared for a moment longer. But didn't answer. He could see something coming from down the street. Two bicycles. Two boys on two bicycles. Two boys with two guitars on two bicycles. And one of them beautiful, to boot.

"Oi," Ed called. "What's this?"

He and Liam came to stop by the front garden. Flanking Dick on their bicycles on either side. And it's funny, Baron thought, because Ed was soft and Liam was shitty. But they were *his* boys. *His* band. They'd beat Dick to a pulp for him, if he wanted it.

But he didn't. Want it, that is. Baron stood up, carrying his guitar by the neck, and went to the gate.

"Dickie dearest is just collecting some money I owe him," Baron said, reaching in his pocket and pulling out the two quid to give him. "For breaking his mummy's washboard."

Liam sniggered at that. Dick pinkened. But took the money, anyway.

"You watch yourself, Waller," Dick said, stuffing his money down into his pocket. Liam wrinkled up his nose, repeating Dick's words in a wheedling tone. For a moment, Dick stared at him. Contemplating socking him, Baron could see.

"Well," Ed said, too loud. "We're off to practice, mate. See you around."

Dick's cheeks turning all ruddy. He locked eyes with Baron, like he meant to say something more. But all he managed was "Ta!" before he took off down the street.

"Give our regards to mummy," Waller called, then sniggered again. Ed, shaking his head, sniggered too. Even Baron laughed at little.

"Christ," he said. "I hate that fucker." Then he looked at the boys. His boys.

"Let me get my coat and my fiddle case," he said. "And we'll be off."

Ed and Liam, both, grinned, nodded. And stood there, waiting. Waiting for him.

<h1 style="text-align:center">54 – 2017</h1>

Matthew knew before waking that Naomi would be gone. The bed beside him had gone cold in her absence. He kept his eyes closed a moment longer, pretending to cling to his own ignorance. Until he just couldn't, not anymore. Kicked the sheets aside. Sat straight. Held his head in his hands.

"Hello?" he called out, but only silence answered him, of course.

Anger and grief seared through him, but only for a moment. He had never been the type of rock star to wreck hotel rooms or destroy guitars. His father, who had once been part of the working classes, had taught him to be better than that, for one thing. *Make a mess,* he said, *and someone else will eventually have to clean it up.* But for another thing, there was no one really to be mad at right now—except perhaps himself. And what other option did he have? He couldn't have lied. Not to her, and not about that.

He rose. Showered. Dressed again. Made his own bed. Put his suitcase on top of it, and began to pack. No use in staying here now another night, he thought. Nothing for him here. No music. No light. He felt his heart squeeze in his chest, tried to will that thought away. He'd have to call the driver, see if he could pick up Matthew early. He needed to get out of here. Needed to go. Needed to forget.

He hefted the suitcase down the steps, then stood there, watching the orange light set over the lake. He felt like a shadow. Hollow. Alone. It was only the sound of his phone, buzzing on the counter, that drew him out of his reverie. He went over to it and looked at the screen for the first time in more than twelve hours. And saw that he had four missed calls and thirty-seven missed texts. All from Kara.

Kara

Matthew?

Kara

I haven't felt the baby moving all day . . .

Kara

Where ARE you? The midwife said to drink some orange juice but it didn't work. Pearl and I are going to the hospital.

Kara

Matthew???

Kara

Matthew, it's okay. They did a scan. It's okay.

Kara

SHE'S okay. Matthew, it's a girl. :)

He clutched the phone between his hands, which shook, now. A girl. A daughter. A girl. His stomach tossed and turned like a ship on the ocean. He could almost see her then, the little girl she would someday be. Kara's skinny legs. His eyes and lips and humor. Tugging on his hand. Needing him. A heavy weight. A scary weight. And real. *Real.*

Sorry, my phone was dead, he typed in haste. *I'm coming home early. I'll see you in a few hours.*

He sent it. And then added, *A girl!!! :)*

Kara sent a stream of emojis back. Matthew called the driver, who said he'd be there in an hour, and then he stared out the enormous window, stunned, watching the sun set.

* * *

He gathered up his guitar, his suitcase, set them beside the front door. Then he went over to those boxes that Naomi had abandoned there. Baron Templeton's journals and letters.

He sat down on the sofa and opened the box again. Avoided the journals this time. Pulled out an envelope, one that bore his father's handwriting on front. In the strange, pregnant silence, he read it. In the strange, pregnant silence, he put it back in its place.

His eye fell on the stack of songs he and Naomi had written together. He was chewing still, mulling still. The song on top was his, mostly, he thought. "Eddie's Song." Or "Answer Song." He still hadn't decided. He lifted up the onion skin of paper and read the words. Felt the memory ringing through him. His father's muddy boots. His little cheek pressed to the dirt floor. The vibrations, how they moved him. He could have taken *that* song, at least, he told himself. Tried to convince himself. What did she know, after all, about fathers? It was *his* song—wasn't it?

He took out his phone, dialed. Chances were that there would be no answer at this time of night. But he decided to take that chance.

To his surprise, his father's voice came sleepily at the other end.

"Matt?" his dad called out, late into the night, at the other side of the ocean.

"Hi, Dad," he said, and for a moment, he didn't know what else to say. Everything was too large and still and strange.

"What time is it there?" his dad asked. Matthew laughed a little.

"Late enough," he said. "It's been a weird couple of days."

"Writing going well?" his father asked. He wasn't sure how to answer that.

"In a way," Matthew said at last. "But I was thinking of throwing out what I have. Starting over."

"Oh?" his dad asked, and there was concern in his voice. Because maybe that meant that Matthew was throwing *it* away, his chance. What might have been his last chance. With the record company. With his career.

"Yeah, I thought—" Matthew hesitated, then laughed again. "I thought maybe you and I could do an album together. If you'd be open to it. I know you usually work alone, since Templeton—"

"I'd love that, Matt," his father said quickly. "I would truly love that, son."

It felt like Matthew's heart was about to burst through his rib cage.

"When?" his dad asked. Matthew squinted.

"Soon? Before the baby comes?" He paused, for only a moment. "By the way, Kara went for a scan. She's—we're having a daughter, dad."

"Ah, a girl!" his father exclaimed. "Cracking!"

If he'd been worried for even a moment that his father would be disappointed to have another granddaughter, then he had worried for nothing. Ed Hammond III was as ebullient as he ever was.

But something weighed on Matthew. Tugged. He looked down at the box. "I've had a strange few days, dad," he said. "I met someone."

A stretch of silence. For a moment, Matthew worried he lost the call.

"A woman?" his father asked at last, cutting right to the point. Matthew bit his lip. Chewed.

"Sort of. Yes. But not any woman. It was—it was Baron Templeton's *daughter*, dad."

"Naomi," said Ed, like he knew. Like he'd always known. "I'd wondered what happened to her. What was she like?"

Matthew couldn't lie. Not to his father. "Brilliant," he said. "Just brilliant."

His father's voice was smaller than he'd ever heard it. "I'm not surprised," he said. For a moment, there was no talking. How could he have told his father that he'd fucked it all up? That she'd left, was lost to him already? He couldn't.

"She gave me something," Matthew said quickly. "To give to you. It's letters. Journals. From Baron Templeton. Your—your letters to him. His thoughts about you." A pause, too long. Matthew didn't know how to explain it, if he even had to. "His *private* thoughts about you."

Silence again, and Matthew worried he'd said too much of the wrong thing. He wondered if his father was going to be defensive, or embarrassed.

But after a minute, Matthew realized that his father was *crying*. So softly that if he didn't know his father—didn't know *better*—he might have thought it was only static. Was only nothing. But it wasn't. It was definitely tears.

"Dad," he said, sadly. His father laughed a little, too.

"Sorry, Matt, I don't know what came over me."

"It's okay, Dad," he said. "It's—I'll give them to you, when you come to New York. They're yours, okay?"

"Who else," his dad gasped at last. "Who else knows—?" And the terror, in his father's voice, and the pain, was almost too much for Matthew to bear. He winced.

"Only me and Naomi," he said. "Not Edelman. Not Kara. Not another soul. We'll keep it that way, too."

"Thank you, son," his father said. And Matthew wondered, then, about every secret his father had ever hidden from the world. What it had cost him, and what it had cost Baron.

"Of course, dad," he said. "You should get some sleep. We'll talk more tomorrow about when you can come out to the city. The record folks will be thrilled." A pause. It wasn't enough. Not yet. "And I'll be thrilled, too."

"Yeah," his father said. He could almost see him, wiping his tears away from his snotty face. Looking soft and very, very old.

"Night, Dad," he said, and hung up the phone.

He looked at the song again, then. And knew he couldn't take it with him. Wouldn't.

Brilliant, he'd told his father about Naomi. And it was true. She might have not been *his*. He didn't have her number, her address. They had no great love affair, the way Baron and Eddie had. Now, they probably never would.

But the music they'd made together . . .

No, he couldn't take it. Not that song. Nor any other. For one thing, the entire sequence wouldn't work without the "Answer Song." It was a leitmotif, wasn't it? You couldn't lift out one piece of the puzzle and keep the whole rest of it intact. Anyway, she would sing it as well as he could, if not better. She would do it justice. And she needed it more than he did. She needed to be the one who would bring it to the world.

He got out his pen and a sheet of paper and started writing, in his tall, neat script:

Sid,

Thank you for introducing me to Naomi. She is remarkable, and incredibly talented.

She would tell you that these songs belong to me. That's a lie. They're her songs. I just did the dictation for her. She's afraid to perform, I think. Stage fright. You're a good manager—remember last year when the record company wanted to cancel my contract? You wouldn't hear of it then. I need you to fight her on this now. You and Cymbeline need to help her get this out there. I had my leg up in the world. She needs one, too.

I've got something in the works with EHIII that should keep the record company happy. Will call you this weekend and fill you in. My love to the missus. Thank you again.

Yours,

Matthew

Matthew closed his eyes for a moment. He could imagine some moment in the future when their paths would cross again. His and Naomi's. Maybe he'd be divorced by then. Or maybe they'd both have wives. Maybe she'd have a Grammy, or maybe he would. Maybe they would meet in the green room at an awards show and have a moment over free champagne—or maybe the moment they'd shared already would be the only one. But he knew that someday, someday, he'd be walking through an airport, with his daughter's hand clutched in his, and "Answer Song" would come on over the muzak—Naomi's voice singing it, delicate and beautiful, and the world would be better for it. His daughter would tug at his hand, asking, "Why are you crying, Daddy?" and he wouldn't have an answer for her. But he'd be glad that the question was there, to be asked.

There was a knock on the door. The driver. Matthew grabbed the file boxes and lugged them to the door. When he opened it, the guy's face was dark in the twilight. The driver held out his hands, took one of the file boxes.

"Christ," the guy said, "What do you have in here? Rocks or something?"

"You know what?" Matthew shot back. "Don't worry about it. I'll carry them myself."

And he did, as lazy snowflakes swirled around them in the deepening night.

55 – 1958

His guitar slung over his back, Baron Templeton jumped on his bicycle and took off after Eddie and Liam. His heart was racing, free and giddy in his chest. It was an important day, after all. They were heading down to Dingle, to Charlie Peck's flat. Eddie had convinced the old codger to try out for the band. It was all real hush hush, of course. Dylan Miranda would have murdered the lot of them if they knew they were about to poach Charlie from him. But sometimes it was worth it, to be murdered, or almost.

They were on their way.

Liam sped up ahead of them around the corner. He was singing "Be-Bop-a-Lua" at the top of his lungs, acting like a maniac. Baron only laughed and coasted on his back pedals, coming to ride next to Ed. The other boy's cheeks were bright as poppies. His eyelashes were delicate, trembling. Beautiful, he was beautiful, with the spring wind against him. But his gaze was hard. Angry.

"What's a matter, love?" asked Baron. Eddie shook his head.

"I don't see why you're giving Dick Ashby money," he said. "I don't see why you're hanging around with that—" There was no word to end the sentence. That's when it struck Baron: jealous. Ed was jealous. And worried that Baron's heart was somehow subdivided. Between Ed. *His* Ed. And foockin' Dick Ashby.

At the road's edge, Baron skidded to a stop. And waited for Ed to stop, too. After a moment, the other boy did. Standing there, straddling his bike. Watching him. Eyes hot and angry.

"I gave Dick Ashby some scratch because I wanted him to leave, Ed," Baron said softly. "I gave Dick Ashby some scratch because he doesn't matter to me, not one bit."

Ed looked at him, sullen, frowning. Chewing over it. "Yeh?" he said. And Christ, if they weren't out on the street, with kids playing all around in this bright spring day? Baron would have kissed him in a second.

"Yeh, ya dope," said Baron. "Now, the way I look at it, it doesn't matter if Dick hangs around or not. Doesn't matter what came yesterday or comes tomorrow. It's a beautiful fucking day, Ed. We're going to go steal Charlie Peck from the fucking Tempests. And be in a band. And make music together. That's what I know is true right now. You ken?"

Ed looked at him a moment longer. Stubborn. But then, at long last, nodded.

"Alright, Barry," he said.

A voice reached out to them from the top of the hill. Liam. Standing there, waving his arms like a mental patient.

"Oi!" he called. "Are you queers coming?"

"Suck it, Liam!" Baron called back. That did it. Ed grinned, then. A real, broad grin.

"Come on, pet," Baron Templeton said. He pumped his bike on up the hill. And after a moment, only a moment, Eddie Hammond III joined him.

January 26, 1977

Baron,

Over the moon yesterday when I got your call. A girl! A bonny girl, Barry. Naomi. It's a beautiful name. I'm glad you weren't the maniac I thought you might be—naming her Baron Junior, eh?

(No jokes, please, about the name of my youngest; me dad would have had me head had I not followed the family tradition.)

Naomi is a beautiful name for a child who I am sure is a stunner, just like her dad.

When you called you asked if I had some sort of advice about the institution of fatherhood for you. Sorry for being so speechless. Never thought you'd be the one asking me for help, Barry. You were always so sure of yourself. Besides, you're the older one. What could I ever teach you? But I guess I have been around that block three times now.

Bear with me: you tell me you might be running off with Peter to find your old man in Trinidad, all for Naomi's sake, and I wish I could warn you off that. For one thing, I still don't trust the bloke (Peter, that is), and I know you think I'm only jealous of the two of you but I swear to you I'm not. He just makes me uneasy. But also I remember when I knocked up Genie, going to me dad, who got me drunk as a pig and told me to marry her. To make it right. He said it was the only way. I think about what it did to you, what it did to us, what it did to the band, the music, and I wish I hadn't been in such a hurry to follow in his path. I love Genie. I love the girls. And Matthew—boy can already play the piano better'n you can. But those old fucks can sometimes be eager for you to repeat their same mistakes. My dad always wanted to be some kind of minstrel, roving from town to town with his Johanna on his back. Sometimes I think he pushed me to it because he was jealous of what we had. The four of us and especially the two of us together. Maybe he wanted me to lose it. I wonder what your old man—whomever he might be—might have to say that could possibly apply to you. It's probably not much. You are a distinct and rare phenomena, Baron.

But fucked if I could ever stop you from doing what you thought was right.

Anyway if I have any advice (which, you, being you, are unlikely to take) it's only this: married or not, merry or not, be there for her. That's all they ever want, isn't it? To be beside you and hear your voice. You don't have to be perfect. You don't have to be straight. Just be your beautiful self, and present, and the rest will take care of itself. I've heard you at your worst, Baron. I know what you think of yourself on your dark days. Weak and ugly, small and queer. Know she will never see that. Your strengths are enough for her. Just don't get scared and don't run off. Stay.

I miss you, you old fairy. Can you believe it's been almost twenty years since the day we met? Not to mention those other firsts. I'll be in the states next year touring, when Matthew is old enough. Let's get the kids together, see if we can arrange a marriage between our great families.

Be good, and when you're bad, if you must be bad—think of me.

Love, always,
Eddie

Playlist

Listen on spotify: https://open.spotify.com/playlist/5e1yWz9BHlajE89VqJBSfL

1. Patti Smith – Gloria: In Excelsis Deo
2. Manfred Mann – A "B" Side
3. Buddy Holly – That'll Be The Day
4. Magnapop – Slowly, Slowly
5. Gene Vincent & His Blue Caps – Be-Bop-A-Lua
6. Julian Lennon – Too Late for Goodbyes
7. Carl Perkins – Honey Don't
8. The Beach Boys – In My Room
9. The Trashmen – Miserlou
10. Heavenly – Cool Guitar Boy
11. Ben Folds (feat. Regina Spektor) – You Don't Know Me
12. Paul McCartney – Too Many People
13. The Rolling Stones – Sing This All Together
14. The Jive Bombers – Bad Boy
15. The Who – Much Too Much
16. Eels – Fresh Feeling
17. Rory Storm & the Hurricanes – Lend Me Your Comb
18. The Cranberries – I Can't Be With You
19. Chuck Berry – Low Feeling
20. Badly Drawn Boy – Never Change
21. Ritchie Valens – My Darling is Gone

22. Estefy Lennon Band – She's a Friend of Dorothy
23. Bruce Channel – Hey! Baby
24. Buddy Holly – (Ummm, Oh Yeah) Dearest
25. Fiona Apple – Across the Universe

Questions for Book Club Readers

1. North chose an unusual structure for this novel. Why do you think they chose it? What might have been some of the challenges and benefits of structuring a book this way?

2. Several characters in *The Chaos Agents* are bisexual. What role does sexuality play in their lives? How does this change depending on the era in which they live?

3. In what way is music an escape for Eddie and Baron? How does this differ from the part it plays in their children's lives?

4. We see the future lives of several characters. What don't we see, and what do you think happens to them when the book is over?

About the Author

From their home in the Hudson Valley, F. Fox North (call them Fox) saves Girl Scout camps, writes songs, climbs trees, and has better taste in music than you do.

Don't look for them online. In fact, don't look for them at all.

Also by F. Fox North

Enjoyed *The Chaos Agents*? Please consider rating it on Amazon: The Chaos Agents - Kindle edition by North, F. Fox. Literature & Fiction Kindle eBooks @ Amazon.com. Want more? A sequel is coming December 27, 2022 in ebook, Amazon exclusive paperback, and hardcover.

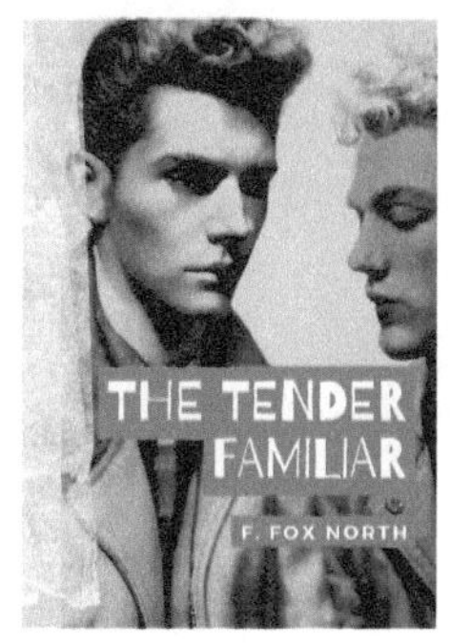

The Tender Familiar (Baron & Eddie: Book 2)
Baron Templeton and Eddie Hammond once formed the backbone of the greatest band of all time.

Then they broke up.

But somewhere in between - amid social change and songs, worries and wives, cats and children - they shared an illicit love affair whose impact would reverberate across history. In this series of interconnected short stories that are searing, sexy, and, above all, tender, F. Fox North returns to the world of Saffron to tell the secret history of two men that the world wanted to tame - but ultimately never would.